# BRYAN
## THE GREAT COMMONER

*From the Wiles Portrait in the State Department*

### WILLIAM JENNINGS BRYAN

*March 19, 1860–July 26, 1925*
*Member of Congress, 1890–1894*
*Democratic Candidate for the Presidency, 1896, 1900, 1908*
*Secretary of State of the United States,*
*March 4, 1913–June 8, 1915*

# BRYAN
## The Great Commoner

BY

J. C. LONG

New York :: London
D. Appleton & Company
1928

COPYRIGHT — 1928 — BY
D. APPLETON AND COMPANY

PRINTED IN THE UNITED STATES OF AMERICA

TO
F. M. S.

# FOREWORD

THE effort is to present the man, to realize his times—their influence on him and his on them.

Acknowledgment is due to many sources, and especially to the Nebraska State Historical Society (Addison E. Sheldon, Superintendent), Charles W. Bryan, Mrs. T. S. Allen (sister of W. J. Bryan), Jane Addams, Samuel Untermyer, Newton D. Baker, Josephus Daniels, H. T. Dobbins of *Nebraska State Journal,* Harvey E. Newbranch, editor of the Omaha *World-Herald,* the Yale University Library, the Harvard University Library, New York Society Library, New York Public Library, Mercantile Library of New York, the Library of Congress, the Department of State and the bibliography given at the end of this volume. The assistance of the persons and institutions named has been in supplying historical data. Mention of these names is made to record appreciation of helpful response to inquiry. It does not imply that any of the persons or institutions are responsible for the material or the point of view of this book.

All of the conversations, statements as to the thoughts of Mr. Bryan, descriptions of scenes, are taken from authentic records, carefully checked. Hence such "story effect" as there may be is not imaginary, but based on evidence.

## CONTENTS

|   | | PAGE |
|---|---|---|
| FOREWORD | | vii |

CHAPTER
I. PANORAMA . . . . . . . . 1
An American Phenomenon—Shipwrecked and Makes a Law—Appears on Republican Platform—Extent of His Fame—Educates Strange Japanese Boy—His Place in America.

II. EVOLUTION OF THE ALPACA COAT . 20
Oxford Foresworn—Courtship from a Baggage Car—Attends First Convention—School Competition with Jane Addams—Sees Lincoln, Nebraska, by Accident—The Passing of the Silk Hat.

III. THE PLAYBOY OF THE WESTERN WORLD 44
*Enfant Terrible* in Politics—Dawes and Pershing in Lincoln—Elected to Congress from Assured Republican District—Poverty in Nebraska—Put on Ways and Means Committee Against All Precedent—Makes National Reputation on Tariff—Defies Cleveland.

IV. THE COUP D'ÉTAT . . . . . . 64
Denounces Cleveland—Benjamin Andrews of Brown University—Harvey's *Coin's Financial School*—Darrow, the Free Silverite—Free Silver Manifesto—Bryan Stumps Country at Own Expense, Hiring Hall—The Staging of Career Before Chicago Convention—Crown of Thorns and Cross of Gold.

## CONTENTS

| CHAPTER | PAGE |
|---|---|
| V. BOOLA BOOLA | 90 |

Rejects a Millionaire for the Democratic Ticket—Makes New York Democrats Change Their Nominee for Governor—Meets Hearst for First Time—The Yale Unpleasantness—Choctaw Indians Rebuke New Haven Civilization.

| | |
|---|---|
| VI. ST. GEORGE | 103 |

Cortland Myers Saves the Republic—An 18,000-Mile Campaign—Thomas Dixon, Jr. and Other Clergy to the Fore—Mark Hanna Assesses Capital—Panic Threatened.

| | |
|---|---|
| VII. MARK HANNA WAVES THE FLAG | 115 |

New York *Tribune* Interprets Deity—Commoner Returns to Private Life—Enlists in War with Spain—Urges Freedom for Philippines—Renominated for Presidency—Anti-Imperialism—Hanna Summons Patriots.

| | |
|---|---|
| VIII. NEIGHBOR BRYAN | 143 |

Chautauqua Nights—Establishes *The Commoner*—Worth $15,000—Becomes a Gentleman Farmer—Set-to with Post Office—"Educates" Congressmen.

| | |
|---|---|
| IX. AN INNOCENT ABROAD | 161 |

Mistaken for King of Italy—Dines with Balfour—Flirts with the Irish Question—Lectures the Czar on Free Speech—Under the Sway of Tolstoy.

| | |
|---|---|
| X. END OF A CANDIDATE | 181 |

Ghostly Appearance at St. Louis—Candidate into Reformer—Disastrous Defeat of Parker—Bathes Publicly in Japan—His Unwilling Triumphal Entry to Tokyo—Ovation on Re-

## CONTENTS

| CHAPTER | | PAGE |
|---|---|---|
| | turn to America—Government Ownership Fiasco. | |
| XI. | THE BATTLE OF GRAND ISLAND . . A Brewers' Holiday—Missouri Goes Republican—The Great Commoner Embraces the Drys—Defeated at Grand Island—Bryan Hires a Hall. | 205 |
| XII. | THE COCKED HAT . . . . . . Rise of the Intelligentsia—Wilson Featured in *The Commoner*—Champ Clark Dodges Bryan—Bryan Writes Embarrassing Letter—Colonel House Offers Information—Cocked Hat Letter Appears—Wilson Draws Breath of Relief. | 224 |
| XIII. | BALTIMORE . . . . . . . Clark Evades Progressivism—Parker Made Temporary Chairman—Bryan Threatens Minority Report—Sends Wire to Candidates—Wilson's Decisive Telegram—Making New York's Vote a Liability. | 242 |
| XIV. | DESERVING DEMOCRATS . . . . Stormed by Office-Seekers—Colonel House Names Big Appointments—The Story of Grape Juice. | 269 |
| XV. | THE FARMER-STATESMAN . . . . New Steps towards Peace in Western World —Who Wrote the Federal Reserve Act? Colonel House Offers Information—Huerta. | 286 |
| XVI. | WAR . . . . . . . . . What Was Said to Dumba—Bryan Hopes for Peace—Colonel House Intervenes Again —Disagrees with Cabinet on Second Wilson Note—"He Kept Us Out of War"—Urges Peace Ratification. | 305 |

[ xi ]

## CONTENTS

| CHAPTER | | PAGE |
|---|---|---|
| XVII. | GRINDING CORN FOR THE PHILISTINES<br>"With the jawbone of an ass, heaps on heaps, I slew a thousand men"—Coolidge and Commoner Defend American Womanhood—Wellesley Girls in Peril—Wisconsin, Abode of Infidels. | 349 |
| XVIII. | THE COMMONER AND AL SMITH<br>In and Out of Tammany—Rise of the City Poor—Bryan, Friend of Rome—Attacks on Commoner at Madison Square Garden—Tammany Misses an Opportunity. | 357 |
| XIX. | THE HOLY WAR<br>Sunset—Challenge from Dayton—At Grips with Darrow—Future of Intolerance. | 372 |
| XX. | IS BRYANISM DEAD?<br>Passing of The Great Commoner—Who Takes His Place?—Changes in the Current World—Ripley to the Fore—Essentials for the Front Page—Basis of His Achievements—Ultimate Effects. | 397 |

BIBLIOGRAPHY . . . . . . . . 405
SOURCES . . . . . . . . . 409
INDEX . . . . . . . . . 413

# ILLUSTRATIONS

| | |
|---|---:|
| Bryan as Secretary of State . . . . . *Frontispiece* | |
| | PAGE |
| Map Showing Origin of Bryan and Lincoln Families | 23 |
| Prosperity or Poverty? Early Cartoon . . . . | 29 |
| Making the Wheels Go Round . . . . . . | 41 |
| Gold and Silver Walk into the Mint . . . . . | 47 |
| Omaha *World-Herald* Reports Bryan Congressional Victory . . . . . . . . . . . . | 53 |
| Atlanta *Constitution* Features Bryan's Tariff Talk . | 67 |
| Davenport's Cartoon of "Honest Money" . . . | 71 |
| *Coin's Financial School*, Sample Page . . . . . | 75 |
| Foreword of *Coin at School in Finance* . . . . | 77 |
| Clarence Darrow Stringing Up Noble Citizens . . | 79 |
| Bryan and His Pet Tiger . . . . . . . . | 81 |
| Democracy Waiting for Something to Pop . . . | 83 |
| Commonweal of Christ Membership Card . . . | 93 |
| Bryan in 1896 . . . . . . . . . *facing* | 94 |
| New Haven *Register* Drawing of Bryan, 1896 . . | 97 |
| News Report on Yale Incident . . . . . . | 99 |
| McKinley and Reed Whistling in the Dark . . . | 105 |
| Music of First Page of "El Capitan" . . . . . | 107 |
| News Report of Rigors of Bryan Campaign . . . | 109 |
| McKinley's Stand on the Gold Base . . . . . | 111 |
| The Story of a Great Convention . . . . . . | 113 |
| Republican National Committee, 1896 . . . . | 117 |
| McKinley and "The Trusts" . . . . . . . | 133 |

[ xiii ]

## ILLUSTRATIONS

|  | PAGE |
|---|---|
| Croker Embraces Bryan | 137 |
| Hanna Taking Care of Willie and Teddy | 139 |
| Chautauqua Map of the United States | 147 |
| Chasing the Bennett Will Bequest | 157 |
| The New Marine Painter | 177 |
| Democracy Must Move Forward (*The Commoner*) | 187 |
| Chart of Railroad Lines in the United States, 1902 | 191 |
| A Temporary Conservative | 193 |
| Rising Over the Horizon | 197 |
| The Return | 199 |
| *Harper's Weekly* Editorial | 201 |
| Bryan Arriving at New York Harbor, 1906 . *facing* | 202 |
| Political Tombstones | 203 |
| The Nebraska Nimrod | 207 |
| Trying to Hold Bryan Back | 209 |
| The Brothers Charlie | 210 |
| Mr. Bryan and County Option | 219 |
| Bryan Announces Campaign on Wet Issue | 221 |
| Miss Democracy Challenges the Dragon | 229 |
| Charley Murphy at Baltimore | 245 |
| The Sacrifice Hit | 259 |
| Welcoming the Little Stranger | 267 |
| Deserving Democrats | 277 |
| Lips That Touch Liquor Shall Never Touch Mine | 283 |
| Pointing Out the Menace | 289 |
| Bryan Organizes a Peace Movement | 299 |
| The Chautauqua Dove | 309 |
| Lecturing to Mexico | 313 |
| Bryan and the Nicaragua Baby | 317 |

## ILLUSTRATIONS

|  | PAGE |
|---|---|
| Britain and the United States Mails | 329 |
| Don't Rock the Boat | 341 |
| Just as You Say, Sir! | 343 |
| The Perennial Courtship | 347 |
| A Democratic Council | 351 |
| Pope Leo XIII, Obituary | 361 |
| A Hard Team to Handle | 363 |
| Political Map of the United States, 1896-1924 | 368, 369 |
| Chart of Election Results, 1884-1924 | 370, 371 |
| Music of First Page of "La Paloma" | 375 |
| Bryan and Darrow at Dayton | *facing* 390 |
| He's Always Seeing Things | 401 |

## CHAPTER I

### PANORAMA

*On the motion of Mr. Hunter, the time of Mr. Bryan was continued indefinitely.*
*Congressional Record,* August 16, 1892

A SHOCK and a grinding sound. A shiver runs through the ship. It is early morning, 3.45 A.M., on November 23, 1911. The *Prinz Joachim* en route from New York to Jamaica has run on a reef.

An American citizen in one of the cabins is deep in sleep. His wife shakes him half awake.

"We are on the rocks!" she cries.

"No," he answers drowsily, "you heard the anchor dragging. We must have reached the Fortune Islands."

She insists that he get up and investigate. He goes on deck and sees the officers and crew busily getting the lifeboats in readiness. The command is given for every one to dress. The citizen returns below and passes the word along. The passengers are deathly still. There is no sound save the shout of orders above, the rattle of boat chains, and the snap of the wireless.

The ship begins to list sharply so that the floor

under one's feet is at an angle. The American glances at his wife and she at him. The communication is brave and reassuring. The thought flashes—"If we are going down, we shall be going together."

Every one gathers on deck. The night is impenetrably black. Rockets arch up into the oblivion, burst—and fall, leaving the ship in a darkness more intense than before. There is no response to these signals, nor to the constant appeal of the wireless.

The passengers face eventualities in stoical silence, save for several Spanish women who kneel on the deck, weep, and pray loudly.

A stream of hot water is turned steaming out of the ship's boiler. Screams are heard from below followed by a plunge, and a second plunge, into the water. Two of the crew have been scalded. Buoys of red fire are thrown over the ship's side, lighting up the scene with a sinister glow for yards around, and the swimmers, now visible, are hauled back to safety. The fleet of lifeboats is revealed standing by in readiness to take off if the ship begins to sink. The red light flickers out. Darkness again.

A response to the S.O.S. comes in. It is New York, 1,100 miles away. Then six other stations along the coast send answer and inquiry, but there is no word from other ships. The American asks why there is silence from the seaward direction. He is told that the law requires only one wireless operator on each vessel. The operator must have his hours for sleep, and there is no one at the key between 1.30 A.M. and 6.00 A.M. The *Prinz Joachim* could go down at any time before six o'clock and a ship only a few miles off would be none the wiser. The American is astounded at this news, and reflective.

The minutes drag on and on. The sea, which has been smooth, begins to be broken with waves. As each billow sweeps against the ship there is a grinding sound at the prow, giving warning. Six o'clock comes at last. Ultimately the call for help is heard by another vessel, and the passengers are saved.

Several months later the American appears before a Congressional committee in Washington. He seeks the passage of a bill requiring ships to carry two wireless operators and always to have some one at the key. The citizen's measure is carried unanimously, and a new safeguard for ocean travelers is thereby put into permanent effect. The citizen's name is Bryan.

Rescue by legislation was no new method to William Jennings Bryan. He spent a lifetime at it. He saw some cause sinking—very well, he would save it. Congress must act. Often, however, the lawmakers ignored his pleas. When the legislatures wouldn't respond he called for volunteers, never daunted. He appealed his case to the public. He shouted, cajoled, campaigned, until the situation was remedied, and if it were not remedied he never gave up.

The wireless law, though it was far-reaching, successful and perhaps one of the most useful acts of his life, was a mere incident in his career. His fight for free silver, his campaigns for the income tax, his drive for the direct election of senators—all these struggles were far sharper, more dramatic, and more colorful than the passing incident of a shipwreck. The securing of the wireless-operator law required only the energy and common sense of an active citizen. Most of his actions exhibited less usual qualities. For years he was the unbidden guest at many a feast and he didn't mind breaking the china. As a young sprig in Congress he defied a President and rebuilt the party. Legend has it that he won the '96 nomination by an amazing oration, but politics isn't built that way. The "Cross-of-Gold" speech was a coup d'état, yet the plans which made it conclusively effective had been laid with a thoroughness which not even the organization politicians realized at the time.

He was a fighter. In the middle years he was also a reformer and at the end of his life he was a mystic. All of these elements were in him from the beginning, though dominating at different periods. Like most men of intense personality, he was many persons, and these incarnations kept rising and subsiding in an unhallowed fashion which disconcerted both his allies and his enemies, even at times himself. He was the artist in politics, in the bravura manner, the manner of his times; and his actions drove the artisans of both parties berserk.

He was not without a sense of comedy, and once went so far as to ally himself with the G.O.P. The incident occurred at Beatrice, Nebraska. Mr.

Bryan was speaking at the Chautauqua in this little town. The tent provided could not begin to hold the thousands who had come to hear him. The committee in charge transferred the meeting place to a hillside. They improvised a stage by taking a large four-horse fertilizer machine and covering it with planks.

As Mr. Bryan stepped on this rural stage, he turned to the audience, glanced downward at the manure-spreader on which he stood, and said, "This is the first time I have spoken from a Republican platform!"

For thirty years he strode the American stage compelling attention. Always he was news, first page news. Whenever his name appeared, one-third of the nation said, "He is a menace." Another third cried, "He is a prophet," and the remainder shouted, "Here is a good show." Denounced, praised, vilified, championed, ridiculed, whatever his lot at the moment he held unabashed the center of the scene. Only Roosevelt and Wilson approached his place in the public spotlight—and at times eclipsed it. But his star rose before theirs, and he was still a luminary when they had passed beyond.

He was twice a member of Congress, three times candidate for the presidency, and for two years Secretary of State. His official life (unless the Thirty Bryan Peace Treaties mark a more permanent advance in international law than is now realized) was too brief to give him an important place in the schoolbooks. This he felt, and felt keenly.

# BRYAN, THE GREAT COMMONER

## PANORAMA

| Year | W. J. Bryan | Political Figures of To-Day | Other Personalities |
|---|---|---|---|
| 1890 | Elected to Congress. | Al Smith, checker, Fulton Fish Market. C. G. Dawes, lawyer in Lincoln, Neb. | |
| 1891 | | Nicholas Longworth, A.B. Harvard. W. E. Borah starts law practice at Boise, Idaho. | |
| 1892 | Wins national attention on tariff speech in House. | Newton D. Baker, A.B., Johns Hopkins. | Gladstone forms Liberal Ministry. |
| 1893 | Leads silver forces in House. | Charles Curtis becomes Congressman from Kansas. | Carter Harrison elected Mayor of Chicago. Mary Pickford born. |
| 1894 | Calls caucus and defies Cleveland. | Herbert Hoover, A.B. Stanford University. Frank O. Lowden marries daughter of G. M. Pullman. Nicholas Longworth admitted to bar. Owen D. Young, A.B. St. Lawrence. | W. H. Harvey writes *Coin's Financial School*. |
| 1895 | Attacks Cleveland on floor of Congress. | Coolidge is graduated from Amherst College. Dwight Morrow is graduated from Amherst College. | G. E. Roberts writes *Coin at School in Finance*. |
| 1896 | Cross-of-Gold Speech. Nominated to Presidency. | C. G. Dawes on Republican National Committee. Owen D. Young begins law practice. A. C. Ritchie is graduated from Johns Hopkins. | |
| 1897 | Chautauqua days begin. | C. G. Dawes, Comptroller of Currency. G. W. Norris, Judge Fourteenth Nebraska District. | Augustus Saint-Gaudens completes Shaw Memorial in Boston. |
| 1898 | Organizes regiment for Spanish War. | Vic. Donahey, Clerk of Goshen, Ohio, township. | G. E. Roberts named Director of the Mint. |
| 1899 | | Frank O. Lowden, professor at Northwestern University. Dwight Morrow enters employ of law firm of Simpson, Thacher & Bartlett. | George Horace Lorimer becomes editor *Saturday Evening Post*. |

# PANORAMA

1890-1925

| General Events | Science and Religion | Stage, Books and Screen | Odds and Ends | Year |
|---|---|---|---|---|
| Strike of Knights of Labor on New York Central. | Lyman Abbott installed at Plymouth Church. Cyanide gold process invented. | Robin Hood, by Reginald DeKoven and H. B. Smith, produced. | | 1890 |
| | | Tess of the d'Urbervilles published. | Bomb thrown at Russell Sage. | 1891 |
| Homestead, Pa., steel strike ends. | Duryea's automobile invented. | Tennyson, Whittier and Walt Whitman die. | Corbett knocks out Sullivan. | 1892 |
| Chicago World's Fair. Savannah, Ga., and Charleston S. C., cyclone. | Briggs suspended for heresy by Presbyterian Church. | | House of Lords rejects Home Rule Bill. | 1893 |
| Pullman car strike and general strike American Railway Union. | Motion picture theaters start. | Trilby, and Jungle Book published. | Coxey's Industrial Army marches to Washington. | 1894 |
| | Roentgen ray discovered. | | | 1895 |
| Jameson raiders defeated. | | Sentimental Tommy published. | H. L. Mencken, valedictorian at Baltimore - Polytechnic Institute. | 1896 |
| | | The Little Minister produced, with Maude Adams. | Klondike gold rush. | 1897 |
| Battleship Maine blown up. | Radium discovered. | David Harum published. | | 1898 |
| Col. Roosevelt sworn in as Governor of New York. | Ronald Ross and Battista Grassi prove malaria cause. | Richard Carvel, and The Gentleman from Indiana published. Floradora produced. | | 1899 |

[ 7 ]

| | | | |
|---|---|---|---|
| 1900 | Runs for Presidency, "Anti-Imperialism" his issue. | James A. Reed elected Mayor of Kansas City. William H. Thompson, Alderman from Second Ward, Chicago. | |
| 1901 | Founds *The Commoner*. | | Queen Victoria dies. |
| 1902 | | Newton D. Baker, City Solicitor of Cleveland. E. T. Meredith founds *Successful Farming*. Carter Glass becomes Congressman. Pat Harrison admitted to bar. | |
| 1903 | Visits Czar Nicholas II. Visits Tolstoy. | Nicholas Longworth elected to Congress. W. G. McAdoo, President Hudson and Manhattan Railroad Co. | |
| 1904 | Announces his leadership of radical wing of Democracy. | Al Smith enters N. Y. State Legislature. Frank O. Lowden member Republican Nominating Committee. F. D. Roosevelt, A.B. Harvard. | Joseph Cummings Chase wins Grunwaldt Poster Competition, Paris. |
| 1905 | | Brand Whitlock elected Mayor of Toledo. | Elihu Root succeeds John Hay as Secretary of State. Alice Roosevelt engaged to Nicholas Longworth. |
| 1906 | Visits the Mikado. Mammoth "Welcome Home" in New York. | Frank O. Lowden member of Congress. | Dreyfus vindicated. |
| 1907 | | F. D. Roosevelt admitted to bar. Charles Curtis elected Senator. | |

[8]

## PANORAMA

1890-1925—(cont'd)

| | | | | |
|---|---|---|---|---|
| Galveston flood. Boxer insurrection in China. | Ecumenical Missionary Conference. Walter Reed discovers yellow fever cause. | | | 1900 |
| Pan-American Exposition at Buffalo. Jacksonville, Fla., fire. McKinley assassinated. | Marconi sends transatlantic wireless. Rockefeller Institute of Medical Research established. | *Tarry Thou Till I Come* published. | Carrie Nation smashes Kansas saloons. | 1901 |
| Martinique volcano. | | | | 1902 |
| Iroquois Theater fire. Pennsylvania coal strike. | Wright Brothers first successful airplane flight. | *The Wizard of Oz*, and *Man and Superman* produced. | Ford Motor Company established. | 1903 |
| Baltimore fire. Daniel Sully, cotton operator, fails. St. Louis Exposition. Russo-Jap war begins. | | *History of Standard Oil*, by Ida Tarbell, published. *The College Widow*, by George Ade, produced. | New York subway opened. | 1904 |
| Port Arthur surrendered to Japanese. | | | | 1905 |
| San Francisco fire. Anthracite coal strike. Czar dissolves Duma. | | *A Man of Property*, by Galsworthy, and *The Jungle*, by Upton Sinclair, published. *The Red Mill* produced. | Harry K. Thaw shoots Stanford White. | 1906 |
| Knickerbocker Trust Company closes doors. | Sage Foundation established. | | | 1907 |

[9]

| | | | |
|---|---|---|---|
| 1908 | Runs for presidency, Government ownership of railroads issue. | James E. Watson, Republican Nominee for Governor of Indiana. Theodore Roosevelt, Jr., A.B. Harvard. | Gatti-Casazza appointed Gen. Mgr. Metropolitan Opera House, N. Y. |
| 1909 | | | Prof. Ferrer executed. Peary finds North Pole. |
| 1910 | Bolts his party on prohibition issue at Grand Island, Neb. | Atlee Pomerene, Chairman, Ohio Democratic State Convention. | Gifford Pinchot removed by Taft and elected to presidency National Conservation Association. |
| 1911 | Offers toga to Champ Clark. | James A. Reed elected to U. S. Senate. | Madero leads Mexican Revolution against Diaz. J. D. Rockefeller resigns as president Standard Oil. Amundsen discovers South Pole. |
| 1912 | Swings Unterrified Democracy to Wilson. | Newton D. Baker, Mayor of Cleveland. Ogden L. Mills, Republican Candidate for Congress, N. Y. State. | |
| 1913 | Becomes Secretary of State. Gives Grape Juice Luncheon. Originates Thirty Bryan Treaties. | Brand Whitlock minister to Belgium. F. D. Roosevelt Asst. Sec'y of Navy. Thos. J. Walsh enters U. S. Senate. | |
| 1914 | Revises Federal Reserve Act. Composes Japan-California difficulties. Opposes bankers' loan to China. | Herbert Hoover, Chairman Commission for Relief in Belgium. Dwight Morrow member J. P. Morgan & Co. | Chas. Chaplin makes screen début with Keystone. |
| 1915 | Dumba Controversy. Resigns on *Lusitania* issue. | C. W. Bryan, Mayor of Lincoln, Nebraska. | |

## PANORAMA

1890-1925—(cont'd)

|  |  |  |  |  |
|---|---|---|---|---|
|  | President Eliot of Harvard becomes emeritus. | *The Circular Staircase*, by Mary Roberts Rinehart, published. | Hudson Tubes opened. | 1908 |
| International Exhibition at Seattle. Hudson and Fulton celebration at New York. | Jeanne d'Arc beatified at Rome. | George Meredith dies. | Lloyd George, Chancellor of Exchequer, introduces British Budget. | 1909 |
| Los Angeles *Times* Building dynamited. Philadelphia street car strike. | Halley's comet appears. |  | Jack Johnson wins over Jim Jeffries. | 1910 |
| U. S. Supreme Court dissolves Standard Oil Company. Mona Lisa stolen. |  | *The Winning of Barbara Worth*, by Harold Bell Wright, and *The New Machiavelli*, by H. G. Wells, published. | Upton Sinclair jailed for violating Delaware blue laws. | 1911 |
| China establishes Republic. *Titanic* sinks. New Mexico and Arizona admitted to Union. |  | Pulitzer School of Journalism established. | Lieut. Becker indicted for Rosenthal murder. | 1912 |
| Peace Palace at The Hague dedicated. Parcel Post started in U. S. Income Tax Amendment. Direct election of Senators Amendment. | Edison talking pictures invented. |  |  | 1913 |
| World War begins. Panama Canal opened. |  |  |  | 1914 |
| Panama Pacific Exposition at San Francisco. *Lusitania* torpedoed. |  | *The Birth of a Nation* produced. | Jess Willard takes heavyweight crown from Jack Johnson. | 1915 |

[ 11 ]

# BRYAN, THE GREAT COMMONER

## PANORAMA

| | | | |
|---|---|---|---|
| 1916 | "He kept us out of war," slogan by W. J. B. | Al Smith, Sheriff of N. Y. County. Newton D. Baker, Secretary of War. | Louis Brandeis appointed to Supreme Court of U. S. |
| 1917 | Volunteers for war service, is refused. | Herbert Hoover, U. S. Food Administrator. Frank O. Lowden, Governor of Illinois. | |
| 1918 | | Al Smith elected Governor of New York. | |
| 1919 | | Calvin Coolidge, Governor of Massachusetts. | G. E. Roberts, Vice President National City Bank. |
| 1920 | Leads Celebration of Eighteenth Amendment. Sounds alarums *re* women's colleges. | F. D. Roosevelt runs for Vice President. | Mary Pickford weds Douglas Fairbanks. |
| 1921 | | Herbert Hoover, Secretary of Commerce. | George Harvey, Ambassador to England. |
| 1922 | | C. W. Bryan elected Governor of Nebraska. | |
| 1923 | Hunts heretics in West Virginia. | Coolidge succeeds Harding. C. G. Dawes, head of German Budget. | President Harding dies August 2. |
| 1924 | Faces Smith forces making final attempt to "bury Bryan." | C. G. Dawes elected Vice President of United States. C. W. Bryan nominated for Vice President. | Woodrow Wilson dies. |
| 1925 | Dayton trial. | Owen D. Young, Chairman American Division, Geneva Federation. | O. P. and M. J. Van Sweringen submit Nickel Plate merger to I. C. C. |

## PANORAMA

### 1890-1925—(cont'd)

| | | | | |
|---|---|---|---|---|
| Attack on Verdun. | Commercial submarine *Deutschland* reaches Norfolk, Va., with 1,000-ton cargo. | | Jeanette Rankin elected to Congress. | 1916 |
| U. S. enters World War. Russian Revolution. | | | | 1917 |
| World War ends. | | | | 1918 |
| Steel strike, soft coal strike, Boston police strike. | | *The Moon and Sixpence* by Somerset Maugham, published. | De Valera visits U. S. | 1919 |
| Prohibition Amendment. Woman Suffrage Amendment. | Radio broadcasting begins in U. S. | *Main Street*, by Sinclair Lewis, and *Outline of History*, by H. G. Wells, published. | | 1920 |
| Arkansas River flood. | | *Second April*, by Edna St. Vincent Millay, published. *Liliom*, produced by Theater Guild. | C. Garland refuses to inherit fortunes. | 1921 |
| Irish Free State established. Knickerbocker Theatre disaster, Washington, D.C. | | *Abie's Irish Rose* produced. | | 1922 |
| Japanese earthquake. | Eclipse of the sun visible in U. S. | *Saint Joan* produced. | | 1923 |
| Reichstag accepts Dawes' plan. | | *What Price Glory* produced. | Leopold - Loeb trial. | 1924 |
| Locarno treaties ratified. | Largest telephone cable in world, New York to Chicago. | | King Tutankhamen exhumed. | 1925 |

[ 13 ]

He was agog with ambition, but there were other impulses which moved him still more strongly even when he knew it meant the destruction of his political hopes. He was swept on by his championship of the common man with an irresistible ardor. Again and again his associates urged him to be quiet about this, to "go easy" on that, to be less definite, more politic, in his conclusions. They frankly told him that his rampaging was costing him the possibility of the White House, and that a little more conservatism might make all the difference. But once convinced of the urgency of a cause, of a wrong to be righted, he could no more stem the torrent of his energy than the Mississippi can be dammed when the levees have broken.

Mrs. Bryan went with him through all of it. From the day when she was suspended from a Presbyterian Academy because of her clandestine meetings with this tumultuous young man, she was his constant inspiration. Once in the closing years at Miami, Colonel House congratulated Bryan on his good fortune in having so able and understanding a helpmate.

"Your marriage was a great romance," said Colonel House.

"Still is," Bryan answered, beaming.

As a husband he needed a good bit of care. His trousers pockets were usually filled with wads of telegrams which Mrs. Bryan retrieved, answered, and filed. He stuffed his coat pockets with paper parcels of radishes which he munched on the long train journeys. These bundles ruined the shape of his clothes. No matter how large his suit case, he couldn't seem to make his things fit into it. Unless Mrs. Bryan was at hand to pack it for him, he would pile in the articles and then step on them until they were sufficiently mashed down to permit the closing of the lid.

He gave lavishly of his time and earnings, a habit which called for watchfulness on the part of Mrs. Bryan. In the years following 1896, when the family began to prosper from the proceeds of his speaking and writing, he, for a considerable period, devoted half of his earnings to various appeals and causes. It was due mainly to their simple manner of living, and the management of Mrs. Bryan, that his estate amounted to more than a million dollars.

She never knew what direction his benefactions might take. One evening in the early nineteen hundreds, the doorbell rang at the Lincoln home and a Japanese youth asked in broken English for Mr. Bryan.

The Commoner went to the door and was informed that the stranger had come to be educated.

Mr. Bryan explained that he did not understand what was meant.

The caller stated that he had written to Mr. Bryan some months ago that he was coming to America to be provided with a university training. He had read Mr. Bryan's "Cross-of-Gold" speech and believed that the man who had written that could accomplish anything.

The silver-tongued orator admitted that he now recalled receiving some such letter, but had answered it explaining that he had three children of his own, and that there were millions more American children who would have a claim on him prior to any from the land of the cherry blossoms. He invited the stranger to stay over night, promising to communicate with the nearest Japanese consul and arrange for the visitor's return passage.

The next morning the newcomer made inquiry about the courses at the state university. He pleaded for the chance to stay just a little while. He arranged for one delay after another, with the result that he lived for five years as a member of the Bryan household until he was graduated from the University of Nebraska, while The Commoner paid the bills.

Other men of Bryan's times had idiosyncrasies, others had showmanship, and some perhaps had somewhere near the same amount of energy. Why was it that Bryan stood out among them?

"A peculiar product of your country," said Herbert Asquith to Walter Hines Page, commenting on The Commoner.

It was also a peculiar remark for the British Prime Minister to make to the American Ambassador with respect to the latter's chief, but it was apt if by "peculiarity" he meant singularity.

The nation itself in Bryan's formative years was

peculiar. It was innocent, yet "on the make," gawky but guileful, sentimental but jingoistic. The times were foxy, especially from 1880 to 1900. The harvest of wealth was ripe, and the reapers were many. The Harrimans, the Pullmans, the Armours, the Hills, were piling up their fortunes. Carnegie, Rockefeller and Schwab were new names. Along with these came a host of successful lawyers—Root, Hughes, Coudert, Stetson, Nicoll.

It was an era of mansard roofs and wrought-iron fences—rococo, romantic, bizarre. James Hazen Hyde was giving parties where monkeys were guests and the humans present danced in evening clothes under gushing fountains. Anna Held was taking her milk baths. Dinners, everyday dinners, were many courses in length. Mrs. Leslie Carter was playing in "The Heart of Maryland," swinging from the clapper of a bell and shouting "Curfew shall not ring to-night." W. A. Clark was building his bulbous palace on Fifth Avenue. In the Chicago wheat pit, Patten and other grain merchants were making and losing millions daily without batting an eyelash.

In the midst of this, the common man was despised and forgotten. The men who set out to grab industrial empires in the gay nineties did so without gentleness, suavity, or qualms. W. H. Vanderbilt was saying "The public be damned." The age called in turn for a commoner as vigorous, as adept, as gargantuan and as reckless, to throw himself into the breech. Bryan, through force of temperament and the drift of circumstance, almost reluctantly became this champion.

In his later years, even his enemies called him The Great Commoner, because he lived his life in epic fashion. He had no patience with those who spent their days condemning individuals. He did not denounce the stage. In fact, he entertained visiting actors at his home in Lincoln. He did not talk against dancing and card playing, nor did he rail at the divorcee. He did not hold with religious sectarianism. His view on the place of religion, stated first at a Protestant church dinner in the early nineties, closely paralleled that of Al Smith. They stood at opposite poles from each other in 1924 and each lost by it. The barrier was mainly that of lack of understanding, the difference in language between the older age and the new.

His personality baffled the reformers because he was essentially tolerant; he was an enigma to the politicians because he believed what he said; and he disturbed the majority of the public because he had more faith in them than they had in themselves. Most of the political reforms (such as the income tax), which he advocated in the face of vilification, alarums, and cries of "Anarchy!", have become an accepted part of the basic law of the land. These measures are not to be overlooked in estimating his place in the American scene. Yet there was a completer, and unconsciously ironic, sense in which he showed democracy to itself—he was The Commoner who enjoyed being one of the common people. The broad-brimmed hat, the alpaca coat, the low collar, the black string tie—these were the visible expressions of a being which exemplified the idiosyncrasies as well as the virtues of "the people."

In the last analysis, it was his integrity and a rare courage which carried him through. He was not afraid of ridicule or of being ridiculous. He was not afraid of making mistakes. A cross between St. George and Don Quixote, Bryan was for thirty years the voice of the nation's conscience—a voice, however, that was neither small nor still.

## CHAPTER II

### EVOLUTION OF THE ALPACA COAT

*I early formed the habit of attending national conventions.*—W. J. BRYAN

WHEN Judge Silas L. Bryan died in the village of Salem, Illinois, on March 30, 1880, the complexion of American politics for the next thirty years was materially altered.

For with the passing of Judge Bryan, there was also ended the plan of his oldest son, William Jennings, to become a student at Oxford.

Bryan at Oxford! One can well imagine the effect which the sophistication and worldliness of that distinguished institution might have had upon The Great Commoner. For, in those days, at least, he was impressionable, susceptible to the ideas and scenes which lay round about him. At that time he was a tall, handsome collegian, popular, ambitious and looking forward to a successful career in law. He was interested in politics, it is true, but he had not as yet allied himself with the cause of the farmer and the oppressed. He had some thought of becoming a United States senator.

In 1880 we do not see him wearing the familiar alpaca coat, the black string tie and the broad-

## EVOLUTION OF THE ALPACA COAT

brimmed hat. Quite the contrary. This spruce young man, who was clerking in a haberdashery shop to earn spending money while at Illinois College, had not neglected the instructions from the fashion plates which he saw in the store. When going among his fellows he wore a close-fitting well tailored coat, a handsome satin tie and a high hat.

Had Bryan not become The Commoner, there would have been no outstanding personality to have challenged the leadership of Mark Hanna, sixteen years later. And had Hanna not feared the threat of Bryan, he probably would not have consented to the nomination of Roosevelt as Vice President. Hanna strongly opposed the naming of Roosevelt and he yielded only to the persuasions of McKinley and other party leaders who urged that Theodore Roosevelt was badly needed to win the West away from Bryan. If Roosevelt had not been Vice President when McKinley was assassinated, a still further train of very different political circumstances would have eventuated, having a marked effect on the destinies of Wilson and of the whole trend and history of the Democratic party. Perhaps La Follette or Hiram Johnson would have become the chief champion of common rights.

When one speculates upon these possibilities, on what might have happened if Bryan had not become The Great Commoner, one gathers some idea of the force and impress which he had upon his age. Is it fair to say that had he become William Jennings Bryan, Oxon., he would never have been a champion of Nebraskanism? It does seem safe at least to assert that he would never have put on the alpaca coat, and, if one may judge by other instances, it seems more than likely that he would have become the polite, distinguished, eloquent lawyer, establishing his residence in the wicked city of Gotham. One can indeed imagine his coming back to reside in Englewood, New Jersey, that abode of New York bankers, and ultimately becoming a partner in the firm of J. P. Morgan & Company, whom he spent much of his life in reviling. His torrential energies would not have been lost in any surroundings, but with the unperturbed Oxford tradition, one cannot imagine his being any whit less urbane than John W. Davis.

That Judge Bryan's death in 1880 made a sweeping change in William's career is evidenced by more than fanciful speculation. His gay apparel was not only the effervescence of collegiate vanity. It was a sign of the steady evolution of the Bryans from pioneer conditions to the position of small town gentry. Like the family of Abraham Lincoln, the earlier branches of the Bryan family had originated in Virginia, pushed westward to Kentucky and then had come up into southern Illinois. "The Bryan, Lillard, Jennings and Davidson families all belong to the middle classes." Mrs. Bryan has stated, "They were industrious, law-abiding, God-fearing people. No member of the family ever became very rich, and none were ever abjectly poor. Farming has been the occupation of the majority, while others

# EVOLUTION OF THE ALPACA COAT

MAP SHOWING ORIGIN OF BRYAN AND LINCOLN FAMILIES

I. BIRTHPLACE OF TOM LINCOLN (ABRAHAM LINCOLN'S FATHER), SHENANDOAH VALLEY, VA.
  1. *Abraham Lincoln's birthplace, Hodgensville, Ky.*
  2. *Gentryville, Ind., Lincoln's boyhood home.*
  3. *New Salem, Ill., Lincoln's home during young manhood.*
  4. *Springfield, Ill., Lincoln's residence as lawyer.*

II. BIRTHPLACE OF SILAS BRYAN (WILLIAM JENNINGS' FATHER), SHENANDOAH VALLEY, VA.
  a. *W. J. Bryan's birthplace, Salem, Ill.*
  b. *Jacksonville, Ill., Bryan's home during young manhood.*
  c. *Lincoln, Neb., Bryan's home,* 1888, *until nearly the close of his career.*

have followed the legal and medical professions and mercantile pursuits."

Considering the few fortunes of those days, and the lack of any so-called aristocratic traditions except in a few eastern centers, this statement of the family's position does not indicate adequately the relative advantage which it had in comparison with its neighbors. Bryan's father, Judge Silas L., had worked his way through college and had made a considerable success in law. The Judge Bryan family in Salem, Illinois, could hardly have been classed as commoners. In so far as there was an aristocracy, they were of it. The judge was a leader in the community, and the owner of an unmortgaged five-hundred-acre farm. More than this, Silas Bryan also kept a small deer park, which was certainly an evidence of conspicuous spending without profitable return.

Into these comfortable circumstances, William Jennings Bryan was born on March 19, 1860.

When William was six, the family had moved out to the farm, affording to the boy the advantage not only of the outdoor life, but of a training which enabled him later amid political scenes to talk to his constituents in their own language. William did chores around the farm, hunted rabbits and seems to have avoided any unusual scrapes.

The religious life in the home was typical of that time. There were always family prayers, and in the family of Judge Bryan there were sometimes prayers twice a day. The judge at one time had been near death's door and had vowed that if he were spared, he would give thanks three times daily for his deliverance. It was his custom in addition to his prayers at home to adjourn court promptly at noon and then and there to kneel in prayer. At one time he was riding his horse near the village square, when the clock struck the noon hour. He immediately dismounted, knelt and gave thanks. There is no evidence that the judge either was insincere or intolerant in his fervent faith. He apparently placed no religious compulsion upon his children, save for a special service for William which the latter did not particularly welcome.

When the judge rode home at lunch time under the row of cedar trees which lined the driveway to the homestead, that was the signal for William to come in from the fields and listen to the reading of a chapter of the Book of Proverbs and to comment thereon. Little Willie, though impressed by his father's devotion, was both embarrassed and bored by this demand upon him to become a Biblical scholar. It was his custom to linger in the fields up to the last possible moment, hoping that, somehow, industrious hoeing might make it unnecessary to be called upon for verbal evidences of piety.

The judge did not forget that he was dealing with a boy as well as a soul. He often took young William squirrel hunting. He bought Will a shotgun with a single barrel, and later a double-barreled gun. William was a good deal of a day-dreamer to own this artillery. On three occasions it came near making an end of him. One day when he was cleaning a gun it went off, blowing a hole through the baseboard. Another time he was climbing a rail fence and had the barrel pointed toward him. The hammer struck a rail and hit the percussion cap, but for some reason did not explode it. On still another occasion, he was driving to the station with a friend, and climbed out of the buggy at a pond near the road to shoot some snipe. In climbing down, the gun was discharged and blew a hole through the back curtain of the vehicle.

At the time of this third explosion, young Bryan and his friend were singing, "For you must be a lover of the Lord or you can't go to heaven when you die." Singing was one of the favorite diversions of the Bryan family. On Sunday they all gathered around the piano. While the mother played, the children sang, led by the judge who carried the air in a capable and enthusiastic tenor voice. These Sunday concerts dealt with hymns and Sunday school songs. On weekdays his father and mother sang the melodies of the time, such as, "When You and I Were Young, Maggie," and "Farewell, Mother, You May Never Press Me to Your Heart Again."

Inspired by these home concerts, young Bryan thought that he would like to learn to play the piano, but his father held the view that the boy had better make music with the hand saw. Such was the status of the arts in Salem, Illinois, A.D. 1875, a condition that was indeed typical. A condition, moreover, which made it possible for Mr. Bryan to remark in later life concerning his failure to study the piano, "If one cannot reach the maximum in entertainment and service, service is the more important of the two."

The schools of Salem were not especially noteworthy, nor did young William rise above mediocrity in his classes. If he was not a brilliant scholar, he was none the less astute. At the age of fourteen, for example, he left the Baptist flock where his father was a communicant and affiliated himself with the Cumberland Presbyterian Church. The Baptists were a struggling congregation in Salem and young William preferred to ally himself with a group which was the more numerous and more influential.

In the later years of his life, Bryan was to feel that in the bosom of the church he could find that security and that certainty of truth which did not exist in the vicissitudes of politics and of worldly ambition. That was not the only motivation in his participation in the Dayton trial, but it was a dominant factor in his choice of work in the latter part of his life. For the fourteen-year-old boy, however, this choice of denominations was logically as much a social matter as a point of faith. The evangelical Protestant religions were the faith of that section of the country, and of that era, in an intense and all-pervading way, but their churches were also the center of most of the social activities. There were no motion pictures, no automobiles, no radios. There were sociables, spelling bees, charades, picnics, and Sunday services. The public depended on its houses of worship both for its salvation and its amusement.

In some families a change in denomination would have been a subject of deep heart-burning in the family (and William's action did pain the judge who made no complaint), but the father was broad in his religious outlook. He entertained the ministers of the various churches at his home, and at haying time sent a load of hay to each clergyman, including the Catholic priest.

As it turned out William's choice of the Presbyterians in Salem was not particularly important for he was to live there continuously only one more year.

The Bryans were proud of their son William, and meant that he should have every advantage. They arranged when he was fifteen years old to send him to Whipple Academy at Jacksonville, a preparatory school for Illinois College. There the boy lived at the home of Dr. Hiram K. Jones, a distant relative. Dr. Jones had been for some years a lecturer of the Concord, Massachusetts, School of Philosophy, and he was considered an authority on Plato.

At this age Bryan's urge towards simplicity had not developed, and the alpaca coat was evidently not even on the boyish horizon. His first expense account records:

> For blacking, bay-rum, etc.......40c
> To the church................ 5c

On further analysis, it appears that of the forty cents, ten cents was for blacking, twenty cents for bay rum, and ten cents for candy. Ah, the sins of the flesh!

Judge Silas back in Salem regarded this expense account somewhat quizzically and wrote to his son regarding the allocation of funds between the church and the world: "It seems to me that this is traveling

From "*Coin's Financial School*"

Cartoon typical of the point of view of that part of the western country which believed that demonetization of silver in 1873 was responsible for the ills of the time.

toward the Dead Sea pretty fast." On another occasion when William wrote home from the academy for money for a new pair of pants, the judge suggested that his son wait until vacation time, adding, "My son, you may as well learn now, that people will measure you by the length of your head rather than by the length of your breeches."

William was anxious by this time to excel in his classroom work and in the extracurricular activities. Oratory was the fashion of the day. But Bryan's attempts in this field at Whipple were discouraging. The homely direct style of speech, full of anecdote and humor, had not yet come into vogue. It was the day of elocution. Bryan entered the first year oratorical competition at Whipple with the Patrick Henry selection, "Give Me Liberty or Give Me Death." He did not win any place and was criticized because his selection was not sufficiently dramatic. The following year he won a third prize at speaking, the high point of his preparatory school efforts.

In athletics he did somewhat better, though he took little interest in collegiate sports which at that time were just coming into vogue. It is recorded that in an alumni day contest at Whipple Academy he won a medal for doing the standing (not running) broad jump in twelve feet, four inches; perhaps time has added to this leap which is set down as nearly a foot more than the intercollegiate record for that year.

In the summer of 1876 following Bryan's graduation from preparatory school there were several incidents which had a strong influence in pointing the direction of his career. The most important of these was the holding of the Democratic National Convention at St. Louis only seventy miles from his birthplace. Judge Silas Bryan and his wife had gone to Philadelphia to attend the Centennial Exposition. William became more and more excited about the Democratic Convention and brought in corn from the farm to the homes of Salem to raise the necessary funds for the round trip railroad fare and other expenses to St. Louis.

His first night on the trip he stayed at East St. Louis, sleeping on a cot in a room with more than thirty others. The next day when he reached the convention hall he learned that it was necessary to have a ticket to get in. For a long while he stood outside fearing that he was never to see the event, but a kindly policeman took pity on him and shoved him into the convention through a window. There he heard John Kelly of Tammany make his famous speech against Tilden, the nemesis of Boss Tweed, who was nevertheless nominated as the Democratic candidate. The uproar which followed the election in the fall when Tilden apparently had the popular vote, though Rutherford B. Hayes was seated by the Electoral Commission, made the incidents of this convention particularly impressive.

In the same summer there was the first nationwide railway strike with bloody rioting in Pittsburgh. Labor came to the forefront in public thought and conversation; and "Labor" was the subject upon which Bryan won his first prize in a college essay contest.

When Judge Bryan sent William to Whipple Academy it was understood that he would enter Illinois College and finish the course there. The Oxford plan was to be for postgraduate work. Young Bryan, alive to the ways of the world, apparently felt that the plain midwestern surroundings of Illinois would not give him all the advantages which one might enjoy.

But the training at Illinois was not as unsatisfactory, or as unequal to eastern opportunities, as some might suppose. Illinois College was a center of Lincoln tradition and Lincoln associations. For many years its president had been Edward Beecher. Beecher was a close friend of Elijah P. Lovejoy, who was mobbed and murdered in his printing plant at Alton where he was publishing *The Abolitionist*. Beecher had been present at this tragedy and had come back to Illinois College aflame with the cause of freeing the slaves and of free speech. He drew about him a faculty of Yale men who became known as a political and educational storm center in that part of the country. William Herndon, later to become Lincoln's law partner, was withdrawn from Illinois College by his father because the old man feared the son was becoming "a red hot abolitionist." The brother of Ann Rutledge, Lincoln's sweetheart, had been a student at Illinois and Lincoln himself had planned to go there because Ann was going to attend school in the same town. Ann Rutledge's death changed his plans and led to Lincoln's giving up the idea of attending college anywhere.

All of these events had taken place, of course, some forty years before Bryan's matriculation at Illinois College, but the tradition was there. If Harvard and Princeton and Oxford had the scholarship, the connections and the *savoir-faire,* Illinois was the institution of those who had saved the Union. It had the tradition of fearlessness, of activity and of idealism.

At Illinois, William Jennings Bryan began to find himself. He was elected vice president of his class. He won a second prize in Latin and a second in oratory during his freshman year. He won a first in essay-writing sophomore year, and in junior year he entered a contest more romantic and more rewarding than any of these academic events. This affair originated in an invitation to attend a tea at the Presbyterian Academy for young ladies, which was located in the same city as Illinois College. Up until that time, all the records indicate that the young man had found his chief interests in oratory, service, the rights of labor, squirrel hunting, eating and fastidious attire.

As he was introduced to the assemblage of proper young ladies, there was one whose gaze particularly caught his eye. Mary Baird was not only the most personable young lady present in the eye of Will Bryan, but his choice was one which any one else might well have made. Her clear-cut features, her oval face, the large, light blue eyes, full curved lips and curly brown hair gave her a distinctive and unescapable charm which made her stand out among her fellow students.

Mary Baird had also the advantage of more experience than some of the others. She was the daughter of a well-to-do merchant from Perry, in the same state, and she had spent a year at Monticello Seminary, one of the best finishing schools in that section. This helped to give her a presence and a manner which strongly appealed to the embryo Commoner, who, as yet, was more interested in the uncommon. Will Bryan, in brief, was immediately responsive to Miss Baird's charms and set forth to pursue her with an even greater zeal than he was ever to show for free silver.

It cannot be recorded that her interest was uncritical. Those were the days when a dark mustache was supposed to set any young feminine heart aflutter, though any one with the clean-shaven comeliness of Will Bryan might well have been considered a catch by any of the young seminary girls. But Mary Baird at that time, as well as later, knew her own mind and was able to see him clearly in spite of the hovering halo of romance.

"His face was pale and thin," she jotted in her journal, "his hair and his smile, I noted particularly, the former black in color, fine in quality, and parted distressingly straight; the latter, expansive and expressive. A pair of keen, dark eyes looked out from beneath heavy brows; his nose was prominent—too large to look well, I thought; a broad, thin-lipped mouth and a square chin completed the contour of his face."

Yet, Will's case was not unfortunate, even though the young lady was acutely observant. He had been well press-agented. Mary Baird had a maiden aunt who knew of Bryan and the Bryan family and was aware that Will was in Jacksonville. She had described him to Mary as "a splendid young man."

When Bryan had appeared at the reception, Mary Baird had at least picked him out as the one who might qualify under the description, asking a companion, "Who is that tall fellow with dark hair and eyes?" And if the young lady was judicial in her opinions, she was not cold to the attentions of the handsome caller.

Her meetings with him became more and more frequent, often without the permission of the school. The girls of the academy were in the habit of walking around the square upon which the academy stood; and the home of Dr. and Mrs. Jones, where Will Bryan boarded, was just across the street.

It came about that the walks of Mary Baird around the square and Mr. Bryan's journeys down town took place at the same time. Miss Baird's mother was spending the year at a sanitarium in Jacksonville. When the young lady went to visit her mother, Mr. Bryan, also, with great solicitude, called at the sanitarium. From there the young people often took afternoon drives. The principal of the Presbyterian Academy learned of these matters and suspended Mary Elizabeth Baird from further participation in the school work for the year. Lest there be scandalous, affectionate farewells, the principal himself took the young lady down to the railroad station and placed her on board the train for home.

He might have been less satisfied with his accomplishment had he been present a few moments later to see emerge from the baggage car, going back into the passenger coach, the future advocate of bimetallism. Will saw the opportunity which the principal's action had afforded him. He pleaded with Mary Baird to be allowed to present his case to Mr. Baird at once so that they might become engaged without further delay.

Shortly after their arrival at Perry, William obtained his desired audience. Fumbling nervously for an adequate beginning for this all-important subject, William, as in later years, turned to the Scriptures.

"Mr. Baird," he said, "I have been reading Proverbs a good deal lately and find that Solomon says 'Whoso findeth a wife findeth a good thing and obtaineth favor of the Lord.'"

Mr. Baird, not to be outdone by any such approach, answered, "Yes, I believe Solomon did say that, but Paul suggests that 'he that giveth her in marriage doeth well; but he that giveth her not in marriage doeth better.'"

The young debater was stumped for a moment, but with a flash of repartee which became characteristic in later years, he found his answer: "Solomon would be the best authority upon this point," he retorted, "because Paul was never married while Solomon had a number of wives."

As a matter of fact, Mr. Baird had taken an instant fancy to his prospective son-in-law. Not long after this he said to the young man, "As long as I shall live, neither of us shall know want." Several years later he loaned William the money to build his first house in Lincoln, though the funds were eventually paid back with interest. Between the two men there was deep congeniality and affection.

William needed this happiness in his life, particularly at this period, for it was in this same springtime of 1880 that Judge Bryan passed away. The Oxford plans went glimmering, because the judge had signed two notes amounting to fifteen thousand dollars for a friend who had defaulted. Technically, the estate might have escaped the obligation, but the children decided to recognize it. For William, the passing of Judge Bryan was more than the dashing of his hopes for a European education. It was the loss of a counselor, a guide for his final year at college and for his beginning in his career, a guide who had been continuously shrewd and sympathetic.

Stirred by his need to make his own way in the world, Bryan threw himself into college activities with more vigor than ever. Out of his limited allowance he spent twenty dollars, not for bay rum, but for additional lessons in public speaking outside the regular classroom work. It was several months after his engagement that he won a prize of fifty dollars for an oration which he invested in a ring, a garnet set in gold, which he placed on the fourth finger of the left hand of Mary Baird—not an expensive gift by modern standards, but not small from the standpoint of the young man's income. In fact, his sole source of funds was the money that he received from home, plus that which he earned by clerking in the haberdashery store. All of the hat store funds were devoted to presents for Mary Baird.

His senior year, beginning in the fall of 1880, was a pronounced success. In junior year he had won first place for an oration entitled, "Individual Power." This entitled him to enter the intercollegiate oratorical contest at Knox College, Galesburg, Illinois. S. S. McClure and John S. Phillips were students at Knox at this time, and Jane Addams was a competitor in the event. Mr. Bryan came in in second place.

Commencement time came and William was valedictorian of his class. He decided to attend the Union College of Law at Chicago, financing his education partly through limited funds from home and partly by working in the office of Judge Lyman Trumbull, a friend of the family. Judge Trumbull was an anti-Douglas Democrat, who had become a United States senator many years before, thanks to the support of Abraham Lincoln. Bryan scrubbed the floors of the Trumbull office, cleaned windows and did other odd jobs to help defray expenses. By

June, 1883, he had completed the course and on July fourth of the same year, he opened his office at Jacksonville with the shingle of W. J. BRYAN, LAWYER.

Those early days were not too encouraging. His chief business was handling minor collections of overdue bills. Early the following year, he took charge of the collection department of the law firm of Brown and Kirby. This, within several months, gave him sufficient funds on which to get married, and on October 1, 1884, the wedding took place.

It was a singular union for that era and region, and its unusual character was made possible, in part at least, by Mrs. Bryan.

Shortly after the wedding, they discussed the best use to make of their spare time. They decided that they would devote it to the study of railroad legislation, political economy and other aspects of government—a formidable program, but perhaps more interesting than evenings in the Masonic Lodge or with the Order of the Eastern Star, or at a table of suburban whist.

Mrs. Bryan joined a German conversation group and took a course in Early English at Illinois College. She also worked at night on the same course of law which Mr. Bryan had pursued in Chicago, and several years later obtained her degree, becoming one of the few women lawyers at that time in the country. She knew her husband's faults as well as his abilities. In an illuminating sentence she has said, "I have never regarded Mr. Bryan as a great letter writer—a little too absent-minded, a little too didactic." But if this preoccupation with general issues, with political philosophy, made him less interesting as a correspondent, she realized that it was a sign of his promise as a public man.

The public man was at this time an exceedingly obscure person. The fancy clothes of college days were beginning to look a trifle worn. It was true that he had a silk hat. Years later a newspaper remarked, "President Wilson instead of knocking Mr. Bryan into a cocked hat, knocked him into a silk hat." Mary Baird Bryan in her *Memoirs* clarified the record of The Great Commoner in this particular. "I wish our descendants to know," she wrote, "that this was by no means the first silk hat in our family. When I first met Mr. Bryan, he was nineteen years old, he was wearing a silk hat as a college boy, and he has had one ever since. . . . I make mention of this that all may know that he is not lacking in this emblem of official dignity." In spite of the hat, the well-turned-out young college man was rapidly turning into the young husband pressed for funds. He was able to live very modestly and put by some small savings, but the only money spent by the family for recreation was in the form of books on the tariff, on politics, and on the financial system of the nation. As Bryan read voraciously the story of the growth and financing of the railroads, as he studied how the farm lands were developed by capital borrowed at a time when the principal could be paid off by X bushels of wheat

## EVOLUTION OF THE ALPACA COAT

only to find that under the gold shortage it would require 2X bushels of wheat to cancel the debt, he began to realize some of the circumstances underlying operations in the Republic.

In the bright college years he had orated fluently of justice, labor, democracy and other subjects in a

*From back cover of "Coin's Financial School"*

> The Middle West and Far West were debtor sections, with properties heavily mortgaged to the bankers.

manner which was florid but without the advantage of experience.

As he began to feel the pressure of the grocery bill, the meat bill and the doctor's bill (for Ruth Baird Bryan had recently arrived) his studies took on a vitality and a personal significance which they had not had before. His dream of being a distinguished Oxford-trained lawyer began to seem very remote indeed and the possibility of being a United States senator was also many years away, especially in this built-up and sluggish portion of Illinois.

Illinois had been a frontier state and the Abraham Lincoln tradition was still vital in Jacksonville, but the social order there was pretty well "jelled." Politicians had built their fences soundly. Bryan attended faithfully the local meetings of the Democratic party, helped in the campaign which kept Congressman Springer in Washington, made speeches and was useful in political odd jobs. But his standing in the community was unimportant. It began to look as if William Jennings Bryan would be just one more lawyer.

In the summer of 1887, he was commissioned to look after some legal business in Iowa and Kansas. He decided to stop off over Sunday in Lincoln, Nebraska, to visit a former classmate, A. R. Talbot. In the breath of the prairies, in the open-hearted hospitality of this new sprawling city, Bryan found a challenge to his temperament which was irresistible. Talbot told him how different things were in the West, how any bright young man could get ahead, how he would be made promptly welcome. This was the kind of atmosphere in which Bryan's spirit could grow like lush corn.

He went back to Jacksonville filled with the prospect of moving out to this new land. There were many reasons against it from the standpoint of logic. Bryan had been raised a Democrat.

## EVOLUTION OF THE ALPACA COAT

Nebraska had been a Republican and a Populist state. To go there would, he thought, mean the end of his political ambitions. And as a financial prospect the outlook was somewhat dubious. Mr. Talbot had offered Bryan a partnership, but on no terms which would mean an immediately assured income. One of Mr. Talbot's main supplies of revenue was the salary which he drew as railroad attorney, which would not play any part in the Bryan finances. It would mean beginning again at the bottom of the ladder. He would start with the prestige of a successful associate, but all would depend upon the amount of business which he might be able to develop.

And yet there was little real debate within him. In Lincoln at the time all were poor and all were rich, according to one's standard of measurement. There were hard work and modest living, but no real poverty. There were early settlers who might claim aristocracy, but newcomers were arriving so thick and fast and the situation was altering so rapidly that accomplishments rather than possessions were the measure of a man. They were all democrats with a small "d," commoners who were proud of the dignity and place of the common man.

By instinct, Bryan realized that these were his people; and on October 1, 1887, the third anniversary of his marriage, he took the train for the land which for more than a generation was to form, and be formed by, his astounding career.

## CHAPTER III

### THE PLAYBOY OF THE WESTERN WORLD

*I'll go romancing through a romping lifetime from this hour to the dawning of the judgment day.*—J. M. Synge

WITHIN a year after Will Bryan established his law practice at Lincoln, Nebraska, he was on his way to the presidential nomination.

He had told Mrs. Bryan when he came to this new country that the decision to live in Nebraska meant the end of his political career, because the state had never been Democratic and was not likely to be.

But Bryan could no more keep out of politics than the Old Soak could pass the swinging door. He had been in Lincoln but a few months before he was on the very inside of all the Democratic operations. Though a newcomer to the city he was elected in 1888 as a delegate from his county to the Democratic State Convention and made his first political speech in the spring of that year.

His avidity for knowledge, especially political wisdom, was insatiable. Later when he became the leader of his party many looked upon him as "the white-headed boy," the darling of fortune who had been catapulted into fame by a smart speech at a lucky time. So it appeared to outsiders. So Woodrow Wilson opined in his early journals, but in those early days in Lincoln Will Bryan was building the groundwork for '96 and all that came afterwards. There was nothing of importance with respect to his party's history with which he was unfamiliar. Back in Illinois he had worked with the organization and studied the annals of the party from the days of Jefferson down. When he moved westward beyond the Missouri he did not permit himself to lose track of the thought of Democracy in any part of the country. He zealously read the New York *World,* one of the most vigorous influences in Democratic affairs. He read the Atlanta *Constitution.* There were newcomers from all parts of the country in Lincoln. Whenever he could he borrowed from them their home-town newspapers, and studied the editorial columns.

He had a thirst for personal acquaintanceship, together with a singular gift for remembering faces and incidents. Human beings were to him as compositions to a musical genius, once seen, never forgotten.

He continued the reading of economic books which he had begun in the initial years of his marriage. Masters of English eloquence, textbooks on economics, biographies, histories, every volume in these classifications on which he could lay his hands was hungrily devoured.

The time was ripe for vigorous leadership. The

Civil War personalities were passing and the younger men of a later day had not yet come to the fore. Jim Reed was just starting the practice of law in Kansas City, Al Smith was a checker in Fulton Fish Market, Hoover was an engineering student, and Newton D. Baker was an undergraduate at Johns Hopkins.

The brains of the country were concerned with the golden field of growing industry where it was every man for himself and the devil take the hindmost. The masses of the population, particularly in the West, were in the condition of financial bondage. In the opening up of the new territory the settlers had incurred long-term debts which had become augmented by the depreciation of prices. From 1866 to 1875 corn averaged forty-seven cents a bushel; for ten years following it dropped to an average of thirty-nine and a half cents; and when Will Bryan came to Lincoln it was sliding down still further until it reached twenty-one cents in 1896, the lowest point in the history of agricultural prices in the United States since the Civil War.

The prices of other farm products had had a similar trend. This had its effect on the earning power of the farmers and the value of the land.

There were various causes which had brought about this decline, but the one most in the public eye when Bryan came to Lincoln was the suspension of silver coinage.

Gold had been established as the sole coin of the nation in 1873. The demonetization of silver had

**THEY WALKED ARM IN ARM INTO THE UNITED STATES MINT.**

From "Coin's Financial School"

The United States had had both gold and silver coinage until the demonetization of silver following the Civil War. This demonetization took place during the time when greenbacks were the common currency, and the event was not generally known until specie payment had been resumed.

appreciated gold and correspondingly had depreciated the values of other products. The man who was indebted for a thousand-dollar gold mortgage in terms of farm products needed double the amount of those products to pay off the mortgage when it came due.

The idea of a joint gold and silver coinage at a given ratio was not a new proposal in the history of the country. It had been the coinage basis of the nation from 1792 until 1873. From 1792 to 1834 the ratio was fifteen to one, and in 1834 it was changed to sixteen to one.

The abolition of silver coinage was passed quietly by Congress in 1873 with the public knowing little about it because the country was on a paper basis. With the resumption of specie payments on January 1, 1879, gold coin was at a premium and the effects of the demonetization of silver began to be felt.

Bryan was thoroughly aware of the history of this matter. He had studied coinage history in other countries and was industriously familiar with the debates reported in the *Congressional Record*.

It was not strange that this tall, dark-haired young man immediately became an authority in the local circles of his party. He not only knew more than they did but he had a grasp of affairs superior to any one they had ever met or were likely to meet. He could cite authority, chapter, verse, and precedent for anything that might come up, yet he was astute enough not to register an air of superiority or to omit interest in purely local affairs. His political friends back in Illinois had trained him too well for that to happen.

Earning money, however, was his paramount problem in the early days at Lincoln. There was a good bit of rivalry for such law business as there was in the city. Charlie Dawes had an office in the same building with him and there were many other smart young lawyers in the town. Bryan kept his living expenses to a minimum by sleeping on a couch in his office, occasionally preparing his own meals, doing all his own office and janitor service. His experience in the collection end of the law business proved useful and in a short time he was picking up enough to make a fair living. He soon had an opportunity to try a case before a jury and won it. This spread the word around that Bryan was a successful lawyer. In the twenty of the jury cases which he tried during his several years of law practice at Lincoln he won nineteen. In the one case which he lost, the attorney for the other side was Charles G. Dawes. Judgment was for $1.27. Bryan's record was not quite as good in equity cases as in jury-pleading but for the short time he practiced he was very successful.

After several months he sent for Mrs. Bryan, who was remaining in Jacksonville until her husband's practice could become established. The young couple soon became active in the affairs of Lincoln. Here was a brighter, livelier group of young citizens than in stodgy Jacksonville. Lieutenant John J. Pershing was in charge of military instructions at the university. Bryan formed the Round Table discussion group for men, and Mrs. Bryan established the Sorosis Club for women. These clubs were not the half-baked, pseudocultural or pseudofraternal bodies which so many groups of the sort became in a later generation. Interest in the discussions was real and sharp. The country was still largely on an agricultural basis, and political and business affairs were a matter of bread and butter. The course which railway legislation might take was not an academic matter but one which affected the land which the club members owned, the price which they could get for their wares, the rates which they would have to pay for connection with the outside world.

The club activity on the Bryans' part was social and nonpartisan. At that time it required no little stamina for them to continue to be Democrats because most of the so-called best people were in the other party. This handicap, however, was somewhat offset by the fact that the Bryans were active Presbyterians.

Although the young lawyer at once made a strong impression in the circles of his own party he was not immediately considered seriously as a political factor in Nebraska because the Republicans and the Populists were apparently able thoroughly to overshadow the Democrats.

Bryan campaigned zealously for J. Sterling Morton, Democrat, in 1888 when the latter was running for Congress. Mr. Morton was defeated by 3,400 votes. Yet wholly undiscouraged by these figures, two years later Will Bryan addressed the Democratic State Convention with as much enthusiasm and vigor as though it were the central influence in the nation.

Undeterred by the defeat of the Democrats for many years, he assailed the Republican party as though it were headed for imminent disaster—if only the voters could be made aware of what was going on.

"The mass of Republicans in this state," he cried, "have deluded themselves with the belief that the Republican party was only flirting with organized wealth, and that it would finally wed the poor man; but the marriage between the G. O. P. and monopoly has been consummated, and what God hath joined together let no man put asunder."

The delegates greeted this sally with enthusiasm and decided that if Mr. Bryan felt in that sort of fighting mood he himself might as well be the candidate for Congress—and be the one to take a licking. There were no serious competitors for the task of running against Mr. Connell, who had defeated Mr. Morton so soundly only two years before.

With the nomination in his hand Bryan was off. He campaigned without ceasing. He spoke in every town and county in the district and made several addresses a day. He attacked the trusts at one place. The tariff was his theme at another point. Again, he expounded on the free coinage of silver. To cap it all, he challenged his opponent to a series of eleven debates. Mr. Connell accepted. Bryan noted that, in the Democratic rallies which occurred prior to these events, he was being watched by Republican lawyers. Accordingly he kept the best of his arguments under cover so that the report went back to Connell that Bryan was saying the same thing at every meeting. But when the debates came on he turned on all his powers of oratory and made a different presentation at each event. By the time of the concluding contest in Omaha his reputation had spread over the countryside and thousands stood outside the assembly hall unable to enter. At one of the debates he was presented with a floral shield and a floral sword of white roses. On the shield was a design of small red flowers spelling TRUTH, and on the sword the letters ELOQUENCE. When the votes were counted on election day, Nebraska for the first time was sending a Democratic Congressman to Washington. Bryan had won his office by a plurality of 6,700 votes.

This playboy of the western world became the *enfant terrible* of Congress within a few months after he had taken his seat. It is customary for a new member to be discreetly quiet for a term or so and learn the ropes, but Bryan had been studying ropes since his college days. Though he was but thirty years of age he had a far more adroit knowledge of the political scene than many of his colleagues, and he was fortunate enough to get into an affray shortly after he arrived at Washington. In fact through his whole life he always seemed to

# BOYD GETS THERE

That Nebraska Will Have a Democratic Governor Is Now Finally Settled.

Prohibition Is Repudiated by the People in a Manner Surprisingly Satisfactory.

Bryan Will Represent the First District in Congress, Having Fully Three Thousand Majority.

A Walkover for McKeighan in the Second—In the Third the Race Is Neck and Neck.

Dorsey Is Still in Second Place—What the Summary Shows—Returns in Full From the Counties.

At midnight Mr. W. J. Bryan sent the following message from Lincoln to the WORLD-HERALD:

LINCOLN, Neb., Nov. 5.—[To My Friends in Douglas County.]—I wish to express my high appreciation of your loyal support and earnest work, which has led to such a splendid victory for tariff reform. The interests of Omaha will receive a full share of my attention and your people will have a warm place in my heart. W. J. BRYAN.

## BRYAN-CONNELL-ROOT.

Fifty-four precincts outside of Douglas county in the First congressional district give:

Bryan .................................................. 4,217
Connell ............................................... 4,585
Root ................................................... 3,054

*From Omaha "World Herald"*

Report of the Bryan victory the day after election in 1890. The 3,000 majority which the paper predicted was more than doubled when the final returns were received.

know when an affray was going on and immediately ran to it as though it were a three-alarm fire. The fracas in this case was the contest for the post of Speaker of the House. Bryan's old friend, Congressman Springer, was battling for Crisp of Georgia. The young Nebraskan joined the Springer forces though the possibility for success in the Crisp contest seemed dubious. Crisp, however, won and Bryan as a reward was placed on the treasured Ways and Means Committee. There was a great deal of criticism of this appointment which was contrary to precedent (nomination was usually on the basis of seniority), but there he was and there he stayed.

As a member of the Ways and Means Committee he was able to appear in many affairs. He was appointed to a committee to determine whether a Republican about whose election there was some question should be seated. He voted in favor of the Republican, stating that the evidence was conclusive in that direction. That side of the House realizing that evidence is not always the basis of decision in such matters was correspondingly grateful, and the young man from Nebraska became a subject of conversation in the councils of both parties. Meanwhile he was not allowing his fences at home to fall into disrepair. He obtained more pensions in his district than all his predecessors put together. Nebraska Democrats had been having little recognition of that sort during the lean Republican years. Bryan cannot, however, be given individual credit or demerits for this accomplishment. The 1890 Pension bill passed by Congress greatly increased the number of those eligible for such aid, so that the number of pensioners in the United States increased from 971,000 to 1,557,000 in five years.

His maiden speech in the House was on the subject of the tariff, on March 16, 1892. He realized that it was a pivotal occasion in his lifetime. It might mean the difference between the immediate making of his career or a long road of mediocrity. Mrs. Bryan and their daughter Ruth were in the balcony. The attendance was small as he started in but the word soon spread around that the tall, dark, dynamic young man from Nebraska was making a talk worth hearing. As his colleagues listened to him they had something of the same mingled surprise and pride of the State Convention which had nominated him. They felt that this was not simply an initial address but the words of a young man who had a certain fire, decisiveness, and belief in the message he was proclaiming. The tariff was an old subject but Bryan made it bite.

For a few moments he spoke without interruption, commenting upon the wool and binding twine schedules. He offered columns of statistics and incisive but solemn paragraphs of theory to prove his point. Members of the House, especially on the Republican side, thought it time to give this brash young man a little hazing during his maiden speech. Such a talk is a trying one for the new Congressman and a bit of medicine administered in the springtime of politics is regarded with much favor by the doctors.

One of the opposition cleared his throat and inquired of Mr. Bryan innocently, "Are you to be understood as opposed to a state or national protection to be extended to the beet sugar industry?"

The sugar beet growers of Nebraska had been seeking a bounty, and the inquirer believed that the young Congressman might do some squirming if called upon to declare himself with respect to an industry of his own state.

Bryan, however, made an answer straight to the chin. "I am, most assuredly. And when it is necessary to come down to Congress and ask for a protection or a bounty for an industry in my own state which I should refuse as wrong to an industry in another state, I shall cease to represent Nebraska in Congress."

Other members peppered him with questions regarding various subsidies, demanding to know whether he wasn't in favor of supporting home industries. He maintained his position and held that he didn't favor any plan which robbed the public till for the benefit of special groups.

Before he was hardly launched on his address he glanced at the clock and saw that his time was nearly gone, used up by the heckling. The House, however, diverted and amused by his parrying, moved to extend his time indefinitely. The press table, realizing that more than a stereotyped address was in the wind, began to stir to life. Other members, seeing the chance to be quoted, stepped into the argument, and the vacant desks became filled as the adjacent offices got word of what was going on.

Mr. Raines of New York brought up a new line of attack.

"Can the gentleman point to any *one* single article produced in the United States in competition with a foreign article that has been increased in price by the McKinley Tariff, or which is not actually cheaper to-day than it was prior to 1860?"

"I have here a statement that the average price of tin plate for 1888 was $4.45 a box. The average price for 1891 was $5.68 a box," the Nebraskan replied.

Mr. Raines, however, had phrased his question carefully. There had been a general decline in prices since the Civil War and by nominating the date 1860 in his query he had considered his ground to be safe. He hastily consulted some papers on his desk. Sure enough!

"I wish to call the gentleman's attention right here," he exclaimed triumphantly, "to the fact that in *1880* the foreign price of tin was $8.28 a box . . . while the price in 1891 was $5.42 a box."

Mr. Bryan appeared to be wholly undisturbed by these figures.

"I am very glad, Mr. Chairman," he answered, "for the matter of information that the gentleman has interjected into the body of my remarks. If he has the statistics in regard to the price in 1870, or in 1860, or in fact if he can give me the price of tin plate in 1592, say, or in 1492 it will be a matter of great interest to my people, and this speech is going to circulate among them."

The New York Democrats gave a roar of applause in seeing that their colleague on the opposite side of the House had grabbed a bear by the tail.

"I believe that the tariff upon tin will result in the establishment of an industry in the United States," Raines shouted. "And will result in cheapening the price to the consumers in the United States."

"The gentleman from New York may well be pardoned," Bryan commented, "as the rest of his party may be, for indulging in prophecy rather than history since 1890."

Mr. Raines withdrew from the debate, but the prodding had been just what Bryan needed as a stimulus. His black eyes flashed with enthusiasm and challenge as he launched into denunciation of tariffs and privilege. Alluding to the Homestead, Pennsylvania, steel strike of the year previous, he said, "When the employee asks for the higher wages that were promised him last year, you find Pinkerton detectives stationed to keep him off, and foreigners brought in to supply his place. . . . Were we not promised last year what the gentleman from New York tells us will come by and by! 'The Sweet Bye-and-Bye' has been the hope of the people for these thirty years; the present has been the enjoyment of the men who made the promises."

By this time the press table was thoroughly awake, and volunteers to tackle the young debater were less eager. Lacking sufficient opposition, Bryan de-

## THE PLAYBOY OF THE WESTERN WORLD

cided to develop some. He noticed Thomas B. Reed, former Republican Speaker of the House, who was sitting through this discussion with conspicuously bored indifference.

"We do not feel unkindly toward our friend from Maine," young Bryan had the effrontery to remark, "the ex-Speaker, although he seems more sensitive to remarks now than when in the chair. We shall not find fault with him if he consumes much of his time, as he gazes around upon the chairs once occupied by his faithful companions, in recalling those beautiful words of the Poet Moore:

"'Tis the Last Rose of Summer, left blooming alone.'"

There was much more of this, none too profound on either side. At last the Republicans felt that the newcomer had proved his mettle. They joined with their opponents in applauding his consummate self-possession and fiery earnestness. Dinner time drew near and the Nebraskan without further interruption or divagation swept into his peroration wherein he prophesied the day when "Democracy will be King."

The next morning the unknown man from Nebraska was known to all the eastern seaboard.

"There was hardly anything else talked about except the wonderfully brilliant speech of the young Nebraskan of the House," the Washington *Post* reported.

"The man who to-day ceased to be a new and young unknown member," commented the New York

*Times,* "and jumped at once into the position of the best tariff speaker in ten years was Representative Bryan, Congressman of Nebraska."

"This speech has been a revolution," stated the New York *World;* "no new member has received such an ovation in years."

The advantage of this event to Mr. Bryan was immediate. It brought him invitations to speak from all over the country and he accepted those opportunities which would fit in best with his political program. He already had in his mind that the issue of free silver was to come to a head shortly. This had been agitated in the House and Senate and was gaining constantly in public attention. He had attended the Western States Commercial Congress in the previous year where free silver was a main issue. He obtained leave of absence from the House a month after his tariff speech to attend the Democratic State Convention at Lincoln where he urged the delegates to support silver.

"Vote this down if you will," he told the convention, "but don't dodge it."

They did vote it down, and from then on Bryan was a man marked for destruction by the gold Democrats.

When the 1892 Convention was held in June, Cleveland was the leading candidate for the nomination. He had been defeated by Harrison in 1888 but remained the outstanding man in his party. Bryan was present at the convention although not as a delegate. The affair was a tumultuous one. Cleveland was a gold Democrat and had the believers in bimetallism against him. He was facing the opposition of Tammany Hall which did not care a great deal about the money issue one way or the other, but did remember that in his previous days in the White House President Cleveland had not been considerate of the Hall in his Federal appointments.

The silver leaders showed themselves unable to cope with Cleveland's prestige and Mr. Bryan thoughtfully observed this incapacity. He was due to speak at the July Fourth celebration of Tammany in New York City the following week and the events at Chicago were enlightening.

It was his first address before a New York audience.

The Hall on Fourteenth Street was still well uptown. The old Croton reservoir occupied what was to be the site of the library at Fifth Avenue and Forty-second Street. Stanford White's Madison Square Garden was in its heyday of popularity and on the date of Mr. Bryan's speech it was harboring a Christian Endeavor Convention, attended by twenty-five thousand young people.

The Great Commoner was to become a hero of the Endeavorers but on this occasion he had an acute political problem on his hands. Bourke Cockran, a leader in Tammany, had urged the support of the organization for the nominee. It was a delicate situation. Mr. Bryan's first advantage in being there was to become acquainted. It would not do to be too definite at this time in support of causes or personalities.

"Mr. Bryan spoke for an hour," the New York *Tribune* reported with some acidity, "in high terms of the Declaration of Independence and its author." The same paper stated that his address "created little fervor." The *Times* was more optimistic and stated that the speaker received "almost an ovation."

The event had accomplished, at any rate, what The Great Commoner wished. Now he had become acquainted with Richard Croker, who sat on the platform with his Tammany sachem's badge around his neck, and Thomas F. Gilroy, ex-mayor, wearing the Grand Sachem's high silk hat. East and West Bryan was now known and known personally. He had to start back to Lincoln and fight for his return to Congress. If that were successful he was ready to take on Grover Cleveland and see who would be leader of the party. It was a valiant contract. Mr. Bryan found on his return to Lincoln that the fame which he had won in Congress was as much a liability as an advantage. The Republicans had recognized his strength and were determined to defeat him then and there. Many of the young lawyers of the city, envious of his success, set to work diligently to win their own places in the sun by achieving the defeat of the silver-tongued orator. The Republican national organization brought up its reserves and threw them into Nebraska. Senator ("Fireworks") Foraker campaigned the district and joining with him was Congressman William McKinley, the wheel horse of Republicanism.

Offsetting these forces and the normal Republican strength was the fortunate circumstance of a local quarrel among G. O. P. leaders. It was clear, though, from the start, that Bryan would have a hard time of it and for hours after the election the result was uncertain. He was returned to Congress, however, by a margin of 157 votes.

He returned with a prestige which went beyond his own party. The sending of McKinley into his territory had been a notable compliment, and the fact that Bryan had won made him a national figure.

He was not yet widely known to the general public, it is true, but the political leaders all knew him, and the political writers. So did Cleveland, though Cleveland could hardly have realized that at the opening of his second presidential term he would have to face a young Congressman who would have the audacity to make a direct attack upon the President.

## CHAPTER IV

### THE COUP D'ÉTAT

> . . . and who shall place
> A limit to the giant's unchained strength,
> Or curb his swiftness in the forward race?
> —BRYANT

WHEN the tall young Congressman from Nebraska walked across the plaza from his home in the northeast section of Washington to the House of Representatives on August 16, 1893, he knew that he was taking his political future into his own hands.

A Democratic President was in the White House with all the advantages of patronage at his command.

The sentiment for admitting silver to coinage again, in order to have a larger supply of currency which would raise the level of prices, had supporters throughout the West and South, and to some extent in the North and East. But the movement lacked effective leadership. Congressman Bland of Missouri had been campaigning on the subject for years. Senator John W. Daniel of Virginia was another veteran in the cause, but Grover Cleveland had routed them successfully and was in full control of his party.

Cleveland was not slow to take advantage of his

victory and had called Congress together in special session, not merely to blockade the program of sixteen-to-one, but to go further and repeal the existing coinage act which directed the Treasury to purchase 4,500,000 ounces of silver monthly for coinage purposes. Under Cleveland's program silver would not be coined at all under any set agreement, much less would it be a standard of value.

Young Bryan was walking to the House of Representatives with the intent of taking the lead and making the major address against the Cleveland program.

This time the House was not apathetic when he began. The members, the press, and the visitors remembered the speech on the tariff. Mr. Bryan did not confine himself to the discussion of theory, but served notice on the President that there was an issue here which would lose him the support of many of his followers.

"The President has recommended unconditional repeal," said Mr. Bryan. "It is not sufficient to say that he is honest. So were the mothers who with misguided zeal threw their children into the Ganges. . . . He won the confidence of toilers of this country because he taught that public office is a public trust, and because he convinced them of his courage and sincerity. But are they willing to say, in the language of Job, 'Though he slay me yet will I trust him'?"

Eloquence, however, did not prevail. The bill passed the House by a large majority and came back to the House with an amendment, on November first. Again Mr. Bryan spoke against the Cleveland measure, pointing out that the President's stand was inconsistent with the declarations of the Democratic platform, and that the price of wheat was falling as a result of this proposed further abandonment of silver coinage.

These addresses placed the Nebraskan in a fighting position which few Congressmen cared to adopt. He was not only ignoring administration policy but was trying to destroy it.

"Every possible argument in favor of free coinage he placed before his hearers in the most forceful style," said the Atlanta *Constitution*. "Bourke Cockran and William L. Wilson declared it was the greatest silver speech ever made upon the floor of the House. . . . The silver men are happy over it to-night. They know that it has strengthened the cause."

Cleveland, however, had the votes and the bill became law. The administration, moreover, could not let such insubordination pass unnoticed.

Cleveland singled Bryan out for discipline. Again this was an unintended recognition of his leadership. With pleasure, even if with trepidation, he accepted from the chief of his party the news of what the punishment would be. The bullet-headed Cleveland, with his heavy curled mustache shaped like the volute of an Ionic column, informed Mr. Bryan that he was in outer darkness, that his political opponents in Nebraska would be appointed to office,

This front-page story of the "Brilliant Bryan" in 1893 indicates the extent of his national reputation three years before the convention of 1896.

and that none of his recommendations to the White House would receive consideration.

When Bryan shortly afterward went back to his State Democratic Convention he found that the President's statements were exact. The Democratic Congressman was ignored by the delegates and on the one occasion when he got the floor he was heavily voted down. Morton, for whom he had campaigned four years ago, was now Secretary of Agriculture. Morton stuck by the administration and sent wires from Washington directing the local Nebraskans how to handle this young upstart.

The Commoner, however, was developing his taste for opposition. The fact that he had dared to face the President of the United States, and was still alive with a good appetite, gave him unlimited zest for new conflicts. He realized that time brings many changes, and he regarded Cleveland's disfavor as an incident. It might kill his chances for Congress again, because it robbed him of his power to reward the faithful, but it wasn't so unfortunate for other plans that he had in mind. Editorial notices all over the country might have a bigger value in national affairs than the control of a few postmasterships. Furthermore, Cleveland had made him a political martyr, and he knew that this would do him no harm in the silver wing of the party.

When he returned to Washington he had a new fight on his hands. It was an unpopular one in the sense of stamping its advocates as "dangerous." This was the battle for the income tax law. On

## THE COUP D'ÉTAT

January 30, 1894, he closed the debate in favor of the bill opposing Bourke Cockran who, though a Democrat, was on the other side of this measure.

"The gentleman from New York," exclaimed Mr. Bryan in the course of the discussion, "said that the poor are opposed to this tax because they do not want to be deprived of participation in it (because of exemption in the lower brackets) and that taxation instead of being a sign of servitude is a pledge of freedom. If taxation is a pledge of freedom, let me assure you, my friends, that the poor people of this country are covered all over with the insignia of free men."

The income tax measure was being discussed in connection with the revenue bill. Secretary of the Treasury Carlisle sent down word that the two measures should be passed separately.

Mr. Bryan promptly called a caucus of his party and obtained an agreement that the revenue bill and income tax matter should be voted upon jointly. This was done and the revenue bill went to Cleveland with the income tax law a part of it.

The President was not in favor of the measure, but did not wish to veto the revenue provisions. The measure, accordingly, became a law with his signature, although the courts subsequently held that its income tax provisions were unconstitutional.

Mr. Justice Harlan dissented from the view of the court in this matter. "It [the decision] cannot be regarded as otherwise than a disaster to the country," said his opinion. "It directly dislocates—

principally for reasons of an economic nature—a sovereign power expressly granted to the general government and long recognized and fully established by judicial decision and legislative action."

Many years later this measure was submitted to the individual states for ratification as an amendment to the Constitution. On February 25, 1913, its ratification was proclaimed by the Secretary of State, William Jennings Bryan.

With the Republican party frankly representing the business groups of the country and with President Cleveland in the same camp, the murmurs of discontent from the South, the rural sections and other groups who felt themselves unrepresented, continued to grow in volume. Most of the Democrats in the election of 1894 ran on the strength of Cleveland's record. As a result, the number of Democrats in the House, which had totaled 219 in 1892, dropped to only 93.

This led to intensive reflection in the political ranks of Democracy. It was desirable to support the President when he had control of patronage for one's constituents, but if supporting him meant that one could not even get elected, that put a new face on the matter. Mr. Bryan wisely did not attempt to run for Congress again. He permitted his name to be used as a candidate for the Senate. Senators were not yet elected by popular vote, though this was another of the measures which he was urging. Since they were not elected by popular vote, but by the legislature, his success or failure in such a race

"HONEST MONEY."

From New York "Journal"

Bryan in attacking the proposed Morgan loan in Congress was expressing a state of feeling very prevalent at the time. Davenport, the cartoonist, was one of the most powerful caricaturists of "the money trust."

would not have a measurable effect on his political future.

The Nebraska legislature went heavily Republican with the logical conclusion that a Republican was sent to the Senate.

Mr. Bryan accepted the post of editor-in-chief of the Omaha *World-Herald* following this event, but he still had a few months of his term remaining in Congress and he improved it by taking a few final shots at Cleveland, which proved to be the most effective of all. The President in his eagerness to establish a gold basis had made the metal increasingly difficult to obtain by his thorough demonetization of silver. He had gone still further by directing the Secretary of the Treasury to redeem all government obligations in gold at the option of the holder, whether the obligation called for gold redemption or not.

The result was that the United States Treasury did not have enough gold on hand to meet the obligations. It had to sell bonds to get the gold to retire these notes, and the retirement of the notes created a still further shortage in currency. The thing worked in a vicious circle.

The government instead of selling the bonds direct to the public, had called upon August Belmont & Company, J. P. Morgan & Company, and their English banking connections, for assistance in floating $65,000,000 worth of 3 per cent gold bonds, with a profit adhering to the bankers for their part in the operations. The contract was put before the

House of Representatives for ratification and Mr. Bryan saw that an opportunity was at hand.

"I want it understood that so far as I am concerned," he said, "when I took the oath of office as a member of Congress there was no mental reservation that I would not speak out against an outrage committed against my constituents, even when committed by the President of the United States.

"The President of the United States is only a man. We trust the administration of government to men, and when we do so, we know that they are liable to err. . . .

"What is the duty of the Democratic party? If it still loves its President, it is its duty, as I understand it, to prove that it has at least one attribute of divinity left, by chastening him whom it loveth. . . .

"Why this sacrifice of interest of the United States? The Government's credit was not in danger; the bonds of the United States were selling in the market every day at a regular premium. The same kind of bonds having only twelve years to run were selling at over 112. What excuse was there for selling a thirty-year bond for 104½? What defense can be made for this gift of something like $7,500,000 to the bond syndicate? . . .

"Has the credit of the country fallen so much in three months that a thirty-year 3 per cent gold bond is worth less now than a ten-year 3 per cent coin bond was then? Nothing has occurred within three months, except the President's message, to injure the credit of the country."

The Cleveland contract was rejected by the House and Bryan had closed his record with a victory.

The vigorous policy of Cleveland in refusing even a compromise position to silver currency, followed by a continuous drop of prices in farm products, forced the monetary question still further into the foreground.

In the East, free silver had a few, but only a few champions. Benjamin Andrews, president of Brown University, published in 1894 a free-silver book entitled *An Honest Dollar*. Andrews was a Civil War veteran who had lost the sight of an eye from a wound at Petersburg; hence his patriotism could not be called into question. He was an ordained minister and a Baptist, hence he could not be called an atheist. But he was a college professor and his views in eastern circles were considered impractical. On the other side of the water, the Right Honorable A. J. Balfour, Moreton Frewen and Archbishop Walsh were urging England to return to bimetallism. This gave the free silver people distinguished authority for their case. On the other hand, it gave the gold standard advocates the opportunity to suggest that the United States might wait and see what England would do about it.

In Chicago, a man named W. H. Harvey had published a booklet entitled *Coin's Financial School* in the form of dialogue and illustrations outlining the arguments in favor of free silver. The book people seldom handled it, and the very poor people seldom ever saw any of it."

## THE FIRST INTERRUPTION.

Here young Medill, of the *Chicago Tribune*, held up his hand, which indicated that he had something to say or wished to ask a question. COIN paused and asked him what he wanted.

He arose in his seat and said that his father claimed that we had been on a gold basis ever since 1837, that prior to 1873 there never had been but eight million dollars of silver coined. Here young Wilson, of the *Farm, Field and Fireside*, said he wanted to ask, who owns the *Chicago Tribune?*

COIN tapped the little bell on the table to restore order, and ruled the last question out, as there was one already before the house by Mr. Medill.

"Prior to 1873," said COIN, "there were one hundred and five millions of silver coined by the United States and eight million of this was in silver dollars. When your father said that 'only eight million dollars in silver' had been coined, he meant to say that 'only eight million silver dollars had been coined.' He also neglected to say—that is—he forgot to state, that ninety-seven millions had been coined into dimes, quarters and halves.

"About one hundred millions of foreign silver had found its way into this country prior to 1860. It was principally Spanish, Mexican and Canadian coin. It had all been made legal tender in the United States by act of Congress. We needed more silver than we had, and Congress passed laws making all foreign silver coins legal tender in this country. I will read you one of these laws—they are scattered all through the statutes prior to 1873." Here COIN picked up a copy of the laws of the

*Specimen page from the pamphlet which sold more than a million copies and was the Bible of the silverites from 1894 to 1896.*

presented the imaginary picture of leading citizens, such as Lyman J. Gage, Professor J. Laurence Laughlin, H. H. Kohlsaat, and others, attending a school presided over by a young boy named Coin. These wise financiers asked foolish questions and Coin gave them enlightening answers indicating the fallacy of the fiscal position of these eminent gentlemen. The use of the names of these personalities helped to give interest and vast circulation to the book. Many believed that the account was authentic and that the bankers of the country were receiving some homely teaching in the fundamentals of economics.

The gentlemen themselves were not pleased. In 1895 George E. Roberts, a newspaper publisher of Fort Dodge, Iowa, printed an answer, a volume called *Coin at School in Finance*. The foreword of this contained denials by Mr. Gage and others that there ever was such an affair as Coin's school, or that they had ever participated in such dialogues as Mr. Harvey alleged. The Roberts book likewise had a large circulation. Two years later, Lyman Gage became Secretary of the Treasury and appointed Mr. Roberts to the position of Director of the Mint. From the Mint he went to the National City Bank of New York, later becoming one of its vice presidents.

The wide circulation of Harvey's original book and the heated denials served to bring the issue more actively to the attention of the mass of the people.

REPORTS from various parts of the country show that many people still understand "Coin's Financial School" to be a report of meetings actually held. For that reason, although a denial ought to be unnecessary, at the suggestion of the Honest Money League of Illinois, this statement is given:

Chicago, May 13th, 1895.

We, the undersigned, hereby declare that we never attended the alleged lectures of Coin reported in "Coin's Financial School", that no such school was ever held and no such lectures ever delivered, so far as we know, and that our alleged participation in the dialogues described in that book is absolutely fictitious.

*[signatures]*

*From "Coin at School in Finance"*

The various prominent men erroneously credited with attending Coin's imaginary school did not care for the publicity. J. Laurence Laughlin of the University of Chicago, and H. H. Kohlsaat, Chicago newspaper publisher, were among those who protested.

Meanwhile Mr. Bryan did not propose to be forgotten. Those who were pondering their Congressional defeats under the régime of Cleveland were looking for a leader. The newspapers had given the man from Nebraska liberal notices and praise but only a few mentioned him as a presidential possibility. The Commoner had not put in ten or fifteen years' study of the political state to no avail. He saw that Congressman Bland and Senator Daniel were recognized as the chieftains of the silver forces and many of the stronger newspapers were predicting that one of these men would be the nominee if the silverites should control the Democratic Convention. But these men had not been able to rally enthusiasm to their cause before, and what reason was there to expect that they might do so in '96? The gold standard advocates might, but probably would not, control the convention. Cleveland having served two terms was not looking for renomination, and Senator David Bennett Hill of New York, the second strongest gold leader, had injured his influence because he had led the fight against the income tax in the Senate.

The main thing for Bryan now was to keep in the public eye, particularly in the eye of the right public. The day after his retirement from Congress, March 5, 1895, he drew up a free silver manifesto and obtained the signatures of many leading Democrats. The name of R. P. ("Silver Dick") Bland headed the list, at The Commoner's request, but the signature of W. J. Bryan was at the

From "Coin at School in Finance"

Cartoon representing leaders of the silver movement stringing up substantial citizens by the thumbs. Note on the right a drawing of Clarence Darrow, who was at that time a free silverite. With him is Governor Altgeld of Illinois, Darrow's law partner.

top of the second column, the right-hand column. When Mr. Cleveland wrote an open letter to Democracy on the subject of the gold standard, Mr. Bryan promptly wrote an open letter in reply.

He attended most of the free silver congresses which were being held in various parts of the country. In this way he became known to the Populist party, which was fast fading but had been able to elect several governors and between thirty and forty members to Congress during the preceding decade. The silver congresses were frequently attended by important leaders of Democracy, such as Carter Glass and Josephus Daniels. In Chicago free silver was particularly strong. There Governor Altgeld was championing the cause and Clarence Darrow, his law partner, was one of the most eloquent advocates of bimetallism.

"Up to 1873," Darrow was proclaiming, "gold and silver were coined on a ratio of sixteen to one; they should be restored to that basis. If it is then found that the ratio is not a proper one, as governed by the laws of trade, the ratio should be changed for convenience until they float together, but in making the change neither the debtor nor the creditor should be asked to bear all the loss. The silver dollar should be made larger and the gold dollar proportionately smaller until they circulate together."

Mr. Bryan, however, knew that congresses of this sort would not acquaint him with all of the men whom he should know. In 1895 he made a tour of

PUR-R-R! PUR-R-R!!
The lonesome Tammany tiger even courts the friendship of the Free-Silver jester.
*Courtesy of "Judge"*

As early as 1892 Bryan was making friends with the Tammany Tiger. This friendship, depicted here in 1899, blew hot and cold at different times in the succeeding years.

the country at his own expense, speaking for free silver. Where no opportune gathering was provided for him to meet the local leaders of the party, he hired a hall. Sometimes there were only a few present, but those few were the political leaders of the party.

At home he had returned in triumph. The disaster of the '94 election had changed the view of the Nebraska Democrats and Bryan had become so strong in his own state that the convention was willing to instruct for him for the presidential nomination, but Mr. Bryan asked that this honor be withheld. North Carolina was formally instructed for him, but Mr. Bryan discouraged talk of his possibilities in advance. He knew politics, political history, the personnel of his party and the logic of events. When the convention came he was ready. The silverites had by far the largest number of delegates present but a debate was due on the issue before bimetallism could be officially adopted as the party plank.

The debate, as at most Democratic conventions, lasted far into the evening.

The day was June ninth and the temperature was appropriately hot. The air in the Chicago Coliseum was stifling and filled with cigar smoke. Rivals of Mr. Bryan, who were, perhaps, not unaware of the trend of the tide, had succeeded in blocking his efforts to become temporary chairman and later permanent chairman of the convention. But this very opposition proved to be a stroke of fortune.

**WAITING FOR SOMETHING TO POP.**

*From the San Francisco "Call"*

Democracy was in a bad way in 1896. Grover Cleveland had alienated his own party and there was severe business depression. The names on the pop corn bags are those of gold Democrats. The free silver wing of the party had been numerous in 1892, but had lacked dramatic leadership. Accordingly many had the opinion that a gold Democrat would be named in 1896.

Some one was needed to make the main and the concluding talk in favor of the silver plank. Since he had been pushed aside from apparently more important appointments, and since the strength of his enthusiasm would be needed in the campaign, Bryan was invited to accept this assignment on the program.

As the time for his speech drew near, almost midnight, he realized that his hour had come. He realized that now, if ever, the logic of events was in his favor. He had a feeling of weakness in the pit of his stomach and a faintness at the thought of all that hinged on his coming address. He went to a counter and bought a sandwich and a cup of coffee to quiet his nerves. Then he came back to the platform. Would things work out as he had thought?

He noticed that Clark Howell at the press table was looking up at him intently. Howell * knew the inside of Democratic affairs and had an able political sense developed in his training on the Atlanta *Constitution*. The reporter scribbled a note on an envelope and handed it up to Bryan.

It read: "This is a great opportunity."

So Howell saw it too!

"You will not be disappointed," Bryan wrote underneath and sent the envelope back.

At last the chairman called for William J. Bryan of Nebraska. When he rose to speak there was

---
* Mr. Howell was also a member of the Democratic National Committee, and of the sub-committee to determine whether Morton or Bryan delegates should be seated from Nebraska. He selected Judge H. G. Lewis of Georgia as the man to place Bryan in nomination.

immediate applause and attention. Here was a man they all knew, though each one failed to realize that the others knew him. Some of the other candidates had a wide acquaintance in certain sections. Some had been heralded by the newspapers, but Bryan's 1895 tour of the nation had made him an acquaintance of virtually every man in the room.

Immediately he began to speak the audience showed interest because his clear penetrating voice reached every corner of the room distinctly. He disclaimed any personal merit in standing as the champion of silver but placed the discussion on the basis of principle. He called attention to the silver manifesto of March, 1895, which had been signed by "a few Democrats." He did not state who prepared that manifesto, but the audience knew.

He replied to the charge that bimetallism would hurt the business interests:

"The man who is employed for wages," said Mr. Bryan, "is as much a business man as his employer; the attorney in a country town is as much a business man as the corporation counsel in a great metropolis; the merchant in the cross-roads store is as much a business man as the merchant of New York; the farmer who goes forth in the morning and toils all day—who begins in the spring and toils all summer—and who by the application of brain and muscle to the natural resources of the country creates wealth, is as much a business man as the man who goes upon the Board of Trade and bets upon the price of grain."

The wage-earners, the small-town lawyers, the storekeepers, and the farmers in the audience nodded their approval.

He pointed to the eastern opposition toward bimetallism and its claim that the silver issue was a sectional one:

"We say not one word against those who live upon the Atlantic coast," Bryan continued, "but the hardy pioneers who have braved all the dangers of the wilderness, who have made the desert to bloom as the rose . . . these people, we say, are as deserving of the consideration of our party as any people in this country.

"Our war is not a war of conquest; we are fighting in the defense of our homes, our families and prosperity," The Commoner cried, his voice vibrant with the injustices which the West had suffered.

"We have petitioned and our petitions have been scorned.

"We have entreated, and our entreaties have been disregarded.

"We have begged and they have mocked when our calamity came.

"We beg no longer. We entreat no more. We petition no more. We defy them."

The audience broke forth into a tumult of applause. Here at last was their Peerless Leader, a man of energy, of imagination, of idealism, and limitless courage.

It was minutes before the Nebraskan could go on with his address. There was no question of holding his audience now, of converting them to his message, or wondering whether they would hear him after the long hours of argument. They hung eagerly on his every word.

He then defined his position on the income tax and in favor of national bank notes as opposed to private notes.

He called attention to the Republican nominee and summoned his party to a victorious campaign.

"We go forth confident that we shall win," he thundered. "Why? Because upon the paramount issue of this campaign there is not a spot of ground upon which the enemy will dare to challenge battle. . . .

"The sympathies of the Democratic party, as shown by the platform, are ever on the side of the struggling masses who have ever been the foundation of the Democratic party. There are two ideas of government. There are those who believe that, if you will only legislate to make the well-to-do prosperous their prosperity will leak through on those below. The Democratic idea, however, has been that if you legislate to make the masses prosperous, their prosperity will find its way up through every class which rests upon them."

More applause greeted this statement. The Commoner was now in the full tide of his message. Only thirty-seven years of age, eager, self-confident, and intent on the cause before him, he made the men about him seem like shadows in the intensity of his personal fervor.

He had come to the final challenge of his address.

"If they dare to come out in the open field," he cried, "and defend the gold standard as a good thing, we will fight them to the uttermost.

"Having behind us the producing masses of this nation and the world, supported by the commercial interests, the laboring interests, and the toilers everywhere, we will answer their demand for a gold standard by saying to them: *'You shall not press down upon the brow of Labor this crown of thorns; you shall not crucify mankind upon a cross of gold.'* "

The convention went mad. Here at last was their defender. Here was the gallant fighter who feared no one, who knew no compromise. After years of being trod upon, ignored, despised, ridiculed, here at last they had their champion—The Great Commoner!

The barrage of applause and shouting, almost a hysteria, knew no let down. Tall bronzed farmers wept, and grasped each other by the hand. Political leaders, less selfless but hardly less excited, wished to be the first to follow in the path of this meteor. Delegate Bush of Georgia, bewhiskered and strong of lung, ran with his standard to the Nebraska delegation. A wild yell from the rear of the hall called attention to Joe Lacy, the Cherokee from the Indian Territory, crashing through the chairs of the New York delegation at breakneck speed in an attempt to beat the Georgian to the Nebraska standard.

## THE COUP D'ÉTAT

Bryan, returning to his delegation, pale with victory and excitement, was lifted high on their shoulders. Alabama led a march of triumph around the delegates' pit. While the frenzied din continued and before the routine of business resumed its course, The Commoner slipped away to his hotel room to await the logic of events.

## CHAPTER V
### BOOLA BOOLA

Students are forever doing such things.
—Henry P. Wright

NO sooner had the Unterrified Democracy adopted this astounding figure from the plains of Nebraska than "the boys" had a foretaste of the unruly St. George who was to lead them for many years into battles for which they had little desire and along paths which were anything but primrose.

Into the little room at the Clifton House, where The Commoner sat on the wooden bed, hard by the old-fashioned pitcher and washbowl, excitedly talking about the "principles of the people" which had triumphed, came committee after committee seeking jobs if Bryan should be nominated and elected, asking questions as to his stand, some hoping at the last moment to commit him to some statement which would prove his unavailability and stem the nomination which was practically settled.

"I understand that you are a hard drinker," said one delegate hopefully.

"You may tell the Convention that I am a teetotaler," Mr. Bryan replied.

So that was that.

Toward noon, news of the ratification of his nomination was brought to the little room. There was no great scene because the event had been virtually assured. But trouble came over the choice of a Vice President. And it was trouble of a far-reaching significance.

"The boys" had learned that John R. McLean of Ohio was willing, nay eager, to run as Vice President. Here was a hopeful and delightful circumstance. Mr. McLean was a man of great wealth, father of Edward McLean who was to be the godfather of the Harding administration and to prove so accommodating in financial matters. The Unterrified Democracy had few persons in its ranks who could be financially accommodating. That made no difference to the mass of the voters, but who was to take care of the organization? The McLean willingness was a godsend.

Not only did this prospective candidate have money but he was also proprietor of the Cincinnati *Inquirer,* a powerful newspaper in Ohio.

When the messenger told Mr. Bryan of the availability of this running mate, The Peerless Leader shook his black mane and, rising to his feet, said that McLean represented the forces of organized wealth, that to nominate him would compromise everything for which the party stood. "If that man is nominated for vice president I would decline the nomination for the presidency. I would not run on a ticket with that man."

There was a moment of blank dismay. It was

all very well to say that sort of thing on the platform, but in the committee room candidates should be reasonable. There was no moving Bryan in the matter, however. He considered the discussion closed and the delegates went sadly back to the convention hall with their message. McLean's name was already in the list of candidates being voted upon, but without the endorsement of The Commoner he would not be able to carry the convention. When the Bryan news came in, Sewall, a shipbuilder from Maine, was named on the fifth ballot.

There followed a period of dubious reception on the nation's part to the candidacy of the plainsman from Nebraska. The Populist party endorsed him a few weeks later, but this made little impression because the Populists' star was already waning. There was at first a tendency in eastern circles to ignore the candidate of Democracy. There were apparently two hopes on the part of the opposition: first, that it might not be necessary to pay much attention to the fellow, and next, that he might not take his platform too seriously. But the tight money issue was a real issue with the people and Bryan showed himself to be a whirlwind campaigner, vivid and vocal.

His invasion of the East started quietly enough. The notification ceremonies were held at Madison Square Garden. The Commoner evidently had far too high an opinion of the critical ability of the city masses and placed too great an emphasis on the exactness of the wording of his message. He did not wish to run the risk of delivering an unguarded

*Photograph by Brown Brothers*

THE PEERLESS LEADER AT THE TIME OF HIS
NOMINATION IN 1896

port he received from the churches in the West and South. "You will find in our cities preachers of the gospel," he said, "enjoying every luxury themselves, who are indifferent to the cries of distress which come up from the masses of people."

These words of denunciation, uttered day after day and evening after evening on improvised platforms in open fields, did not have the reasoned carefulness of the Madison Square speech but they got attention. Even business men who were opposed to him stood on the edges of the crowd and were fascinated by the fervent voice and the flashing eyes of the Nebraska Jeremiah.

Bryan sensed that he was gathering strength, and when at Wilmington he received the affront of his campaign, he was ready to meet it. It came suddenly and amazingly. The Democrats had nominated John Boyd Thatcher as the candidate for governor in New York State. As Bryan arrived at Wilmington he received a copy of the evening paper which announced that Thatcher had come out for the gold standard and would not support the silver plank in the Democratic platform. Bryan was beside himself with anger and lost no time in getting the Democratic State Chairman on the long distance telephone.

"Unless Thatcher is removed from the ticket," he said to the chairman, "my engagements in New York are canceled. The Democrats of New York will nominate a man who will stand by the Chicago platform or I will not enter the State. If New York wants to repudiate the platform of the party, we shall repudiate New York."

The thoughts of politicians are long, long thoughts, and a vista of possibilities opened before the chairman at the other end of the wire. Bryan had been a failure at Madison Square Garden but he had now dropped his manuscript and was sweeping the bushes like a forest fire. He was not getting the ear of the sturdy burghers, but the burghers were Republicans and where would New York Democracy be if this tornado of the plains should by any chance win out? The chairman pleaded, explained, argued, but finally agreed that the nominee for governor would be quietly asked to refuse the nomination when it was officially presented to him, and a silver candidate would be named.

Such matters travel underground with amazing rapidity, even though they may not be officially public at the time. Word went around that The Commoner was dominating his own party and that the Madison Square wet firecracker had begun to dry out. It was also known that he had spent a Sunday afternoon with John Brisben Walker, editor of the *Cosmopolitan,* at that time a journal of opinion of considerable circulation and influence. At the Walker home he had had tea with a tall, large-faced, quiet young man who had recently startled New York newspaper circles with his management of the New York *Journal.* Bryan in alliance with Hearst was another political enigma of the times!

It was not strange that when he determined to

*From New Haven "Evening Register"*

This portrait, drawn during the 1896 campaign, was one of the first, if not the first, newspaper sketches made of The Great Commoner.

campaign New England that the Yale boys were out in full force to attend the New Haven meeting, and that they were there to make trouble. He spoke on an outdoor platform erected on the Commons hard by the Center Church. Every space of the several blocks of lawn was occupied by listeners. It was a mixed gathering. In Yale at the time were Percy Rockefeller, Payne Whitney, James W. Wadsworth, Jr. (later senator from New York), E. S. Harkness, Herman Kountze and W. F. Jelke, sons of the men who were controlling the financial forces against which The Commoner was making his campaign. On the other hand, there were hundreds of workers from the factories of New Haven, most of them perhaps out to see a show, and some earnestly interested in what the young candidate might have to say.

The Peerless Leader lost no time in getting under way. "If the syndicates and corporations rule this country," he said, "then no young man has a fair show unless he is the favorite of a corporation."

Applause and yells for McKinley came from the Yale boys.

". . . People have been terrorized over by financial institutions until in some instances it is more dangerous to raise your voice against the ruling power than it is in an absolute monarchy."

Great applause and more yells.

As he tried to continue the shouts of undergraduates increased and cries of "McKinley" interrupted him at every turn. Finally a brass band which had been playing for a drill in another part of the square came nearer and the silver-tongued orator was unable to compete with the baser metal.

Unfortunately for the undergraduates, such inci-

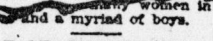

### YALE "JOLLIES" HIM.

At 2:18 the Old Guard Band struck up in front of the New Haven House and the moving procession showed that the Boy Orator was on his way to the Green. It made its way through Temple Street and up the aisle through the human passageway, and, at 2:25, Mr. Bryan, accompanied by Alexander Troup, ex-Mayor Crandall of Norwich, ex-Mayor J. B. Sargent of this city, and several members of the State Central Committee, took his place on the platform. James B. Martin called for three cheers for Bryan and they were given lustily. They were, however mingled with hundreds of hisses by Yale men and at one time it looked as though the cheers would be drowned.

J. B. Sargent then stepped to the front and began to talk. He said: "Fellow-citizens—This magnificent election——" and then the clamoring and babble of human voices became inaudible to even the persons within four feet on the same stage. Just then the stage rail broke at the rear of the staging, and two or three occupants fell off to the ground.

There was momentary confusion, but finally Mr. Bryan stepped forward and raised his hands in an attitude imploring for silence. It was more than a minute before anything like order was restored. He took his start on the southeast corner of the stand and stood waving his hands and waiting for the tumult to subside. Yale men in the crowd kept up a continued roar and Bryan at last took his seat again on the platform. Hundreds of Yale men set up their "Brek-ke-ka-kax, ko-ax ko-ax, and the crowd surged to and fro in front of the stand. It was evident that the Yale noise-makers held the situation in their hands and were going to "bully" the Boy Orator.

### BRYAN'S SPEECH.

*From New Haven "Evening Register"*

The New Haven *"Evening Register,"* which was supporting Bryan, minimized the Yale incident. This item is taken from a front-page story (which occupied the entire page) of Bryan's visit to New Haven. The opposition papers emphasized the Yale matter as a just rebuke to a dangerous demagogue.

dents receive publicity. Many newspapers pointed out that after all Mr. Bryan was the duly nominated candidate of one of the two major political parties, and entitled to courtesy. The affair was commented on in all parts of the country. Whether the Indian tribes had been scouted for new blood to strengthen the sons of old Eli is not known, but at any rate the Choctaws of the Indian Territory held a mass meeting and produced this resolution:

RESOLVED, that we contemplate with deep regret the recent insulting treatment of William Jennings Bryan by students of a college in the land of the boasted white man's civilization, and we admonish all Indians who think of sending their sons to Yale that association with such students could but prove hurtful alike to their morals and their progress toward the higher standard of civilization.

*The Yale News* itself felt that the dignity of the institution had not been properly represented in the affair, and on the following day commented: *"The News* must deprecate the expression of horse-play—this is the true light with which the animus must be regarded—which prompted the demonstration at yesterday's political meeting. The action of Yale men present plainly showed a lack of seriousness for the dignity of the speaker, as a public man, everything political aside, and thoughtful and fair-minded consideration will unanimously condemn and regret the exhibition regardless of party affiliation."

Yale also deemed it advisable to disabuse Harvard of any notion that such an uncouth exhibition was countenanced at New Haven. The Yale news letter in the *Harvard Crimson* the following week stated: "This has been greatly deplored throughout the university, though it was by no means as serious as many newspapers have represented it to be. At no time in his talk was Mr. Bryan interrupted, the cheering and noise occurring before he had commenced to speak, and merely delaying him a few minutes."

Evidently that was the proper note. Henry P. Wright, the acting president of the university, held the view that the situation demanded the lighter touch, feeling that Yale boys will be Yale boys.

"I do not regard the matter seriously," said Dr. Wright's statement, "because I am sure it was not premeditated. Boys will be boys, you know, and it was really nothing more than a boys' outbreak. Students are forever doing such things, thoughtlessly enough, I am sure. I am very sorry indeed that it should have happened, for it places the University in a false light, where the antics of college boys are not understood."

Mr. Bryan himself received the whole incident in reasonably good temper. He was due to speak the next day at Hartford, the next at Springfield, and for every day many times a day before the campaign closed. He was to face many more difficult and tempestuous matters than the Yale incident. In spite of the mutual regrets of the participants, however, the New York *Sun* lent its blessing to the affair and praised the Yale boys for their moderation.

"They ought to have done it," said the *Sun,* "and

the sentiment to which they gave utterance was honorable to them. . . . These decent students, the reports agree, did not offer any personal violence to Mr. Bryan or anybody else. They did not throw rotten eggs or otherwise assail his dignity, but merely shouted their college cry [*sic*] and yelled derisively."

## CHAPTER VI

### ST. GEORGE

To renne hedlynge without feare vpon all ieopardies, as communly passionate persones doth.
—*The Pilgrymage of Perfection*

BRYAN was getting stronger daily. The amusement of his opponents which had followed the farce-comedy at Yale was deepening to uneasiness.

It had been thought at the start of the campaign that the Cleveland Democrats would put up an independent ticket on a gold platform and would split Bryan's strength in two so that there would be no doubt whatever of McKinley's election. A gold candidate was put up late in the campaign, but he carried only one election precinct in the nation.

Metropolitan papers had also assured the public that the man from Nebraska was nothing but a silly, handsome boy with a gift for eloquence. Hence during the early days of the campaign, The Peerless Leader found his opposition to be chiefly that of ridicule.

But the supposedly inexperienced campaigner had begun to register his force upon the opposition. His action in New York State in making his own party withdraw their nomination of their gold Democrat for governor and name another candidate, was a demonstration of audacity and power of personality which made the old stagers in both parties gasp.

Mark Hanna back in Ohio launching the Republican campaign, saw that something needed to be done and that right quickly. He passed the word along that this man Bryan with the dangerous doctrines of the income tax, direct election of senators, and other perilous ideas, was a menace to the Republic. Bryan was the same man with the same known ideas who had been invited to speak on "Patriotism" on the same platform with McKinley only two years before at the Chicago Union League Club, the fortress of western Republicanism. Times had changed and votes were in peril.

Some of the eastern clergy were among the most useful in starting the cry of anarchism, because they could do so with an air of holiness and avowed nonpartisanship which Mr. Hanna did not possess. The Reverend Cortland Myers, later of Boston and Los Angeles, but then at the Baptist Temple in Brooklyn, took up the cry.

"This pulpit is absolutely nonpartisan," he said. "I must be heard and will be heard against all dishonesty and anarchy and kindred evil. I love the blood-stained banner of the cross, and it is ever in danger. I love every stripe and every star of Old Glory, and it is at this moment in danger. I must speak every Sunday from now on until November. I shall denounce the Chicago platform. That platform was made in Hell."

### WHISTLING IN THE DARK.

*From Washington "Post"*

Political opponents of McKinley were fond of emphasizing his resemblance to Napoleon. Mr. Reed, shown in the picture, was the Republican Speaker of the House whom Mr. Bryan had called "The Last Rose of Summer."

But the young Bryan continued unabashed in his ardor. He knew as well as Hanna the underlying issues of the campaign. He knew that since the days of Lincoln the people had had no measure of control over their government in protecting their interests while men like Armour, Hill, Vanderbilt and Gould went unchallenged in amassing fortunes created in part by their genius and in addition by the mere means of capital uncontrolled by any force representing the public welfare. Ideas which were to be accepted as matters of course twenty years later were regarded as anarchistic. The strengthening of the Interstate Commerce Commission, limitations on the wash sales and watering of stock, and other regulatory practices were still in the future. The Peerless Leader knew that they must come and that the public would eventually demand better protection from its government.

The extent of his '96 campaign was a phenomenon which has never been equaled in American political history. In the space of three and a half months The Great Commoner spoke in Kentucky, Tennessee, North Carolina, Virginia, West Virginia, Delaware, New York, Pennsylvania, New Jersey, Connecticut, Rhode Island, Massachusetts, Vermont, Maine, Ohio, Indiana, Michigan, Illinois, Missouri, Iowa, Wisconsin, Minnesota, Montana, Nebraska and Kansas. He traveled more than 18,000 miles and in that time talked to more than 4,800,000 persons.

No town was too small and no audience too humble to warrant his attention. He spared himself

# EL CAPITAN.
## MARCH.

JOHN PHILIP SOUSA.

*Courtesy of The John Church Company*

"EL CAPITAN" WAS THE MARCHING TUNE OF THE CAMPAIGN OF 1896

not at all wherever an opportunity presented itself to proclaim his thoughts. He seldom slept for more than three or four hours at a stretch and often not that. He had a cot in his campaign car and left directions that he should always be wakened whenever there was a group that had come down to hear him. He was often up for the day by five o'clock in the morning and spoke from fifteen to twenty times before dark.

Reporters assigned to cover his course begged him to treat himself with more consideration lest he break down before the election came on, but Bryan smiled and suggested that perhaps it was they who were growing weary. Among the representatives of the press who were traveling with him were Julian Hawthorne, James Creelman, Alfred Henry Lewis, and Richard V. Oulahan. Many of this press staff were officially hostile to the silver candidate, but they continually were faced with scenes with which the ordinary run of ridicule could not cope.

The train drew up at a little frame railroad station at two hours after midnight. Near it was a speaker's stand of plain pine boards, decorated with flags and bunting. Flaring gasoline torches mounted on yellow pine posts threw a sallow light on the front rows of hundreds of plainly clothed men and women who had driven for miles to hear The Great Commoner. The cold autumn wind swept down across the prairie and the audience, wrapped in blankets, shivered.

There was a quick intake of the breath as a tall,

## ST. GEORGE

Bryan and described him as "a mouthing, slobbering demagogue whose patriotism is all in his jaw bone."

In spite of the war cries of anarchy and the opposition of the pulpiteers, Bryan's following grew. On

MCKINLEY: "I wish this base had a little more 'protection' about it."

From New York "World"

*McKinley's reluctant stand for gold as the sole currency basis was not popular at the time, even though subsequently justified.*

his last trip through the East he threw what was well nigh a panic into the heart of conservative New England. In Waterbury, Bridgeport and Boston his audiences numbered more than fifteen thousand.

On the invitation of President Andrews, who had written *An Honest Dollar,* he spoke at Brown University, in Providence, Rhode Island. The action of Andrews was an example of the courage and self-sacrifice which it meant for many of that day to embrace Bryanism. Richard Olney, Cleveland's Secretary of State, was on the Board of Fellows of Brown; John D. Rockefeller, Jr., was in college at the time, and Andrews deepened the ire of his Board of Trustees (already none too favorable to him), by inviting this so-called enemy of the Republic within the college gates.

In spite of all, Hannaism was not going over. The bloody shirt argument which had been useful since the Civil War, namely, waving Old Glory and denouncing the Democratic candidate as the delegate of rebellion, was beginning to wear thin. The Republicans used it, but it was not having its old time effect. Nonpartisan journals were stating the issue with entirely too much candor. The *Literary Digest* presented it this way a few days before the election:

"To many American journals it seems that the presidential campaign, no matter what its immediate outcome, has forced the question of so-called plutocracy to the front, which no single election will solve or relegate to the ranks of minor political issues in this country."

As election day drew near, the Republicans, who had looked upon the campaign as a walk-over, in the early days, now feared for the election of their candidate. Then Mark Hanna played his trump card. He sent forth the word that all the financial world should be taxed. He made an assessment on all national banks. There were no laws in those days with respect to the amount or source of campaign contributions, and the river of gold poured in for the McKinley cause.

Hundreds of thousands of handbills were printed

*From St. Louis "Republic"*

*Enormous contributions were made to the McKinley campaign fund by business interests which feared Bryan's election.*

bearing the legend, "Free Silver Will Bring on Another Panic." Bankers were told to inform their customers that in the case of Bryan's election the future of American business would be in grave doubt.

In Steinway, New York, the president of a large factory called his workers together the night before election and said: "Men, you may vote as you please but if Bryan is elected to-morrow the whistle will not blow Wednesday morning."

Similar warnings were given all over the country, and the business world worked itself up into a state of panic which was communicated to its employees indirectly, even when not directly stated. The Peerless Leader gave a glowing picture of the promised land, but it was a new and unfamiliar territory. The people hesitated on the threshold, a little dubious and more than a little afraid. Would The Great Commoner be able to overcome this hesitancy?

It was a night of excitement and anticipation as Bryan awaited the returns in the little frame house on D Street. Exhausted by his colossal campaign, he sought rest in bed, while Mrs. Bryan sat in the library below analyzing the returns.

The room was decorated mainly with pictures of political heroes. Full length portraits of Washington, Jefferson, Jackson and Lincoln hung on the walls. There were steel engravings of Webster and Calhoun. There was a painting showing Henry Clay addressing his colleagues in the United States Senate. Would there ultimately be among these portraits a painting of The Peerless Leader, labeled "President of the United States"? Or would the enemies whom he had made obliterate him entirely from the political landscape, as they had promised to do?

## CHAPTER VII

### MARK HANNA WAVES THE FLAG

*There must be no scuttle policy.*—McKinley

THE brilliance of the skyrocket was ended. The "light in the west" had faded to embers, and would appear no more. Bryan was done for. This disturbing, dangerous, and crack-brained candidate had sunk into the oblivion from which he would never again emerge.

Such was the view of the metropolitan press and of the George F. Babbitts of the time, when the election results were announced. This was the first of the many Bryan burials which were to occur in the ensuing twenty-five years, and it was the most enthusiastic. On each succeeding occasion the mourners were less jubilant because less certain that Mr. Bryan would, himself, be aware of his demise. Bryan had lost, and the New York *Tribune* gave the foremost of the eulogies at the grave; for bitterness and extremism it set a pace of abuse which no subsequent critic was ever able to equal, and review of it to-day makes the diatribes of Mencken sound like the trilling of a choir boy. Referring to the Chicago platform, this paper remarked:

It has been defeated and destroyed, because right is right and God is God. Its nominal head was worthy of the cause. Nominal, because the wretched, rattle-pated boy, posing in vapid vanity and mouthing resounding rottenness, was not the real leader of that league of Hell. He was only a puppet in the blood-imbued hands of Altgeld, the anarchist, and Debs, the revolutionist, and other desperadoes of that stripe.

But he was a willing puppet, Bryan was, willing and eager. Not one of his masters was more apt at lies and forgeries and blasphemies and all the nameless iniquities of that campaign against the Ten Commandments. He goes down with the cause, and must abide with it in the history of infamy. He had less provocation than Benedict Arnold, less intellectual force than Aaron Burr, less manliness and courage than Jefferson Davis. He was the rival of them all in deliberate wickedness and treason to the Republic. His name belongs with theirs, neither the most brilliant nor the least hateful in the list.

Good riddance to it all, to conspiracy and conspirators, and to the foul menace of repudiation and anarchy against the honor and life of the Republic. The people have dismissed it with no uncertain tones. Hereafter let there be whatever controversies men may please about the tariff, about the currency, about the Monroe Doctrine, and all the rest. But let there never again be a proposition to repeal the moral law, to garble the Constitution, and to replace the Stars and Stripes with the red rag of anarchy. On those other topics honest men may honestly differ, in full loyalty to the Republic. On these latter there is no room for two opinions, save in the minds of traitors, knaves, and fools.

Meanwhile there were some six and a half million persons—and one besides—who felt differently

From "Harper's Weekly"

The Republican National Committee, Mark Hanna holding the fan. Hanna was Chairman and the brains of the 1896 and 1900 campaigns. T. C. Platt, with pointed beard, was the Republican boss of New York.

about the matter. Singularly enough, the one extra person was Mark Hanna, Chairman of the Republican Campaign Committee, capitalist, and practical politician. Hanna did not take overseriously the ideas of Bryan, or, for that matter, of any candidate. He believed in personalities and he admired accomplishment. The person who came nearest to winning Hanna's astounded admiration at this time, after Major McKinley, was none other than William Jennings Bryan.

It required the experience of a political expert to realize the amazing accomplishment of The Peerless Leader. True, he had lost, but the margin had been a thin one. On the surface McKinley's vote of 7,107,000, to Bryan's of 6,511,000 looked like a heavy majority. Actually the victory had been very close, because the big surpluses for McKinley had been rolled up in New York, Pennsylvania, and Illinois, industrial states where the forces of money, organization and Republican traditions were most potent. And those votes were sadly needed, for The Peerless Leader had garnered 956,000 more ballots than Cleveland had received four years before.

In fact the Republican National Chairman realized that if fewer than 20,000 votes had been changed in the proper states, the *Tribune* would never have had an opportunity to write its editorial. A difference of 142 votes in Kentucky would have changed that state to Bryan. He needed but 9,000 votes, out of more than 500,000 cast, to carry Indiana. California was a doubtful state with a difference of only 962 needed to win it for The Great Commoner. Slightly more than 5,000 votes in West Virginia and 1,000 votes in Oregon would have won over those states. With these changes involving fewer than 20,000 ballots, Mr. Bryan would have been elected President.

This close race for the presidency had been achieved with a poverty-stricken campaign chest, with defiance of the old-time leaders, with a rival Democratic ticket in the field, and with an improvised organization in many of the states where the disgruntled Cleveland Democrats had taken the attitude of Senator Hill of New York who wrote to a friend: "I am a Democrat still, very still."

For the coming four years Mark Hanna and all good Republicans held their breath and prepared for 1900.

If there was bitterness in the East, or at any rate the organized effort to create it, in order to hold the Babbitts in the paths of righteousness, the feeling between the two candidates was one of courtesy and friendliness.

The Great Commoner spent the two or three days following the election in his bed, completely exhausted. The months of speaking, of nights without continuous rest, left him with sleep as his chief desire. From time to time Mrs. Bryan came in bringing dispatches of election returns. For a time the news looked good, but more often the disappointment on her face told him the story even before she read the messages. When notified on Thursday by his campaign manager of the Major's election he sent this wire:

> Senator Jones has just informed me that the returns indicate your election, and I hasten to extend my congratulations. We have submitted the issue to the American people and their will is law.—W. J. BRYAN.

William McKinley in turn replied to the vapid boy from Hell in these words:

> I acknowledge the receipt of your courteous message of congratulation with thanks and beg you will receive my best wishes for your health and happiness.—WILLIAM MCKINLEY.

This friendliness on the part of the candidates was commented upon in many papers and proved to be disappointing in a number of quarters where bitterness prevailed. But the generosity of the President-Elect was eventually repaid. The time came, and not far off, when McKinley had need of Bryan's support in a national crisis.

To Bryan in '96 and '97, even though he had not won his hoped-for victory, events indicated that within a term or two he would probably be elected. He had demonstrated to his own party, as well as to Mark Hanna, that he had a personality and a vote-getting power which had accomplished more than any figure in American history since the Civil War from the standpoint of individual leadership. There was no question as to who would be nominated in

1900 if Bryan desired to run. And in his second attempt he would have a band of six and a half million followers who had come close to the gates of victory. Only unforeseen circumstances could dam the tide of the enthusiastic West which at last saw an opportunity to put one of its citizens into the White House, and to have written into the law of the land principles which recognized the needs of that part of the country.

Nor was this enthusiasm limited to the interests of one section of the nation. In the South there was the hope that the man with the cotton patch would attain to a place in the government which had been withheld from him since the days of the Civil War. Cleveland had been a Democrat, but a Democrat of northern training, tradition and sympathies, while Bryan understood the poverty and the needs of the South and was looked upon as one who could relieve them.

Circumstances soon began to operate to minimize the chief Bryan plank and to justify the stand of the Republicans in insisting on a gold basis. Gold, which had been growing scarcer and scarcer, depressing farm prices and placing the creditor class of the nation in almost insuperable bondage, suddenly became plentiful. The cyanide process of production was discovered which made it possible to use ore hitherto unprofitable. The vast Transvaal mines in South Africa were being opened up by the British. On top of that came the discovery of the Klondike, setting the whole western world crazy in the rush for gold, de-dramatizing silver, and bringing in new floods of the golden metal.

The purposes of bimetallism were being accomplished by unforeseen means. The price of corn increased from twenty-one cents per bushel in 1896 to thirty-five cents per bushel in 1900.

Though the force of the bimetallic platform was vitiated by these circumstances, Bryan remained a hope for millions of people. Even in the East he had hundreds of thousands of followers. Henry George, the Bertrand Russell of his age, said after the defeat of '96, "What did free silver matter, the people have lost again." The fight was going on. Benjamin Andrews at Brown University was continuing to preach the awakening of public conscience and consciousness. In 1897 his Board of Trustees asked for his resignation and placed the pastor of Rockefeller's church in the chair of the Baptist institution, but Andrews' days were not ended. Soon there occurred a vacancy in the chancellorship of the University of Nebraska, and The Peerless Leader saw to it that the call was extended to the eastern college president who had fought for Democratic policies in 1896.

The Peerless Leader, resting until time for the next campaign, felt some degree of relief. He foresaw in himself, for the moment at least, "the picture of a citizen by his fireside, free from official responsibility." So he predicted the situation a few days after the election, but his fireside was to see little of him. His brother Charles was hard at work building a political organization. He himself was in demand as a speaker in all parts of the country. He was also engaged in the preparation of a thick volume entitled *The First Battle*.

On Mrs. Bryan's shoulders fell the burden of being the wife of a public man. She rose every morning at five o'clock and opened the mail. There were at times as many as twenty-five hundred letters a day. She divided these into piles, those which Mr. Bryan should see, those which she could answer, and a chaff of communications which needed no reply. The Bryans had a hard time financially during this period, because the expenses of the campaign had eaten into their savings, and revenues from his books, articles and speeches had not yet attained to the profitable schedule which they later realized. Hence on Mary Baird Bryan, the favored only daughter and finishing-school graduate, fell the burdens of secretary, advisor, cook, general houseworker, and mother. She handled it all cheerily and with gusto.

At seven o'clock she awoke the children (who now numbered three) and Mr. Bryan. By seven-thirty she had on the table a breakfast of typical western proportions: eggs, sausages, waffles, and even sometimes in season sliced tomatoes and radishes. Mr. Bryan was very fond of these latter delicacies and on his lecture tours he would carry a package of raw radishes on the train with him. If he were a guest in a home and radishes were served, it was customary for such hostesses as knew his preference to make up a package for him to carry along. There was a romantic touch to the waffles. During his courting days he had written to Mary Baird: "So you have learned to make waffles. I am so fond of them."

Following breakfast the children were hustled off to school. Much of the housework was chored away while Mr. Bryan went over the letters, and the remainder of the day was devoted by Mrs. Bryan to answering correspondence, most of which her husband would sign. The elder daughter, Ruth, helped out by acknowledging the hundreds of letters received from parents who had named their children for The Great Commoner. More than once letters came in enclosing the photographs of triplets who had been named respectively William, Jennings, and Bryan.

Gifts poured in supplying an amazing exhibit of Americana. One of the choicest of these was a large watermelon in a gilded laundry basket. Scores of rabbit's feet were forwarded to The Commoner. A stuffed alligator was another present. Among the livestock offerings were a dog, four live eagles, and a mule.

There were demands as well as gifts. Many wrote in and desired repayment for the election bets which they had lost. One correspondent stated that he had bet his cow on the election and now his children were left without milk; would Mr. Bryan kindly send a new cow at once. Another letter writer complained that during the visit to his city,

Mr. Bryan had been greeted by a salvo of explosions. The explosions had damaged his incubator and the eggs had failed to hatch. Would Mr. Bryan kindly remit.

All these communications had to be handled with tact and thoughtfulness. Aside from the desire to deal kindly with admirers, there was a political hazard involved. One of these problems soon came to light:

When Mr. Bryan happened to be away on a lecture trip he received a letter from a widow in the South stating that she was shipping to him a railroad carload of watermelons. There had been a very heavy watermelon crop in the South, she said, and she needed to get a favorable price for these articles in order to support her family. Would Mr. Bryan kindly sell these for her and remit? Mrs. Bryan was at her wit's end what to do about this communication, especially when the freight office called her up and asked her where they should deliver the shipment.

She hurried down town to the local markets and tried to make a sale. The widow wanted two hundred dollars for the lot which was a theoretical market price at the time, but melons were not moving at any price in Lincoln any more than in the South. Mrs. Bryan tried to sell the carload to local stores, but most of the folks in Lincoln had their own gardens and did not purchase melons in great quantities at the neighborhood stores. By the time Mr. Bryan got back from his lecture trip, the freight office, Mrs. Bryan, and the southern widow were in a state of turmoil. Fearful lest the melons be completely ruined before a sale was made, Mr. Bryan offered them at auction and realized about one hundred dollars which he sent on to the widow. Whether or not this watermelon plan was of political origin was never determined, but the story of the wronged widow robbed of her melon money by the grasping Democratic leader was liberally reported in all parts of the country.

Meanwhile there were disturbances on the national scene of far more importance to the future of The Great Commoner. McKinley in his message to Congress on December 6, 1897, had foreseen that trouble was brewing with respect to Cuba, and predicted that a protectorate of the United States might eventually be established with respect to that country along the lines of the Monroe Doctrine.

"I speak not of forcible annexation," he said, "for that is not to be thought of. That, by our code of morality, would be criminal aggression."

The country was aroused by the cause of the revolutionists in Cuba who were trying to throw off the Spanish yoke. McKinley was opposed to war, but the newspapers, especially the New York *Journal* and the New York *World,* were beating the tom-toms. Into a state of high excitement and public sympathy fell the spark of the sinking of the battleship *Maine* in the harbor of Havana. Immediately it was charged that this had been done by the Spaniards. Regretfully, and urged by the force of public opinion, the President called for a declaration of war. Bryan instantly volunteered his services.

McKinley, thankful that he was to have behind him a united country, asked Senator Allen from Nebraska what assignment should be given to The Great Commoner. Political advisors, however, kept the Major from making a direct answer to Mr. Bryan and no reply was ever sent to his message. Mark Hanna was not going to have any war heroes in the Democratic camp. The bloody shirt and the waving of the flag were to be reserved for Republican purposes.

Bryan, however, was made a colonel by the governor of his state and organized the Third Nebraska Volunteer Regiment which was mustered into service on July 13, 1898. The Great Commoner was a commanding figure as he rode out before his troops on his shiny black Kentucky horse into the hollow square formed by the waiting regiment.

His troops were encamped at Panama Park in Florida, and suffered there from typhoid fever and other ills due to the lack of knowledge of sanitation of the day, the decayed beef supplied by the government, and the mismanagement of the War Department in omitting to supply necessities. The colonel bought many supplies for his men out of his own pocket, and his tent was a center for relief work until he himself came down with fever. Neither before this nor after his recovery did his regiment have an opportunity to get to the front.

Charles Willis Thompson, a leading political observer, made the comment, "The Republican administration was taking no chances on his getting away with any military glory and it marooned him in Florida until after the war."

Twenty years later Theodore Roosevelt was also to offer his services to the country, and a Democratic President remembered a valuable precedent in not replying.

Bryan saw the war with Spain as a noble attempt to give freedom to an oppressed people and add to the spread of democracy throughout the world. On land and on sea America scored prompt and decisive victories. In the Philippines the rebel troops were aiding the United States. General Aguinaldo, the head of the Philippine forces, was prevailed upon by Admiral Dewey and the representatives of the United States State Department to join as an ally with the Americans.

Before he had enlisted Bryan had said at Omaha on June 14, 1898, "History will vindicate the position taken by the United States in the war with Spain. In saying this I assume that the principles which were invoked in the inauguration of the war will be observed in its prosecution and conclusion. If a war undertaken for the sake of humanity degenerates into a war of conquest we shall find it difficult to meet the charge of having added hypocrisy to greed.

"Is our national character so weak that we cannot withstand the temptation to appropriate the first piece of land that comes within our reach?"

## MARK HANNA WAVES THE FLAG

Immediately hostilities ceased toward the end of 1898, The Great Commoner saw that the administration had no intention of applying the same rule to the Philippines as had been proclaimed for Cuba. He promptly resigned from the army since the warfare was over, and held himself in readiness to demand that independence be assured in both cases. He did not have to wait long for a specific statement of President McKinley's intention. On December 21, 1898, McKinley issued a proclamation to the Philippines asserting the sovereignty of the United States over them. The reception of this move in the Islands was one of astonishment and sense of betrayal.

Aguinaldo met the proclamation by a counter one in which he denied the claim of the United States, asserting that the country had been reclaimed from the Spaniards by the blood and treasure of his countrymen.

The women of the Cavite Province brought a petition to General Otis, Commander of the American Forces in the Philippines, stating that after all the men were killed off, they would shed their blood for the liberty and independence of their country.

Active hostilities broke out on February 4, 1899. Senator Hoar of Massachusetts, in a communication to the Springfield *Republican,* stated that the aggression came from the American side: "The outbreak of hostilities was not their fault, but ours. We fired upon them first. The fire was returned from their lines. Thereupon it was returned again from us, and several Filipinos were killed. As soon as Aguinaldo heard of it he sent a message to General Otis saying that the firing was without his knowledge and against his will; that he deplored it and that he desired hostilities to cease, and would withdraw his troops to any distance General Otis should desire. To which the American general replied that as the firing had begun, it must go on."

The American public, though elated by the victories of Dewey, Sampson, Schley and Roosevelt, were still lacking a justification of war upon the Filipinos after all the previous sentiments about liberating the oppressed in Cuba. The President, twelve days after the outbreak in the Philippines, gave the public the message for which they were instinctively seeking.

"Our concern was not for territory or trade or empire," he announced, "but for the people whose interest and destiny, without our willing it, had been put in our hands."

Such were the words of the executive, as incredible as they may sound to a more realistic era. That was to be the platform: no selfish motive or desire for land actuated the country, no seeking of power, merely a kindly disposed feeling to be our brother's keeper, a duty actually thrust upon the country while it was looking the other way.

Even some of the Republican senators were shocked at the imperialistic policy of the administration and its bold change of position between Cuba and the Philippines. Senator Hoar in particular opposed this course and violently objected to the signing of the treaty which would cede the Philippines from Spain to the United States.

The success of McKinley's administration and of all the peace parleys was threatened by this opposition. If Bryan demanded that the Democrats in the Senate should take a similar position the issue could not come to a settlement. Much to the surprise of Senator Hoar and other Republicans, The Peerless Leader came out with a demand that the treaty should be signed because it was easier to do justice to the Philippines and promise them independence after they were the property of the United States by treaty than if their international status were still in debate, due to the treaty not being signed.

Senator Hoar, wise in years of political experience, realized that with the power in the hands of the administration to do with the Philippines as it liked, there was not much doubt as to the outcome. Bryan had let his friendliness for McKinley, his desire to do the right and the grand thing, and his love of peace euchre him into an embarrassing situation.

He did not, however, stay in one situation for more than five minutes at a time. He campaigned up and down the country, denouncing imperialism and demanding that McKinley, now that the peace treaty was signed, at least give assurance that the Philippines at some definite future time would be set free.

Mark Hanna smiled in his office in Cleveland, Ohio. Three years before he had feared that no man in the country might be able to stop the course of The Peerless Leader by the time 1900 was reached. The danger was not over but two strange shifts in the luck had risen up to cast a shadow on the "light in the west." The gold discoveries had minimized the silver issue, and the excitement of war had brought their usual change and forgetfulness in the public feeling. The fervor and idealism of '96 were forgotten in the successful roar of cannon and in the blare of bands playing Sousa marches of victory.

Another political leader had appeared on the horizon galloping out of the East. Theodore Roosevelt, the hero of San Juan Hill, had been elected governor of New York and wanted to run again. Senator Platt, the Republican boss of New York State, had found that Roosevelt did not take orders and consequently Platt was determined to put him out of politics.

Hanna in the meantime was worried over the strength of The Peerless Leader in spite of the circumstances of the past four years. The public at the moment was militant in its mood, but what might not this prairie orator accomplish in rousing the farmers and masses everywhere to a state of idealism (impractical in Hanna's mind) unless some one could be found to wave the flag? He deferred to the ability of Major McKinley but could McKinley a second time stand up against the Bryan attack? Would McKinley alone, essentially a man of peace, be willing to act the rôle of military hero? Some

*From New York "Journal"*

Roosevelt's part in the Spanish War had made him the most dramatic figure in the Republican camp. It will be noted that the British issue was then in politics, as later. Hay and Pauncefote were the American and British negotiators of a treaty affecting the use of the Panama Canal by Great Britain.

one was needed on the ticket who would dramatize the war for the westerners, and Roosevelt was offered to him as the man. Hanna did not like Roosevelt and did not understand him. He thought that all Republicans should be good fellows together, and this fellow was a maverick. While he was complaining to his friends that McKinley favored the addition of the Rough Rider to the ticket he was also sending word to Senator Platt that he would yield to the view that Roosevelt must run for the vice presidency, with McKinley as candidate to succeed himself.

This pleased Senator Platt immensely. It would get Roosevelt out of the State of New York and would place him in a position which hitherto had been a political burying ground. Roosevelt resisted the suggestion and thought he foresaw it would have a disastrous affect on his own political career, but the insistence of the party managers that this was the only way to defeat Bryan and his policies persuaded T. R. to enter the race.

By the time of the Republican nomination there was no doubt that imperialism would be the issue of the campaign. McKinley's statement did not equivocate. When notified of his nomination, he said: "There must be no scuttle policy. We will fulfill in the Philippines the obligations imposed by the triumph of our arms, by the treaty of peace, and by international law, by the nation's sense of honor, and, more than all, by the rights, interests, and conditions of the Filipinos themselves. . . . The Philippines are ours, and American authority must be supreme throughout the archipelago."

In Kansas City the Democrats accepted the challenge. They named "anti-imperialism" as the leading plank and called on Bryan to head the ticket. The incidents of this meeting gave little comfort to the Republicans, for Bryan had won a strong ally in New York State which had been his greatest problem in 1896. Richard Croker, leader of Tammany Hall, came out strongly in support of Bryan. Croker, the wily Irishman, had realized that the "high-brow" politicians in New York such as Senator Hill and Cleveland, were not going to get anywhere, nationally or locally. They were merely thin replicas of Republicanism. Croker, too, like Hanna, recognized the tremendous personal accomplishment of The Peerless Leader in the '96 campaign, and saw that this was Democracy's best bet. Accordingly he instructed Senator Hill to endorse Bryan's policies in Kansas City. After all, the Tammany Chief figured, what difference does it make what the national policies are if the local elections are won and the local boys cared for? Hill was even more than ever anxious that Democracy should turn to a gold standard platform. Bryan did not personally attend the Kansas City Convention but the leaders talked to him on the long distance wire and asked if he would be willing to run if a reiteration of the silver plank were omitted, or a gold plank included. He said that under those circumstances he would refuse to be a candidate. They urged upon him the view that silver had become an obsolete issue, but he stood fast and the majority report favored his position. At this point Senator Hill desired to frame a minority report and fight the thing through to a finish. Mr. Croker sent the message from New York that the delegation of that state would vote for the majority report, and Hill faded from the picture.

Croker was wise enough to know that Bryan could not be won by promises of support, rewards, or other common coin of politics. Tammany Hall had nominally supported him in '96 but with no great warmth. Some way must be found to reach the heart of The Great Commoner, and New York's Irish boss had not reached his position by accident. He sat down and wrote to The Commoner that a few days before he had been laid up by an accident and had an opportunity to read Mr. Bryan's book entitled *The First Battle*. He told how this had changed his political outlook and he stated that he was supporting him for the presidency because he believed that Bryan was in public life because of his interest in the public welfare and not in it for pecuniary advantage. This message had the expected effect, possibly it was at least half sincere. At any rate Bryan had the zeal of a missionary for his convert and as long as Croker remained ruler of the Hall, The Commoner and Tammany were good friends.

Some of the Democrats hoped that Bryan would be able to find another issue. Many were disappointed that he could not find something which

## MARK HANNA WAVES THE FLAG

**BRYAN:** "But this is so sudden. Mr. Croker."
*From New York "World"*

*While the cartoonist usually portrayed Mr. Bryan as embarrassed by his friendship with Tammany, The Commoner himself always apppeared to be openly and unreservedly cordial to Croker, who was the leader of Tammany at the time of the 1900 campaign.*

would be more acceptable to everybody. They went along with him on anti-imperialism, hoping that the reiteration of the income tax and other planks adopted at Chicago in '96 and repeated in the 1900 platform might pull in votes which would not be with Democracy on anti-imperialism solely. The

Republicans were talking about the "full dinner pail," a theme which proved to be as stirring as the flag of a successful war.

But The Great Commoner, once started on an issue, was like a locomotive thundering down the tracks without brakes. Nothing stopped him. His cause filled his complete horizon. He could see no reasons against it and he could not understand why it would not be self-evident to every human being.

In his speech of acceptance at Indianapolis he was specific to the last comma as to what he would do with respect to the new conquests.

"If elected," he said, "I shall convene Congress in extraordinary session as soon as I am inaugurated and recommend an immediate declaration of the nation's purpose: first, to establish a stable form of government in the Philippine Islands, just as we are now establishing a stable form of government in Cuba; second, to give independence to the Filipinos, just as we have promised to give independence to the Cubans; third, to protect the Filipinos from outside interference while they work out their own destiny, just as we have protected the republics of Central and South America and are, by the Monroe Doctrine, pledged to protect Cuba."

While Roosevelt and Bryan were the dominant political figures for more than a score of years they were never opposing candidates for the presidency, yet in this campaign Roosevelt carried the burden of the work for McKinley, did the stumping of the country for him, and carried the position of the

## MARK HANNA WAVES THE FLAG

Republicans much further than they had dared to place it.

Roosevelt stood for the manifest destiny argument and occasionally spoke of unselfishness, but he bound his campaign down to one simple issue.

NURSE HANNA: "My, what a difference there is in children."

*From Cleveland "Plain Dealer"*

Mark Hanna, Chairman of the Republican Campaign Committee, is shown holding the squalling Teddy while McKinley sits quietly on the floor engrossed in his "Second Term Reader."

"Don't haul down the flag," he shouted as he addressed audience after audience.

Meanwhile the silver-tongued orator was opposing the claims of jingoism by an appeal to the enlightened sentiment of the American public and in this appeal he allied with him many who had not been willing to endorse him in the free silver days.

He won Andrew Carnegie to his cause and Carnegie forever after was an admirer of The Great Commoner though the admiration was reciprocated only to a limited degree. In fact, Bryan in later years resigned from the chairmanship of the Board of Trustees of Illinois College because they accepted the Carnegie Pension Fund which he held would work to tie the tongues of the teachers in their discussions of economics.

Never at any period in his career did Bryan have an issue in which he believed more deeply, never did he express himself with more fervor in the elaborate periods of the age.

His challenge to the American people to a higher conception of Democracy, issued at Indianapolis after defining his stand on the Philippines, was voiced in terms which have not been surpassed in political campaigning. Manifest destiny?

"I can conceive of a national destiny," he declared in reply to the imperialists, "separating the glories of the present and the past—a destiny which meets the responsibilities of to-day and measures up to the possibilities of the future.

"Behold a republic," he continued, "rising securely upon the foundation stones quarried by revolutionary patriots from the mountains of eternal truth—a republic applying in practice and proclaiming to the world the self-evident propositions that all men are created equal; that they are endowed by their Creator with inalienable rights; that governments are instituted among men to secure these rights and that governments derived their just powers from the consent of the governed."

Was that American policy? or was it to be thrown aside as the American nation asserted its superiority over another race and attempted to rule it? Don't haul down the flag? Was America still to be ruled by an old-world conception of what constituted patriotism?

"Behold a republic standing erect while empires all around are bowed beneath the weight of their own armaments. Behold a republic whose flag is loved while other flags are only feared."

Was it necessary to the grandeur of the American people in their own desire to feel a sensation of the glory of being great, to realize that desire only through aggression? "Behold a republic," The Great Commoner urged, "increasing in population, in wealth, in strength and in influence, solving the problems of civilization and hastening the coming of a universal brotherhood—a republic which shakes thrones and dissolves aristocracies by its peerless example and gives light and inspiration to those that sit in darkness."

It was the nation coming of age that he was addressing as he went from town to town, riding the sleepers as in the days of 1896, wearing out the reporters who tried to keep up with his energy in speaking twelve to fifteen times a day and all hours of the night. He was talking to farmers who had dreams of riches in their new lands; to workmen who were fed with stories of the opportunities of rising from the bench to the superintendent's office; to an adventurous, acquisitive people who had just begun to realize their mass power as a military force. Such was the mood, in so far as there can be any general mood, of the vast middle class who had had all the thrill of seeing brass buttons in an easy war which had brought much flourish of trumpets and few sorrows. He was talking to a country which in the upper financial ranges was peopled by business men who regarded the nation as their oyster, by writers of the mauve decade who had reached the last extreme of the *précieuse*. In the church audiences he was talking to citizens led, in many instances, by preachers who were advocating a sensational evangelism, who were filling their churches by discussion of crime, who had an adeptness at identifying the popular prejudices of the day with the will of the Almighty.

Before this conglomeration of souls he held up this vision: the ideal of a nation living up to its highest possibilities. "Behold a republic," he cried, "gladly but surely becoming the supreme moral factor in the world's progress and the accepted arbiter of the world's disputes—a republic whose history, like the path of the just, is as the shining light that shineth more and more unto the perfect day."

Teddy roared, "Don't haul down the flag."

## CHAPTER VIII

### NEIGHBOR BRYAN

Nor rural sights alone, but rural sounds,
Exhilarate the spirit, and restore
The tone of languid nature.
—Cowper

STRONG in the youthful confidence that the American public would renounce jingoism and glory in the opportunity to bestow freedom upon the Philippines, Mr. Bryan awaited the election news with a confident heart.

The record indicates that he was in error. It was a swashbuckling age, the age of Kipling. The British poet, shouting about the White Man's Burden, and T. R., the picturesque Rough Rider, had captured the imagination of the public. The people were drunk with "the glory of being great." They saw the stars and stripes flying over the seven seas. The appeals for the magnanimous, the democratic, and for the liberating gesture, fell upon deaf ears. Mr. Bryan's vote was slightly less than in 1896, and he had a net loss of two states. South Dakota reverted to Republicanism; Kansas and his own Nebraska decided to march with the brass band. But Kentucky returned to the Democratic column and stayed there for twenty-four years.

It was a baffling time for the young political leader just forty years old and twice defeated for the presidency. Times were changing and his political experiences had shown him that he had not entirely caught the drift. He had twice made a grand fight and tried to carry everything before him in a *tour de force,* but not enough of the voters had come with him. The country was too large, too diverse, and the motives of the people too complicated for him to win in that fashion. The truth of the matter was that up until 1900 he was not in any thoroughgoing sense a commoner. He had adopted the string tie, the worn suit of clothes, and all the other trimmings of the common people, but by temperament he had little in common during his campaign or in preceding years with the plowhorse or the man who walked behind him.

Bryan in 1896 and in 1900 was brilliant, incandescent, in the fire of his oratory and intensity of his thought. Events had piled up one on top of another, giving him virtually no time to live the lot of the common man, had he desired to do so.

But now there was a breathing spell. For a time it looked as though he might settle down to the life of a prosperous country squire. He became "just folks" with the neighbors on D Street in Lincoln, yet one suspects that even in this placid time he sensed there was a difference between himself and the masses. One can see him stirring about, attending meetings, supervising the building of his new home out in the country, presiding at the Round

Table Club in Lincoln, lecturing on a Sunday evening in the little Westminster Presbyterian Church near his home, all the time giving a good and sincere imitation of a commoner, and yet all the time having that extra voltage which set him apart from the ordinary run.

The political outlook was dark. The price of corn in 1900 under the Republican régime had risen to thirty-five cents. Gold production continued to pour in from the Klondike and also from the Transvaal, providing more currency, creating a rise in prices, and doing away with the underlying circumstances which had made free silver an issue.

While the 1896 campaign had been followed by a deluge of communications from Bryan admirers, sometimes as many as twenty-five hundred letters arriving in a day, after 1900 the Bryanites apparently felt that the game was up, and they permitted him to return undisturbed to his private life. Yet, in his section of the country, he remained until the end of his days the dominant political figure. In 1900 he was the only American living west of the Missouri who had a national and international reputation. The older leaders had all been in the East and the younger men were still for the most part obscure. Al Smith was clerking in the Commissioner of Jurors' Office in New York City. Newton D. Baker was city solicitor for Cleveland, Ohio, and due soon to be its mayor; Hoover was a mining engineer, traveling from Mexico to Canada, to Australia, to South Africa—wherever engineering problems arose. G. W. Norris was a Nebraska judge, but had not yet served his first term in Congress; Vic Donahey was clerk of Goshen County Township, Ohio, and Borah was practicing law in Boise, Idaho.

Lincoln, itself, had lost its two other citizens who were to win international fame. Pershing had been moved to another army post, having acquired by this time the rank of captain, and Charlie Dawes was down in Washington as Comptroller of the Currency, a reward which came to him for his work on the Republican National Committee in 1896.

Hence, alone in his glory and his responsibility—for he took it as such—Bryan continued unofficially to be the spokesman of the farmers and small tradesmen for his part of the country, and to some extent for the entire nation. Being a spokesman in itself does not provide food and clothing for a healthy family, and Bryan now had two daughters and a son to be provided for. He had some thought of returning to his law practice until he discovered that his oratorical gifts were enormously profitable on the Chautauqua platform, and enabled him to take in an income far ahead of that of any normal legal practice of that region. To become well-to-do as a lawyer in that part of the country, he would have needed to take on railroad or other corporation business, which would have been distasteful to him as the champion of people opposed to the trusts.

On the other hand, the Chautauqua gave him a chance to know and to meet vast masses of people,

"THE CHAUTAUQUA BELT"
From "World's Work"

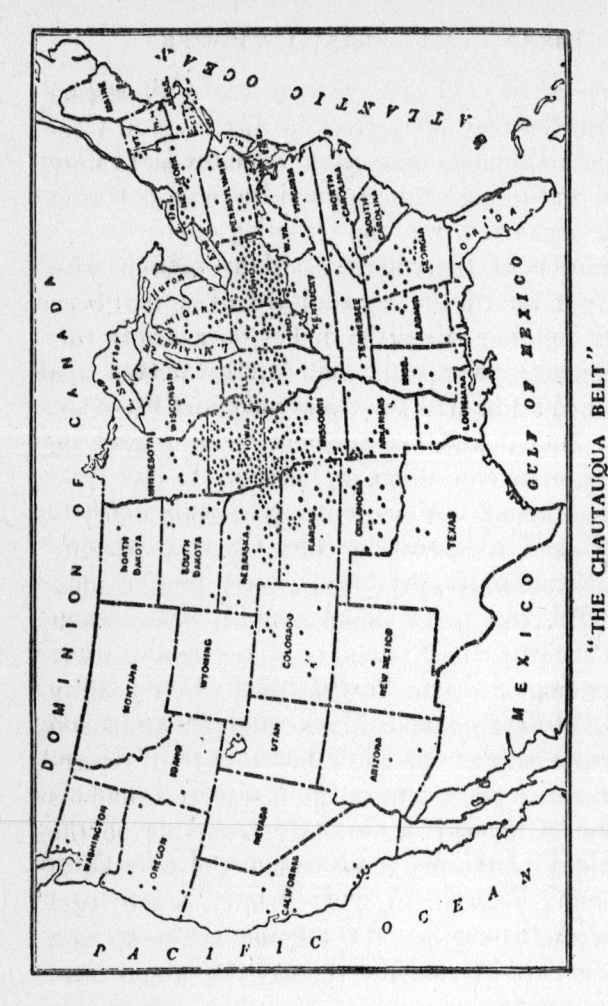

THE DOTS INDICATE THE TOWNS IN WHICH SUMMER ASSEMBLIES ARE HELD EVERY YEAR

This map of the Chautauqua movement is a fair indication of Chautauqua in 1900, though the chart was made in 1912.

an acquaintanceship and experience which were in line with the real interests of his life.

Chautauqua, taking its name from the Lake Chautauqua gathering, where the idea was first thoroughly organized, was the traveling opera house of that section of the country. Many regions which could not afford the expenditure of a permanent theater building raised the money once a year for a Chautauqua session to be held in a great tent. Admission could be had for twenty-five and fifty cents. Entertainment and management were usually supplied by some entertainment bureau. In later years the Chautauqua was one more gibe with which the papers liked to thrust at The Great Commoner. As a matter of fact, virtually every man in public life in America had availed himself of the opportunity to earn an income and reach the public through this medium. Taft, Peary, Mark Twain, Glenn Frank, Stefansson and Mark Sullivan are among those who have appeared on Chautauqua platforms.

The series of entertainments usually included a well-known speaker, a novelty act, and an operatic troupe among the major attractions. Lillian Nordica, Emmy Destinn, Madame Sembrich, Schumann-Heink, and Emma Calvé are among the singers who have appeared in community auditoriums or under the big canvas.

But none of them had the continuous pulling power of Bryan. Season after season, year after year, whenever he appeared, no tent could be found large enough to hold the crowds which came. His hearers felt that they were listening not only to an address of unusual sparkle and power, but they sensed in the speaker a sympathy and understanding of their ways of life and their needs. It was in the Chautauqua days of the early nineteen hundreds that William Jennings Bryan began to emerge as The Great Commoner. His talks were no longer hurried addresses from the back platform of trains, or busy stops where political committees had to be met and listened to. He could now mingle among the people as one of them and take the time to get acquainted. He became guide, counselor, and friend for a vast countryside. Here again his amazing memory for faces, names, and the personal fortunes of all of his bearers, was useful. Folks—the people all about him—became his dominant interest and preoccupation.

Not long after he began his Chautauqua and lyceum lecturing, he was a good enough business man to make a deal with the managers always to go on a percentage basis, frequently 50 per cent of the gate receipts. He always told them that he didn't want them to lose any money, and that if no one came to hear him they needn't pay him a cent. The managers were very anxious to risk contracting for several hundred dollars a night rather than accept Mr. Bryan's kind offer, but the percentage basis was the usual thing. It is said to be in Carthage, Missouri, that he first exceeded a revenue of one thousand dollars for one lecture.

This occasion was on a broiling midsummer day.

The mammoth tent seated several thousand and thousands more stood listening outside under the open air. The sun beat upon the canvas making it as golden as grain and as hot as the furnace of Shadrach, Meshach, and Abednego, but the faithful remained unperturbed, waiting for their Commoner to begin his message. As he rose to start his address, there was a bugle call in the offing, and there appeared riding, two by two, two hundred citizens mounted on two hundred white horses. The cavalcade rode up the center aisle of the tent, saluted, and then withdrew to the outer wall until the address was over.

The Commoner, with tears of joy in his eyes, greeted the horsemen at the conclusion of the meeting. It was merely a demonstration on the part of his followers as a tribute to his leadership, which they hoped would continue for years to come.

This event and the enormous audiences which he was getting everywhere determined him definitely to adopt lecturing as his primary means of income. He usually spoke without charge on Sundays, and never charged for any church sermons, of which he preached many.

On January 3, 1901, The Great Commoner began a publishing venture which lasted for twenty-two years, an unusual record when one considers that the periodical was a personal journal, built wholly round the life and interests of one man, and carried on with very little advertising effort, and little of the brains or attractiveness of competent journalism.

## NEIGHBOR BRYAN

This venture was *The Commoner,* a weekly journal of opinion, which gave The Peerless Leader a speaking range throughout the country even greater than the extent of his own lecture tours. From the beginning, he was astute enough to quote small-town papers all over the nation as a weekly feature, and they in turn scanned *The Commoner,* not only to see if they were being quoted but also for material for return of courtesies.

The paper sold for one dollar a year, and had an advance paid subscription demand of 17,000 copies. Ultimately, 175,000 copies were printed of the first edition, and for a number of years the circulation went up and down over the 100,000 mark. The circulation in the second year was 140,000.

*The Commoner* succeeded through the personal devotion of Bryan's admirers, and the vigor of the presentation of political messages, rather than from entertainment or popular presentation. Most of its issues, in fact, were as dull as *The Nation* and other political papers of the day. Only in occasional crusades did it draw wide general attention, and then it was quoted by the metropolitan press as well as by the small-town periodicals.

It had a home department which ranked well enough with the newspapers of the time, being rather in keeping with the style of the day, filled with anecdotes, sentimental thoughts and poetry, which represented a wide range of talent geographically.

In fact, Mr. Bryan's interest in public service made him less stringent with respect to the arts, and his tolerance appeared here in full flower to a degree which was nothing short of appalling.

"We are a nation of writers and a nation of poets," he did not hesitate to say in a midsummer issue of the paper in 1901; "there is hardly a state in this Union but that may count among its citizens several poets of recognized standing."

The publication was a singular combination of virtues and faults. At the end of the first year, the editor said: "The advertising has been limited, because I have rejected some advertising as unfit for a family paper; second, because I have not cared to advertise trust-made goods—and with the growth of trusts this class amounts to more and more. While the exclusion of trust advertisements reduces the revenue of the paper, I can discuss the trust question without having to consider the effect of the editorial on my income."

Yet, though there was this purity with respect to trust advertising, *The Commoner,* like many newspapers and nearly all the religious papers of its day, reeked with patent medicine advertising. One might see in many an issue a large display of Dr. Harris's $20 Electric Belt, guaranteeing "to cure rheumatism, neuralgia, lumbago, paralysis, dyspepsia and all stomach troubles." Again, there was the Elixir of Life revealed by a Dr. Pierce, and many similar nostrums.

In its main field of political comment and criticism it wielded from the beginning a distinct power. At the masthead was carried this statement:

"*The Commoner* will endeavor to aid the common people in the protection of their rights, the advancement of their interests, and the realization of their aspirations."

Week after week, this political gadfly buzzed around the operations of Congress and of state governments, keeping their activities in the public view. Nor were these matters always presented with the crusading or ponderous method. *The Commoner's* column of brief and pointed paragraphs became known and feared wherever politicians congregated, feared for their humor which was frequently more effective than the longer, more serious editorials. One finds, for instance, this comment in one of the early issues: "A $60,000,000 River and Harbor Bill is not unexpected. High water and corroding tides have weakened Congressional levees, and they must be properly reënforced before November, 1902."

The course of the magazine was not entirely an untroubled one. The publisher had been sending free copies to various members of Congress, in addition to those who had subscribed for it. Some had made complaint to the Post Office Department, asking to be protected from receipt of this annoying magazine, thereby furnishing the opportunity to spread the rumor that the Post Office Department had found it necessary to look into the circulation methods of Mr. Bryan's publication.

It was a political maneuver of the type which might have been successful with either a more reserved or a more vulnerable publisher. Mr. Bryan was neither. He immediately blazed forth in his paper about political persecution, and in no time at all had dug up enough inefficiencies and injustices on the part of the Department so that it was ready to yell quits.

The Great Commoner was finding life beautiful and worth while in most respects. His family life was happy, and he was establishing through his paper and platform a definite place for himself in public affairs. The only shadow was the fact that death was taking some of his old associates. "Silver Dick" Bland had gone and Judge Trumbull; and on March 11, 1902, Altgeld, who had supported the young Bryan in '96, also passed to the beyond. Bryan attended the funeral service. Dr. Frank Crane preached the main sermon, Clarence Darrow, Altgeld's law partner, gave the eulogy, and Bryan spoke at the grave.

But in spite of these sadnesses, and of the political reverses which he had suffered, his outlook was always brightly toward the engaging concerns of the present and the sunny possibilities of the future. He had a grand time in *The Commoner* belaboring the Republicans for their sins. Twenty years before his famous letter inquiring about jobs for deserving Democrats, he criticized the appointment of the son of Justice Harlan of the Supreme Court to the attorney-generalship of Porto Rico, and of the son of Justice McKenna, also of the Supreme Bench, to the office of Inspector-General of Volunteers.

He attacked President Eliot of Harvard for eulogizing nonunion strikebreakers. He championed religious freedom, and it wasn't until many years later that he noted that American womanhood was in danger. In 1901 he wrote in his paper, "Civilization has nothing to fear from the new woman, who aspires to an intimate acquaintance with the things which deeply concern society." Unfortunately, this cryptic sentence was not amplified.

His attitude towards Roosevelt was one of encouragement rather than jealousy. He kept egging him on to more "trust-busting," rather than objecting to T. R. for stealing the Bryan policies.

With respect to the negro, his point of view was distinctly southern, influenced not only by his political associations, but also by his frequent visits to North Carolina. He strongly deplored the luncheon invitation of President Roosevelt to Booker T. Washington, president of a negro college. Concerning this, he wrote in *The Commoner*, "The action of President Roosevelt, inviting Professor Booker T. Washington to dine at the White House was unfortunate, to say the least. . . . The fact is that in none of the Southern States has an attempt been made to take from the negro the guarantees enumerated in our Constitution and in the Bill of Rights."

The power of this paper made Bryan an additionally perplexing factor in the political scene. In 1902, one finds him saying kind things about Tammany and Richard Croker. He also published in the columns of *The Commoner* the opinions of William Randolph Hearst concerning Jefferson. The opinions were favorable. The Jeffersonian cult, it should be said in fairness, was not confined to any one politician, and *The Commoner* joined with other Democratic papers in the establishment of Jefferson as an ideal even more than in discussion of his political philosophy.

While all these things were going on, Mr. Bryan was making money rapidly for those days and for a commoner. In fact, some of his readers were critical about the vast revenues which they thought that Editor Bryan might be drawing from his paper. They received fifty-two issues for a dollar, and there was very little advertising, but they had been reared to look for signs of wealth in business enterprises and they did not hesitate to inquire just how much Mr. Bryan was making out of his publication. In February, 1903, he, accordingly, obliged these inquirers with a statement of his personal finances.

He was taking out less than $5,000 annually from *The Commoner*. He reported that he had received about $3,000 by inheritance, and had saved another $3,000 prior to his nomination for the presidency. His royalties on books had amounted to $34,000, but half of this had been pledged to campaign committees. During the past five years he had lived simply, and had given $21,000 to political reform movements. The net result was that he was worth between $15,000 and $20,000 besides his house and land.

*From St. Paul "Daily Pioneer Press"*

*In 1903 a political friend of* The Commoner's *left him $50,000. The widow contested the will and the newspapers had a good story.*

Bryan had at last reached the point where he could afford to become a country gentleman. He had determined to buy some land several miles from town in a section called Normal and he decided to build thereon a home which he thought would be better for his children than living in the city. He always prized the days which he had spent as a child on the farm. The house he planned was in the architecture of the General Grant school; it was amply and substantially built. "Fairview," as he called it, became an oasis for persons of note traveling across the country, whatever their political affiliation. Both Bryan and Mrs. Bryan enjoyed the rôle of hospitality, and Fairview, with its lively youngsters, became known in all parts of the country. Its barn was spacious and its laborers were well paid. In fact, they were so well paid, some getting as high as $150 a month, which was a lavish sum, especially for those days, that Fairview itself was a financial loss. But it gave The Great Commoner an ampler scene, a more natural setting, a more expansive ground than the house on D Street.

It gave him the sense more definitely than ever of being not only a brilliant political leader, but a successful, substantial commoner and farmer.

Fairview was the comfortable foundation of most of his future activities, a source and haven of strength. At Fairview were held the first marriage of his daughter Ruth, and her second marriage to a British army officer. Here, too, Grace Bryan was married. After moving here Bryan attended the Presbyterian Church less frequently when at home. He, his wife and children communed at the little Normal Methodist Church about a half mile from his house.

A momentarily disturbing note in the midst of

this calm was occasioned by the will of a Philo Sherman Bennett, leaving $50,000 to Mr. Bryan. The widow promptly sued to break the will. Mr. Bennett was a wholesale grocer of New Haven, Connecticut, who had been an enthusiastic free-silver advocate. He had been on the New Haven reception committee when Bryan first visited that city in 1896, and had followed up the acquaintanceship. Shortly before 1900 he had called on Mr. Bryan in Lincoln to discuss the provisions of his will which would distribute an estate worth $300,000.

Mr. Bennett proposed to leave $100,000 to the widow, certain amounts to relatives, and about $80,000 to public causes. In the latter item, he included the $50,000 bequest to The Commoner with the purpose of enabling Bryan to continue on the lecture platform and to give free lectures. Mr. Bryan at this conference, which occurred before the 1900 campaign, said that he would not accept the money personally if circumstances proved to be such that he did not need it. Neither would he accept the bequest if the widow should object. Mr. Bennett replied that he had provided amply for Mrs. Bennett and if Bryan refused to accept the money personally, as an executor of the estate he should distribute the funds to public causes. When Mr. Bennett died in 1903 Mrs. Bennett objected strenuously both to the terms of the will and the naming of Mr. Bryan as an executor. The hostile press painted lively pictures of The Commoner attempting to rob the poor widow. Mr. Bryan announced that he would not accept any of this money for himself, but that as an executor he would defend the will and would allocate the $50,000 to public causes. The widow lost her suit. Mr. Bryan distributed the funds, and calm reigned again at Fairview.

## CHAPTER IX

### AN INNOCENT ABROAD

Integer vitæ scelerisque purus
Non eget Mauri jaculis neque arcu.
—Horace

WHILE the simplicities of the righteous American Middle West appealed to Mr. Bryan as a symphonic theme for his political orchestration, the scene was not adequate to satisfy his interest and his energies.

It was patriotic and soul-warming to extol the virtues of the common man, even of the ordinary, middle-class citizen in Lincoln, Nebraska, and The Peerless Leader did this with sincerity and poetic fervor. Yet, he was himself an uncommon man, and days spent at *The Commoner* office, under Chautauqua tents, or before women's clubs provided too little drama for his teeming energies.

By 1903 the furors and aftermath of the 1900 campaign had passed. Free silver, due to the unforeseen vast influxes of gold, had become a dead issue. Vox populi was doing very little talking because its mouth was liberally stuffed with food. America was placidly continuing to occupy the Philippines and no political candidate was going to get far with that theme. Yes, Nebraska had become a somewhat tedious place and America itself offered no issues to which the people would listen.

It was not strange that Mr. Bryan's thoughts turned toward Europe. A trip to Europe. The project offered delightful and picturesque opportunities. Mrs. Bryan thought that it would be good for their young son. Mr. Bryan still believed that if a choice had to be made between service and entertainment, service was the more important of the two. Fortunately, he felt that the European trip would be educational both for himself and for his family, so that it was possible for him to embark on the picnic of his life while charging it up in his own mind to the benefit of his family—thus running true to form as a typical American husband.

But, perhaps even to his surprise, his journey proved to be much more far-reaching than that of the typical American. He was to find himself received everywhere with the dignities and attention of a high officer of the state. While he held no political office at the time, it was evident that Europe at this time, as well as on later trips, always regarded him as one of the dominant forces of the country, who might at any turn of the wheel of fortune become the head of the government.

Mr. Bryan, his wife, and William, junior, set sail for England on November 17, 1902. He was armed with introductions, which were to lead him into personal conversation with such diverse persons as the Czar of Russia, Margot Asquith, Pope Leo

XIII, Mr. and Mrs. Sidney Webb, Leo Tolstoy, and Sir Alfred Harmsworth (later Lord Northcliffe). On board the boat The Peerless Leader was his usual busy and untirable self. The captain took him on a tour of the steamship, and the point which impressed him most was the sweat and grime of the stokers, "who kept the fires aglow while the passengers above compared experiences and discussed questions, individual, national, and international."

And one may believe that there were questions discussed on this voyage. One of Mr. Bryan's table mates was Charles Michaelson of the New York *Journal;* another Edgar Wallace of the London *Mail.* There was also an assortment of English nobility and members of parliament, likewise a Mr. Wetmore, a Chicago grain merchant, and a Father O'Grady from the Argentine Republic. With all of his fellow travelers Mr. Bryan improved the occasion by getting from each some added data to increase The Great Commoner's generous and assorted store of information. Father O'Grady enlightened him upon religious work in South America, while Mr. Wetmore supplied statistics on grain transportation. For Mr. Bryan, whose mind had been a tumult of activities, whose energies had been poured forth on this and that campaign, and in combating this or that issue for the preceding twenty years, this trip afforded an opportunity for reflection and a course of observation which had a strong effect on his policies all his life.

When he arrived in England, his sojourn was a triumphal procession. The British, with their usual prescience in diplomatic affairs, were not going to lose an opportunity to cement a friendship which might be valuable later on. The American Ambassador, Joseph Choate, gave a dinner for his countryman. On Mr. Bryan's right at this affair sat the Right Honorable Arthur J. Balfour, at that time the Premier and a bimetallist. Mr. Moreton Frewen, also a bimetallist, was additionally congenial to Mr. Bryan because of his knowledge of the Bible. Frewen was working with the protectionist party, of which Joseph Chamberlain was the leader. Mr. Frewen had found a Bible passage, which he was using on the stump, namely: "Go unto Joseph; what he saith to you do." The dinner was a jolly occasion. Mr. Bryan told many anecdotes and tilted with the Conservatives present on their tariff policy. He glowed with enthusiasm as he talked with these men of affairs and had the opportunity to fence with minds who had spent a lifetime in thinking about governmental matters. He faced here no provincial prejudice of Boston, New York or Philadelphia, but an interested group who were eager to hear the opinion of one section of America and who regarded with an almost envious wistfulness the simplicity, eagerness and fire of this emissary from the new world.

There seemed to be nothing which Mr. Bryan's eyes and ears did not absorb. Of all of his encounters in the British capital, the least successful seems to have been that with Margot Asquith. What he made of her one can only surmise, because it appears in his records simply as a notation that Mr. Asquith was out when he called and he had tea and conversation with Mrs. Asquith. The encounter does not appear at all in Margot's published journals. It is a pity. One wonders what she made of this dark-haired, handsome, evangelical gentleman, who had little of the drawing-room grace of her acquaintances, and yet who had all the assurance of one who has been the standard bearer of a leading political party, and all the gracious self-confidence of a kindly and honest spirit.

Perhaps some other lion was engaging her attention at the moment, for she evidently learned little from him. Years later, she is found in America conversing with President Harding about the history of lecturing in the United States, and jotting down in her notes the engaging statement that lecturing was started in the United States by the Chautauqua movement. Presumably, up to that time, these unlettered whites and Indians had not known the pleasures or pains of the lecture platform.

Mr. Bryan was tireless in listening to British speeches. He studied their oratory with all the zest of a technician. He traveled to Cardiff, Wales, to hear Joseph Chamberlain speak on the tariff. He went to a Liberal meeting in the suburbs of London to hear Mr. Asquith. He visited a meeting of the Free Food League to get a line on the oratory of the Duke of Devonshire and Lord Goschen. He had been warned in advance that the Duke was the only English statesman who ever took a nap during the progress of his own speech, but Mr. Bryan listened to the deliberate and logical presentation of this speaker and decided that he had a battering-ram effectiveness.

He also attended a meeting at which Lord Rosebery was speaking and was invited to sit on the platform. While he was on the stage he noticed a child of unusual beauty sitting just in front of him, and asked a man at his side whether the boy was a fair sample of the English race. The neighbor replied that the youngster was an excellent representative and was the child of John Burns, the British Labor leader.

Mr. Bryan's contact with Lord Rosebery and Mr. Burns was not, however, at an end. One of the London newspapers observing that an unidentifiable visitor had called at the Labor leader's house, published this account of the affair:

> Just before ten o'clock this morning a hansom cab plentifully bespattered with gilt coronets stopped outside the residence of Mr. Burns, Lavendar Hill. . . . We believe the visitor was Lord Rosebery; he certainly bore a striking resemblance to that childlike peer. Possibly, however, it was only the King of Italy. In diplomatic circles it has been known for a long time that His Italian Majesty intended to visit the municipal Mecca for much the same reasons that induced Peter the Great of Russia to come to England. It was known also that he would come in some sort of disguise. That Mr. Burns' visitor this morning was a person of im-

portance is evidenced by the fact that a constable in uniform and two or three other men (probably secret service officers) were in waiting when the cab drew up.

The gilt coronets and the secret service officers were the product of the imagination of the reporter. His guesses also were slightly wide of the mark, for the visitor was Mr. William Jennings Bryan of Lincoln, Nebraska.

In Burns, Bryan found a kindred spirit, a man of the people, and at the same time a citizen having humor and education. Bryan's admiration of Mr. Burns's young son, which had been expressed wholeheartedly and without knowledge of the boy's identity, also helped to cement the ties between the English Labor leader and The Great Commoner.

His interest in the sufferings of labor and others of the poorer classes was not dulled or betrayed by the courtesies which he received at every hand from those in high places. He spent a week-end at the vast country estate of Sir Alfred Harmsworth and he received the social attentions of much more ancient houses, but his eyes were not led away from those things which he wished to see most. He spent not a little time with Beatrice and Sidney Webb. From then on, he obtained much information on municipal ownership. From the Webbs, from Burns, and from a visit to Scotland was developed and was nourished his interest in the public ownership of public utilities, which was to play a large part in his political campaigns in the years to come.

No, The Peerless Leader did not succumb to the delightful charms of upper-class England, much as he enjoyed them. His eye continued to be for "the people's cause," and on his arrival in Ireland he noted that his time was too brief to enable him "to look into the condition of the tenants in the various parts of the Island." But if he was not able to settle the Irish question thus briskly, he had one grand good time. John Dillon gave a great dinner at the Mansion House on behalf of this half-Irish delegate from America. Among those present was Archbishop Walsh, who had written a pamphlet on free silver in 1896 which had been generously quoted by the Bryanites at that time. Also present were John Redmond, Michael Davitt and High Sheriff Thomas Powers.

This affair was followed several days later by another dinner at the National Liberal Club in London, where the guests included T. P. O'Connor, William Redmond (brother of John) and James Devlin. In the midst of all this entertainment, The Peerless Leader was evidently impressed with the beauty and charm of his hostesses. This was never with any thought of disloyalty to Mrs. Bryan. The political scavengers of early campaigns and scandalmongers of a later date hoped to find in the life of The Great Commoner some incident, some *affaire* which might serve their purpose, but Bryan's devotion was centered throughout his life on the woman of his youthful choice, and his flirtations were with the body politic.

But he was appreciative of London's womanhood. Mrs. Bryan had charm, intelligence, interest in the affairs of the day, and a ready wit, but most of his acquaintances and neighbors in America, men or women, were not as gratifyingly equipped. Hence, one finds him commenting that "Lady Harmsworth is one of the most beautiful women in the kingdom"; "Mrs. Chamberlain is a charming and accomplished woman and justly popular with the Britons as well as with the Americans who visit England"; and again he refers to the wife of T. P. O'Connor as "a beautiful Texan."

He made a special trip to Scotland to study municipal ownership, and there spent much time investigating the public utilities, finding out how Glasgow furnished water, gas, electricity, street car service, and model tenements to the public at cost. He had also found that water and light were under city operation at Birmingham and that in Belfast the railways were under city control. Commenting on these charters in his dispatches to America, he said: "Any surplus earned over and above the dividends allowed must be used in reducing the price paid by the consumer. I feel that our money magnates would be at a loss to find words to express their indignation if any such restriction was suggested in America and yet is it not a just and reasonable restriction?" He foresaw the storm clouds that would gather if he dared to advocate any such practices in America. Perhaps it was the very enmities which such a policy would create which led him to pursue the possibilities of the suggestion further. When "special privilege" was angry Mr. Bryan felt that this was a sign that the public interest was being fought for, safeguarded. But the issue went deeper than this. The very existence of danger seemed to impel him to take up the sword and attack it. He was a Robin Hood, a soldier of fortune entering upon, even seeking affrays, in the people's behalf. He was not, it is true, committed to government ownership especially because of his interviews with John Burns and the Webbs, or because of his observations in Scotland and Ireland. Nevertheless, as his trip went on his reports contained less and less about beautiful hostesses and more about attractive government-owned railroad systems. He noted that in Switzerland, in Holland, in Belgium, and in Denmark the railroads were largely government-owned. This was also true, he found, in Germany and in Russia.

But in Russia his mind turned to another and more far-reaching issue—that of universal peace. In Russia, at the start of his journey, he had something of a vacation from his constant research in statistics and practices in municipal affairs. The country was strange and he was impressed by its color and its differences. He visited the art gallery at Moscow. He had not written home about the other art galleries in Europe, but of the one at Moscow he made the comment, "In this gallery the nude in art is noticeable by its absence." He does not comment on the subject matter of the paintings in the gallery of St. Petersburg, but calls attention to its collection of cameos, jewelry, and precious stones.

Russia began by being a holiday for him. He went horseback riding in the parks of St. Petersburg. He met Prince Hilkoff, head of the Siberian Railroad, who had crossed the plains of Nebraska by wagon in 1858, and he obtained a personal audience with the Czar who was heading a government in which the monarch was supreme.

It was an audience of a type which one may guess the Czar had not had before and never had again. Into the throne room of the palace at Tsarskoe Selo, shortly before noon on a midwinter day, was ushered, clad in a full-dress swallow-tail, as the occasion demanded, Mr. William Jennings Bryan of Nebraska.

He chatted freely with the Czar of All the Russias and did not hesitate to put his host on the defensive. The young Romanoff, slender and erect with boyish face, light blue eyes, hair brushed back over his forehead, a blond mustache and beard, found himself in the position of some young medico who was being called upon to explain his therapeutics.

Emperor Nicholas II started out by trying to give Mr. Bryan as favorable an impression of Russia as possible. He said that 65 per cent of the adult men of Russia could read and write and that the number was increasing at the rate of about 3 per cent per year. He based his figures on the records of the recruits to the army, which represented all conditions and sections of the Empire.

Mr. Bryan received this information with interest and gratification, but felt called upon to call the attention of the Czar to a decree which he had issued a year back, promising a measure of self-government to the local communities.

The Czar looked out of the windows at the snow which was sparkling on the ground and then replied, "Yes, that was issued last February, and the plan is now being worked out."

Mr. Bryan then followed up his statement with some comments on free speech.

Nicholas II hastened to turn the discussion to the proposals which the Emperor had submitted to The Hague, asking for the formation of a court of arbitration. He then went on to speak of the friendly relations which had existed between Russia and the United States, and said that the attitude of Russia with regard to recent Jewish massacres had been much misrepresented. He asked Mr. Bryan to carry that thought to the American people.

Having discussed with the Emperor these incidents and policies of the Romanoff régime, and having called to the Emperor's attention the fact that certain of his promises had not yet been put into effect, Mr. Bryan of Lincoln, Nebraska, returned to his hotel, where Mrs. Bryan was awaiting him.

"What did you talk about?" she asked him.

"Free speech," The Peerless Leader replied.

"Free speech to the Czar! surely not."

"Yes, free speech. I thought he needed to hear about it, and he seemed quite interested."

The Great Commoner was impressed by the simplicity and open-mindedness of the Emperor and wrote home to the effect that it was Russian officialdom rather than the Russian throne which was threatening the well-being of the Empire.

Yet there was another living in this Empire far closer in sympathy to The Great Commoner's point of view, and living the type of life which Mr. Bryan could understand. This was Count Leo Tolstoy, whom The Great Commoner described about the time of his visit as "the intellectual giant of Russia, the moral Titan of Europe, and the world's most conspicuous exponent of the Doctrine of Love." One hundred and thirty miles south of Moscow Tolstoy was living in quiet retirement upon his estate near the village of Yasnaya.

The circumstances of his life were vastly different in origin from those of Mr. Bryan, yet his condition at the time was similar. Both believed passionately in the inherent dignity of the common man. Both found it necessary to live away from the great cities in order to maintain serenity of mind. Both believed deeply and religiously in the doctrine of love and of nonresistance.

Tolstoy was seventy-six; Bryan was forty-three. The younger man was not as convinced of nonresistance and was not so tremendously certain of the appeal of the doctrine of love then as he came to be later.

Yet his surroundings and training pointed him in that direction. Nebraska had outgrown the frontier stage, that stage when every man carries a gun. It had achieved its civilization, its belief in law and order, and like other thriving and orderly communities it considered that bloodshed was a silly and wasteful method of settling disputes. These things could all be adjusted if only enough time were allowed. Nietzscheism, the dream of the coward on horseback, had no place among such people, who could not understand the feverish adulation of a weakling for a giant. Bryan was in no danger of being enthralled by the militarism of Europe. Nebraska would take care of that. But nonresistance, that was a hard doctrine to swallow for one whose life had been spent in crusading. The Peerless Leader, accordingly, approached this visit with just as many questions on his tongue as he had ready in his journey to the Czar of All the Russias. Mr. Bryan, of course, knew of Tolstoy's theory from his books, but he wanted to see the man at first hand. He wanted to challenge his ideas face to face.

The Count received his visitor at the door. He was wearing a grayish blue blouse belted in at the waist and skirts reaching nearly to the boot tops. His trousers were baggy and stuffed into his boots. He was an impressive figure about five feet eight inches in height with a large head and flowing Russian beard coming down in two long gray wedges. His forehead was unusually wide and high, and his large blue eyes were set wide apart. His eyebrows were heavy, his mouth large and the lips full.

As this Russian of titanic energy gazed on Mr. Bryan he gave his hand a warm clasp, which conveyed a sense of kinship. After showing his visitor around the place and taking him for a walk and a horseback ride, he settled down to converse with the man from Nebraska. Mr. Bryan was ready.

"Do you draw any line," The Great Commoner asked, "between the use of force to avenge an injury already received, and the use of force to protect yourself from an injury about to be inflicted?"

"No," Tolstoy answered, "instead of using violence to protect myself, I ought rather to express my sorrow that I had done anything that would make any one desire to injure me."

This was drastic doctrine for The Peerless Leader and went further even than the kind of pacifism which he had extolled. He was fond of quoting Carlyle to the effect that "thought is stronger than artillery parks." He also believed in the doctrine of *integer vitæ*, that he who led an upright life needed no arms for his defense. But Tolstoy, who had spent his life in the midst of court intrigue and bloodshed, was well aware that a sentiment so exalted held true only if one's fellows were equally civilized. His was the belief of complete self-abnegation. He held no delusion that either thought or integrity would necessarily carry one successfully through all dangers.

Looking out over the vast snows of barren Russian country, Mr. Bryan tried to apply this equally stern philosophy to the needs of his own life and country. Morally, it fascinated him. He was already familiar with Tolstoy's ideas, it is true, but to see the man before him, to hear from his own lips this creed of self-immolation was a breathless experience.

How far would Tolstoy go with it? Bryan did not propose to let any loophole, any mental reservation of the Russian escape notice, if there were any reservations.

"Do you draw a line," he asked Tolstoy, "between the use of force to protect a right, and the use of force to create a right?"

Had not America gone to war with Spain to defend Cuba? Might not Cuba's action be considered the defending of a right and America's aid help to create the right? But Tolstoy was consistent and inflexible.

"No," he answered, "that is the excuse generally given for the use of violence. Men insist that they are simply defending a right when, in fact, they are trying to secure something that they desire and to which they are not entitled. The use of violence is not necessary to secure one's rights; there are more effective means."

But The Great Commoner was not satisfied. He had still another question, with which he thought to drive the philosopher to the wall.

"Do you draw any distinction," he asked, "between the use of force to protect yourself, and the

THE NEW MARINE PAINTER.

*From Washington "Evening Star"*

Tolstoy as early as 1903 was giving lessons to this artist who by 1913 became accomplished in the Tolstoy school of marine painting.

use of force to protect some one under your care—a child for instance?"

But again Tolstoy defended his complete pacifism without budging.

"No," he replied. "As we do not attain entirely to our ideals, we might find it difficult in such a case not to resort to the use of force, but it would not be justifiable. And, besides, rules cannot be made for such exceptional cases. Millions of people have been the victims of force and have suffered because it has been thought right to employ it, but I am an old man and I have never known in all my life a single instance in which a child was attacked in such a way as it would have been necessary for me to use force for its protection. I prefer to consider actual rather than imaginary cases."

There was much more talk at the Tolstoy farm. There were, in fact, hours and hours of it. There were long walks over the snowy countryside, and the philosopher of the Old World found great pleasure in the flashing-eyed, eager, talkative Commoner from across the seas.

Bryan in turn was won by Tolstoy's magnetism, the dignity of his presence, and the compelling logic of his position. The reckless completeness of Tolstoy's vision gripped The Peerless Leader's religious zeal, though he drew back at its practical applications.

Yet, while never accepting Tolstoy's theories in their completeness, while never willing to carry to the last ditch the doctrine of nonresistance, he felt

## AN INNOCENT ABROAD

continuously from then on the compulsion of the Tolstoy influence. It hovered over him as an inspiration and a superconscience. It strengthened his religious and idealistic convictions, and made him, as the years went on, less and less a realist, as the term "realist" is generally understood.

The contact between Tolstoy and The Commoner did not end with his visit. They continued their correspondence and the admonitions of the Russian St. Francis were actual as well as implied. In 1907 he wrote to Mr. Bryan, "I wish with all my heart success in your endeavor to destroy the trusts, and to help the working people to enjoy the whole fruits of their toil, but I think this is not the most important thing of your life. The most important thing is to know the will of God concerning one's life, *i.e.*, to know what He wishes us to do and fulfill it. I think that you are doing it and that is the thing in which I wish you greatest success."

For a time the pacific words and the searching of heart recommended by the older man did not have a particular bearing on Mr. Bryan's life. The years immediately before him after his European visit were too filled with a multitude of conflicts for him to give much thought or comment to the problem of whether it was right to employ physical force.

He was to become involved immediately on his return in the 1904 campaign. After that came 1908. Then the sunset of his personal political fortunes when he threw over the Wets in the Democratic party in a violent and courageous encounter at Grand Island, Nebraska. Yet, if he was not to be President, it was ordained that he was to become Secretary of State, and when those days came it was easy to see that over the hand which wrote the Bryan treaties and over the hand which penned the early Wilson notes to Germany hovered the hand of Tolstoy.

## CHAPTER X

### END OF A CANDIDATE

*I have kept the faith.*—W. J. BRYAN

THE Commoner returned to Lincoln no more pacified and no more ready to settle down than when he had left. In fact the trip had only served to stimulate his political interest and show him how much there was which might be done before the millennium.

From the Webbs and the Scottish cities he remembered the lessons in municipal ownership, from the Irish Labor party he had an example of never-say-die, and from Russia he had the recollection of the peace projects of the Czar and the pacifism of Tolstoy.

The trip had been profitable in other ways. His dispatches regarding his tour had been syndicated by the enterprising Mr. Hearst, and had made a pretty penny for both the publisher and The Peerless Leader. To be exact, after Mr. Bryan got settled back at Fairview and had his syndicate and royalty statements, he found that his surplus property of $20,000 several years back had increased to something over $100,000. His only extravagance was his farm. He was continuing to pay his hired men as high as $150 a month. Between the good wages, the good nature of the proprietor, and experimentation with high-grade cattle, Fairview still did not turn in a profit.

This, however, was the least of The Commoner's concerns. Money came to him readily because of his irresistible interest as a public character, and his matchless gifts as an orator. He continued to give freely to political causes, societies and educational purposes which attracted his interest. Since the days when he was struggling for a bare existence, his income had been wholly a subordinate consideration. Mrs. Bryan kept track of that end of things, and his mind was free for whatever imperative cause seized his attention at the moment.

There were but a few months after his return home until the next Democratic Convention. He wisely announced that he would not be in the running, having been unsuccessful in carrying the standard on the two preceding occasions. But he did expect to have something to say about the nomination of the candidate. Richard Croker, leader of Tammany Hall, had written to him after the 1900 defeat stating the belief that Bryan would nevertheless some day be President. This was one of the few letters that The Commoner received from the East after 1900 and, in fact, one of the few communications which came from any source at that time expressing faith in his political future. He always remembered Croker's thoughtfulness, and he expected that the New York delegation would support the Bryan policies at the convention, whoever the nominee might prove to be.

## END OF A CANDIDATE

Though The Great Commoner was in partial eclipse his influence was not ignored; and delegation after delegation came to Fairview seeking to win his favor for their candidate. Among these visitors were supporters of William Randolph Hearst who had a grievous tale to unfold. It appeared that Mr. Hearst, seeking the nomination, had obtained the endorsement of the Illinois State Convention in a narrowly won victory. The opposition, however, had succeeded in naming delegates to the national convention who were hostile to the Hearst candidacy. The Commoner was receptive to the thought of acting upon the untoward state of affairs and proceeded to Chicago to call upon the publisher. Hearst, however, was unwilling to disturb the situation by precipitating a further controversy. Perhaps, like so many persons both before and after, he felt that The Commoner's day of influence was past. At any rate, he held that it would be improper for him to criticize the Illinois Convention, even in its unfortunate choice of delegates, since the convention had at least endorsed him. Bryan was not satisfied with this view and carried on the fight to have the pro-Hearst delegates seated at St. Louis. In this he was successful, but he went no further in support of Hearst who had cooled the Bryan ardor by the refusal to fight.

By the time the convention opened at St. Louis in June, Bryan had not yet determined where he would throw the weight of his influence, and the tide of his popularity in fact was at ebb. The

Hearst forces were calling him an ingrate for not responding to their wishes, and Senator David Bennett Hill was on the rampage again. He had not forgotten how Croker had called him off in 1900 from his project of trying to insert a gold plank in the Democratic platform. He was at present determined to nominate an old school Democrat and to break the power of The Peerless Leader. Bryan was in a difficult position because he had not made up his mind on a strong man to fill his shoes. When he got the floor at the convention, he mentioned several names that he considered satisfactory, and concluded by seconding the nomination of Senator Cockrell, a man relatively obscure in the party circles. Mr. Hearst was put into nomination, and seconded by Clarence Darrow.

In the midst of the controversy Bryan was taken suddenly ill, and upon calling a physician at his hotel he learned that he had an attack of pneumonia and must not leave his bed.

Once Bryan was out of the way the old school Democrats had no opposition and were able to nominate Judge Alton B. Parker of New York on the first ballot by a total of 679 votes out of a thousand cast, or twelve more than needed under the two-thirds rule. Mr. Hearst had 181 ballots, including all of California, Illinois, Iowa, and several small states, with a few scattering votes from states where the unit rule did not obtain.

Elated by this victory, Parker wired the convention of his irrevocable support of the gold standard. The original plan had been to tactfully omit reference to silver or gold. The delegates were debating the wisdom of taking as drastic a stand as this when suddenly they were aghast to find on the platform the tall and shaking figure of William Jennings Bryan. Some one had brought the news of what was taking place to his hotel room. He had waited for a moment until his nurse and doctor were out of the way, had dressed and come over to the hotel.

Riddled with fever, his frame and voice shaking with emotion, he turned upon the delegates and cried out, "I have kept the faith."

He denounced the faint hearts who were willing to turn back the wheels of time for the sake of what was erroneously believed to be a few more votes. He warned them that the public never rallied to an apostate. He dared them to repudiate the silver doctrine and he assured them that he for one would never turn back the pages of history and forsake the liberalism to which the party had pledged itself in recent years.

In a moment he had left the hall as quickly as he had appeared, but the temper of the convention had changed. Many delegates were on their feet yelling that the Parker nomination should be rescinded. After the hubbub had settled down somewhat, it was found that the judge's telegram had been partially garbled in repetition, and that the candidate was less uncompromising than had been at first supposed. Cooler heads realized that it would be difficult **to** explain to the nation the nomination of a candidate in the afternoon and the canceling of the ballot in the evening. Parker's nomination stood.

Pneumonia germs were no more powerful than New York *Tribune* editorials in the attempt to bury The Great Commoner. Within a few days he was up and around again and back at his editorial desk in Lincoln.

The experiences at St. Louis had left him in a grim humor. He was resolved to support the ticket and to bide his time. Hitherto he had tempered his views, so he thought, and been moderate in his criticism in order to make haste slowly and not to embarrass the party.

But from now on he determined to lay aside the rôle of political chief in the more limited sense, and to become the reformer, the educator, the physician and the prophet of the body politic. Not only did he determine upon this course for himself, but as usual he had no hesitancy in advising the world what it might expect. While Judge Parker was trying to lead his party back to the good old days of Grover Cleveland, The Peerless Leader opened up the July twenty-second issue of *The Commoner* with the challenge headed, "Democracy Must Move Forward."

My selection as standard-bearer of the Democratic party in 1896 and again in 1900 [said this editorial] made me the nominal leader of that party, and as such I did not feel at liberty to engraft new doctrines upon the party creed. I contented myself with the defense of those principles and policies which were embodied in the platform. Now, that

# The Commoner.

WILLIAM J. BRYAN, EDITOR AND PROPRIETOR.

Vol. 4. No. 27.   Lincoln, Nebraska, July 22, 1904.   Whole No. 183.

## DEMOCRACY MUST MOVE FORWARD

THE FAMOUS ISSUE OF "THE COMMONER" WHEREIN BRYAN
ANNOUNCED HIS LEADERSHIP OF THE RADICAL WING
OF DEMOCRACY

the leadership devolves upon another and I bear only the responsibility that each citizen must bear, namely, responsibility for my opinions, my utterances, and my conduct, I am free to undertake a work which until now I have avoided, namely, the work of organizing the radical and progressive element in the Democratic party. . . . I invite the Democrats, therefore, to consider a plan for the government ownership and operation of the railroads.

For a few months, until the presidential campaign was over, Bryan remained fairly quiet on these issues and put in most of his time campaigning for the Democratic ticket, omitting reference to the money issue and advising the voters to cast their ballots for the party of Thomas Jefferson. When the election returns came in, the warning issued at St. Louis proved justified.

Parker won no states away from the Republican columns. Maryland was narrowly Republican in the popular vote, but a majority of Democratic electors were chosen. He lost from the Democratic side the states of Colorado, Idaho, Missouri, Montana and Nevada. His vote was 1,500,000 less than Bryan had polled in '96 and even less than Cleveland had rolled up in years when the population was considerably smaller.

The Great Commoner felt his stand had been vindicated, and he set forth on his new campaign for government ownership of railroads. Week after week in *The Commoner* and on the stump he cited the experience of Europe· and the sins of private ownership to prove his contention.

## END OF A CANDIDATE

The issue with him was no idle theory born of schoolboy or scholastic zeal. It was an attempt to grapple with a menace which was real in his part of the country and more sharply realized than in eastern sections where there were more sources and ramifications of industry and power. The railroads permeated the whole economic life of Nebraska and neighboring states. If there was a contest in politics, underneath it was fundamentally a contest between two railroads for domination. The railroads went into each small town and chose the ablest attorney to represent them. If another strong personality appeared in the community and needed to be dealt with, he, too, was retained. The communities were at the mercy of the railroads because they were the only rapid means of communication, the contact with the markets of the world. The rail lines had come into these different cities upon urgent petition. True, they might have come there anyhow, and also true that the towns were important to the road. But the railroads, concentrated in management, were able to capitalize their favorable positions.

They were ever present in the state legislatures. There, issues were fought out between different groups with the hands of different railroads pulling the strings. Legislators were bought and paid for in quantity lots. The initiative was not all on one side. Local politicians learned the game and many who had not been paid introduced bills which might be uncomfortable unless the introducer were properly recognized and adequately persuaded to forget the matter.

While the wrongs and the responsibilities for the condition were widely distributed, the fact remained that the railroad companies had these communities by the throat. Mr. Bryan realized that his proposals were difficult, but to his mind they were by no means impractical. He regarded government ownership of railroads as preferable to, and no less practical than, railroad ownership of governments.

There remained two or three years, however, until the next presidential campaign. He knew that the public can get tired of having too much of one man, and again the simple pleasures of Lincoln, so ideal to contemplate, began nevertheless to pall. He planned for a world-wide trip and this time started from San Francisco, visiting the Orient. His initial visit was to Japan, a trip which proved useful to him later when he became Secretary of State. Again on this journey as on his European trip, he was received with official honors wherever he went.

Social life in Japan proved difficult for The Great Commoner who by this time had developed considerable girth as well as height. He was about as large as the average Japanese house, and was regarded as a curiosity not only because of his national fame but also because of his magnificent and tremendous physique. It became virtually a neighborhood holiday whenever he took a bath, and this event was attended by many spectators at a respectful distance watching behind screens, until the visitors

# END OF A CANDIDATE

| VANDERBILT SYSTEM | | PENNSYLVANIA SYSTEM | | GOULD-ROCKEFELLER SYSTEM | | MORGAN-HILL SYSTEM | |
|---|---|---|---|---|---|---|---|
| Road | Mileage | Road | Mileage | Road | Mileage | Road | Mileage |
| New York Central System (Including the main line, the Beech Creek, the Fall Brook, the Mohawk and Malone, the New York and Harlem, the Rome, Watertown and Ogdensburg, the West Shore, and many others.) | 3,107 | Pennsylvania R. R. (east of Pittsburg & Erie).. (Including the New Jersey lines, the Allegheny Valley R. R., the Philadelphia and Erie, the Northern Central, and many others.) | 5,530 | Controlled by the Gould-Sage interests Missouri, Pacific and Iron Mountain............ International and Great Northern............ Wabash................ (Including the Wheeling & Lake Erie, and the Omaha and St. Louis.) St. Louis and Southwestern............ Texas and Pacific........ | 5,372 891 2,098 1,203 1,619 | Controlled jointly Northern Pacific........ (Which owns twenty-three million acres of land.) Great Northern........ Chicago, Burlington and Quincy............ Erie................... Lehigh Valley........... | 3,487 5,417 8,171 2,005 2,178 |
| Lake Shore & Michigan Southern........... | 2,084 | Pennsylvania R. R. (west of Pittsburg & Erie).. (Including the Pennsylvania Company, the Peoria and Western, the St. Louis, Vandalia & Terre Haute, the Pittsburg, Chicago, Cincinnati and St. Louis, the Cleveland, Akron and Columbus, the Grand Rapids and Indiana, and others.) Long Island............. Baltimore and Ohio...... (Including the Cleveland, Lorain and Wheeling, the B. & O. Southwestern, and others.) | 4,405 | | | | |
| Michigan Central........ (Including the Canadian Southern.) | 1,635 | | | Rockefeller and Gould interests | | Controlled by Mr. Morgan | |
| New York, Chicago & St. Louis. (Nickel Plate) (Including the Pittsburg and Lake Erie.) | 523 | | | | | Philadelphia and Reading (Including the Central of New Jersey.) Hocking Valley......... (Including the Toledo and Ohio Central, and the Kanawha and Michigan) Chicago, Indianapolis and Louisville........... Southern Railway...... (Including the Central of Georgia, the Alabama, Great Southern, the Cincinnati, New Orleans and Texas Pacific, and the Mobile and Ohio.) | 1,677 882 546 10,627 |
| Chicago & Northwestern (Including the Chicago, St. Paul, Minneapolis & Omaha and the Fremont, Elkhorn and Missouri Valley.) | 8,769 | | | Missouri, Kansas and Texas............ Denver & Rio Grande.... (Including the Rio Grande Western.) | 2,480 2,301 | | |
| | | | 391 4,025 | | | | |
| Cleveland, Cincinnati, Chicago & St. Louis. (Big Four)........... Boston and Albany...... Lake Erie & Western ... | 2,387 304 725 | | | Total Mileage........ | 10,924 | | |
| | | Total Mileage........ | 14,351 | | | | |
| Total Mileage ....... | 19,524 | | | | | Total Mileage......... | 37,590 |

| CONTROLLED JOINTLY BY THE PENNSYLVANIA AND THE NEW YORK CENTRAL | | BELMONT SYSTEM | | HARRIMAN-KUHN-LOEB SYSTEM | | IMPORTANT INDEPENDENT SYSTEMS | |
|---|---|---|---|---|---|---|---|
| Road | Mileage | Road | Mileage | Road | Mileage | Road | Mileage |
| Chesapeake and Ohio..... Norfolk & Western....... | 1,616 1,685 | Louisville and Nashville. Nashville, Chattanooga and St. Louis............. | 5,188 935 | Union Pacific............ (Including the Southern Pacific, the Oregon R. R. and Navigation Co., and the Oregon Short Line.) Chicago and Alton....... Illinois Central.......... Kansas City Southern.... | 15,103 918 5,000 873 | Atchison, Topeka and Santa Fe........... Chicago, Rock Island and Pacific............. St. Louis and San Francisco.............. Colorado and Southern... Chicago, Milwaukee and St. Paul............ Pere Marquette......... Atlantic Coast Line...... Seaboard Air Line ...... Plant System........... New York, New Haven and Hartford........ Boston and Maine....... | 7,481 3,818 2,887 1,142 6,461 1,747 2,177 2,600 2,207 2,098 3,338 |
| Total Mileage........ | 3,301 | | | | | | |
| | | Total Mileage ........ | 6,123 | | | | |
| | | | | Total Mileage....... | 31,954 | | |
| | | | | | | Total Mileage..... | 35,896 |

*From "World's Work"*

By 1902 a few railroad systems had already obtained control of most of the trunk line mileage of the country. This chart indicates the situation which Mr. Bryan thought should be handled through government ownership.

were advised that such observation was not an American custom and was disquieting to even so public a man as Mr. Bryan.

He also encountered difficulties on being received by the Emperor. Custom demanded that the caller at the throne room follow a specific procedure. Mr. Bryan arrived to find the little Emperor ready to receive him. He was directed to bow, then advance halfway to His Majesty, bow again, then proceed and bow yet a third time as he took the extended hand of royalty. The bowing from the waist was none too easy for The Great Commoner, though he always kept himself in fair condition when at home by felling trees. The most difficult aspect of the meeting was the requirement that conversation must consist only of answers to questions asked by His Majesty. Bryan had chatted with Emperor Nicholas, but the Mikado was courteously formal and no opportunity was offered for the discussion of free silver, labor conditions, or the other matters of state.

Bryan, however, called assiduously on leaders of all classes in the country and obtained, as usual, vast quantities of information concerning the land which he was visiting. The Japanese boy whom he had educated had spread his fame in advance and The Great Commoner was beset with petitions by other boys also eager for an education in America. One young man, realizing that The Peerless Leader was an important person in his own country, and not wishing to omit any title, addressed a communication to him as "My Lord, Your Grace, the Duke."

Bryan visited the father of his Japanese protégé, who was engaged in the occupation of farming. Even these intimate visits were difficult because of the local custom of taking off one's shoes when going indoors. It was permissible to wear a particular type of house slipper. This did not help Mr. Bryan

## END OF A CANDIDATE

The Only W. B.—"I Wonder If I Can Stand It Until 1908"

*From Seattle "Post Intelligencer".*

During Bryan's *1906* trip abroad his friends hoped that he might forget government ownership, since they felt he could carry the country in the coming election on the basis of his personal popularity, if he did not scare the populace with strange doctrines.

much because no Japanese footgear could be found approaching his size. For a time he paid calls in his stocking feet, but he caught cold as a result of this and finally compromised by purchasing the largest pair of Japanese felt slippers which he could find and cutting away the toes. He thus appeared at state and other functions with the sole of the slipper under his instep, but with the large sock-covered Bryan toes sticking out in front.

The visit to Japan was an opportune gesture of good will, and was so regarded. The Russo-Japanese Peace Treaty had recently been signed in America and Admiral Togo had just come back to Japan after attending the Peace Conference which had been so favorable to his country. Mr. Bryan was invited to the official reception and dinner to the Admiral upon his return. He reached Tokyo the morning of the reception and sought for transportation to take him to Uyeno Park, the place where the event was to be held. He made his wants known to a Japanese interpreter who secured a ricksha man for him. As Mr. Bryan squeezed his bulk into the flimsy vehicle, the man grabbed up the shafts and started on his journey. Soon Bryan saw that to his horror he was in the midst of a parade. Admiral Togo had arrived on the same train and was being escorted to the reception.

The Great Commoner gesticulated to the man, trying to indicate that he was to be taken out of the parade, but his gestures were simply understood to mean more speed. The ricksha man raced forward and got nearer to the front in the procession. Mr. Bryan redoubled his sign language, but again with the same result.

By this time The Great Commoner was acutely embarrassed because he was riding in the midst of the officials of state shortly behind the Admiral's conveyance. He made one last attempt to make his transporter understand, and the man with a gallant burst of speed carried the ricksha to the front of the procession where for the several miles between millions of cheering natives rode The Peerless Leader from Nebraska, followed by the Admiral of the Japanese Navy!

As he reached the park he was relieved to find certain of the city council who understood English, and he was able to make abject apologies and explanations which were smilingly received.

In the evening he attended a banquet given to the Admiral, and once again an embarrassing situation arose. All present had paid tribute to the Japanese naval leader. The time came to drink a toast. Those present lifted their champagne glasses, but there was a gasp of alarm as Mr. Bryan was seen to raise a glass of water. Some one grasped his arm and whispered hastily that such a toast would be considered as an insult.

The Great Commoner was equal to the delicate situation.

"You won your victories on water," he said, turning to the Admiral, "and I drink to your health in water; whenever you win any victories on champagne I shall drink your health in champagne."

At Japan, as on his previous trip, he was writing home about the existing conditions. In one dispatch he reported, "In some reforms Japan has moved more rapidly than the United States. . . . The Japanese Government also owns and operates a part of the railroad system. . . . I traveled on both the government and private lines and could not see that they differed materially so far as efficiency was concerned."

At the Philippines he was greeted with great acclaim. The colonial sympathizers wanted to justify their position and those seeking independence were eager for a sight of the man who had espoused their cause. The American colony at Manila gave a vast reception for him at the Elk's Club. In the midst of this there was a great stir and Emilio Aguinaldo came forward to greet The Peerless Leader. The conversation of the two men dealt with friendly formalities while the audience and the reporters waited with eager ears. But Mr. Bryan was unwilling to embarrass his own government and to bring false hope to the Filipinos when he was not in a position of authority.

In his visit to the southern part of these Islands his enthusiasm for the native was somewhat modified if not dampened. He was invited to call upon Datu Piang, a leader of the region, and had an opportunity to see a district leader, Philippine style. Datu held court on a barge manned by forty oarsmen. He greeted the arriving Commoner with a salute of more than fifty guns. To emphasize his appreciation of the visitor he had the barge brought to shore, and as he sat in state he smoked a cigar and was flanked on either side by a brown-skinned

*From Nebraska Historical Society*

An indication of the favorable Bryan sentiment in the West. The cartoon was included in a presentation booklet at a reception given to him on August 30, 1906, by the Commercial Travelers Anti-Trust League.

native bearing an open umbrella of red silk trimmed with wide yellow fringe. He did not appear to be especially oppressed.

While The Great Commoner did not feel free to make any commitments, he wrote home, "What is needed is an immediate declaration of the nation's purpose to recognize the independence of the Filipinos when a suitable government is accomplished."

His trip continued on through the Orient and around to Central Europe, and finally to England. His reception in the British Isles was as friendly as before. The British press admired and marveled at his tremendous vitality. One paper commented, "His energy is expended in doing things, not romping."

Meanwhile another presidential campaign was coming due in the states. Parkerism had been defeated so disastrously that none of the eastern Democrats were looked upon as possibilities. News services had been carrying dispatches from day to day of the honors paid to The Great Commoner in all the capitals of the world. Both the Republican and Democratic newspapers were picturing him as the logical candidate for Democracy. The brewers, who were strong supporters of the Democratic war chest, were alarmed at The Peerless Leader's toast to Admiral Togo. Bryan was known to be a teetotaler but this rejoinder had been heralded around the world and served to emphasize to them that he could not be counted upon to fight their battles and might at any time be a danger.

# HARPER'S WEEKLY
## JOURNAL OF CIVILIZATION

Vol. L.   New York, Saturday, September 1, 1906   No. 1591

## THE RETURN

*The finely printed tags attached to the bouquets are from Emperor William, King Edward, the Pope and Czar Nicholas.*

In spite of these considerations there was no other likely candidate in sight.

As Mr. Bryan was seated in a hotel in London, it was announced that there was a caller to see him by the name of Mr. Hayne Davis. The Commoner's face lighted with pleasure. Davis had been a loyal friend for many years. A native of North Carolina, he had been on the Democratic State Committee and had later practiced law in Tennessee and in New York. Mr. Davis, in 1904, had been the press representative of the Interparliamentary Union and had advocated a union of nations applying the idea of the United States to the world at large.

Mr. Davis did not lose much time in stating his message. He pointed out to Mr. Bryan the political situation in the United States, but urged that Roosevelt would not be running again and Taft, the heir-apparent, was a conservative. Bryan, the Democrats thought, could sweep the country by storm.

But Davis urged The Great Commoner to temper his radicalism. Especially government ownership of railroads. He pointed out that the people did not understand it and that it would serve only to galvanize the opposition.

Mr. Bryan heard these words with disappointment. He had been planning upon government ownership as the next great project which he would bring before the people, but he knew that Davis was sincere, astute and honest to the core. He realized that the proposal was made in good faith and pos-

# HARPER'S WEEKLY

Vol. L.   No. 2593

*EDITED BY GEORGE HARVEY*

THIRTY-SIX PAGES
AND A COLORED SUPPLEMENT
NEW YORK CITY, SEPTEMBER 1, 1906

Terms: 10 Cents a Copy — $4.00 a Year, in Advance
Postage free to all Subscribers in the United States, Canada, Mexico, Hawaii, Porto Rico, the Philippine Islands, Guam, and Tutuila, Samoa

*Entered at the New York Post-office as second-class matter*

HARPER & BROTHERS, PUBLISHERS
NEW YORK CITY: FRANKLIN SQUARE
LONDON: 45 ALBEMARLE STREET, W

## COMMENT

To WILLIAM J. BRYAN—*Greeting:*

As we pen these words you are dancing over the billowy waves under the protection of the German flag, on your way to home, sweet home. Presently you will be borne majestically into the most impressive of harbors, and remain at anchor long enough to explain to the customs officer why you found it necessary to purchase a suit of clothes manufactured by the pauper labor of Europe. Then you will go on deck, and the brass will crash and the trumpets bray along with a varied collection of statesmen eager to be kodaked while grasping your large, glad hand. It will be a grand reception. Even now the clans are gathering from Nebraska to Maine. A pity it is that bickerings and jealousies are but too apparent in many councils, but all are pardonable as springing from a laudable purpose. It is the highest ambition of each and every member of the multitude, from JEFFERSON M. LEVY up and down, to let you know how fully he appreciates your greatness, and to let the public know how graciously and fraternally you recognize his appreciation. When some years ago ULYSSES S. GRANT landed in San Francisco after passing around the world, he was It. But you are more than It; you are They. You are not only the original, undiluted, and uncompromising radical of old, as you yourself have said, but, by the grace of THEODORE ROOSEVELT, you are by contrast the personification of conservatism. For the first time shivering plutocracy joins with rag-tag and bob-tail in doing reverence to <u>one who was described not long ago as a statesman who never made a statute, a lawyer who never tried a case, a soldier who never fought a battle, and a farmer who never turned a furrow.</u> Wide and deep, however, is the belief now in the hearts of your countrymen that all you lacked was the opportunity, and that the time of realization of glorious possibilities is rapidly approaching.

*The underscored lines in the editorial indicate the type of opposition which Bryan faced. The legislative record and his abilities as a lawyer were matters of established record.*

sibly in good judgment. He promised that he would see what he could do.

A super-Democratic ovation met him as he came up the bay to the Statue of Liberty. Tugboats blew their whistles and an official reception boat came down to the entrance of the harbor, loaded with the leaders of Democracy, the officials of the state, and his closest friends from Lincoln.

He was scheduled to speak at Madison Square Garden the following night. It turned out to be typical Democratic weather—roasting, sweltering, hot, with not a breath of air stirring.

Before the meeting Mrs. Bryan turned to him and said that she hoped he was not going to read his speech.

He said that he felt that he ought to do so as he did not wish anything he said to be misrepresented.

She pointed out that he would probably be misrepresented anyway and she begged him not to read his paper. She said that he never won his audience when he did so and that he would lose all the possibilities of this opportunity to at last win New York to his support.

But as in the case of his Madison Square talk in '96 he again disregarded Mrs. Bryan's advice and for paragraph upon paragraph and page upon page he read his manuscript.

The effect was disastrous. The audience stirred restlessly and many went out. It is true that he had the press of the country in mind rather than the immediate audience. But the day was not saved

*Photograph by Brown Brothers*

BRYAN RETURNING FROM EUROPE IN 1906

## END OF A CANDIDATE

there either. He had borne in mind the request of Hayne Davis as far as he could, and had buried his views away down in his speech, but he could not bring himself to be entirely quiet on the issue which was burning within him. Reading quietly and without emphasis he came to these paragraphs:

*From Detroit "News"*

The two prior *defeats* were among the main obstacles to success in 1908.

"I have already reached the conclusion that the railroads partake so much of the nature of a monopoly that they must ultimately become public property. . . . I do not know that the country is ready for this change. . . . I prefer to see only the trunk lines operated by the Federal Government, and the local lines by the several state governments. Some have opposed this dual ownership as unpracticable, but investigation in Europe has convinced me that it is highly practical. . . . As to the right of governments, federal and state, to own and operate railroads, there can be no doubt."

The next morning the headlines screamed: "Bryan Out for Government Ownership!"

The edge had gone from eastern enthusiasm. Bryan, at the next convention, was nominated by acclamation, but the sureness of victory had disappeared. The rank and file were not happy, not knowing into what wilderness their Moses might lead them next. The Great Commoner was not dismayed. He had thrown aside the advice of caution and political wisdom, but he was storming the country in a cause in which he believed heart and soul. Whatever the result, he had kept the faith.

## CHAPTER XI

### THE BATTLE OF GRAND ISLAND

*I do perceive here a divided duty.*
—*Othello*

AS Bryan sat in the reception room at Fairview listening to the election returns, he laughed and chatted with the reporters, more indifferent in manner to the outcome of the contest than any others present. If he won, the people had at last recognized what he stood for. If he had not won, it was just one more engagement in his career. There was no longer the eager excitement of youth which felt that all of a lifetime hung upon the result.

Ever since 1904, when he had declared himself the moral leader of his party, regardless of consequences, he had put aside the equation of personal victory. If he had become more middle-aged, less flashing and more self-assured (if that were possible), he also had a greater kindliness, a greater sense of proportion and a more benign attitude toward the scene before him.

The geniality of the candidate who had taken on weight with the years, and lost hair, made him appear like some great happy field god, at home in his own country whether or not accepted by the majority of the nation. As he sat in the Fairview reception room, surrounded by lacquered Japanese cabinets, under the oil paintings of Jackson and Jefferson, resting his heels on the pelt of a lion, he was slightly irritating to the temper of a Chicago newspaper man who complained that the telegraph service provided at Fairview was entirely inadequate.

Mr. Bryan smiled and continued to converse with his guests. He had reason to smile for the Lord had prospered him, as the overfurnished reception room of Fairview bore witness. It was the custom of the times to have plenty objects of art in one's drawing-room, and the Fairview interior indicated that the Bryans had traveled far and had done well.

The Chicago reporter repeated his complaint that the telegraph facilities in Fairview were not satisfactory.

Mr. Bryan discussed the change in the times since the early days of his campaigning, the development of the West and the tremendous growth of the trusts which, together with the power of the railroads were leading to an ever increasing concentration of wealth. He pointed out that whatever the present situation, it was clear that there would need to be many improvements in the machinery whereby the people protected their rights before Democracy was fully realized. He discussed these issues in a quiet, friendly way as much to kill time as anything else, passing out coffee and sandwiches to the reporters, knowing that they had no ears at present for political principles, wishing only to get the election returns and add a note of local color.

THE BATTLE OF GRAND ISLAND

*From Newark "Evening News"*

Will he bag the elephant?

The Tammany support of Bryan at the 1908 Convention had been a mixed blessing. It was actively used against him in the eastern opposition papers.

For the third time, the Chicago reporter objected to the lack of telegraph facilities at Fairview.

Mr. Bryan had built a little telegraph office at one corner of the field in front of the house, in order to save the reporters the inconvenience of rushing back and forth between his estate and the town, which was three miles away. The Chicago newsman, however, felt that this was not a large enough station and better accommodation should be provided.

"I am sorry that you are not satisfied," The Peerless Leader said, at last recognizing the complaint of the young man; "perhaps after I have run two or three more times for the presidency, we shall be able to do better."

Returns were not favorable. Bryan picked up the states which had been lost by Parker, including Colorado, Nebraska and Nevada. He also won the new state of Oklahoma. His vote was 6,409,000 compared with the 5,084,000 of Parker. He polled nearly 100,000 more than in 1900, but not quite as many votes as in '96. His numerical losses were heaviest in the southern states which he carried as in previous years. The vote on both sides in 1908 was much lighter than in '96, due to the comparative apathy with respect to the election. In Alabama, for example, the vote in '96 had been 131,000 for Bryan to 54,000 for McKinley. In 1908, it was 74,000 for Bryan to 25,000 for Taft.

In Maryland, as in 1904, a majority of Democratic electors were chosen, though he lost by the slight difference of 605 votes in the popular total, in which 232,000 ballots were cast. As the popular vote is recorded by taking the highest vote cast for any elector, the personal popularity of one elector may

## THE BATTLE OF GRAND ISLAND

**TRYING TO HOLD BRYAN BACK**

*From Florida "Times Union"*

*The old Populist party which had supported Bryan in 1896 put its own ticket into the field in 1908. Tom Watson, the leader of Populism, had not welcomed the rise of "the light in the west." While the 1908 campaign was the dying gasp of the Populists, it served to take some votes away from Bryan in closely contested states.*

at times give a misleading picture. In Missouri, he lost by a few more than 600 votes difference out of nearly 700,000 ballots. He was nowhere near as close to winning the nation as he had been in '96.

His self-election as the Cassandra of his party announced after the 1904 affair had made many elements wary of him and they had conspired to bring about his defeat. The organization had been

[ 209 ]

with him earlier because he carried them along to local successes, even if not getting elected himself, but any man who felt that he was independent of political considerations was not too good a fellow with whom to do business.

The brewing interests were strongly against him and undoubtedly helped to keep him from winning the state of Missouri which he had carried by large majorities in '96 and 1900. Bryan also believed that they had worked against him in all the larger cities and were primarily responsible for his defeat for the third time.

Prohibition had been an embarrassing issue for him throughout his political career. He had sidestepped it in his early days believing that there were more vital issues and knowing that he would have been put out of business early in the game if he had advocated it as a young man. He had stayed away from the question for nearly twenty years and he had been repaid by the Wets by an attitude of distrust and with lack of support. The dry sentiment was growing apace throughout the South and Middle West. Prohibition had become state-wide in many states and all over the country county option, namely, the opportunity for an entire county to decide whether it would be wet or dry, was a usual thing. Not so in Nebraska. There the option was decided in each town. The result was that any village might be dry, but saloons could be established at the village line and the purpose of the law defeated even for the local unit.

# THE BATTLE OF GRAND ISLAND

**THE COMPLETE OUTFIT IN DUPLICATE.**
Taft—Blamed if he hasn't a brother Charlie, too. Well, this is no handicap race at any rate.

*From Minneapolis "Journal"*

*Taft had a brother Charlie who was a millionaire. This was supposed to be a political liability.*

Bryan did not make his decision immediately, but as he mulled over the political scene, he realized that the prohibition wave was coming, that he could help to bring it about, and that all the tradition of his family and his people demanded that he get into the fight. He knew that it would make him personally forever politically ineligible. He also knew that he was the most likely leader to take hold of this movement if any one were going to. If he did not take a stand, what less powerful person in the party could be expected to do so? The brewers had thought that he was a dangerous man for their cause. Very well. No gauge of battle lay on the ground indefinitely before his eyes.

He did not have many months to wait before the opportunity presented itself for him to declare his stand. The State Democratic Convention was to meet at Grand Island, Nebraska, on July 26, 1910. The issue of prohibition was certain to come up. Governor Shallenberger, a Democrat, had signed the Daylight Saloon Law which required all saloons to close at 8.00 P.M. Many of the faithful were enraged at Shallenberger's stand and might have quietly transferred their allegiance to Republicanism, but the Republicans had gone one degree worse. They had come out with the endorsement of county option. If the Democrats should come out for county option, that would mean a Nebraska united in progress toward a dry condition. But that was not likely to happen as those familiar with Nebraska history knew.

The wet issue had been a turbulent one from territorial days. From 1854 to 1858 Nebraska had only the Democratic political organization. It was composed mainly of native-born Americans from New

## THE BATTLE OF GRAND ISLAND

England, New York and the Middle West. It passed a prohibition law as early as 1855. By 1858 the young Republican party was organized in the territory, made up to a large extent of German settlers who were with the Republicans on the slavery issue. To win them more securely, the Republican leaders declared against prohibition and repealed the law in 1859.

By 1874, the subject had become an issue again. Republican Yankees came from New England with strong convictions on the dry issue. A wave of Christian evangelism swept the country, and especially the West, giving impetus to the dry cause. The Republicans who had gained in numbers and for many years had had a majority, found themselves compelled to recognize the prohibition sentiment. In 1889, a strong Republican legislature brought in the question of constitutional prohibition. All the Democrats in the legislature except two voted against it and there were enough Republicans opposed to result in the loss of the measure. The Democratic party kept outbidding the Republican party for the support of the Wet element, with the result that it attracted a large part of the German, Bohemian, Irish and Polish vote. The leadership of the party before 1890 was distinctly wet, and the attitude of the Democratic press was pro-liquor.

When Mr. Bryan ran for Congress in 1890, the main issue in the contest for the state offices was prohibition. The young candidate tried to leave the subject severely alone. The Omaha *World-Herald,* which was supporting him, said, "He [Mr. Bryan] never fails to announce that he is against prohibition." This was putting it rather strongly. He never failed to admit that that was his political stand and the stand of his party whenever a demand was made upon him to state a position. He accepted the traditional attitude of the Democrats of the time against "sumptuary legislation," though he stated that personally he was a teetotaler.

An embarrassing incident arose during this campaign at the Bar Association banquet, held in Lincoln. Mr. Bryan, though a newcomer to the city, objected to the use of liquor at the event.

This gave the Republicans a great opening. They charged him with being a prohibitionist and then waited to see whether he would repudiate his party or abandon his principles.

The young Commoner answered in his next public speech: "The use of wine at the Lincoln banquet was abandoned for two reasons. First: Some of the expected guests were known to have a weakness for the flowing bowl which would result in their intoxication. Second: It was a question of having the banquet without wine or without women. Many of the guests at that banquet could do without wine, but none of them could do without the refining influence of woman, so wine was abandoned and woman triumphed. If this be treason, make the most of it."

Rivers and floods had rolled under the bridge since the days when William Jennings Bryan was an obscure Congressional candidate. For twenty years, in fact, he had been the dominant political figure in his state and for fourteen years the chief power in his party both in the state and in the nation. As he set forth for Grand Island, he realized what it would mean if he should not succeed in the drastic step to which he was trying to convert his party. It was hard to turn aside the possibility that some time again he might be wanted as the nominee for the presidency, though that issue was pretty well settled. But it was harder still to relax his grasp on the control of state affairs which had been his for so long. Bryan might be defeated in the nation, and he had once failed to carry Nebraska in a presidential campaign, but the whole world knew that in Nebraska he was first citizen. It was pleasant at the fifty-year mark to look forward to a life of arranging affairs, or being a kingmaker, even if one were not seeking office one's self. It was hard to go against friends who had campaigned with him through a lifetime, but his party was wrong and if he did not correct it it would sink into a twilight of defeat. Norris and similar oncoming radicals in the Republican camp would gain the leadership and establish themselves as the real representatives of the people.

Bryan's views were well known before the convention opened. There was consternation and anger among many of "the boys" who felt that this last attempt to take nourishment away from them was just a little too thick. Bryan's repeated attacks on big business had resulted in the Republicans getting most of the supplies of the larder, but as long as Democracy remained safe in the arms of Bacchus, "the boys" knew whence their bread and butter and *spiritus frumenti* were coming. They did not propose to stand for county option, but they were divided on the policy which they should take in handling the situation and in dealing with The Great Commoner's prestige and oratorical power. Mayor Dahlman, of Omaha, was present, ready to demand a plank seeking definite opposition to county option. Governor Shallenberger took the stand that if a county option bill should be passed, he would not veto it. R. L. Metcalf, a lifelong friend of Mr. Bryan, and for many years editor of *The Commoner,* wanted to introduce a compromise platform.

The convention met on a typical Democratic day under a roasting sun in a huge khaki tent. Mr. Bryan walked in with the Lancaster County delegation and was greeted by mingled cheers and catcalls. Several of the leaders conspicuously stayed away from his delegation. Congressman G. M. Hitchcock, later a senator, made the first hostile move by offering a resolution to prohibit the introducing of platform planks with accompanying speeches unless submitted as a section of the majority or minority report of the Committee on Resolutions. The effect of this was that Bryan would not be permitted to speak to his subject at all until time for the committee reports. The Great Commoner was on his feet instantly trying to introduce a modifying amendment. The chairman ordered a roll call on the amendment and Bryan lost by 465 to 394. A wave of cheers greeted the defeat of the man who had led them for twenty years.

The dominant forces introduced their plank against county option. Shallenberger introduced his less committal position. The Bryan plank was presented reading, "We favor county option as the best method of dealing with the liquor question."

Evening had come by the time The Great Commoner had an opportunity to reach the platform with his minority report. His followers tried to make up for the slights of the day by a demonstration in his behalf. He waved them to quietness and started with conciliatory words saying that he did not come to his present action by any desire to disturb party harmony nor to take the rôle of a dictator.

"It is already being heralded abroad," he said, "that I am to be turned down at home, and that fact is to be used as a taunt whenever I go up and down the country."

He stated that he had no apology for his conduct and attitude toward the brewers. If he had any to make, it would be to the fathers and mothers of the state for remaining silent so long.

He notified his hearers that he proposed to appeal to the Democrats of the state. He reminded them that delegates to conventions were made up of representatives chosen by sparsely attended county gatherings.

"County option is not only expedient," he said,

"but it is right. This is a moral question. There is but one side to a moral question. Which do you take?"

In closing he made an appeal to those who had worked with him for so long. He said he would never sound a retreat, and if the standard were to be given over to the enemy, let it be put in other hands. Early the following morning there was a roll call on the Bryan plank. It was lost by a vote of 647 to 198.

Dahlman's opposition plank was also lost and Governor Shallenberger's position was supported by popular acclaim.

Both candidates set forth on a state-wide struggle to secure the nomination for governorship in the party primary. The number of votes cast in this event were more than 20,000 greater than in the primaries two years prior. It was charged that the Republicans in order to put the Democrats into a thoroughly Wet position voted for Dahlman in the Democratic event. At any rate, Dahlman led Shallenberger in the primary by 71 votes.

All seemed to be going well for the victor until Friday before the election. On that day, there appeared a brief announcement by Mr. Bryan in the Lincoln newspapers which stated that he had hired the local auditorium and would address the people of Lincoln on Monday evening, dealing with political subjects. Long before the hour for speaking to begin, the crowds were flocking toward the auditorium. By eight o'clock the hall was filled. Hun-

MR. BRYAN—NOW, WHAT AILS THE CRITTER?

From Minneapolis "Journal"

Nebraska Democracy kicked over the traces when Bryan came out in support of county option. County option meant the right of a county to decide whether it would or would not permit saloons. Under the plan of township option (then in practice in Nebraska) the saloon-keeper could set up his place at the edge of the village, even though the village were dry.

dreds stood in the back of the building unable to gain an entrance. Listeners hung in the wings of the stage and overflowed on to the stage, leaving only room for the speaker. There was no chairman. Mr. Bryan appeared alone in the center of the platform.

Hundreds of Republicans as well as Democrats had come to hear him. Mr. Bryan, with a glint of humor in his eyes, took occasion to lecture his audience on sound Democratic doctrines and the shortcomings of the Republicans. If the latter were going to come to his affair, he was not going to lose the opportunity to shed a little enlightenment.

This meeting was unimportant on the surface, and yet it was the culmination of years of struggle. For more than a century, the Prohibitionists had campaigned in America. Long before the formation of the Anti-Saloon League, women's clubs and organizations, church societies, both Protestant and Catholic, had campaigned for the cause. The Great Commoner himself never claimed the credit for results which years of campaigning, endurance of ridicule, and self-sacrifice by thousands of citizens had brought into being. But with the addition of The Peerless Leader to the ranks of those who were bringing the movement to a head, the beginning of its accomplishment was near.

At this meeting in Lincoln, on October 31, 1910, The Great Commoner launched his nation-wide campaign against the liquor movement. Here, he for the first time came out vehemently and whole-

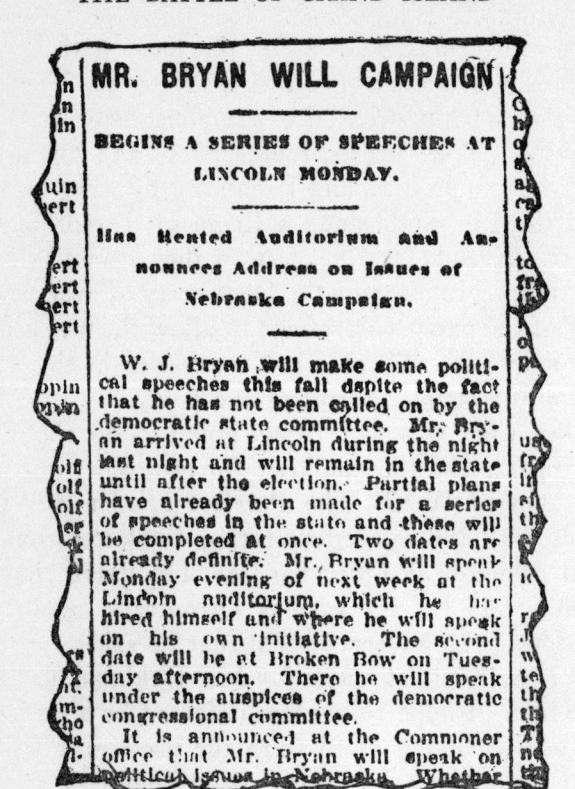

> **MR. BRYAN WILL CAMPAIGN**
>
> BEGINS A SERIES OF SPEECHES AT LINCOLN MONDAY.
>
> Has Rented Auditorium and Announces Address on Issues of Nebraska Campaign.
>
> W. J. Bryan will make some political speeches this fall dspite the fact that he has not been called on by the democratic state committee. Mr. Bryan arrived at Lincoln during the night last night and will remain in the state until after the election. Partial plans have already been made for a series of speeches in the state and these will be completed at once. Two dates are already definite. Mr. Bryan will speak Monday evening of next week at the Lincoln auditorium, which he has hired himself and where he will speak on his own initiative. The second date will be at Broken Bow on Tuesday afternoon. There he will speak under the auspices of the democratic congressional committee.
> It is announced at the Commoner office that Mr. Bryan will speak on political issues in Nebraska. Whether

*From Nebraska "State Journal"*

The beginning of Mr. Bryan's campaign on county option which led him ultimately to the support of national prohibition. Note the ominous first sentence in the story.

heartedly for the prohibition cause, and the fight was on.

"The liquor business is on the defensive," he declared to the audience in the Lincoln auditorium;

"its representatives are for the most part lawless themselves and in league with lawlessness. They are in partnership with the gambling hell and the brothel. They are the most corrupt and corrupting influence in politics, and I shall not by voice or vote aid them in establishing a Reign of Terror in this state. Even before the election, they are impudently attempting to question the Democracy of every member of the party who refuses to allow them to censor his speeches. They will, if successful in this campaign, insist on controlling the party."

But what was Mr. Bryan going to do about his own party and the candidate for governor, who was an avowed Wet? The Peerless Leader met that issue with the same devastating frankness that he had exhibited in other battles. He stated that he would vote for the various Democratic candidates excepting the governor. On that he said:

"I shall neither speak for Mr. Dahlman nor vote for him. I hope to see him defeated by a majority so overwhelming as to warn the brewers, distillers and liquor dealers to retire from Nebraska politics and allow the people to act upon the liquor question as they do upon other questions.

"But whether Mr. Dahlman is elected or defeated I shall continue my protest against the domination of our party by the liquor interests. I shall contribute whatever assistance I can to the effort which will be made to put an end to the spree upon which our party seems to have embarked. I am not willing that the party shall die of delirium tremens.

## THE BATTLE OF GRAND ISLAND

An appeal will be made from Philip drunk to Philip sober, and I am confident that the appeal will be successful, that the party will rise again to the high plane upon which it has conducted its campaigns in this state for nearly two decades and appeal once more to the conscience and moral sense of the people."

Dahlman was defeated in the election by close to 20,000 votes, while most of the other Democratic candidates were elected.

On January 16, 1920, the Eighteenth Amendment to the Constitution went into effect. The Great Commoner was the chief speaker at the celebration ceremonies at Washington, taking for his text, "They are dead which sought the young child's life."

## CHAPTER XII

### THE COCKED HAT

> Don't inquire about how the fight is going to go—make it go the right way, if you can.
> —W. J. Bryan to Champ Clark

AS the thunderings of The Great Commoner reverberated year after year across the rolling plains of Nebraska and over the poverty-stricken brown and white cotton patches of the South, the echoes began to be heard in the corridors of the intelligentsia.

How much Bryan had to do with the muckraking period of 1908-1912, and how much America's criticism of the industrial age arose from a general sense of being thwarted on the part of the common man, one can hardly determine.

Certain it is that The Peerless Leader for at least twelve years was the most dramatic and the most vocal forerunner of this movement. Roosevelt in the Republican camp had also taken up the cry of "trust-busting," but Roosevelt's ancestry, education, family connections and independent income tempered his attacks on big business and for a time left Bryan as the only undisputed, authentic commoner.

Yet the spirit of revolt was finding a voice in language which was more in keeping with modern times, in criticisms which were more specific, better ordered and more acute than the outcries from Fairview.

Edward Aylsworth Ross had written that singularly penetrating book *Sin and Society*, a volume bound in scarlet and purchased by many a college sophomore under the impression that he was buying an American Boccaccio. But it was also read by virtually every college student before his graduation. Walter Rauschenbusch had published *Christianity and the Social Crisis*, which went much further than Mr. Bryan both in denunciation of the established order and in means suggested for its remedy. By 1911 and 1912 Ray Stannard Baker was exposing the sugar trust, writing in the *American Magazine*. Charles Edward Russell in *Hearst's Magazine* was pillorying business in his articles "Mysterious Octopus," after he had been doing two years of this sort of thing in *Hampton's Magazine*. George Creel in *Collier's* was telling its readers about "Denver's Uprising Against Misrule." Lincoln Steffens was hammering away in *Everybody's* against "The Sovereign Political Power of Organized Business."

The vocabulary of the world had changed since 1896. The words "plutocrat and anarchist" had been revised to "conservative and progressive."

The intelligentsia were using the language of the day and to some degree they had the votes. The Peerless Leader himself felt instinctively that in a sense the world was slipping away from him, not his special world of the small town perhaps, but his complete grasp of the forces and the language of protest. He realized that he was not the logical candidate to carry the Democratic standard in 1912. He had, as has been noted, virtually thrown away this possibility when he came out for national prohibition. He was also an unlikely candidate because he had already run three times. But more than this, he felt that the middle years were upon him and that it was time to give other and younger men their opportunity.

Other men very strongly felt the same way about it. Governor Wilson was quite sure that no one so uncouth was fitted to lead Democracy amid the complicated problems of the age. Champ Clark, Speaker of the House, and many others thought that the leadership should turn to them. And yet in spite of his isolation from the life and thought of the larger towns and cities, in spite of his lack of acquaintance with the idioms of the new era, there was a blazing quality to his leadership, an unabated vigor to his convictions and a magnetism in his personality which made him, in spite of all, the dominant, unescapable figure in his party.

Months before the Baltimore Convention, which came at the end of June, 1912, letters poured into Mr. Bryan urging him again to be a candidate. In addition to these, there was the wish of Mrs. Bryan. As the quarrel between Taft and Roosevelt developed and a split in the Republican party seemed likely, she urged him to be the candidate. As he thought of the thousands of miles of campaigning

## THE COCKED HAT

which they had done together in all corners of the country, as he realized that month upon month and year upon year Mary Baird Bryan had risen at five o'clock in the morning to answer political correspondence and tried to keep all his supporters in line, this advice must have been the hardest of all to resist. He knew that even if he decided to campaign for the nomination, the probabilities were against him.

Mrs. Bryan says in her *Memoirs,* "I wanted him to take the nomination; I wanted him to be president; I wanted him to conquer his enemies. We had worked so long and so hard." But if Bryan could see the larger wisdom of not urging himself for the candidacy, he also realized that the temper of the country was at last turned against the reactionaries. He knew that the Democrats must not be dominated by the Parker wing of the party and that the record of any one who should run must be clear-cut on this point.

Colonel House, of Austin, Texas, at that time one of the younger progressive leaders in that state, also realized that the time had come to look for a satisfactory candidate. Bryan had lived next door to the House family in Austin during the winter of 1898 and 1899, and the acquaintanceship of the two men had been continued since that time, with little love existing on the part of Colonel House who regarded The Peerless Leader as a fanatic.

Nevertheless, the Colonel wrote in his diary in

1910, "I felt it was practically impossible to nominate or elect a man that Mr. Bryan opposed."

The Colonel at that time already had the vision of himself as the power behind the throne. In Texas, while campaigning on behalf of various governors, he had refused to accept any office and contented himself with the thought of what he had accomplished in bringing others to the forefront. It is perhaps human that he overestimated his part in many of these affairs, especially in the information which he at this time tendered to The Great Commoner about the political state of the nation, as one who might present Moses with a copy of the Ten Commandments.

His initial step was to ask Mr. Bryan for suggestions as to a likely candidate, and the latter mentioned Mayor Gaynor, of New York, as a possibility. The mayor was something of a commoner in his own style. He had led the fight in trying to get a fair deal between the City of New York and the traction companies. He had a large family. He wrote delightful letters to children. His candidacy would have been picturesque and human.

But apparently the mayor did not appreciate the importance of the dapper man from Texas. Colonel House called on Mr. Gaynor, explained his mission, and thought that he had made arrangements for the mayor to make an opening campaign speech in Texas on invitation of the Texas legislature. The legislature later, by arrangement with Colonel House, extended the invitation. When a newspaper wired

THE DEMOCRATIC PARTY WILL NOW HAVE A FINE OPPORTUNITY TO SHOW HOW IT IS DONE.

From Des Moines "Register and Leader"

Taft in the White House was proving ultraconservative. The muckraking era was in full swing. The country looked to Democracy to take the leadership of liberal opinion.

Mr. Gaynor about this, he replied that he had no notion of doing so and had never heard of any such proposal.

Perhaps the mayor feared the Greeks bearing gifts. Perhaps the matter had entirely slipped his attention. In either event, the incident was highly displeasing to the gentleman from Texas, and his efforts on behalf of the New York mayor ceased then and there.

Colonel House turned to the cause of Wilson, but there was another man of the hour who appeared at the moment more logical. Champ Clark, of Missouri, was the Speaker of the House. He was a man much of the Bryan stamp. He had joined with The Great Commoner on the free silver issue when both were Congressmen in 1892. He had supported Bryan in all his campaigns and Bryan had occasionally spoken for him. He was also a Chautauqua lecturer, whose favorite topic, "Richer Than Golconda," dealt with the literature of the Bible.

Yet because Clark was of the Bryan school, he was not in touch with the new spirit of the day any more than The Great Commoner; and his progressivism was open to question.

In the Clark-Wilson controversy the part of Bryan was supreme and The Commoner effected a decision in national history, not only by the aid of the situation, but more particularly by his own virtuosity in politics, and by his intuition of the needs of the hour, even though many of its complications had drifted beyond his comprehension.

## THE COCKED HAT

Bryan felt at home with Clark, and yet feared his devotion to progressive causes was inadequate. Clark had given reason for this feeling of doubt. In 1910 the insurgent Republicans and the majority of the Democrats were trying to overthrow the rule of Speaker Cannon in the House of Representatives. When the issue was put to a vote, twenty-three Democrats under the leadership of Representative Fitzgerald voted with the standpat Republicans. Many indignant Democrats were for reading these men out of the party, but Clark intervened. "We haven't got enough Democrats in the party now," he said, "so what's the use of throwing any one out just because he doesn't agree with us on one point." But the one point was a vital one in the politics of the period. Clark had an eye on the nomination and he did not wish to do anything which would alienate support.

There was still another issue which was to prove embarrassing to this candidate for Democratic leadership. Schedule K on the tariff schedule had been introduced to protect the woolen manufacturers. The radical Republicans and many of the magazines of the day had raised an outcry against it. This was the kind of challenge which would have been gunpowder in the nose of Bryan. He could not understand the lukewarm attitude of his friend Champ Clark who was neglecting to take a stand on the issue.

Clark, in fact, was afraid of progressivism, of being identified with so risky a train of thought. At least, he didn't want to tie up too specifically with any particular element. When interviewed by the *World's Work,* he said, "Yes. I class myself as a progressive. It's in the air—everything is progressive these days."

Yet the ties of friendship and the memories of old battles together made The Great Commoner feel that here was a man who might be the future leader of Democracy. On the twentieth of March, 1911, Mr. Bryan held his annual birthday "at home" and dinner, a day later than usual for this occasion, because the nineteenth was on a Sunday. It had been customary to make this affair a political get-together of some importance, and Bryan invited Clark to be the speaker of the occasion. In view of the coming campaign this was a high compliment. But the Speaker accepted with some reluctance. He was familiar with Fairview, its fields of corn, the ornate architecture of the homestead, the tents on the lawn filled with plain people, the living room decorated with the portraits of Democratic heroes. He knew the Lincoln auditorium where the dinner was served on tables made of boards across wooden horses, like a mammoth church supper. That sort of thing might be all right, but it hadn't won the day thus far.

What he wanted to know was whether Mr. Bryan, his host, was going to get out of the way so that some one else could be nominated in the 1912 Convention. Three times Mr. Clark got The Peerless Leader to one side and brought the conversation

## THE COCKED HAT

around to this point and three times Mr. Bryan stated that he was not a candidate.

There was little talk on Mr. Clark's part of the people's wrongs or of a triumphant democracy or of the burdens of the masses. It was clear that his problem first and last was, "Who is going to be nominated?"

Bryan's attitude was tolerant. Even though approximately the same age as Clark, he was in many ways much older in political experience. He was ready to transfer the mantle of his leadership to another. If he sensed Clark's eagerness for the nomination, he was honest and sympathetic enough to remember his own longing for the prize, especially in the days of '96. He did not hold the desire for the office to be a fault in his friend, but he saw the great mistake that Clark was making even from the practical standpoint, in sidestepping issues.

So it was that two months later, on May 5, 1911, The Peerless Leader wrote to Champ Clark a letter which reveals more than any other document the political philosophy, the audacious strategy, and the reckless idealism which made The Great Commoner a dominant influence in public affairs as long as he lived. As one reads the letter, one realizes how completely Bryan recognized that he was about to resign the leadership of his party, and how generously he was pointing the way for his possible successor. Had this been a letter for general publication it might have seemed merely an idealistic statement for public consumption. But it was a personal communication from Bryan to a lifelong friend. It said the kind of things that one would not say to an acquaintance, and it gave the ripened experience of a long career with a generosity which could have been better appreciated. He wrote:

My dear Clark:

I venture to make a suggestion for your consideration. I believe the fight over wool will prove a crisis in your life as well as in the party's prospects. A leader must *lead;* it is not always pleasant to oppose friends, and one who leads takes the chances of defeat, but these are the necessary attendants upon leadership. Wilson is making friends because he *fights*. His fight against Smith was heroic. He fought for the income tax and for a primary law. The people like a fighter. You won your position by fighting and you must continue to fight to hold it. Enter into the wool fight. Don't be content to take polls and sit in the background. Take one side or the other and take it *strong*. If a tax on wool is right, lead the protectionists to victory. You can do it and it will make you strong with that wing of the party. If free wool is right, as I believe it is, lead the fight for it and get the credit for the victory, if victory comes. Don't inquire about how the fight is going to go—make it go the right way, if you can. If you fail you lay the foundation for a future victory. The right wins in the end—don't be afraid to wait. My opinion is that you will not have to wait long, but whether long or not, one can better afford to be defeated fighting for the right than to win on the wrong side.

I hope you will pardon this intrusion upon your thoughts, but the party needs your assistance. A blast from your bugle may save the day, and it will, in my judgment, strengthen you personally.

Regards to the family.

Yours,<br>
BRYAN

Mr. Clark did not care for the advice, and had as little communication with Mr. Bryan as possible during the intervening months. In fact, it was apparently the Clark view that Bryan's influence was done for. There is no other way to account for his studied indifference to the Bryan support, though his managers campaigned vigorously to secure the Nebraska delegates and Mr. Bryan did not oppose this movement, until at the time of the convention. The Nebraska delegation went to the Baltimore Convention pledged to Clark.

In the meantime, Woodrow Wilson and his friends were becoming concerned at the indifference which they had shown to Mr. Bryan in the past. In 1908 Wilson had refused to sit on the same platform with The Peerless Leader at a meeting in New Jersey, and it was not until March 13, 1911, that Wilson met The Great Commoner face to face. Bryan was speaking in New Jersey just a week before his birthday dinner in Lincoln. Governor Wilson evidently thought that it was about time that he make the acquaintance of the Nebraskan. Not only did he attend, but he invited Mr. Bryan to take dinner with him and his family that evening. No great mutual friendship developed between the two men at that time. Mr. Wilson sat, and with finger tips pressed together, talked of the new freedom in terms of the scholar and historian. Mr. Bryan expanded in anecdote and oratory in a manner which Governor Wilson did not usually find to be happy.

As the autumn drew on, Colonel House made continual efforts to interest Bryan in the Wilson cause. He wrote in his diary that he considered it his mission to "nurse Bryan and bring him around to our way of thinking."

In November, Mr. Bryan decided to take a vacation trip to Jamaica, the occasion on which he was shipwrecked. Just before he sailed, House called on him and discussed the qualities which made Mr. Wilson deserving of Democratic support. Mr. Bryan smiled and invited the Colonel to keep him informed concerning political conditions and to send him clippings.

The Colonel embraced the opportunity zealously and for the next several weeks, while enjoying the tropical breezes of the West Indies, The Commoner's mail contained frequent messages from the Colonel, each telling more and more about Governor Wilson. Nor was the opportunity lost to say a word or two now and then in derogation of Mr. Clark. On November twenty-fifth Mr. Bryan received this message: "There is some evidence that Mr. Underwood and his friends intend to make a direct issue with you for control of the next convention, and it looks a little as if they were receiving some aid from Champ Clark and his friends." A

## THE COCKED HAT

week later another note from E. M. House brought the word that Mr. Hearst was taking a hand in the political situation. "I learned," said The Commoner's correspondent, "that he [Hearst] was favorable to Underwood or Champ Clark and was against Governor Wilson."

Things were apparently going along very nicely. Just before he left Jamaica, Bryan wrote to Mr. House: "I shall attend the Washington banquet on the eighth of January and will have a chance to learn how things are shaping up.

"I am glad Governor Wilson recognizes that he has the opposition of Morgan and the rest of Wall Street. If he is nominated, it must be by the Progressive Democrats, and the more progressive he is, the better.

"The Washington banquet will give him a good chance to speak out against the trusts and the Aldrich currency scheme."

On his arrival in the United States, The Commoner went down to Raleigh, North Carolina, to visit his old friend, Josephus Daniels. With Daniels, he felt at home. Here was neither the supercilious polish of the East, nor the smartly worded theories of the intelligentsia, nor the bitter opposition of those who disliked him. Josephus Daniels was folks. The Daniels had family prayers. They attended the Edenton Street Methodist Episcopal Church, a huge homely structure which seated close to a thousand worshipers every Sunday. Here was a part of the country where Evangelical Christianity was the order of the day and where every respectable citizen was a Democrat. This was home.

Mr. Bryan sat in the comfortable rocking chair in the study and talked of old times and what the future might bring forth. There was a ring at the front doorbell. Mr. Daniels answered it and after some conversation came back into the living room introducing a young man who announced himself as a reporter for the New York *Sun*.

The reporter handed Mr. Bryan a dispatch and asked for his comment on it. The dispatch contained a letter more than four years old, but just made public.

Princeton, New Jersey<br>
April 29, 1907

My dear Mr. Joline:

Thank you very much for sending me your address at Parsons, Kansas, before the Board of Directors of the Missouri, Kansas and Texas Railway Company. I have read it with relish and entire agreement. Would that we could do something, at once dignified and effective, to knock Mr. Bryan once for all into a cocked hat!

Cordially and sincerely yours,<br>Woodrow Wilson

The Peerless Leader did not hesitate in his comment, nor did he in the stress of the moment commit himself to any position which might in the future prove embarrassing.

"You may wire the *Sun*," he said, "that you have seen Mr. Bryan and he says that if Mr. Wilson wants to knock him into a cocked hat, Wilson and the *Sun* are on the same platform. That's what the *Sun* has been trying to do to him since 1896."

These sentiments of Governor Wilson were no particular news to Mr. Bryan. As far back as 1897, Professor Wilson had commented, "We might have had Mr. Bryan for president because of the impression which may be made upon an excited assembly by a good voice and a few ringing sentences, flung forth just after a cold man who gave unpalatable counsel has sat down. The country knew absolutely nothing about Mr. Bryan before his nomination and it would not have known anything about him afterward had he not chosen to make speeches."

Again in 1908, Dr. Wilson remarked, "Mr. Bryan is the most charming and lovable of men personally, but foolish and dangerous in his theoretical beliefs."

Bryan had overlooked the personal slurs of Mr. Wilson and had cheered on the New Jersey governor in his fight against the trusts, commenting on them in detail in *The Commoner*.

Accepting the eastern newspaper view of Mr. Bryan as a pettifogging, ambitious windbag (who nevertheless had influence with the corn belt vote), the Wilson managers were in a state of great excitement at the publication of the Joline letter. Wilson himself was considerably worried. He telephoned his secretary, Mr. Tumulty, to come to Washington, and there a conference was held with other leaders, including Senator O'Gorman and Dudley Field Malone. Josephus Daniels was asked to explain to Mr. Bryan the circumstances that lay back of the Joline letter, to patch things up as best he could.

This was the day before the Jackson dinner. On the following evening, January 8, 1912, the assembled dignitaries of Democracy sat in state in the banquet hall of the New Willard Hotel. They might be dirt farmers or just plain city folk for 364 days of the year, but on Jackson day, with boiled shirts and hearty appetites, they were accustomed to sit down to celebrate the principles of the party.

On this occasion the air was electric. It was particularly so for Senator Underwood, Governor Harmon of Ohio, and Champ Clark, Speaker of the House, all of whom had that much better chance of being nominated the following summer, if the Wilson-Bryan situation was not smoothed over at this dinner.

When Bryan came into the reception hall, there was a perceptible stir. There was nothing in his manner at that moment to indicate what his attitude would be. His greeting to Mr. Clark was courteous but not exceptionally friendly. Clark, himself, had the feeling of being brushed aside.

As Governor Wilson rose to speak, the audience wondered whether he would ignore the late unpleasantness or what his attitude would be. What would be the governor's manner toward The Peerless Leader who was "known because he made speeches" and whose "theories were dangerous"?

The audience did not have long to wait. Governor Wilson turned to The Great Commoner and said, "When others were faint-hearted, Colonel Bryan carried the Democratic standard. He kept the fires burning which have heartened and encouraged the democracy of the country."

When Mr. Wilson was seated, Bryan put his arm around the shoulders of the New Jersey governor.

Before leaving the governor after the dinner, Bryan told Wilson not to worry about the Joline letter.

"I, of course, knew," he said, "that you were not with me in my position on the currency."

"All I can say, Mr. Bryan," Woodrow Wilson replied, "is that you are a great big man."

## CHAPTER XIII

### BALTIMORE

We are sailing for England.
—Colonel House

CLARK'S love for Bryan did not advance as the spring of 1912 approached. It seemed clear that Clark would have the ultimate support of Hearst and the New York delegation led by Charley Murphy, at that time the Chieftain of Tammany Hall, and those ninety votes looked better than the influence of Nebraska.

The affectionate interchange between Bryan and Wilson at the Jackson day dinner had not been to his liking, and further the tone of the eastern papers had fooled him into believing that The Great Commoner was a voice from the past.

Meanwhile, Bryan was becoming increasingly dubious regarding the conduct of his old associate. Clark was wearing the string tie, the baggy suit and the ample hat of Esau, but his voice was the voice of Jacob.

The Wilson managers during this period, especially Colonel House, were doing their best to keep the Nebraskan in a happy frame of mind. Bryan made a trip to New York in April, 1912, and stopped at the Holland House. The Texas Colonel was among the first to telephone him. A breakfast appointment was arranged.

There in the midst of silver and fine linen the Colonel earnestly presented the case of Governor Wilson to Mr. and Mrs. Bryan. He told how Wilson had fought the trusts, how he was hated by Wall Street; all the arguments which he had been writing for the past several months.

If Colonel House seemed unaware that *The Commoner* had been printing the story of Mr. Wilson's activities, week by week, for a number of months before he had approached Bryan on the subject, at least the visit was more complimentary than the indifference of Mr. Clark.

Why did not Bryan announce his support of Wilson at once? Colonel House pressed the point home again and again, but The Peerless Leader was not to be stampeded. His position as arbiter of the party, wrapped up, as he believed, with his duty as the people's champion, would be much minimized if he let a victory for either side come about so easily.

Mr. Wilson, though a leader of progressivism in the East, did not have the rural touch. His spirit was with the common people, but he did not bring his person too closely in touch with them. He had discovered that Mr. Bryan was "a great big man," but his enlightenment had been too recent for The Peerless Leader to feel entirely sure of the new admirer.

More than this, there were several crises ahead which would test the caliber of the different candidates, and if these crises did not come of themselves, Mr. Bryan intended to see to it that they were developed.

A Democratic victory seemed certain. Roosevelt had come back from Africa foaming at the mouth at Mr. Taft and determined to secure the Republican nomination. Many outsiders thought that Roosevelt would be the Republican candidate, but The Great Commoner, an old stager on the political platform, knew that Taft as President could insist upon his own nomination. It was a repetition of 1896 with the laugh this time on the Republicans. With Taft running for office, Roosevelt would either put his own independent ticket into the field or would sulk at Oyster Bay and welcome a Republican defeat.

Bryan was a newspaper correspondent at the Republican Convention in Chicago. He saw the strength of the Roosevelt delegates and realized that at last the thunderings from Nebraska had become a political issue which the people not only understood but intended to translate into terms of political action. He realized that if the Democrats nominated a conservative, Roosevelt would be elected and the new Progressive party would occupy the position which The Peerless Leader had been trying to create for Democracy throughout his whole public life.

ON GUARD AGAIN.

*From New York "World"*

Charley Murphy was boss of Tammany Hall at the time of the Democratic Convention at Baltimore. He and Hearst and Wall Street were supporting Clark.

As these thoughts passed through his mind in his room in a Chicago hotel, a telephone call came in. It was Josephus Daniels, who always seemed to be opportunely present at the crises in Mr. Bryan's life, and did not a little to bring them about.

Mr. Daniels brought the news that the Democratic National Committee had met and had nominated Alton B. Parker as temporary chairman for the Democratic Convention in Baltimore. Mr. Daniels asked Mr. Bryan what the latter thought of the selection.

When Mr. Bryan was a small boy his mother had talked to him seriously on the matter of profanity and had expressed the hope that her son would never be guilty of that transgression. Accordingly, Mr. Bryan's answer was Christian though emphatic. He told Mr. Daniels that he would not only criticize the selection but the committee that made the selection.

Parker! Parker who represented the New York gold Democrats! Parker, the attorney for Thomas Fortune Ryan, traction magnate, stock manipulator! Parker, the man who had polled several hundred thousand votes less than the poorest record made by Mr. Bryan! It was incredible.

The Peerless Leader was himself again. He may have been ridiculed by cartoonists from coast to coast; true he had been defeated three times by the people whose will he extolled; and again true that his old-fashioned, individual, spread-eagle idealism was being overshadowed by the literary parlor

## BALTIMORE

Democrats of the new age. But this was a situation that he and he alone could handle.

He tore down to the telegraph desk and sent this wire to each of the leading candidates:

> In the interest of harmony, I suggested to the Sub-Committee of the Democratic National Committee the advisability of recommending as Temporary Chairman some progressive acceptable to the leading progressive candidates for the presidential nomination.
>
> I took it for granted that no committee-man interested in Democratic success would desire to offend the members of a Convention overwhelmingly progressive by naming a reactionary to sound the keynote of the campaign.
>
> Eight members of the Sub-Committee, however, have over the protest of the remaining eight, agreed upon not only a reactionary, but upon the one Democrat, who, among those not candidates for the presidential nomination is, in the eyes of the public, most conspicuously identified with the reactionary element of the Party.
>
> I shall be pleased to join you and your friends in opposing this selection by the full Committee or by the Convention. Kindly answer here.

Would Clark respond to this challenge? The Peerless Leader wondered. And what would be the answer of the educated governor of New Jersey when an actual fight was at stake with the precious ninety ballots of New York to be considered, for one could hardly oppose the Parker nomination and expect Judge Parker to permit the New York ballots to be cast in one's favor!

It was not a pleasing wire for any of the possible candidates to receive. It was not sent to Underwood and Harmon, who were frankly in the conservative wing of the party. Governors Foss of Massachusetts, Marshall of Indiana and Baldwin of Connecticut were all possibilities, but they declined to join Mr. Bryan in his crusade. Governor Burke of North Dakota lent his support.

When The Peerless Leader received Mr. Clark's answer, it must have decided him finally in his choice.

In Mr. Clark's reply was this keynote statement: "The supreme consideration should be to prevent any discord in the Convention."

One can see the amazement on The Great Commoner's face as he read this reply. With the Democratic progressive victory in sight, with the actual moment at hand when the causes for which he had fought for sixteen years were about to be realized, his old associate and would-be commoner from Missouri talked of the supreme issue being to prevent discord! Governor Wilson wired:

You are right. Before hearing of your message, I gladly stated my position in answer to a question from the Baltimore *Evening Sun*. The Baltimore Convention is to be the Convention of progressives—the men who are progressive in principle and by conviction. It must, if it is not to be put in a wrong light before the country, express its convictions in its organization and its choice of men who are to speak for it. You are to be a member of the Convention and are entirely within your rights in doing everything within your power to bring that result about. No one will doubt where my sympathies lie and you will, I am sure, find my friends in the Convention acting upon a clear conviction and always in the interest of the people's cause. I am happy in the confidence that they need no suggestion from me.

The Peerless Leader was accused then and later of having tried to stampede the convention in his own direction, but he was too wise a politician, were this the case, to have given any candidate an opportunity to put himself on record in the way which Mr. Wilson had embraced.

The Wilson star rose high at that moment. But Mr. Bryan was fresh from the lessons of the Republican Convention, and knew well that mere progressive enthusiasm would not carry the day in a political convention, even though it be the convention of his own beloved Democracy.

The task set before him was not simply to provide Wilson enthusiasm—in fact, the primaries in his own state had instructed the delegation for Clark—his task was to create a situation which would permit him to support Wilson and to so arrange events that the convention would not dare to name any other candidate.

There were many men anxious to bring about the Wilson nomination, some selfishly and others unselfishly—but who could really accomplish it? McCombs, McAdoo and Tumulty were doing a good job in the East along with many others, but their western influence was limited.

Colonel House, the country gentleman from

Texas, with his liberal leanings and his Republican tailor, had no stomach for the coarse fare of a convention of the Unterrified Democracy. He was accustomed to going to Europe every summer for his health and he feared that a Democratic Convention would literally make him ill.

"We are sailing for England," wrote the kingmaker to Woodrow Wilson, as the Baltimore Convention opened.

So, upon the shoulders of the stout, evangelical, politically-scarred war horse from Nebraska rested the task of nominating the candidate of Democracy.

By the time Mr. Bryan had arrived at the Belvedere Hotel in Baltimore, the Clark forces were aware of the fact that something must be done to conciliate The Peerless Leader. Perhaps a little limelight would suit him. They must show that they were all friends together.

Mr. Bryan was hardly installed in his room when he received a call from Senator Vardaman of Mississippi. This bearer of the olive branch for Clark and Parker was a wise choice. He was an old friend of Bryan and had all the scenery of a back-country Democrat. His hair was minus in front and in back came down over his collar in a heavy cascade. He wore a ten-gallon, broad-brimmed, Texas cowboy hat.

He announced to Mr. Bryan that if The Peerless Leader would only stop opposing Mr. Parker, the Clark forces would see to it that Bryan was made permanent chairman of the convention. Bryan stood up on hearing this message and glared coldly at his visitor. It is not strange that he regarded this sophomoric attempt at political maneuvering as an insult.

Vardaman, however, was both hurt and surprised at Bryan's hostile attitude.

"I thought," he said, "that our personal and political relations were intimate enough to permit me to talk about the matter to you."

Bryan melted, smiled at his old friend, put his hand on his visitor's shoulder and said that he did not mean to offend. But Vardaman returned to the Parker forces with nothing accomplished.

The next step of Mr. Bryan was to hunt up Judge Parker and request that the latter refuse to let his name be put in nomination as temporary chairman, stating that the main function of this office was to give the keynote of the convention, and that the Parker keynote would not be in tune with the pitch ultimately to be adopted. It was Mr. Parker's turn to be insulted.

The Great Commoner then tried to enlist Senator O'Gorman and later Governor Marshall as candidates for the office, but each refused. He finally persuaded Senator Kern of Indiana to permit him to place his name before the convention in opposition to Parker.

The convention was held in the Fifth Regiment Armory. The walls were covered with red, white and blue bunting, while the factory-like windows were draped in yellow and white. On the wall at the speaker's right was a huge portrait of Thomas Jefferson, under which was the quotation, "He never sold the truth to serve the hour."

As Mr. Bryan came out on the platform there was a vast roar of applause; it lasted for many minutes. In speaking for Senator Kern in contrast to Parker, he turned to the portrait of Jefferson and used the quotation beneath it. Yet it was clear that the Bryan style of oratory did not have its old-time compelling appeal. His oration for Kern had this concluding paragraph:

"We have been traveling in the wilderness. We have now come in sight of the Promised Land. During all the weary hours of darkness, Progressive Democracy has been the people's pillar of fire by night. I pray you, delegates, now the dawn has come, do not rid our Party of the right so well earned—to be the people's pillar of cloud by day."

He expected the peroration to sweep the convention before him and put Kern into the chair, but the words were received with indifference. Perhaps a goodly share of the delegates didn't know what he was talking about. The only pillars many of them had heard of were the pillars on the Dime Savings Bank. Bryan realized that he had not made a great impression and Senator Kern did also.

Kern with quick wit immediately arose and turned to Judge Parker, who was on the platform, asking the judge to join with him in withdrawing from the contest in order that the convention might

## BALTIMORE

agree upon some one who could receive its united support.

There was a moment of acute silence while the entire audience waited for Mr. Parker's response. It did not come. Then the senator turned to Mr. Murphy, the permanent chairman of the New York delegation, asking him to urge Judge Parker to withdraw. Mr. Murphy also remained silent.

Following that, the senator from Indiana announced that he would withdraw, but if there was going to be a contest he would make the issue a real one by putting into nomination for the temporary chairmanship the name of William Jennings Bryan.

The vote stood for Parker 579—for Bryan 508. As an initial move the vote on the surface was a failure, and the family of The Great Commoner were downcast, but he went briskly from delegation to delegation, unperturbed, shaking hands, giving the atmosphere that all was well, and finally returning to his hotel. There he found the beginning of the deluge. He had opened the convention with the issue dramatized between the progressives and the opposition, and the country was awake to the battle that was going on. The telegrams had started. There was a constant parade of messenger boys to the Bryan headquarters, sometimes bringing only handfuls of wires and at other times basketfuls. Mr. Bryan received in all 1,182 telegrams and the total number of wires sent to the delegates exceeded 110,000.

Action in the convention responded quickly. Bryan was visited by a second delegation from the Clark forces, this time composed of several men. They urged him eagerly to accept the permanent chairmanship of the convention, pleading that they would prove that in its permanent aspects the gathering was progressive at heart. But The Peerless Leader was not fooled. The task of permanent chairman is largely that of pounding the gavel, an operation which would, in fact, shelve him quite effectively. Mr. Bryan told the committee that those who owned the ship should furnish the crew, and that when his friends controlled a convention they never asked the minority to supply the officers.

Hardly had this situation been met than the announcement came up to the room that Charles R. Crane and Francis J. Heney, Progressive Republicans, were calling to see him. Roosevelt had not yet put his Progressive ticket into the field and The Peerless Leader thought that the visit was meant to draw his support from the Democratic party, or at least to lead his mind in that direction. He saw sharply the to-do that the newspapers could make about a private meeting with these men, no matter what statements both might make afterwards. Directing that they should not be permitted to come up, he hastened down to the hotel lobby, shook hands with each man, expressed pleasure at the courtesy of their call, then hastily and conspicuously withdrew.

By this time the Parker and Clark delegates were

thoroughly aroused to the dangerous position in which they found themselves. The vote between Bryan and Parker had been a Pyrrhic victory. It had done the thing they least wanted, namely, to emphasize that there was a division between conservative and progressive in the Democratic party. It became most important to persuade The Commoner to accept some kind of olive branch. Hence the delegation which had asked him to become permanent chairman of the committee was succeeded the following morning by yet another committee which urged him to be chairman of the Resolutions Committee. With ominous blandness, Mr. Bryan thanked them for the offer, but said that the majority should furnish the chairman, as he might find it necessary to present a minority report. The Peerless Leader was well aware of the import of his presumably innocent words. Great God, a minority report! The committee went away profoundly disturbed.

They accomplished the next best thing by persuading Mr. Kern, whom Bryan had put in nomination, to act as chairman of this committee, and when Bryan agreed to serve on the subcommittee, they all breathed easier.

At the Resolutions Committee meeting he made as an initial suggestion that once a platform had been tentatively agreed upon, it should be held until after the naming of the candidate for President so that he might be consulted about the platform before it was adopted.

One of the delegates asked in surprise whether any candidate would object to a platform which the convention would adopt.

"Our candidate did in 1904," Mr. Bryan reminded them.

During Wednesday and Thursday The Commoner sat with the committee and worked for the incorporation of the principles which he had fought for in previous campaigns. His favorite phrase on the trusts first used in Chicago in 1899 went into the platform again. "A private monopoly is indefensible and intolerable."

Governor Beckham of Kentucky advocated the inclusion of a plank for a single presidential term making the President ineligible for reëlection. Mr. Bryan had first introduced this thought in the days when he was a Congressman, and in his campaigns he had also stated that he would not be a candidate for a second term, believing that this permitted the President to act unselfishly.

The early days of the convention were taken up with various details prior to the actual work of nomination. The Commoner's contest with Parker had been an opening gun, but it had not sufficiently emphasized the ineligibility of Clark nor, on the other hand, called forth from him or his managers any vigorous progressive statement or action.

Thanks to the organizing work of Charles W. Bryan, W. J.'s brother, The Peerless Leader was in continuous touch with the trend of sentiment in the various delegations. It was clear that the ninety

## BALTIMORE

New York votes bound by the unit rule would be swung to Clark after the first few ballots, as soon as it became evident that Harmon did not have a chance.

Clark was due to come into the convention with more votes out of the 1,088 total than any one else. The sudden casting of ninety votes in the direction of the Speaker would under ordinary circumstances start the landslide which would mean prompt nomination. The problem was to so discredit the New York ballots that when they were voted they would be a liability rather than an asset. Bryan believed that, in fact, they were a liability. August Belmont, the New York subway financier, was one of the leaders of the delegation from that state, and The Commoner regarded Charley Murphy, the Tammany leader, as merely the paid tool of the business interests. Both of these men were friendly with Parker and with Thomas Fortune Ryan who held his residence in Virginia and was a member of the Virginia delegation.

Still it was difficult to establish the sinfulness of being a millionaire or friendly with the same, though The Peerless Leader felt that the situation was all wrong and that no candidate could command progressive enthusiasm or respect who had Wall Street affiliations.

There were others who shared this view who would have preferred to see Democracy nominate a candidate tarred with the Wall Street brush. At this time in Oyster Bay, one of the Roosevelt boys was remarking: "Daddy is praying for Clark."

But how could Bryan make the convention realize the situation as he saw it and as it would be seen by the world at large? It was Charlie Bryan who found the answer. Charlie's suggestion was so radical that Bryan hesitated to adopt it. This was on Wednesday evening. He asked his brother to consult with other friendly delegates and get their view by the next day. If he took action he wished to do so on Thursday evening because the balloting would begin some time on Friday. When Thursday came, the opinions which Mr. Charles Bryan had received regarding his suggestion were discouraging. None wished to dare it. Yet it was the one thing that had been suggested which might bring the result.

Late Thursday evening The Commoner went to the convention hall with the decision to act on his brother's recommendation even though his judgment was not supported by those of his oldest and most trusted advisors. The great expanse of the Fifth Regiment Armory was in a bedlam. Dozens of men had been speaking for the record, nominating candidates in fulsome language which demanded periods of applause which were largely mechanical though prolonged. Whistles, horns and rattlers were the order of the day. Delegates were moving from group to group, each trying to convert his neighbors to his own way of thinking. The platform was bare, bare at least of any interest. According to Mr.

THE SACRIFICE HIT.

*From Minneapolis "Journal"*

Bryan's sacrifice hit in the famous anti-Murphy resolution enabled Wilson to come home.

Bryan's later accounts of it, he walked up to the rostrum as any one might and secured the permission of Ollie James, chairman, to address the gathering.

To others the appearance seemed much more sudden. Champ Clark, who was getting reports over in Washington, later said that Mr. Bryan appeared as through a trap door. Cardinal Gibbons subsequently remarked to Mrs. Bryan, "Madam, your husband stepped out like a great lion."

At any rate, the audience suddenly realized that there in the center of the vast, barren stage The Great Commoner was standing with something to say. There was a hush of expectation and of apprehension. He held in his hand the copy of a resolution which he offered to the convention. This is what he read:

RESOLVED, that in this crisis in our party's career and in our country's history, this convention sends greetings to the people of the United States, and assures them that the party of Jefferson and of Jackson is still the champion of popular government and equity before the law.

As proof of our fidelity to the people, we hereby declare ourselves opposed to the nomination of any candidate for president who is the representative of or under obligation to J. Pierpont Morgan, Thomas F. Ryan, August Belmont, or any other member of the privilege-hunting and favor-seeking class.

Be it further resolved that we demand the withdrawal from this convention of any delegate or delegates constituting or representing the above named interests.

## BALTIMORE

The convention was instantly in a tumult. Every Clark man promptly saw the significance of the resolution, but the situation was worse than that. Hadn't Democracy struggled long enough with poverty without going out of its way to insult the hand that carried the feed bag! This was 1896 all over again. Just when a comfortable, well-fed victory might have been enjoyed, this maniac with his radical mouthings was to snatch it all away. Many of the delegates were hysterical with rage. One of them rushed to the platform, shook his fist in Mr. Bryan's face and frothed at the mouth. He stood there trembling with rage, denouncing The Peerless Leader until carried away by friends.

Mr. Bryan, seeing Urey Woodson in a box, one of the Parker men who had sided with the judge in 1904, called out to him: "Urey, when your machine ran over me, it moved so slowly that I was able to inspect the works from the inside and I am now telling the convention what I saw."

The excited conversation, the shouting, and the swearing from all over the hall made a continuous roar punctuated by an occasional shrill tenor which rose above the sound:

"I will give $25,000 to any one who will kill him," screamed one delegate, leveling his arm toward Mr. Bryan.

"Why doesn't somebody hang him?" another yelled in reply.

Then to make matters worse, Bryan stepped over toward the mass of shaking fists and asked for a roll call. He said that he was willing that the second part of the resolution be omitted. The Wall Street delegates could stay, but the convention must register its opposition to them. In the midst of the din, it is not known how many heard this amendment, but the roll call was held. Charley Murphy cynically realized that New York itself must vote for the resolution. He turned to Belmont and said, "Augie, listen and hear yourself vote yourself out of the convention."

The resolution was carried by a vote of about four and one-half to one. Its effect was not only to galvanize the convention into a painful awareness that the progressive issue must be met, but also its national influence was immediate.

The balloting began on Friday evening. The first vote was:

> Clark ................... 440½
> Wilson ................ 324
> (remainder of 1,088 scattering)

Bryan was in the Resolutions Committee room at the time, but the Nebraska vote, according to instructions, was cast for Clark. New York was voting for Harmon, its original choice. There was still no definite indication of alliance between the Clark forces and New York support.

On succeeding ballots up until the tenth, both Clark and Wilson continued to gain.

On the tenth roll call when New York was named, Charley Murphy announced, "Ninety for Clark."

This was the signal for the great demonstration of the Clark forces. The Missouri delegation picked up Genevieve Clark, the speaker's seventeen-year-old daughter and carried her on their shoulders around the convention hall. They marched, leading a snake dance around the auditorium, which was agitated by waving banners, cheers, cowbells and clappers. Mr. Bryan came in from the Resolutions Committee room and took his seat unobserved with the Nebraska delegation. This was the peak of Clark's possibilities. Would the convention nominate him then and there or had the value of the New York votes been punctured as The Commoner had planned? The tenth ballot, with the New York vote included, registered Clark 556, Wilson 350½.

On no succeeding ballot did the Clark votes rise any higher.

Yet the danger was by no means over. Clark was continuing in the lead even though not having a two-thirds vote and Governor Wilson had picked up only 26½ votes in ten ballots.

There was a danger of there being a landslide in the direction of a dark horse, perhaps toward Marshall of Indiana or some other candidate not identified with the disputes at issue, and yet thoroughly unsatisfactory from the standpoint of progressive leadership which Mr. Bryan was determined to obtain.

As he sat with his delegates during the next three ballots, he decided that the time had come to declare his choice.

"Nebraska," was called by the clerk for the fourteenth time.

"Mr. Chairman," said Mr. Bryan, rising from his chair near the Nebraska standard.

"For what purpose does the gentleman from Nebraska rise?" asked the presiding officer.

"To explain my vote," Mr. Bryan replied.

Several delegates shouted, "Regular order!"

"Under the rule nothing is in order but the calling of the roll," said the presiding officer.

"How does the gentleman vote?"

"As long as Mr. Ryan's agent—as long as New York's ninety votes are recorded for Mr. Clark," Mr. Bryan announced, in his penetrating, bell-like voice. "I withhold my vote from him and cast it—"

There was an uproar which drowned out The Peerless Leader's words. W. J. Stone of Missouri urged that Bryan be allowed to go on. There were shouts of opposition, but the presiding officer put Senator Stone's motion, which was carried.

Mr. Bryan pointed out that Nebraska was a progressive state and would want her delegates to follow out the spirit more than the letter of their instructions if a choice had to be made on that basis. He referred to the resolution adopted by the convention.

"The vote of the State of New York in this convention," he said, "as cast under the unit rule, does not represent the intelligence, the virtue, the democracy or the patriotism of the ninety men who are here. It represents the will of one man—Charles

F. Murphy—and he represents the influences that dominated the Republican Convention at Chicago and are trying to dominate this convention. If we nominate a candidate under conditions that enable these influences to say to our candidate 'Remember now thy Creator' we cannot hope to appeal to the confidence of the Progressive Democrats and Republicans of the nation.

". . . speaking for myself, and for any of the delegation who may decide to join me, I shall withhold my vote from Mr. Clark as long as New York's vote is recorded for him. And the position that I take in regard to Mr. Clark, I will take in regard to any other candidate whose name is now or may be before the convention. . . .

"I will now announce my vote."

But there were many who did not intend that he should announce it, not at the end of a peroration.

Governor McCorkle of West Virginia demanded to know whether Mr. Bryan would refuse to support the candidate if a candidate should ultimately be named who had New York's endorsement. The Commoner did not fall into the trap which would have labeled him as a bolter if he had answered in the affirmative. He indicated that he would support whoever might be named by the convention.

"Are you a Democrat?" a delegate shouted from the audience.

"Some gentleman asked me if I was a Democrat," Mr. Bryan replied, "and I would like to have his name, that I may put it by the side of Ryan and Belmont, who were not Democrats when I was a candidate for the presidency."

The opposition continued to stall for time and to try to get Mr. Bryan into the position of losing his temper or in some other way to embarrass his influence.

"Mr. Chairman," complained Delegate Knox of Alabama, "have we not anything to do in this convention except to listen to Mr. Bryan's speeches? He has already made four speeches."

"Now I am prepared to announce my vote," said Mr. Bryan, after more interruptions, "with the understanding that I shall stand ready to withdraw my vote from the one for whom I am going to cast it whenever New York casts her vote for him. I cast my vote for Nebraska's second choice, Governor Wilson."

On the fifteenth ballot, the results stood Clark 552, Wilson 362½.

Wilson continued to gain slowly through the remainder of Friday evening and all day Saturday. Bryan from the moment of changing his vote, did not leave the convention hall while the meetings were in session. He refreshed himself frequently with a bottle of water and some sandwiches, keeping an alert eye on the proceedings. At one time some Clark supporters brought in a banner quoting some friendly remarks which Mr. Bryan had made regarding Mr. Clark in 1910. Bryan started for the

### "WELCOMING THE LITTLE STRANGER!"

*From Boston "Journal"*

*Wilson's nomination was even more of a surprise to the business world than to the public at large.*

platform to explain the circumstances. The chairman refused to recognize him and also ordered the banner taken from the hall.

Neither Woodrow Wilson nor Champ Clark was present at the convention. The Speaker was busy over at Washington where Congress was in session and he did not plan to go near Baltimore unless his delegates advised it. Towards Saturday evening it appeared that the Wilson vote would soon pass that of Clark.

There were telephone conversations back and forth between Washington and Baltimore coming with redoubled urgency as the situation became apparent. Hour after hour dragged on and finally the convention adjourned until Monday morning.

As the force of cleaners were trying to put the vast hall in order after the night's debacle, there was a newcomer who arrived at the hall, deciding to see at this last moment if there was anything that could be done.

His face turned gray with disappointment as he learned that the meeting was over.

The newcomer was the Speaker of the House of Representatives, Champ Clark.

When the meeting opened on Monday morning, William G. McAdoo, on the twenty-seventh ballot, challenged the vote of his delegation (New York) and demanded that those of its members who so desired be allowed to record themselves for Woodrow Wilson. Among those who so voted were Abram Elkus, McAdoo and Samuel Untermyer. The tide was now turning rapidly. On the thirtieth ballot, Wilson polled 460 votes, compared with 455 for Clark.

On Wednesday, July third, Woodrow Wilson of New Jersey was nominated on the forty-sixth ballot.

Mr. Bryan caught a train to take him to a July Fourth Chautauqua engagement and Colonel House continued with his European tour.

## CHAPTER XIV

### DESERVING DEMOCRATS

> Then came there unto him all his brethren, and all his sisters, and all they that had been of his acquaintance before, and did eat bread with him in his house.—JOB 42:11

AT last, after the terrific storm and stress of years of campaigning, The Great Commoner was jubilantly happy. Only a naturally rebounding temperament could have stood up under the constant effort, disappointments, and criticism of his years of political activity without losing serenity.

Through all those years he had preserved an independence and a sweetness of spirit which was commented upon by some at the time and by all when he was safely in another world. Yet, it had been hard on many occasions to maintain the cheerful front of the happy warrior.

At last the periods of defeat had ended in the tremendous Wilson victory. Many of the newspapers tried to create and encourage the idea that The Peerless Leader was jealous of the man he had put in power, that bitterness was arising between them. But there was none of this in the heart of The Great Commoner, and none of it ever developed in his actions. The Democrats had won! That was the thought which suffused him day after day, before the actual taking possession of office occurred.

David F. Houston, and House, noted Bryan's unabashed jubilation in the early days of the victory, and noted it with a certain feeling that it was indelicate. In fact, the honesty of The Great Commoner's sentiments, and his constant habit of being himself, proved trying to many of his associates in the early days of the victorious régime. To Bryan these little coldnesses made little difference, were barely observed in the first few months of 1913. His people were going into the Promised Land, and he had ultimately led them there. That was enough for him. Certainly he had no pangs of jealousy for the man who was to sit in the White House. He had for him rather the great, expansive love of a father, saying to his son, "Well done."

To the eastern Democrats, to Colonel House, and to a number more who had their eyes on the control of the administration, the matter was not so simple.

There was even considerable discussion of whether Mr. Bryan should or should not be included in the Cabinet. It is not likely that any one entertained very serious doubts as to the ultimate decision, but it was a pleasant thought with which to play. The Great Commoner had made it possible for all of them to have office, and it was interesting to traffic with the idea of whether they would give him anything or not. The "they" consisted of the great number of voluntary advisors surrounding the President. Colonel House had come back from Europe and hastened to advise the President-Elect to get in touch with Mr. Bryan and discuss Cabinet appointments with him. He advised the President to offer Bryan the Secretaryship of State, but also to suggest that Mr. Bryan could be of great service if he would be willing to go to Russia. There were other bright thoughts for getting Mr. Bryan out of the country, some suggesting that he might be willing to take the ambassadorship to England. All in all, however, it was felt that perhaps The Peerless Leader's influence might be useful, perhaps even necessary to the success of the administration, and former Governor Wilson invited him to luncheon at the Sterling Hotel in Trenton to discuss the question of appointments.

As The Commoner listened to the stern-faced President-Elect, who sat opposite discussing the program of the administration and the personnel to be gathered around him, Bryan foresaw some of the issues that would inevitably arise.

When Wilson, doubtless with a sense of bestowing a decoration, invited Mr. Bryan to take the office of Secretary of State, The Commoner hesitated, anticipating one difficulty which might obtrude itself, and that right quickly.

Without answering whether he would accept the post or not, Bryan inquired whether it would embarrass Mr. Wilson if, as Secretary of State, he did not serve wine and liqueurs at official dinners. The Commoner had always been a teetotaler, he and his wife and their families before them. He had finally committed himself to prohibition by law as well as by personal choice. He knew that however people might view his stand on prohibition by law, there would be thousands and thousands of friends who trusted in him who would not be able to understand his departing in his own home from principles in which he so firmly believed.

It was hard to jeopardize the first place in the Cabinet so soon after the day had been won, but this was a matter which he knew must be faced, and he put it squarely to his chief. It was not a pleasing or easy question for the Democratic governor, who was also a Presbyterian elder. He told Mr. Bryan to use his own judgment in the matter.

The Peerless Leader did not accept the office that day but did so shortly afterward.

Meanwhile, the question of what Democrats were most deserving of high places was continually under discussion, by Colonel House, David F. Houston, W. G. McAdoo, William F. McCombs, and in all corners where Democrats foregathered.

Later on some of these same gentlemen were to feel very much perturbed at Bryan's activities in trying to find places for the faithful.

"Mr. Bryan is a spoilsman and is in favor of turning the Republicans out and putting in Democrats," Colonel House later noted in his memoirs. Walter Page, Ambassador to England, complained bitterly about an inquiry by the Secretary of State regarding a minor job in the American Embassy which was held by an Englishman. After Mr. Page recorded his protest at any change, he noted that Bryan said nothing further about it. In fact, through the records of most of the men who became Cabinet officers, one finds the complaining comment that The Great Commoner was asking them about jobs, though if they were sufficiently cold in refusing the requests, The Peerless Leader said nothing further about it. Why, they obviously felt, could he not mind his own affairs?

In these early stages, however, none of them had as yet secured their own jobs, and, hence, the matter of seeking appointments had not yet reached the stage of being undignified. The good Colonel from Texas was as busy as a bee advising the appointment of various persons. These were not, as one might have gathered from the quotation above, persons from the Republican party, but they did include three lifelong friends and political coworkers, namely, David F. Houston, Secretary of Agriculture, Thomas W. Gregory, Attorney-General, and Albert S. Burleson, Postmaster-General—all from the Lone Star State.

The other members of the Cabinet included William G. McAdoo, Lindley M. Garrison, and W. C. Redfield, in the Treasury, War, and Commerce Departments. These were all easterners. The only close associate of Mr. Bryan was Josephus Daniels, named as Secretary of the Navy, who had been a supporter of the Bryan wing of the party for many years.  Franklin K. Lane, in the Interior, was an admirer of The Great Commoner though not a close associate.  In all of these instances the House influence was very strong, though Mr. Gregory did not become Attorney-General until after J. C. McReynolds, Wilson's first appointee to that office, had been appointed to the Supreme Bench.

The Great Commoner had served his purpose, and it was desired to consult him on these matters as little as possible.  In fact, it was hoped in some circles that the Cabinet and the government might be composed of college professors and certain well-to-do Democrats, who had had enough acquaintance with the cosmopolitan world and enough astuteness to have acquired something of the metropolitan manner.  The fewer persons around like Mr. Bryan, with his embarrassing geniality and his still more embarrassing harping on the common people, the better.  Walter Page, then editor of the *World's Work,* and logically in line for an important appointment, was particularly stricken when he learned of the two more rural appointments in the Cabinet.  He had frequently expressed adverse opinions of Mr. Bryan in his magazine, and he was especially dashed to learn of the appointment of Mr. Josephus Daniels of Raleigh, North Carolina, coming only a few miles from Mr. Page's own home village.  The Pages of Aberdeen had their own ideas of who should be first in Rome, and they would not include that man from Raleigh who had built up a newspaper from nothing to a point where it was one of the dominant organs of the South.

If Mr. Bryan were left out of all this discussion, he, nevertheless, was himself in the midst of a maelstrom of applications from all parts of the country. Wilson, the dapper Colonel, the frenzied McCombs, the lean-faced McAdoo, the intellectual Page—all of these men were virtually unknown to the rank and file of the party. Bryan was the man whom they had followed for sixteen years. Bryan was the man whom they had followed at Baltimore. Bryan at this juncture was the leader of his party, and they looked to him to "come through."

Even as the young Republicans had pestered Lincoln, so Bryan found hordes of office-seekers on his back. Years before, he had criticized Justices Harlan and McKenna for getting appointments for their relatives, but the years had also taught him that the successful party must have rewards for the faithful. And he wanted them to be rewarded. For many, it had meant real sacrifice and loss of social prestige to have supported him at various times in the past. And, where this was not the case, there were thousands of those who had worked diligently in season and out preparing the way which had led to ultimate success.

And there were jobs to be had.

Aside from the War and Navy Departments, he had noted in *The Commoner* a number of years before that the President had the following appointments:

| | |
|---|---:|
| State Department | 318 |
| Customs | 743 |
| Post Office | 4,015 |
| Pensions Office | 747 |
| TOTAL | 5,823 |

It was all very well for the men who had not borne the storm and stress of the battle, who probably would not know how to do so in future campaigns, to be aloof about granting appointments. Some one had to look after these matters, and Mr. Bryan found himself willy-nilly very much the people's provider.

Several months after being in office, he wrote to the Receiver of Customs in San Domingo, who had been appointed through the influence of Mr. McCombs, "Now that you have arrived and are acquainting yourself with the situation, can you let me know what positions you have at your disposal, with which to reward deserving Democrats? . . . You have had enough experience in politics to know how valuable workers are when the campaign is on; and how difficult it is to find rewards for all the deserving."

This letter was written on August 20, 1913, and unearthed by the New York *Sun* on January 15, 1915. By that time, most of the bigger deservers in the East had had theirs, and a considerable howl went up through the land. Before and after these communications and criticisms, however, The Commoner carried on his work of seeking appointments

THE EMPLOYMENT AGENT.

From New York "World"

After Colonel House had filled the de luxe jobs for the new administration, Mr. Bryan was allowed to receive the applications of the commoners.

for his friends, doing so at times with some embarrassment, and always being just a little surprised at the coldness of many of his colleagues.

All this, however, was at the start a very faint shadow on the bright sunshine of events. The inauguration day came. Mr. and Mrs. Bryan were occupying the President's suite at the New Willard. The Commoner went down to the Capitol for the ceremonies, and as he reached the stand a great roar of applause greeted him. As he passed into the grandstand erected for the ceremonies, people put their arms on his shoulders and fervently shook his hands.

Colonel House was not present at the inaugural address. The President-Elect had telephoned him and invited the House family to join the presidential family and accompany them to the ceremonies. The Colonel sent his wife, but he, himself, went over to the Metropolitan Club and loafed around until the affair was over. "Functions of this sort do not appeal to me," he wrote in his journal, "and I never go." Following the meeting, the new Secretary of State learned some of the inconveniences of being like other men in a Democracy. He gave his carriage number to an attendant, but the conveyance was not forthcoming. The fact that it was the vehicle of the Secretary of State seemed to have little effect on the situation. Finally, some one, apparently in charge, called him over and placed him in an automobile.

Mrs. Bryan held back, as it had not been customary for wives to ride with their husbands in the inaugural procession, but he turned to her and said:

"You have helped me win this and I want you with me."

As the cars rode up Pennsylvania Avenue, cheers were given for the President, and again, when the Bryan automobile passed between the banks of people, the thousands of persons present shouted and clapped, giving The Commoner the greatest ovation of his life. He beamed with happiness and was touched at the tribute. Turning to Mary Baird Bryan, who had gone with him through all the years of work and hope, he said:

"It is worth sixteen years of hard work to have devotion like this, isn't it?"

Then followed a dinner at the White House, which included about two hundred of the new Democracy, including the Texas Colonel, who apparently did not include dinners in the events which bored him. Following this initial occasion in Washington, the Secretary of State again tried to get transportation, but the silver tongue which had moved millions was unable to attract the attention of a Washington cab driver. But, after all, what were a few blocks of unexpected walking on a day like that? The Commoner and Mrs. Bryan walked back to their rooms at the Willard accompanied by Mr. and Mrs. Edward Goltra of St. Louis. Goltra had married the sister of one of Mr. Bryan's early law partners. He had stanchly supported the young Commoner throughout his career, and it was a heartwarming occasion for the silver leader at last to be accompanying his followers in the corridors of official Washington.

The signs continued to be auspicious. After talking it over with Mary, The Commoner decided to engage the John A. Logan house, a beautiful brick structure with white windows, very different from the plain little boarding place they had occupied in Washington more than twenty years before. To this location they moved many of the objects of art which they had collected, or which had been given to them in the Orient, and to this residence also came the paintings of the nation's orators which had adorned the home in Lincoln.

The first Cabinet meeting was another step in the new life which was to him acutely and delightfully memorable. It came at eleven o'clock in the morning of March fifth. Every one was there well ahead of time, all aglow with the thrill of the work before him. Josephus Daniels walked around the room exclaiming, "Isn't it great! Isn't it wonderful!"

Mr. Bryan beamed at all. He beamed at Houston, who had been a Cleveland Democrat and opposed to the silver leader for a score of years. He beamed at all the other late strangers, who had come to the top of the party in the past few years.

The President entered, and after preliminary social conversation, he brought up the matter of office-seekers, and said to the Cabinet:

"Gentlemen, I shall have to give my attention to the graver problems of the nation, and I shall not have time to see the swarms of people who want office. I shall have to ask you to sift the applicants for me and to make your recommendations."

Mr. Bryan smiled, and remarked to the Cabinet that they need not be surprised if he asked them to find places in their departments for his supporters. He pointed out that he was in a different position from any of those present.

"Six million people have voted for me for President three times, and many of them," he added with a twinkle in his eye, "would like to serve the nation."

At home he had a rather definite idea of the large number that were doing the seeking. Mrs. Bryan, as usual, was standing by and interviewing the rank and file of the petitioners for office. She made a card catalogue of their names with their lists of qualifications, and in time the work became so well organized that the names which were presented represented the top selection of those who had done the work. Yet, in spite of all the furore which was made about the matter, there were a number of the Secretary's closest, lifelong workers for whom he could not secure substantial appointments.

While he was obliged to consider office-seekers, the phrase of "deserving Democrats," in connection with The Great Commoner, was more important as an apt alliteration than as a dominant interest in his official life in Washington. He realized that some one had to keep the home fires burning, and it fell upon him to handle the job. He felt it both necessary and proper to take up these matters with his close associates and presumable intimates in the government, and assumed that he might go into the subject frequently and as a matter of routine business without its being laid up against him in future memoirs.

His main energies and interests were stored up and used for more important events. His responsibilities came quickly. He had to make decisions affecting Americans in all parts of the world. Singularly, one of his first official acts was to cable to our embassy in Rome in regard to funeral ceremonies to be held over the body of J. Pierpont Morgan. Morgan, whom Bryan had so steadfastly reviled! Morgan, who, at least in Bryan's belief, had used the full force of his financial power to defeat the cause of silverism! Morgan, the emblem of Wall Street, was lying in Rome while The Great Commoner arranged the services.

Soon came the issue which Mr. Bryan had foreseen, the first official luncheon of the State Department, a farewell function to Ambassador and Mrs. Bryce, who were leaving for England. The affair was held in a private room at the Hotel Willard. It was a small luncheon, covers being laid for only eighteen. There was the white-haired Ambassador Bryce, Ambassador Jusserand of France, with his double-pointed brown beard, chiefs of all the embassies.

When the guests were all seated, Mr. Bryan rose,

"LIPS THAT TOUCH LIQUOR SHALL NEVER TOUCH MINE!"

From New York "World"

Roosevelt's milk habit and Bryan's grape juice were a sore trial to the Wet forces in each party.

and with full consciousness of how this would ultimately be reported to the outside world, he craved the indulgence of his guests for a few moments.

He told them of his conversation with President Wilson before taking office. He explained the view of millions of Americans regarding the use of alcohol, and pointed out that he could not himself depart from that view if he were to be true to his principles and his traditions. He expressed the hope that he might make his hospitality none the less true and real without serving wines, and asked his guests to understand this omission.

Applause followed the address, and the meal proceeded with White Rock and grape juice as the chief beverage.

The Russian Ambassador turned to his dinner partner and said that he had not tasted water for years, but that Mr. Bryan had forewarned him and he had taken his claret before he came.

This event raised the storm which was expected, and once again The Great Commoner was standing in the midst of the hurricane of criticism which he had faced in his free silver, his anti-imperialism, his government ownership, and the other campaigns. He knew what was coming, but he could not do otherwise.

The eternal crusading urge in his temperament always drove him on, at war with his love for comfort, friendliness and admiration.

It required courage of a singular, indomitable

pioneer sort on the part of Mrs. Bryan also. A few days after this luncheon, she noted in her diary:

"I hope the example may do good. It is hard to stand against prevailing customs."

## CHAPTER XV

### THE FARMER-STATESMAN

Wide was his parish, and houses fer asonder.
—CHAUCER

THE appointment of Bryan as Secretary of State had been distasteful not only to the better tailored members of the Cabinet, but to a large section of the eastern part of the country. His ideas did not suit the views of the seaboard, or, at any rate, the more influential elements on the Atlantic coast. He was essentially a farmer-statesman, and opposition to him came not only from those who felt he would be incompetent in office, but also from those who feared he would be much too competent in specific directions.

The difficulty in dealing with him lay in the fact that he was not ashamed of being a commoner. He did not blush to be called a farmer or the representative of farmers, and his strength lay in the fact that this was not a pose but a conviction. He was not dazzled by office nor by the favors of the so-called great. All that was far back in his history. He was not inexperienced in the ways of the world and their governments. He had twice been received by the officialdom of Europe, he had been to Mexico a number of times, and he had traveled the Orient. In his office as Secretary of State and in the Cabinet he was thoroughly aware of the various courses he was adopting, and pursued them with diligence and understanding. It had been customary in Congress to lull the Bryan areas of the country with soft words and fine promises, but The Peerless Leader was at last in office and he proposed to see that the principles for which he had stood for a generation should not be ignored.

The Wilson administration opened with many problems in the forefront; some were legacies from the Taft administration, and others were issues which Democracy had been urging for a number of years and were just coming to fruition. Roosevelt had utilized much of Bryan's thunder, translating it into eastern terms, and beating The Commoner at his own game. Then Taft had come in and action lagged. The Wilson administration, accordingly, rode in to find a difficult yet opportune situation.

The form of the currency had again come to the forefront. The increased volume of gold had made bimetallism unnecessary, and events had also shown that an increase in the currency was a far too simple remedy for the ills brought about by unrestrained control of the money power in the hands of a few. The country had had a bad panic in 1907. There was a tradition that a panic occurred every seven years, with the public holding the bag. Another such disaster was due in 1914, and Wilson was expected to do something to head it off. The limelight had been further played on the situation by the Pujo Investigating Committee of the House of Representatives in the 1912-1913 Congress. Samuel Untermyer, for years a friend of The Great Commoner, had been the counselor and investigator for this committee. He had dramatized to the public the uses and misuses of money power by pointing to many specific instances.

The Republicans had recognized the inadequacy of the financial system of the country, and Senator Aldrich had worked for years on a Federal Reserve plan. This differed from the one ultimately adopted in various vital points, but whatever there might be in its essentials the public was not in the temper to accept it, because it came from the pen of Aldrich who was judged to have a prejudicial view and to be one of the insiders in Wall Street.

Senator Robert L. Owen of Oklahoma also had been working on the problem for many years. The Wilson administration was preparing a Federal Reserve Act from the Democratic viewpoint. Carter Glass was preparing a bill in the House, in his capacity as Chairman of the Banking and Currency Committee.

McAdoo was concerned in the project as Secretary of the Treasury. Bryan was involved only in so far as the measure was a national policy and concerned the welfare of the people at large. From the early days of the campaign Colonel House had busied himself with this subject as with other major issues. As in the case of his desire later on to take over the

*From Minneapolis "Journal"*

While both parties wanted a Federal Reserve System, Aldrich on the Republican side feared that anything supported by Bryan would be crack-brained, while Bryan feared that any program supported by Aldrich would sell out the country to Wall Street.

essentials of Mr. Bryan's department, so he had the desire to handle the Federal Reserve matter for the President. Twenty days after inauguration the Colonel took a drive with Carter Glass, and urged him not to allow the Senate committee to modify any of the essential features of the Glass measure. The Colonel promised to bring up the President and the Secretary of the Treasury as reserve artillery if the Senate, meaning Mr. Owen, did not yield.

He had not counted upon the counterbatteries of Untermyer and Bryan.

Earlier in the year he had discussed the problem with Governor Wilson. Mr. Wilson expressed the view that Bryan would not approve a bill of the Glass-House nature. The Colonel suggested that it was better to contend with Bryan's disapproval and fail to get any bill at all rather than to get one which was not sound.

House had kept at this matter diligently. He talked over what should be done about the Federal Reserve System with Henry Clay Frick, Otto Kahn, Frank Vanderlip of the National City Bank, J. P. Morgan (the younger), and other leading financiers. It was logical that the experience of these men be consulted and House was strongly influenced by their views. When Mr. Morgan came to him with a currency plan fully formulated and printed, however, he felt that it would be more adroit to have the script typewritten to permit of correction.

All this was taking place during the winter and after the drive with Carter Glass. The Colonel wrote in his diary: "I spoke to the President about this after dinner and advised that McAdoo and I whip the Glass measure into final shape, which he [the President] could endorse and take to Owen as his own. My opinion was that Owen would be more likely to accept it as a presidential measure than as a measure coming from the House Committee on Banking and Currency." Both House and Glass realized that the measure which they had in hand contained two factors which were against the long declared policy of Democracy and needed all the prestige of the presidential office to put it across. The objectionable points were that the Glass bill permitted banker representation on the Federal Reserve Board, a situation which might tend to put the power of the government back of the issues of private bankers, rather than resulting in the control of the banking power by the government, which was one of the presumable aims of the Act.

Further, the Glass measure provided for the issuance of Federal Reserve notes by the private banks rather than by the government.

Senator Owen was firmly opposed to having the bankers on the Federal Reserve Board. He held that one would not expect to place men holding railroad offices on the Interstate Commerce Commission or representatives of protected industries on the Tariff Commission. In the beginning, Glass and House had the ear of the President and apparently convinced him of the wisdom of their approach to the matter. Mr. Glass did not welcome the volunteered intrusion of the Colonel into the situation, but it apparently helped his cause none the less for a season.

Meanwhile, Mr. Bryan was swamped with the affairs of the State Department and with the landslide of political office-seekers. While he was not active in forming the provisions of any bill on the subject in its early stages, he was being kept advised on the matter by other elements in the party, who believed that Democracy could not afford to repudiate its stand of many years on certain features of the bill. Senator Owen had visited Samuel Untermyer in New York, and at his home had also talked with Vanderlip, A. Barton Hepburn, Paul Warburg, and other financiers whose views he wanted, and to whom he wished to make clear that the government was not hostile but aimed to be impartial. Toward the latter part of May, Bryan became restive on the situation, feeling that the matter might reach a crisis in public before he could get a chance to present his views to the President. He tried to see Wilson on the matter but the President wished if possible to avoid discussion on the subject, fearing that he would not agree with The Great Commoner and that there would be a break in the party.

Wilson wrote to Carter Glass on May 15:

"Mr. Bryan has twice indicated his desire to discuss currency matters with me; but, if I may venture to say so, I think his talk should be first with you.

## THE FARMER-STATESMAN

Bryan did not argue the point. He knew of the visits of bankers to Washington, and, inevitably, that their point of view had been consulted along with others. He believed, however, that Wilson was not influenced in any sinister way, though he feared that unconsciously the banking view had prevailed upon the President.

Instead of indulging in debate on this point, however, The Great Commoner turned to the shelves of his library and read aloud to Tumulty from the party platforms:

"From the 1896 platform:

"We therefore denounce the issuance of notes intended to circulate as money by national banks as in derogation of the Constitution, and we demand that all paper which is made a legal tender for public and private debts, or which is receivable for dues to the United States, shall be issued by the Government of the United States, and shall be redeemable in coin.

"From the 1900 platform:

"We are opposed to this private corporation paper circulated as money but without legal tender qualities and demand the retirement of the national-bank notes as far as Government paper or silver certificates can be substituted for them.

"From the 1908 platform:

"We believe that in so far as the needs of commerce require an emergency currency, such currency should be issued and controlled by the Federal Government."

Tumulty, as an experienced party man, realized that Bryan held an unassailable position. As Bryan himself got into the matter and reviewed these pledges more specifically, he hesitated as to whether it would be best to retire silently or whether he ought not to bring all his power to bear to see that these pledges were carried out, no matter who might be affected.

Tumulty, aware of the seriousness of the situation, urged Bryan to say nothing further until the President had an opportunity to talk the situation over with Mr. McAdoo and Mr. Glass.

Meanwhile, Owen was rallying his supporters and had informed Untermyer of the turn of events. Accordingly, there arrived at Mr. Bryan's home on the following day this attorney and friend, who begged the Secretary of State to go with him at once and call on the President.

The Great Commoner was only too willing because the Untermyer support was an important leverage for the cause. Mr. Untermyer was one of the few New York Democrats to break away to the Wilson cause on the roll call at the convention, and the President was not unmindful of this incident. The President listened carefully to his visitors' presentation and became convinced of the rightness of the position regarding banker representation. He was willing also to accept an arrangement for making the Federal Reserve notes government notes without abandoning the protection that would be behind them as private bank notes.

## THE FARMER-STATESMAN

The President called in Mr. Glass, Mr. McAdoo, and others concerned with the bill, and explained to them the necessity of making the changes.

At the next Cabinet meeting The Great Commoner turned to the President and said: "Mr. President, we have settled our difficulties and you may rely upon me to remain with you to the end of the fight."

Meanwhile, there were gentlemen in Congress who realized that here was an opportunity to put Bryan forward and to minimize the power of the administration: an attempt was made to reintroduce the issue of silver, and Mr. Bryan's name was invoked in this cause.

The Great Commoner was true to his pledge, however, and on August 22, 1913, he wrote his assurances to Carter Glass as follows:

My Dear Mr. Glass:

The papers have reported members of Congress as presenting views which were alleged to be mine. I do not know to what extent these reports may exaggerate what has been said and done; but you are authorized to speak for me and say that I appreciate so profoundly the service rendered by the President to the people in the stand he has taken on fundamental principles involved in currency reform that I am with him in all the details. If my opinion has influence with any one called upon to act on this measure, I am willing to assume full responsibility for what I do when I advise him to stand by the President and assist in the passage of the bill at the earliest possible moment.

Very truly yours,<br>W. J. Bryan.

While Bryan was ready enough to come to the firing line on any issue which affected the principles of the party, his chief interest was in the cause of peace. He had not forgotten his visit to Tolstoy, or Tolstoy's letter to him. He believed that most wars were drummed up by special interests against what would be the wishes of the people if enough time were given to bring out the true facts. His part of the country lay far beyond the Alleghenies. To his people war seemed a bad dream of the past, and in A.D. 1913 it seemed impossible for the future. Norman Angell had demonstrated in his book that war could not happen again because it would be too costly. Bryan had traveled enough abroad to realize that this cheerful millennium would not come about without a new arrangement between the nations for dealing with hostile acts at the time they arose.

He had been in office but a few weeks when he set about the greatest work of his official life, a work which has not yet been tested in practice, nor has yet been repudiated, but which marks a milestone in international peace and law.

On the twenty-fourth of April, 1913, William Jennings Bryan, Secretary of State, called a meeting in the reception room of the State Department. Among those who attended were Jusserand of France, with his double-pointed, brown beard, the kindly, white-haired Bryce of England, the suave Bernstorff of Germany, and the almond-eyed Chinda of Japan; in fact, the ambassadors and ministers of the entire world.

From Des Moines "Register and Leader"

The specialists in peace-making were somewhat bellicose in advocating their own plans.

An atmosphere of great formality and expectancy prevailed as the American Secretary began to state the purpose of the meeting. Was this to be some new plan of world aggrandizement? Were they to concur in some program for Mexico? What was up?

Mr. Bryan presented each delegate with a written outline of the agenda, which was a proposal for a series of international treaties on a new basis. He proposed that the essence of these treaties be that a year's time be permitted for nations to discuss all matters in dispute before resorting to arms.

Recognizing that this was a radical and back-country idea which could hardly appeal at first glance to the sophisticated chancellories of the world, he opened the discussion with a story.

"A man was complaining to a friend," he said, "that he found it impossible to drink moderately because of the numerous invitations which he received from others. The friend to whom the complaint was made suggested that the difficulty might be remedied by calling for a sarsaparilla whenever he found that he had all the whisky he wanted. But the complainant demurred, 'That is the trouble; when I get all the whisky I want I cannot say sarsaparilla.'"

Mr. Bryan pointed out that at the time when investigation is most needed between angry nations, it is difficult for either party to seek for it lest the request be construed as weakness or cowardice. Accordingly, he called both for the investigation of all disputes, and, secondly, for permanent international commissions between nations, to whom all such disputes would be referred.

He provided that such a commission should be made up of one citizen from each nation to be chosen by that nation; for another citizen to be chosen by each nation from a foreign nation; and a fifth person to be selected by agreement of the two contracting countries. He provided finally for the reservation by each nation of the right to decide for itself at the conclusion of the investigation what action it would take.

The policy of international effort towards the preservation of peace was not new. In 1899 the adoption of a general arbitration agreement had been proposed at the first Hague conference. All the great powers were in favor of such a measure at that time except the Imperial German delegates, who prevented it from going through.

Again in 1907 the issue had been brought before The Hague, urgently advocated this time by the Czar of Russia. Again, the influence of Germany was used to block the proposal.

Mr. Bryan tactfully avoided references to what had taken place in the past, but pointed out that the difficulty with treaties of arbitration was that they left exceptions in respect to questions of honor, independence, vital interest, and the interest of third parties. These exceptions cannot be eliminated, he held, but often an automatic provision for discussion of them would serve to clear up a situation.

"The nations have had machinery for war," Mr. Bryan pointed out; "they could go to war in a week, but, strange to say, they have no machinery for the adjustment of disputes which defy diplomatic settlement. They are compelled to rely upon good offices or mediation, with nothing to prevent acts of hostility before either can be offered. The Peace Treaty plan furnishes the machinery, and it can be invoked as soon as diplomacy fails. The time may come when all questions without exception will be submitted to arbitration; until that time, the treaty providing for investigation in *all* cases is the best assurance we have against war."

Such was the nature of the proposal which the farmer-statesman made to the delegates of the powers of the world.

The reception on the part of the delegates was one of amazement and pleasure. Most of the ambassadors said that, of course, they would have to take the matter up with their home governments, but a number said that they felt free to express the views that their governments would welcome the suggestion.

Bernstorff was silent. Later, when some of the other powers had agreed to such a treaty, he stated that Germany would accept it in principle but would not sign it.

By many critics of Bryan in the Wilson administration the idea was pooh-poohed. Page thanked his lucky stars that this country had no such agreement with Germany at the time the United States entered the war.  Professor Seymour, the compiler of the House memoirs, also pointed out later, "Had Germany signed this treaty, it would not have been possible for the United States to enter the war on the submarine issue until after the lapse of a twelve-month, except on the ground that German use of submarines constituted acts of war against the United States."  As a matter of fact the delay was longer than provided for in the Bryan plan, for the *Lusitania* disaster occurred on May 7, 1915, and the United States' declaration of war on April 6, 1917, a difference of two years, without the assistance of a possible commission to determine the point at issue.

If certain unofficial parties considered that the Bryan program was worthless, his statesmanship had at least the endorsement of those in power.  The Commoner had submitted to the President a written outline of his plan and the matter had been discussed with the Cabinet, prior to the calling of the meeting at the State Department.  Bryan had also proved wiser than his chief in such matters, in lining up the Senate Committee on Foreign Relations for his plan before broaching it either to the diplomats or to the public.  His old friend and free silverite, Senator William J. Stone of Missouri, was chairman of this committee.

With the officialdom of the government solidly behind the plan, it was reported back to the capitals of the world with the full weight of the favor of this endorsement.

The acceptance of the program was almost worldwide. Salvador was the first to sign on the seventh of August, 1913. Several other Central American countries followed suit shortly after.

On July 24, 1914, Brazil, Argentina, and Chile signed simultaneously.

On September fifteenth of the same year, Mr. Bryan effected treaties on the same basis between the United States and France, Great Britain, Spain and China, bringing into arbitration agreement in one day 900,000,000 people.

By the end of that year, the United States had established Bryan treaties with thirty nations, with only these important powers not participating: Belgium, Austria-Hungary, Germany and Japan.

No disputes or threats of war with the contracting parties have occurred to put these treaties to the test, but they have been written into the history of the international law of the world.

To The Great Commoner they were and remained the realest achievement of his life, and when he read time and again in the press that he was no statesman and understood nothing about such matters, he smiled and warmed himself with the thought that all of the treaties were ratified, without serious dispute, by the United States Senate.

## CHAPTER XVI

### WAR

*Every subject's duty is the king's;
but every subject's soul is his own.*
　　　　　　　　*King Henry V*

WHILE Bryan was laying his far-spreading plans for world peace, trying to set a new mark in history as a Christian statesman in the most literal following out of that phrase, while he was emulating the doctrines of his hero Tolstoy, his office was beset with more threats of war than had confronted any Secretary of State in America's history.

At the very opening of the administration China was in a turmoil, Mexico was unsettled, and Japan was offended at the adoption of California's alien land laws.

Bryan found that while it might be easy for Tolstoy on his remote Russian farm to practice the doctrines of nonresistance, it was not a simple matter to observe these principles as Secretary of State of the American Republic. In his initial dealings with these crises and for the first year of his administration his handling of issues seemed both practical and successful.

The first trouble bobbed up in March, shortly

after the inauguration. China was in a state of distress and the government was seeking a loan. J. P. Morgan & Company had been interested in the six-power loan to China, but were unwilling to continue their interest unless the American government was willing to lend support to enforce the stipulations of the contract. Henry P. Davison, of the Morgan Company, and Willard Straight called upon The Commoner at the Department of State and presented their case. The Secretary was not favorable. He was determined that his administration should be one of peace and that the last thing he would consent to would be the possibility of a war in which the United States would set out to collect a banker's loan. At the meeting of the Cabinet following this session, he strongly recommended to the President that the United States refuse to participate in this action.

The Cabinet endorsed the Secretary's stand on the matter, and Bryan had cleared the first hurdle which offered the possibilities of controversy.

Less than a month later, however, a new trouble arose. California had passed an alien land law which prohibited Japanese immigrants from holding title to real estate in that state. The pride of Japan was deeply offended and the government of that country issued a note which had in it the threats of war. The sentiment of the country was considerably divided on the issue, some feeling that California was well within her rights, others supporting the view that the state had precipitated an issue which involved the foreign policy of the nation and was out of its province. The difference of opinion was not along party lines but rather on a geographic basis. Traditional Democratic policy in the support of states' rights would have favored a program of noninterference with what California had done, but the President and the country at large were anxious to avert war, especially as there was some thought that Japan was desirous of provoking a conflict before the Panama Canal should be opened.

While the President neglected the Cabinet in the latter years of his administration, he consulted them faithfully during the early days. At the Cabinet meeting on April twenty-second, he introduced the matter of the California situation, and asked what should be done. Mr. Bryan believed that the heart of California was in the right place, and that if a referendum of the people in that state should be held they would vote either to modify the law or leave it to the hands of the national government. Other members of the Cabinet were not so optimistic and held that if the referendum should go the wrong way the situation would be doubly bad.

Some one suggested that California instead of naming the Japanese or Mongolians specifically, could prohibit landholding by "those ineligible to citizenship."

The Secretary of State did not think that would help much. "I would oppose the insertion of that phrase," he said, "unless the President has a different opinion. In that case, I might have another opinion. I am here solely to help and to carry my part of the burden."

After the discussion wandered considerably without reaching any conclusion, the President turned to Bryan and asked him if he would not go out to California himself and try to adjust matters. The Great Commoner stirred uneasily and said that he was not anxious to do so but would if it were thought best. His colleagues, only too glad to shift the burden of a delicate situation, thought that was just the thing to do. Had he not visited Japan? Was he not well acquainted in California? Was it not particularly the function of the State Department to adjust a matter of that sort?

Hence The Peerless Leader left the pleasant surroundings of Washington for one of the stiffest tasks of his career. He had in the background of his mind the thought that the Democrats in their platform had demanded the enactment of an exclusion law. He himself in *The Commoner* had been pointing out for a number of years the impossibility of mingling Mongolian and Anglo-Saxon blood and, particularly, the hazard to the standard of American labor from the cheap competition of the Asiatic races.

He made arrangements, however, with the governor of California to give him a hearing before the legislature on the theory that no harm could be done by having a frank discussion between the personnel of the state government and a representative from the national authority. As soon as he

WAR

*All ready in the event of possible hostilities*

From Philadelphia "Inquirer"

One of Bryan's earliest diplomatic tasks was to adjust the differences between California and Japan.

arrived at Berkeley, he consulted with local leaders and then went to the legislature where he delivered a message to them, describing the problems of the situation. He obtained the consent of this body to work out any plan which would save the face of the Japanese and at the same time essentially protect the rights of the state against the inroads of foreign labor. Word that an agreement in principle had been reached was made public and the world heaved a sigh of relief. The press of the country for once endorsed the capabilities of The Great Commoner even while differing on the extent and permanence of what had been accomplished. The New York *World* commented, "If Secretary Bryan's errand in California was to prevent alien-land legislation, it was a failure; if it was to persuade the Californians to enact a treaty in harmony with our treaty with Japan, it was a great success."

Japan, however, was not in a mood to be satisfied. When Bryan returned to Washington he found that the official forces of the government were almost as worried as when he had started. President Wilson, in the Cabinet meeting on May fifteenth, said that he had not seriously considered that war might result until he had a short time before noticed the extremely nervous and excited attitude of the Japanese Ambassador. Secretary of War Garrison spoke up and stated that he had been surveying the matter of defending the Philippines and suggested that some ships then in Chinese waters might be sent to Manila and that these could prevent the Japanese from crossing to the United States possessions.

Some of the Cabinet members murmured at this suggestion and Garrison indicated that the views of his colleagues on military matters were not particularly competent.

The Great Commoner turned on Garrison at this speech and shouted that army and navy officers could not be trusted to say what should or should not be done except in actual time of war. He pointed out that the Cabinet was discussing not how to wage war, but how to keep out of it, and that if ships were moved about it would be an incitement and a threat.

Some of the Cabinet went further and thought that the ships in the East might be brought back home. The President was opposed to this, but suggested that they stay where they were without maneuvers. He held that the biggest problem at the present moment was Ambassador Chinda and he asked the Secretary of State to get in touch with the Ambassador as soon as possible. Again this was felt to be a happy move and the Cabinet turned to less vexing problems.

The following day before the Secretary had an opportunity to carry out this mission the telephone rang. The message was from Ambassador Chinda expressing a desire to call in person upon the Secretary. Shortly after this Chinda arrived. The occasion was tense. The little brown man, with a face shaped like an acorn, was suave and diplomatic in his language, but his hands and voice shook as he presented the compliments of his government.

The Great Commoner preserved as best he could an air of calm and turned the discussion to the pleasant days he had spent in Japan, to his admiration for the Japanese people, and to the humorous occasion when he had unwittingly participated in the parade of Admiral Togo.

Chinda, a little less nervous, but still realizing

that he must press forward with his errand, stated the indignity which Japan felt had been imposed upon her by the terms of the California law naming her citizens as undesirable.

The Great Commoner pointed out that this was not the essential aspect of the situation, that California had peculiar economic problems, that living conditions in the two countries were different, and that any action, of course, would have to be in line with the existing treaty between the United States and Japan.

The Ambassador was not satisfied. His government felt that the name of Japan had been aspersed and all that Mr. Bryan said did not create any relief for the dignity of his country.

The Great Commoner expressed the view that this was not a matter concerning dignity of country, but of landholding rights on the parts of individuals. If any injustice were to result it would be a matter which could be undertaken in the courts. Presumably existing holdings would be protected and any commitments already made would be followed out.

The discussion went back and forth for some time on this basis without The Great Commoner budging essentially from his position or the Japanese Ambassador letting go of his contentions.

Chinda pressed the issue as to whether or not the California law essentially would stand, and Bryan indicated that it would. Chinda arose and said, "I suppose, Mr. Secretary, this decision is final."

Bryan, with a flash of inspiration, smiled, extended

# WAR

**WHAT MEXICO NEEDS.**

*From Chicago "Daily News"*

*Wilson was encouraged in his "watchful waiting" policy in Mexico by the views of his Secretary of State, who believed that friendly treatment would get further than firearms.*

his hand, and said, "There is nothing final between friends."

Chinda resumed his seat and before the session closed, it was agreed that some statement could be

[ 313 ]

worked out which would satisfy the dignity of the Japanese government without interfering with our economic arrangements.

It seemed as though there could never be a meeting in that Cabinet Room in the White House undisturbed by rumors of war. The Great Commoner attended these sessions with feelings of joy which were nevertheless overcast with dread. Democracy had entered into the promised land but in the situation there seemed to be a portent of disaster for the aims which he cherished. The long wooden table of the Cabinet Room, surrounded by the comfortable chairs, the view out of the French windows over the White House gardens, the whole note of simplicity should have promised peace, quiet and prosperity. But on May 23, 1913, just after the Japanese affair had been settled, Mexico came into the foreground. Huerta had obtained the president's chair of the southern republic by murder. As head of the Mexican army he had taken the former president and vice president personally and put them to death. This was in February, 1913. President Taft had left the problem of recognition to the new administration. Many business interests of the West were anxious to see Huerta accepted by the United States Government. Delegations called at the State Department. Mr. Bryan held that if Diaz (the former president) after thirty years of dictatorship had not been able to control the country by terrorism, what reason was there to believe that Huerta in a far weaker position would be able to do so? He further held that he had never been accustomed to consider public questions as separated from morality and from the principle of popular government and he did not propose to change that position.

Huerta had continued, however, for three months without an American endorsement and it began to look as though he might be able to obtain financial loans which would keep him in office. This was the issue in the May twenty-third meeting of the Cabinet. Several members thought that Huerta might as well be recognized, that one Mexican was about the same as another. The President and the Secretary of State held that constitutional methods must be respected and that if this country recognized the existing régime such recognition would be giving encouragement to a loan which might fasten Huerta upon the Mexican people for a long while. In that event the United States would have a moral responsibility. Bryan was asked to consult the British and French Ambassadors on this point and then warn them that they could not enforce a loan guaranteed by pledge of customs duties.

Through June the trouble was still brewing and the Japanese matter was still more or less in the air. The Japanese government had sent word that it was not satisfied with the proposed adjustments and tried to keep the matter open.

John Lind, former Governor of Minnesota, on the recommendation of Mr. Bryan, was sent to Mexico as an emissary to discuss with the authorities a possible working out of that situation. Bryan was of the opinion that most of the candidates for presidential office in Mexico were simply soldiers of fortune, in some cases little better than bandits. He preferred Carranza, a Constitutionalist who favored orderly government with the protection of the rights of the mass of the Mexican people. Such, at any rate, was Carranza's reputation with The Great Commoner and a large part of the American press.

By August it was clear that Lind's good offices were not getting anywhere and the President appeared before a joint session of Congress on the twenty-seventh of the month, urging Americans to leave Mexico even though he would do all that he could to safeguard their interests and lives in that country if they remained. He stated that he would act under the law of March 14, 1912, forbidding the exportation of arms or munitions to either party in Mexico. He stated the position of the government by saying, "The steady pressure of moral forces will before many days break the barriers of pride and prejudice down, and we shall triumph as Mexico's friends sooner than we could triumph as her enemies." This was doctrine that went straight to the heart of The Great Commoner.

Since no improvement of the situation was noted as the weeks wore on he sent a memorandum to the President in October, desiring to keep this principle uppermost in the President's mind.

The first announcement of the Monroe Doctrine [Bryan wrote] was intended to protect the republics of America from the political power of European nations—to protect them in

*From Louisville "Times"*

The Commoner amazed the country in July, 1913, by proposing a treaty with Nicaragua, which would create virtually a protectorate.

their right to work out their own destiny along the lines of self-government. The next application of that doctrine was made by Cleveland when this government insisted that European governments should submit their controversies with American republics to arbitration even in the matter of boundary lines.

A new necessity for the application of the principle has arisen, and the application is entirely in keeping with the spirit of the doctrine and carries out the real purpose of that doctrine. The right of American republics to work out their own destiny along lines consistent with popular government is just as much menaced to-day by foreign financial interests as it was a century ago by the political aspirations of foreign governments.

If the people of an American republic are left free to attend to their own affairs, no despot can long keep them in subjection; but when a local despot is held in authority by powerful financial interests, and is furnished money for the employment of soldiers, the people are as helpless as if a foreign army had landed on their shores. This, we have reason to believe, is the situation in Mexico, and I can not see that our obligation is any less now than it was then. We must protect the people of these republics in their right to attend to their own business, free from external coercion, no matter what form that external coercion may take.

Meanwhile yet another problem had been handled in the State Department in a manner which suggested that imperialism may appear less harmful when one is in the government than when in the opposition. This issue was the case of Nicaragua and proposals were made under Secretary Bryan which proved to be the *modus operandi* for many years to come.

During the Taft régime American troops had landed in Nicaragua, and the adjustment of that issue was left to the Wilson Administration. On July twentieth the terms of the proposed Bryan agreement were made public. In Bryan's opinion these terms were not inconsistent with his former anti-imperialism. He had always espoused the protectorate in Cuba as contrasted with McKinley's declaration of sovereignty in the Philippines. Nevertheless the imperialists hailed with applause the Bryan proposals which recommended:

That in return for $3,000,000 in gold Nicaragua would yield a canal right of way to the United States and certain islands for a naval base.

That Nicaragua should not declare war without the consent of the United States.

That no treaties should be made with foreign governments which would give them a foothold in the western hemisphere.

That the United States should have a right to intervene with armed force to preserve Nicaraguan independence, or to preserve life and property.

The Republican press heartily endorsed this stand as well as the papers which steadily supported the administration. Within a short time after this the treaty was negotiated though not ratified in modified form until many months later.

From late in 1913 until the following spring the administration had some rest in its foreign policy. The eastern press continued to be critical of the Bryan-Wilson policy in Mexico, yet until April it appeared that the United States might avoid being actively involved.

But early one morning—at two-thirty o'clock—The Great Commoner was aroused from his slumbers in his home in Calumet Place by a cable message which informed him that the German steamship *Ypirango,* carrying munitions, had arrived at Vera Cruz, Mexico, that morning.

Bryan at once put in a call for the White House where he was connected with Joseph Tumulty, secretary to the President. He outlined the situation to Mr. Tumulty and stated that he believed drastic measures should be taken at once to prevent the delivery of these munitions.

Forgotten for the moment were all the Tolstoy admonitions about nonresistance, or the pacifists' doctrines which his mind had accumulated. Aroused from his sleep, and appealed to by the urgency of the situation, he was once again the old campaigner eager to meet the situation quickly and drastically.

In a few moments Secretary Daniels was heard on the same wire, having received the identical information. Shortly after that the President, who had been roused, came in on the conversation.

"Mr. President," Bryan informed his chief, "I am sorry to inform you that I have just received word that a German ship will arrive at Vera Cruz this morning at ten o'clock, containing large supplies of munitions and arms for the Mexicans and I want your judgment as to how we shall handle the situation."

"Of course, Mr. Bryan, you understand what drastic action in this matter may ultimately mean in our relations with Mexico?" the President answered.

"I thoroughly appreciate this, Mr. President," Bryan said in a ringing voice which assured Wilson that there would be no weakening from that quarter, "and I fully considered it before telephoning you."

There was a pause for a moment and then the President asked for the view of Secretary Daniels, who agreed with the position of The Great Commoner.

"Daniels," said the President upon hearing this, "send this message to Admiral Fletcher: 'Take Vera Cruz at once.'"

Fortunately, the Vera Cruz incident turned out to be a temporary one. Unwilling to embarrass our relationships with other countries the pretext of taking the city, which was publicly emphasized, was that of an insult which had been offered to the American flag. Having prevented the landing of the munitions, the American forces were withdrawn and there was no further active trouble with Mexico until The Great Commoner had retired from office.

But within several months after this, in July, 1914, a shot was fired in Serbia which exploded the European War.

Bryan, the ambassador of peace, found himself as Secretary of State in the bloodiest period in the world's history.

His sympathies were evenly divided. Ruth, his elder daughter, had married a British army officer and was living in Egypt. His son had married a girl of German descent from Milwaukee, where pro-German sympathies were very strong. While the eastern seaboard was for the most part hotly pro-Ally, the country at large did not regard the issue as its affair.

After the opening weeks many western newspapers did not carry the war on the front page, except when there was some big new drive.

Even the belligerent Roosevelt in the early weeks following the outbreak of war felt that the affair did not concern the United States.

In the September 23, 1914, issue of the *Outlook* Roosevelt wrote:

> Our country stands well nigh alone among the great civilized powers in being unshaken by the present world-wide war. For this we should be humbly and profoundly grateful. All of us on this continent ought to appreciate how fortunate we are that we of the western world have been free from the working of the causes which have produced the bitter and vindictive hatred among the great military powers of the old world. . . . It is certainly eminently desirable that we should remain entirely neutral and nothing but urgent need would warrant breaking our neutrality and taking sides one way or the other.

Bryan had not much interference from Colonel House during the early part of the administration, but from now on the Colonel's shadow was to come continually between Secretary Bryan and his chief.

House's intrusion into State Department activities was cautious. He was far from being an admirer of The Great Commoner but he knew that Wilson had a feeling of affection and loyalty for The Peerless Leader which might be aroused if not carefully treated. He wrote to the President on April 5, 1915, objecting to the idea of Bryan's offering his good offices of mediation to the belligerents and particularly urging that if it were done it should come from Wilson himself without the thought that Bryan had instigated it. He advanced the view that in that event neither the people here nor abroad would take it seriously.

"You and I understand better and know that the greatest sort of injustice is done him," wrote the Colonel to the President, "nevertheless, just now it is impossible to make people think differently."

In November, 1914, Bryan went to Lincoln to vote and he saw that the temper of that section of the country was largely neutral and did not realize that the War concerned it at all.

When he arrived at Washington the Sunday following election, he could sense the difference in the atmosphere, the distorted importance that is given to rumors in any capital city, the undue significance that is given to passing remarks and the nervousness over international relationships.

He had planned to go to church, but he received a call from Colonel House who urged that some matters of great moment were pressing. Bryan was amazed to find that House foresaw war and The

Great Commoner held that the very fear of war and the planning for it would help to bring it about. House was strongly for increasing the army, at least by approving plans for a large reserve force. The Peerless Leader looked at his visitor with alarm and suspicion. He knew that Ambassador Page in England was writing directly to Wilson and to House, ignoring the State Department, and he feared that House was being swayed in the direction of war. He stated that he did not believe there was the slightest danger to this country from foreign invasion even if the Germans were successful. The attitude of Page, House and certain other of the eastern Democrats was making his position increasingly difficult. Many times he was not told what was going on or what was being said. He had to fight against an atmosphere of distrust, not, as far as he knew, from Wilson, but from various of Wilson's advisors and colleagues.

Less than three weeks later he had another call from the Texas Colonel, who explained a plan which he had for a league of Latin American powers, a Pan-American League of Nations. Mr. House showed Bryan a pencil memorandum of the plan which had been written by President Wilson at House's suggestion. The Colonel's proposal was that he should feel out the ambassadors of Brazil, Argentina and Chile with respect to their views on this program.

The Great Commoner acquiesced, though he had in the background of his mind the thought that the thirty treaties already enacted with various countries virtually did away with the necessity for the House plan. He turned the conversation to the Russian treaty, a proposal by the Venezuelan minister, and to prohibition.

Several days later the Colonel called again and expounded his pet plan. Mr. Bryan listened politely and then thought it an opportune time to speak of the problems within the organization of the party and the need for getting a job for a certain faithful Democrat. But the Colonel was not interested.

Hardly a week went by now without Bryan being forced to wonder whether he or Colonel House was Secretary of State. In the early days of the administration House had buzzed around in the Department of Agriculture and later had busied himself with keeping Carter Glass and Senator Owen informed on financial matters, but now on top of the South American affairs the dapper Colonel was injecting himself into the relationship of the United States with European powers.

Late in the afternoon of January 13, 1915, Bryan had a call from the Colonel which brought perhaps the most drastic disappointment of his career. House informed The Great Commoner that he had spent the day talking with the British Ambassador and the representatives of other nations with respect to the possibilities of peace. House said that he had taken up with Wilson the proposition that he should go to Europe as a peace emissary and that the idea had been approved.

The Commoner could not conceal his disappointment and surprise. Who in the administration had been the one to work for peace? Who had been active in the peace movement in the United States and abroad for many years? Who had negotiated thirty peace treaties involving most of the world's population? The decision to ignore the record of The Great Commoner in favor of House was a stunning slight.

Mr. Bryan said that he considered the work of a peace emissary to come properly within his duties and that he had planned to do that himself. House explained that his trip was to be distinctly unofficial with the purpose of sounding out the powers and that a much franker exchange of views could be obtained if an unofficial delegate made the approaches.

Bryan replied that if this were to be an unofficial task Colonel House was the one best suited to do it.

Two weeks later the Colonel was around again. This time he was proposing a commission form of government for Mexico, with the Latin American powers and the United States acting jointly in charge of the country. Bryan thought that this might work out as a last resort but he was fundamentally opposed to any step which might lead to conquest or involve war.

Meanwhile the tendency to ignore Bryan increased. There had been several leaks of news which had been charged to the State Department though afterwards this was proved not to be the case. It led, however, to Page telling Bryan practically nothing, to ambassadorial meetings in the home of the Assistant Secretary of State with the connivance of House and without the knowledge of Bryan, and to a general disposition upon the part of certain members of the Cabinet to ignore his powers. Daniels remained a staunch friend. The President always listened sympathetically and attentively to what The Great Commoner had to say. Franklin K. Lane, Secretary of the Interior, also saw the way that things were drifting and tried in a tactful way to heal the disagreements and the mutual distrusts. Lane wrote to House on May 5, 1915 saying, "I am growing more and more in my admiration for Bryan each day. He is too good a Christian to run a naughty world and he doesn't hate hard enough, but he certainly is a noble and high-minded man and loyal to the President to the last hair."

House had gone abroad by that time but had not found a cordial reception to his mission.

"Everybody seems to want peace," he wrote the Secretary of State, "but nobody is willing to concede enough to get it. They all also say that they desire a permanent settlement so that no such disaster may occur hereafter, but again there is such a divergence of ideas as to how this should be brought about that for the moment it is impossible to harmonize the difficulties."

Then on May 7, 1915, there occurred an event which changed the whole temper of Washington and eventually of the nation. The Cunard liner, the *Lusitania,* was sunk by a German submarine and 117 American citizens lost their lives.

The Great Commoner went to the Cabinet meeting four days later in trepidation as to what this might mean for the people of the Republic. He walked into the Cabinet Room with a heavy heart and took his accustomed seat at the right hand of the President.

Mr. Wilson opened the discussion of the *Lusitania* incident, reading a message from Colonel House:

It is now certain that a large number of American lives were lost when the *Lusitania* was sunk. I believe an immediate demand should be made upon Germany for assurance that this shall not occur again. . . . If war follows, it will not be a new war but an endeavor to end more speedily an old one.

President Wilson then read a memorandum of a note that he proposed sending to Germany. Bryan was aghast at the procedure of his chief in taking up with the Cabinet the House telegram and the proposed German note without having consulted the Secretary of State on the problems and implications involved. Without waiting for any thought on the matter from Bryan, several of the Cabinet members expressed the view that a strong message should be sent to Germany at once. Bryan had previously written to the President a memorandum pointing out that while America had been pressing the issue with respect to submarine warfare she had not been mak-

## A SPRING OFFENSIVE

From Brooklyn "*Daily Eagle*"

The administration and the State Department had to recognize the existence of anti-British as well as anti-German sentiments. The British had aggravated the situation by interference with the United States mails.

ing as stringent recommendations with respect to the British blockade.

At the Cabinet meeting he again asked what was going to be done about British interference with our exports. The President thought that this was not an opportune time to take up that problem.

Mr. Bryan then commented that certain of the Cabinet members seemed to be pro-Ally.

"Mr. Bryan, you are not warranted in making such an assertion," the President said angrily; "we all doubtless have our opinions in this matter but there are none of us who can justly be accused of being unfair."

The Cabinet meeting ended with the decision that the President should send a firm note to Germany, demanding pledges of security for neutrals.

The tense atmosphere of Washington, which realized the ultimate possibility of the incident, was felt throughout the State Department and especially by its Secretary. Matters were made more acute by the action of Dumba, the Austrian Ambassador, who brought a new and disturbing note into the situation.

Dumba was a little man who looked like a miniature edition of J. P. Morgan (the younger). His head was the same shape, his eyebrows were bushy. He had a similar contour of jawbone and of features, except that the mouth hiding behind the white mustache was soft and indecisive.

Several days after the *Lusitania* event Dumba called at the State Department and asked to talk with Secretary Bryan on this subject.

He asked The Great Commoner how this varied so differently from the offenses of the British blockade.

"Because the American people cannot regard the holding up of merchandise by Great Britain in the same light that they regard the taking of life by the sinking of the *Lusitania*," Mr. Bryan contended.

Dumba stated that Germany was anxious to maintain friendly relations with the United States and wanted to know that if assurances were given for the future whether it would not be possible to arbitrate the question as far as past transactions were concerned.

Bryan said that he did not feel authorized to discuss the subject without getting the President's views, but that he might say to the German government that there was no desire for war in this country and that we expected Germany to answer the note in the same spirit of friendship that prompted ours.

Dumba followed up this conciliatory statement with a suggestion that it would be easier for Germany if she could say that she expected us to insist upon the same spirit of freedom of trade with neutrals. Mr. Bryan was not receptive to that thought. He pointed out that a specific issue was being discussed with Germany and that this country could not be embarrassed by advice from Germany as to how it should proceed in its attitude toward the Allies. Mr. Bryan further suggested that Germany ought to be willing to assume that the United States would live up to its previous position with respect to neutral rights which had already been advanced in memoranda to Great Britain.

The Austrian Ambassador inquired softly whether he could have any confidential assurances that the United States would insist on such rights.

Mr. Bryan said that no such assurances ought to be necessary. He suggested that if Germany wished to justify her own position to her own people she could set forth whatever she might desire in a statement to them, saying that she took it for granted that we would insist upon our rights as neutrals. If, however, Germany tried to tell the United States how it should deal with Great Britain, the situation would become extremely complicated.

The Ambassador finally abandoned the attempt to get a promise from the Secretary of State with respect to the country's attitude toward the British. His next line of attack was to ask whether the United States would agree to refuse clearance to ships which carried explosives and ammunition.

Mr. Bryan said that Germany was at liberty to make any suggestions that she thought proper in her reply, but that the United States could not consider these suggestions in advance.

As the Ambassador left, the Secretary dictated a memorandum of the conversation and dispatched it to the President. To his summary he added several suggestions.

"I believe that it would have a splendid effect if **our note to Great Britain can go at once**," he said;

"it will give Germany an excuse and I think she is looking for something that will serve as an excuse. . . . I have no doubt Germany would be willing to so change the rule in regard to submarines as to exempt from danger all passenger ships that did not carry munitions of war."

Bryan also enclosed a statement from Ambassador Page, which expressed enthusiasm at Wilson's first *Lusitania* note and also indicated the extent of the Ambassador's pro-British sympathies.

"I am glad to note," Secretary Bryan said dryly in his comment to the President on this matter, "that it will not take a generation to regain the respect with the loss of which we were threatened."

A few days after this colloquy and the report of it by Mr. Bryan to the President, the Secretary was dumfounded to learn that the German minister Zimmermann had told Ambassador Gerard that Dumba had sent a telegram saying in effect that the *Lusitania* note was "not meant in earnest and was only sent as a sop to public opinion." The effect on the administration was staggering. Both Gerard and Colonel House expressed the view immediately that Bryan could have said nothing of the sort. The Great Commoner sent for Dumba and demanded what he meant by putting any such construction or interpretation on their conversation.

Dumba claimed that Zimmermann had misrepresented him and that he had not said so.

Mr. Bryan did not stop to discuss the evidence of the alleged cable, but demanded that he communicate with the German government immediately correcting the misconstruction.

The harm had been done, however, and Germany's reply to the Wilson note was truculent and unyielding.

Bryan attended the Cabinet meeting on June first under a great strain. He realized that some of his associates did not believe his account of the Dumba incident. He was further alarmed by the fact that the affair had made Dumba himself unacceptable to the American government with the complication that free communication between Germany and the United States became increasingly difficult because of the fear that the American view would be misrepresented in forwarding to Berlin. Meanwhile the President had not sent any note to England with respect to Great Britain's constant violation of United States claims arising from the blockade. The President spent most of the time discussing Mexican affairs. He was in the mood to give the support of the United States to some Mexican leader who could work out a solution of that country's problems. Cabinet opinion was widely divided as to what should be done. Bryan still preferred Carranza, but took little interest in the matter compared with other problems that were at hand. Other members of the Cabinet held similar views, none expecting to find any ready solution of the Mexican dilemma. The President expressed impatience at what he considered a change of mind on the part of the Cabinet with respect to firm action in Mexico.

He then read to the Cabinet his second note with respect to the *Lusitania*. Bryan again brought up the point that the United States had been pressing the issue in one direction but had not balanced it with equivalent insistence of our rights with respect to the Allies. He likewise realized that as the note was read, Wilson was veering further and further away from conciliation to a condition which seemed certain to lead to war.

On April twenty-third he had written to the President, "The fact that we have not contested Great Britain's assertion of the right to use our flags has still further aggravated Germany and we cannot overlook the fact that the sale of arms and ammunition, while it could not be forbidden under neutrality, has worked so entirely for the benefit of one side as to give to Germany, not justification, but an excuse for charging that we are favoring the Allies."

Again on May ninth he had sent a memorandum to the President stating: "A ship carrying contraband should not rely upon passengers to protect her from attack—it would be like putting women and children in front of an army. . . . I learned from Mr. Lansing last night that the *Lusitania* carried ammunition."

He had tried during the discussions of the past month to minimize the immediate issue raised by the President's initial reply. In the light of that there was some basis to Dumba's interpretation, and in so far as there was a basis, the policy had the endorsement of the White House. In a memorandum to the President on May twelfth, Bryan stated: "The words 'strict accountability' having been construed by some of the newspapers to mean an immediate settlement of the matter, I deemed it fitting to say that that construction is not a necessary one. . . . Germany has endorsed the principle of investigation * embodied in the thirty treaties signed by as many nations. These treaties give a year's time after the investigation and apply to all disputes of every character. From this nation's standpoint there is no reason why this policy should not control as between the United States and Germany. I believe such a statement would do great good."

President Wilson, before the second German reply, was highly receptive to this communication by Mr. Bryan. He wrote The Great Commoner on May thirteenth, suggesting that the executive department should give out an interpretation of the situation as contained in a memorandum which he enclosed. This memorandum said in part: "A frank issue is now made, and it is expected that it will be made in good temper and with a desire to reach an agreement, despite the passions of the hour—passions in which the United States does not share—or else submit the whole matter to such processes of discussion as will result in a permanent settlement."

Later the same day, Mr. Wilson sent Secretary Bryan a further message stating that he had heard something indirectly from the German Ambassador

---

* Germany had, however, as stated elsewhere, definitely refused to sign any such treaty.

which indicated that there was no hope of bringing Germany to reason if there was the slightest indication of weakening on the part of the United States or if the note was thought to be merely the first word in a long debate.

"In the meantime," the President wrote, "I trust you will pardon me from changing my mind thus. . . . If we say anything of the kind it must be a little later, after the note has had its first effect."

Mr. Bryan was not satisfied with this statement of the President's, and in fact feared that it indicated a change of mind which would lead the country rapidly into war. On May fourteenth he addressed the President, suggesting that the government should issue a warning to American citizens with respect to taking passage on British boats pending negotiations over the *Lusitania* affair. The President disagreed with this suggestion, holding that the public already knew the danger and that it would weaken our position with Germany.

In view of all this which happened shortly before the first June cabinet meeting at which the President virtually ignored the Cabinet view on the European crisis, Bryan thought that it was time to resign.

On Saturday, the fifth of June, he called on McAdoo (Secretary of the Treasury and son-in-law of the President) to go over the whole situation and say why he thought he ought to withdraw from the Cabinet. McAdoo urged him not to do so, feeling that this would tend to emphasize the difference of opinion in the government and weaken the position of the United States in international affairs. On Monday the President asked him to come to the White House and discuss the matter. When Bryan arrived he found Mr. McAdoo with the President, and again they both urged him to reconsider his decision.

The Commoner felt that since Germany had "accepted in principle" the idea of the Bryan treaties to submit all matters in dispute to a neutral commission to be considered for a year, if necessary, before war should result, that this instrument should be employed under the existing circumstances.

The President did not share Bryan's faith in the good intentions of the German government. And later the Kaiser had said to Colonel House that Germany would never think of signing such an agreement. "Our strength," said the Emperor, "lies in being always prepared for war at a second's notice. We will not resign that advantage and give our enemies time to prepare."

But the vision of nonresistance and the faith of Tolstoy had possession of The Great Commoner, who passionately believed that wrongs existed on both sides of the conflict and that if only a moratorium could be obtained the masses of the people in each country would demand peace with the specific terms to be adjusted by negotiation.

Wilson did not feel that such a procedure was practical, and Bryan determined to go ahead with his decision to resign.

## WAR

When the morning of Tuesday came, The Commoner realized for the first time the full impact of the fact that after only two years of service he was no longer a part of the government which he had done so much to create. The thought was almost intolerable. He called the White House on the telephone and asked whether it would be desirable or agreeable for him to attend the Cabinet meeting.

There was a pause at the other end of the wire while the President repeated the question to Bryan's former colleagues.

The answer came urging him to come.

He lost no time in getting to the White House. As he entered the Cabinet Room all the members stood up, including the President, and greeted the Secretary of State. His resignation was already on the table, as well as Wilson's second note to Germany demanding prompt satisfaction.

As a final modification he had asked that this clause be inserted in the second Wilson note: "If the Imperial German Government should deem itself to be in possession of convincing evidence that the officials of the Government of the United States did not perform these duties with thoroughness, the Government of the United States sincerely hopes that it will submit that evidence for consideration."

The purpose of this additional phrase was to give an opportunity for further discussion, rather than forcing the issue to a head.

The discussion at the Cabinet meeting had to do

with the note as a whole, rather than with the Bryan modification.*

The other members of the Cabinet were none too clear as to what the policy of the country should be, or what the President meant in his notes.

"How far do you propose to go?" Houston asked the President. "Do you demand that Germany give up the use of the submarine in her efforts to destroy British trade? . . . This war will present many new problems. England is violating the three-mile blockade. She is blockading at a distance."

The President asked Houston to write him a memorandum on this matter. Bryan sat with his eyes closed and said nothing. He had been writing memoranda for the past month.

As the meeting came to a close Bryan asked if the Cabinet would lunch with him at the University Club. Lane, Daniels, Burleson, W. B. Wilson, Garrison and Houston accepted.

Throughout the luncheon Bryan had little to say. He realized the wedge that this step would drive between him and his associates. He knew that it

---

*Colonel House, who was not present at the time, reports the version of this incident given to him by Attorney-General Gregory. According to his view the Bryan Amendment and the entire message were on the table throughout the discussion, and the implication is drawn that Bryan accordingly knew that his Amendment was going to be accepted. There is additional evidence, however, which shows that the Cabinet did not know what would be decided upon when the meeting was over. Apparently the President gave no assurance of changing his mind. That evening he telephoned to David F. Houston, Secretary of Agriculture, to discuss changes in the note. While Bryan knew that his proposal was before the house, he had no evidence to make him think that it would be accepted.

AND THEN HE ROCKED IT.

*From New York "World"*

*One of the most famous war-time cartoons representing the view of those who felt that Bryan should have buried his own views and stuck by the administration.*

would severely weaken his influence with his party, and he was aware that all the batteries of the hostile press would be turned on him again with the purpose forever to blacken his name in history.

"Gentlemen," he said, turning to his colleagues, "this is our last meeting together. I have valued our association and friendship. I have had to take the course I have chosen. The President has had one view. I have had a different one. I do not censure him for thinking and acting as he thinks best. I have had to act as I have thought best. I cannot go along with him in this note. I think it makes for war. I believe that I can do more on the outside to prevent war than I can on the inside. I think I can help the President more on the outside. I can work to control popular opinion so that it will not exert pressure for extreme action which the President does not want. We both want the same thing, peace."

"You are the most real Christian I know," said Lane, turning to him. Burleson nodded in accord.

"I must act according to my conscience," Bryan continued. "I go out into the dark. The President has the prestige and the power on his side."

The irony of history swept before The Great Commoner's eyes. He broke down at the thought that all he had done was going to end only in vilification.

"I have many friends who would die for me," he said aloud to the Cabinet members, who looked at one another and stirred uncomfortably.

# WAR

**JUST AS YOU SAY, SIR!**

*"I ask the American People to sit in judgment on my decision to resign."*
—William Jennings Bryan.

From Chicago "*Herald*"

*Bryan was at the low ebb of his newspaper popularity following his resignation from the Cabinet.*

While Bryan's guesses as to what would happen were partially correct, the country turned out at that time to be closer to him than it was to the cause of war, even though the papers denounced his so-called "peace-at-any-price" policy, and the press of the eastern seaboard especially was against his contention that these matters could be discussed or that American citizens should be warned against traveling on the boats of belligerents.

Bryan's resignation—which was offered on the grounds that the Wilson policy did not allow opportunity for further discussion—was weakened by the recognition of his suggestion in the Wilson note, but essentially the difference between the view of Wilson and himself remained the same.

As has been pointed out the discussion of the submarine affair lasted over a longer period than would have been required under the Bryan treaty plan.

The Peerless Leader remained loyal to the administration while differing with its foreign policy. When the campaign of 1916 came on a year later, the public had been lulled into thinking that there was no danger of getting into the conflict. Mr. Bryan went to the 1916 Convention and sounded the keynote of the campaign which ended in Wilson's reëlection.

"The Democratic party," he said, "is able successfully to defend every action of the administration. We have put more laws of importance to the people on the statute books than any dozen Republican administrations. No president since Jackson has had to face such a tremendous attack on the part of predatory wealth as Woodrow Wilson. The currency laws we passed have broken the grip of Wall Street on the politics of the United States. I have differed with the President on some points of his policy in dealing with the Great War, but I agree with the American people in thanking God we have a president who has kept—who will keep—us out of war."

"He kept us out of war" became the slogan of the campaign, and the Bryan country together with California returned Wilson to office.

In fact, Bryan enthusiasm was so strong that the proceedings in the early part of the convention were continually interrupted by the applause of delegations calling for "Bryan." He realized that this was an obstruction to the necessary business of the event and hit upon the expedient of placing a chair under the stage where he could hear everything and yet not be seen. In this voluntary exile he placidly remained until the end of the convention.

This period made a break in The Great Commoner's life in more than political ways. He had decided to settle permanently in Florida. It was better for his health, and his rejection at Grand Island had made many rifts in lifelong Nebraska friendships.

Pulling up stakes in the autumn of 1916 was hard not only for him but for Mary Baird Bryan. These were to be her last days in Fairview as a permanent home (though the house was never sold). "I shall never forget those days," she wrote in her journal, "quite as beautiful as summer. The 'fodder in the shock'; blue mist on the horizon; a reddish-gold globe of a sun pushing through the mist; frost on freshly plowed fields; shivering weeds by the roadside; rabbits running to cover. I saw and loved them all."

Events moved swiftly following the election, with Germany making more and more demands rather than receding from her position. The President, on April 2, 1917, asked the Congress to declare a state of war. The news came to Bryan at Albany, Georgia, and he wired the offer of his services to the President as a volunteer in any capacity.

"The quickest way to peace," he concluded, "is to go straight through supporting the Government in all it undertakes, no matter how long the war lasts or how much it costs."

The Great Commoner retired to his Florida home, sallying forth only for occasional lectures, and devoting his time and funds to various war efforts and charities. When peace came he was an enthusiast for the League of Nations and also for the signing of the Treaty.

At the Jackson day dinner held as usual at Washington on January 8, 1920, he stepped back into public favor as quickly as he had left it, and without realizing that his position would be so heartily cheered.

Wilson had had the view that the League of Nations without its Article X, which was the force clause, was useless. He had sent a letter to the Jackson dinner condemning United States Senator Lodge, who had been the chief opponent of the League.

### THE OLD FRIEND OF THE FAMILY WHO WAS JUST INVITED IN TO CHAPERON THE JACKSON BIRTHDAY PARTY.

From New York "Tribune"

In 1920, after the War, it was again recognized that Bryan remained a strong force in his party. This was further emphasized by his stand on the League of Nations announced at the Jackson Day Dinner.

Bryan spoke at the dinner for a prompt ratification of the Treaty and the adoption of the League with or without reservations in order that the world might get back solidly to a condition of peace. "I was willing to ratify the League as it came to us though I did not like Article X. It is clear that all must be lost unless we accept reservations. I prefer to take them and so go into the League."

He awoke next morning to find that he was in the midst of Republican as well as Democratic approval. Even the Republican New York *Tribune* said "Good boy!"

## CHAPTER XVII

### GRINDING CORN FOR THE PHILISTINES

> And he found a new jawbone of an ass and put forth his hand, and took it, and slew a thousand men therewith.—JUDGES 15:15

THE War was over, but its after effects were hysteria and Belshazzar feasts.

People were possessed with an insanity to get away from themselves. President Wilson had said that the heart of the world was broken, and Shaw had written on the same theme in his "Heartbreak House."

The closing days of the Wilson administration were a riot of spending, succeeded by the Veterans' Bureau scandal and other peccadillos of the Harding régime. Workmen were wearing twelve-dollar silk shirts while the intelligentsia in self-defense adopted the former blue shirt of the laborer.

Those whose temperaments were not satisfied by or equipped for reckless expenditures of money revenged their disenchantment in other ways. Some of these indulged in heresy hunting of various sorts. Chasing bolshevism was a prevalent form. Hillis at Plymouth Church saw bombs hidden behind every pew. Senator Lusk of New York put a gag law on the school system.

Calvin Coolidge, Vice President of the United States, viewed the plight of American womanhood with alarm. He wrote three articles for the *Delineator* under the heading of "Enemies of the Republic," which told how sinister doctrine was being taught at Barnard, Radcliffe, Wellesley, Boston University, Simmons, and other women's colleges. Bryn Mawr and Smith seemed safe, so was Mount Holyoke.

The Great Commoner did not escape from the hysteria. To his home in Florida there came word from all over the land that the faith of the younger generation was being destroyed. A Baptist preacher informed him that at Columbia a professor began his course in geology by telling his class to throw away all that they had learned in Sunday school. A Methodist preacher reported to him that a teacher at the University of Wisconsin was telling his class that the Bible was a collection of myths. Things were as bad or worse in the women's colleges.

So Mr. Bryan set forth on his own pet campaign and carried the fight to the door of the colleges.

In the summer of 1920 he hurled out his denunciations from the Tent Evangel at Amsterdam Avenue at 110th Street, only a few blocks from Columbia University.

The tent was filled to capacity when Bryan came on the platform to speak. Most of the audience were deeply religious men and women, poorly dressed, eager and fervent. They looked up to the heavy-set, tall speaker on the platform with eyes of

From Detroit "News"

Democracy, struggling to find a leader more successful than Cox, seemed to see the same face in all directions.

almost fanatical zeal and hope. In the rear of the tent, at the fringes of the crowd, were Columbia students and other curiosity seekers.

The Great Commoner was getting old. The flesh around his cheek bones and jaw was no longer firm. His forehead and the crown of his head were completely bald, only gray fringes of hair over his ears and at the top of his collar remained. The lines around his mouth were tired, except when he got into the full stride of his speech. He wore the familiar gray alpaca suit, "boiled" white shirt, low collar, and black string tie.

A pitcher of ice water and a glass stood on the table at his side as he spoke.

"It has come to a point," he told his audience, "where the young folks in some of these eastern colleges vote whether or not there is a God. I am told that in Bryn Mawr in one of the class rooms there the vote was twenty-three for God and forty-three against."

The audience gasped as The Great Commoner poured himself a glass of ice water.

"At Ann Arbor, Michigan, there is a professor who argues with his students against religion and asserts that no thinking man can believe in God and in the Bible," Mr. Bryan continued.

"One of my friends, a Congressman, tells me that his daughter upon returning from Wellesley told him that nobody believes in the Bible stories now."

Mr. Bryan went on naming Vassar, Barnard, and **many other** institutions of learning where in his opinion the faith of the fathers was being undermined and destroyed. Throughout that summer and for two or three years to come he went up and down the land, describing the perils that beset American womanhood, joining with Mr. Coolidge in viewing with alarm the institution of the American college.

To those who knew The Great Commoner, his religious training and his personal faith, his agitation on this subject was not a surprise, but the methods and arguments he used during this period gave them painful pause. Later when he stood at Armageddon at the Dayton evolution case they applauded the gallant war horse in his final battle.

But on April 13, 1923, there occurred an event at Charleston, West Virginia, which indicated the extent to which Mr. Bryan was pursuing his heresy hunting.

A bill had been introduced into the West Virginia legislature prohibiting the teaching of evolution in the schools of that state. Mr. Bryan had been invited to address the legislature for the proponents of the bill.

His address on this occasion advocated the doctrine of education by legislation, especially by use of the veto power.

"A few scientists," he told the West Virginia lawmakers, "demand the right to teach *as true* unsupported guesses that undermine the religious faith of Christian taxpayers.

"It is no infringement on their freedom of conscience or freedom of speech to say that, while as individuals they are at liberty to think as they please and to say what they like, they have no right to demand pay for teaching that which the parents and the taxpayers do not want taught. The hand that writes the pay check rules the school."

Many who had carried the torch for Bryan through a generation of politics were aghast when that doctrine was transmitted to the world. What madness had come upon The Peerless Leader that he upheld man as taxpayer as the ultimate arbiter? For years The Peerless Leader had been the proponent of the inherent dignity of Man, as laborer, taxpayer or in whatever capacity.

He had fought the trusts on the ground that they curtailed human liberty.

He had not felt that justice was done when Christian Taxpayer Mark Hanna had raised great funds to educate the people in the direction of the gold standard. He had not cared for the idea that the man who holds the pay roll is the man who holds the votes when eastern manufacturers had told their laborers how to cast their ballots.

He had been so incensed when the trustees of Brown University ousted E. Benjamin Andrews because of economic views that he saw to it that Dr. Andrews became chancellor of the University of Nebraska.

*O' Weep for Adonais!*

The educational world which had respected The Great Commoner's personal faith and had not resented his criticism of their views rose in protest at this demand that the legislatures should dictate what should or should not be taught in the schools. President Kenneth C. Sills of Bowdoin College, Maine, had met the issue when it came up in his state with these words:

"To one who knows Maine and its traditions it seems incredible that such a law should even be thought of . . . the very idea of legislating against science and against the pursuit of truth is preposterous and stupid, and contrary to the freedom and liberty of thought and speech in which we people of the State of Maine have taken such pride."

Mr. Bryan did not win on the West Virginia vote but that did not deter him from arousing Christian taxpayers elsewhere.

He called on the president of the University of Wisconsin with respect to the professor who had been teaching that the Bible was a collection of myths. President Van Hise, who had been through a generation of campaigning with La Follette in shaking off the domination of special interests in that state, regarded his visitor with amazement. He lectured The Great Commoner on educational freedom and made no reference to the professor in question.

The Peerless Leader was undeterred and went from Kentucky to Minnesota, from Florida to Georgia, appearing before most of the state legislatures of the country, trying to have enacted into law a statement of what could not be taught in the schools.

He became obsessed with the taxpayer argument. In the State of Nebraska at the time there were 650,000 qualified voters, of whom but 97,700 were income taxpayers, Christian or otherwise. There were but 169,100 persons owning their own homes, a total possible maximum of 266,800 taxpayers (assuming that the figures do not contain duplications), Christian or not. Those who opposed him pointed out that even a majority of the taxpayers would not necessarily concur with a majority of the voters and in an issue of that sort who should be considered?

The question was also raised as to whether The Great Commoner would be satisfied if the Christian taxpayers in any state failed to carry out his beliefs and whether such a vote would prove that they were right.

But Bryan was intent upon his theme and his purpose. The implications and ramifications of the doctrine of the pay check seemed not to worry him. Along with Vice President Coolidge he was anxious to save the young women in the colleges so that they would not be led astray and taught doctrines which would undermine the Republic and their own immortal souls.

Meanwhile the students at Vassar, at Wellesley, at Smith and elsewhere were being graduated, were marrying, and settling down in Cleveland Heights, Germantown, and Montclair, New Jersey; and those who had been so obsessed with the welfare of American womanhood eventually turned to other matters.

## CHAPTER XVIII

### THE COMMONER AND AL SMITH

"Like,—but oh how different."—WORDSWORTH

AS much as many of the cohorts of Democracy squirmed when marching under the banners of The Great Commoner, the results were always worse when they ignored his leadership.

In the 1920 campaign Bryan's attitude on ratifying the League had run counter to Wilson's. His dry enforcement plank had been voted down in the convention at more than eight to one, and he refrained from campaigning actively for Governor Cox.

Democracy suffered the most smashing defeat since the days of Parker. There was very likely in the latter instance little relationship between the repudiation of The Commoner's views and the poor showing at the polls; there were nevertheless many political leaders who looked at the results and were willing to have the counsels of The Great Commoner once again.

He had become something of a local power in Florida. He had been living in that state since 1916 and was one of its most distinguished all-year citizens.

When time for the 1924 Convention came along it was logical that Bryan should go on the state ticket as delegate at large to the Democratic Convention.

The delegation as a whole went to the convention instructed for McAdoo, but Bryan ran several thousand votes ahead of his ticket and might have been swayed in the direction of any candidate had he felt that there was a winner on the horizon who would represent the principles for which the party had stood over a period of years.

In New York's delegation there was a candidate, Alfred E. Smith, then in his second term as governor of the state, who in many respects was the logical recipient of the Bryan toga, altered and re-trimmed to suit city sophistication.

Smith was a man who said of himself, "I have not been a silent man, but a battler for social and political reform."

Smith stood in the same relationship to the city multitude as Bryan had stood in respect to the tenant farmer and the small-town business man in 1896.

Smith had the same quick, warm responsiveness to humanity and to political conditions which The Great Commoner possessed. Each man trusted to the heart and to his own understanding of specific situations, more than to the book.

Between Smith and the nomination stood three shadows: wetness, Catholicism, and Tammany Hall.

If Smith had been willing to stand for law enforcement and forego his Wet connections, the problem of getting the support of The Great Commoner would have been possible of solution. Bryan approached the 1924 Convention with an open mind. Even in his seconding speech for McAdoo he repeated his performance of 1904 by listing several men who would be satisfactory to him. The New York delegation, however, feeling strong in Madison Square Garden in their home city, could only remember 1912, and forgot the history of The Peerless Leader and New York over the long period of years.

They assumed that he was anti-Catholic, that he was a member of the Klan, and that he was unalterably opposed to Tammany Hall.

In these suppositions there was a lack of political sagacity and knowledge which proved costly.

Bryan had been accustomed in his youth to seeing his father deliver a load of hay to every clergyman in the town including the Catholic priest. As early as 1890 he had taken occasion to declare himself on this issue. When he was running for Congress that fall he sent the following communication to an Omaha newspaper:

> WEEPING WATER, NEBRASKA
> October 18, 1890
>
> Editor *World Herald,*
>     Omaha, Nebraska.
>     Your dispatch just received. I belong to the Presbyterian Church, but do not belong to any anti-Catholic society. I

respect every man's right to worship God according to his own conscience.

W. J. BRYAN

In *The Commoner* he had shown considerable interest in Catholic affairs. The paper in one issue in 1903 devoted a full page to the death of Pope Leo XIII, and had as the leading editorial "The Whole World Mourns." On his trip to Europe in 1906 he had called on Pope Pius X, and written an admiring sketch of the prelate for an American newspaper syndicate.

He was well aware of the large section of the Democratic party which was Catholic in faith, and had fought to have this situation recognized. Shortly after Wilson's election, when Colonel House had called upon The Commoner in Miami to discuss Cabinet appointments, Bryan suggested that one member ought to be of the Roman Catholic faith. Colonel House answered that the appointment of Joseph Tumulty as secretary to the President ought to cover the situation. Mr. Bryan did not think so.

When the Klan became active after the War, The Great Commoner refused to have anything to do with it. His name was evoked by it many times and certain klaverns were named for him, but he refused to acknowledge the tribute.

In fact, in the attitude of Bryan and of Smith with respect to the relationship of the state and religion there was a close paralleling of views:

# POPE LEO XIII IS DEAD

Pope Leo XIII. was taken ill July 4. On the evening of that day a number of cardinals were summoned to the vatican. For several days the pope lingered between life and death, showing a most remarkable vitality and the attention of the world has been fixed upon the proceedings at his bedside. At 4:04 p. m. Monday July 20, the pope passed away.

For a quarter of a century Pope Leo XIII has been the head of the Roman Catholic church. He was regarded by many as one of the greatest popes and universally he was understood to be one of the ablest and most conscientious of public men. The enormous demands made upon him by his church were not sufficient to prevent him from participating in an intelligent consideration of the world's proceedings and many were surprised that he had an intimate acquaintance with the merits and the history of all great controversies throughout the world. Among the many descriptions of Pope Leo none is more interesting and instructive than that which appeared in the Louisville Courier-Journal. In this it is said:

"As a scholar, the pope ranked among the first men of his day. In all departments of learning his efficiency was remarkable. As a poet he was recognized to possess genius, and a number of his compositions were of the highest order.

"Personally the late pontiff was tall and slender, and his hair was snow white. His face had the kindliest of expressions, and his smile was ready when there was anything amusing said. He possessed a keen wit, tempered by his charitable wish not to wound the feelings of others. His manner was high-bred and finished, and he possessed a most charming courtesy, which placed all who saw him at their ease. He delighted to chat on literary topics and to the last found pleasure in reading the great authors of antiquity. His experience in life had been so vast that his remarks were full of a quiet wisdom. He impressed every one who met him. His personal habits were simple to a degree, for he lived the life of an ascetic. His industry and power for work were extraordinary, and the labor he daily went through while pope was enough to exhaust a much younger and stronger man."

Reverting to the history of Pope Leo, the Courier-Journal writer says:

"Joachim Vincent Raphael Lodovico Pecci was born March 2, 1810, at Carpineto. He was sent to the Jesuit college at Viterbo in 1818, where he remained till 1825, when he entered the Collegio Romano, just restored by Pope Leo XII. Two years later he was matriculated as a divinity student at the Gregorian university. In 1832 he won the degree of doctor of theology and entered the College of Noble Ecclesiastics, where those who design to serve the pontifical government diplomatically or administratively are trained. In 1837 he was made subdeacon, then deacon, then priest. In 1838 he was made delegate, or governor of the province of Benevento. In 1841 he was appointed governor of Spoleto. In 1843 he was made apostolic nuncio, or papal ambassador. To Belgium and titular archbishop of Damietta. In 1845 he was made bishop of Perugia, where he arrived in 1846. In 1854 he was made a cardinal. In 1877 he was appointed camerlingo. In 1878 he was chosen pope to succeed Pius IX. deceased."

The methods of choosing a successor to Leo are described in a most interesting way by the Courier-Journal writer. This writer says,

"The selection of the sovereign pontiff is a most important event, both for the church and the secular world. Catholicism teaches that Christ Himself chose the first pope, St. Peter but left no record in the scriptures as to how the succeeding popes should be elected From this it follows that the supreme pontiff the vicar of Christ, has the power of determining the method of election of his successors. It is a much mooted question whether the pope has the divine right to appoint his own successor or not. However under the present system he has not. The present method was established by Pope Pius IX.

"Ten days after the death of Pius IX. which occurred on February 18__ Cardinal Pecci was elected pope by the card___ and took the title of Leo XIII.

"The next conclave will follow the death of Leo XIII. and its tendencies that will dispute for the pre-eminence in that conclave are three: First, either no deviation from the policy of Leo XIII., a conciliatory one; or, second, a gradual change; third, the assertion of the claim for the restoration of temporal power in Italy, together with a disinclination to sacrifice all else to this one point, as has been done by Leo XIII.

"As an extreme concession the new pope might carry on the contest on legal grounds, encouraging Italian Catholics to take a more active part in political elections. There is some fear in higher Italian Catholic circles that Italy may become a republic.

"It is almost unnecessary to say that the next pope will be an Italian.

"The sacred college of cardinals is composed at present of sixty-seven members, the canonical number being seventy. Twenty-two reside at Rome. Only thirty of the sixty-seven belong to nationalities outside of Italy. As to nationality they stand: Italians, thirty-seven; French, eight; Austro-Hungarians, seven; Spaniards, five; Germans, two; Prussian-Pole, one; Irish, two; English, one; Portuguese, one; Belgian, one; American, one; Australian, one.

"Well informed sources in Rome eliminate all of the thirty-seven Italian cardinals except four and possibly five as impossible for election to the papacy.

"The four cardinals who are considered to be 'papabili' and out of which number it is confidently expected there is one upon whom the papacy will fall, are as follows: Girolamo Gotti, Serafino Vannutelli, Domenico Svampa, and Guiseppe Sarto. Cardinal Rampolla, the secretary of state to Pope Leo XIII. is considered by some a possibility. Cardinal Rampolla's position has naturally made him some enemies. His influence in certain quarters, however, is very great and it is not at all unlikely that he will select the candidate and quietly throw all of his strength toward electing him when the conclave meets. Thus he would be retained as secretary of state under the new pope if his candidate succeeded.

"The vatican, the residence of the pope, is one of the most interesting buildings in the world.

"He who is elected pope retires to the vatican, a custom inaugurated by Pius IX. In fact, Pius was living in his palace at the time of the Italian occupation of Rome, in 1870.

"In the course of the day as it became clear that the capture of the city was imminent, the pope retired to the vatican, never to leave it again. His successor Leo XIII., who was elected in the vatican, has continued the traditions of Pius IX., and since his election in 1878 has not gone outside of the vatican. This 'imprisonment' is purely voluntary and is meant as a dignified protest against what, from the vatican standpoint, can only be regarded as a usurpation: a seizure by violence of the possessions of the church.

"As a rule, the conclave of cardinals is held in the palace where the late pope has died. On the death of Pius IX., owing to the circumstance of the Italian occupation of Rome, it was proposed and at first even voted to hold the conclave abroad. Malta, Spain, the Tyrol, France and even England, were suggested. None of these countries, however, made any offer or guarantee, and in the second congregation (preliminary of the cardinals to arrange for the conclave) the motion was rescinded by a large majority It is now clearly understood that the Italian government will undertake to guarantee the orderly procedure of the conclave, so that a proposal to adjourn to a foreign country is not again likely.

"The conclave proper, i. e. the cardinals in their elective capacity only assemble after the funeral of the deceased pope This is an elaborate affair, lasting several days—eleven days in the case of Pius IX.—and accompanied with much ceremonial.

"On the death of the pope, the cardinal samerlengo approaches the bedside and taps the deceased three times on the head with a silver mallet, calling him by his Christian name. Thus the present pope would be addressed, not ad Leo, but as Gioacchino Naturally receiving no answer the samerlengo turns to the court and formally announces 'Il Papa e veramente morto' (the pope is really dead).

"The cardinal vicar then causes placards to be affixed to the doors of the Roman basilicas and churches, announcing the death of the pope and ordering all church bells to be tolled for an hour and solemn obsequies to be celebrated. On the second day the body of the pope is embalmed. The

---

*Bryan, always friendly with the Catholic element in the Democratic party, devoted considerable space in "The Commoner" to news of especial interest to the Roman Catholics.*

| BRYAN | SMITH |
|---|---|
| For the good of the State and the welfare of the Church, the moral and the civil law have been separated. To-day we owe a double allegiance and "render unto Cæsar the things that are Cæsar's, and unto God the things that are God's." | Your Church, just as mine, is voicing the injunction of our common Saviour to render unto Cæsar the things that are Cæsar's, and unto God the things that are God's. |
| Their governments are concentric circles and can never interfere. Between what religion teaches and what the law compels there is, and ever must be, a wide margin, as there is also between that religion forbids and what the law prohibits. | In the wildest dreams of your imagination you cannot conjure up a possible conflict between religious principle and political duty in the United States. |
| In many things we are left to obey or disobey the instructions of the Divine Ruler, answerable to Him only for our conduct.<br>—Early Address in *Memoirs* | I believe in the absolute freedom of conscience for all men and in equality of all churches, all sects, and all beliefs before the law as a matter of right and not as a matter of favor.<br>—*Atlantic Monthly,*<br>May, 1927. |

His relationship to Tammany Hall had also been an in-and-out affair. Under the leadership of

## THE COMMONER AND AL SMITH

*Boston Herald Nov. 1900*

**CROKER--You're driving beautifully, Colonel.**

*From Boston "Herald"*

Again in 1924 Bryan faced the familiar problem of what his attitude would be toward Tammany Hall. In 1900 and 1908 their contacts had been friendly. In 1924 Tammany took the lead in indicating what the relationship would be.

Croker and Nixon this political body had supported Bryan and he in turn had endorsed its judgment.

In 1902 he commented in *The Commoner*: "Mr. Croker showed good sense as well as devotion to the party's interest when he threw his influence to so excellent a man as Mr. Nixon and caused him to be selected as leader of Tammany. Mr. Nixon represents that element of the organization which has stood for clean government and has opposed the use of political position for private gain. He is a man of honesty, character and ability, and his leadership will silence much of the criticism that has been aimed at the organization in recent years."

Never had there been a leader from the South and West so aware of the problems of New York Democracy, so open-minded towards its beliefs and history, and so able, if he so desired, to win measurable support for any candidate whom he might support.

But Tammany was leery, just as Hill had been leery, and Champ Clark. They wanted nothing to do with this man. Whenever Bryan rose to be heard in the vast expanse of Madison Square Garden he was greeted by hisses and catcalls. The New York crowd had the galleries packed with Smith rooters, who yelled for their candidate at every opening, even though they could not garner the votes.

The convention was in a constant hubbub from the time that it opened. The floor was littered with papers and grime. Butcher boys ran up and down the aisles, dragging at the end of a rope baskets full of pop bottles, chewing gum, and cheap cigars.

Apart from the noise and din, in a private room, the platform committee was trying to draw up its planks. A minority wished to specifically condemn the Ku Klux Klan, but Bryan supported the view of the majority who felt that to single out such a group would only serve to dignify it and to concentrate attention on the religious issue. The Tammany

## THE COMMONER AND AL SMITH

Tiger, however, smelled Protestant blood and wanted specific condemnation of the Klan in reprisal for the intolerances of that organization. The majority report won.

Bryan's talk for McAdoo came on the thirty-eighth ballot when he rose and obtained the consent of the chair to speak, on the technicality of explaining his vote. It was the last time that he addressed a convention of his party, and the hosts of the occasion did all they could to make the event a bitter one. The Great Commoner was not too deeply enamored of McAdoo. Their friendship was bound by long years of association, but The Peerless Leader realized that the Klan support of Wilson's son-in-law was more of a liability than an asset. It was also true that in his latter days the President had been cold to the man who had put him in office. Wilson's cordiality to Bryan lasted longer than toward most of his associates and there was a nominal friendship between them up to the end of Wilson's active days. But there were some pretty deep scars in that association. If there were a chance, however, to woo Mr. Bryan to the Smith cause, the Madison Square galleries did all they could to prevent it.

As the veteran rose to speak, the New York delegates and their friends drowned his opening remarks with jeers and cries of derision.

"This is probably the last convention of my party to which I shall be a delegate," said The Great Commoner.

Loud hand-clapping greeted this announcement.

"Don't applaud," Mr. Bryan cautioned them, "I may change my mind."

He went on to state that there were various men who might be fitted to bear the party standard, and began to name several of them. Cries of "Smith! Smith!" interrupted him.

As he went on with his address, some one yelled, "What about free silver?"

"There is a statute of limitations even in politics," Mr. Bryan answered.

At length, as he came to his peroration, he was greeted by a chorus of hoots as he seconded the nomination of William Gibbs McAdoo.

Perhaps The Commoner's days were done. Perhaps this was his political swan song which his opponents had been promising for thirty years. Perhaps he was wholly and completely discredited.

Yet when the ballots were counted, his candidate had more votes than any other in the field, nearly one-half the total, while Smith received at no time more than one-third.

The feeling had gone too far for either the McAdoo or Smith forces to yield to the other. The Great Commoner who adjusted so many political differences was not called upon to aid in this affair, and the New Yorkers had no one to whom they might turn to carry the convention their way. They saw it at last, but they saw it too late.

Early in the morning after the Democratic manner, the convention decided on John W. Davis as candidate for the presidency.

## THE COMMONER AND AL SMITH

When the powers behind Democracy realized what had been done, a note of alarm ran through the camp. Mr. Davis had been an attorney for J. P. Morgan & Company, and had had a long career identified with corporate interests. The New York element of the convention had tried in every way to make clear to Bryan that he was not wanted. Putting two and two together, it seemed possible that a very awkward situation might develop in party circles.

The wiseacres decided that the thing to do was to try to get Charles W. Bryan, The Commoner's brother, to run as Vice President. C. W. Bryan had been governor of Nebraska, and had run some fifty thousand ahead of his ticket, going in as governor of the state with a Republican legislature, even as had Al Smith in the East.

The brother was dubious about taking the nomination, and the leaders became increasingly anxious. Charlie went to his brother with the problem, debating what he should do.

The Great Commoner was too old a hand at the political scene to be worried about what had recently taken place. He advised his brother to go on the ticket and make it that much better. Davis had a distinguished record in respect to labor, as well as being an attorney for business, and The Commoner promised to give the ticket his hearty support.

The attempt to appeal to East and West by a team which stood for conservatism in the presidency and Bryanism in the vice presidency did not work.

The opportunity to bring together Bryan and Smith, two leaders whose temperaments and outlook had much in common, even though wide apart in tradition, had passed.

Once again the party found itself far from the Democratic millennium where in peace the tiger and the donkey shall lie down together.

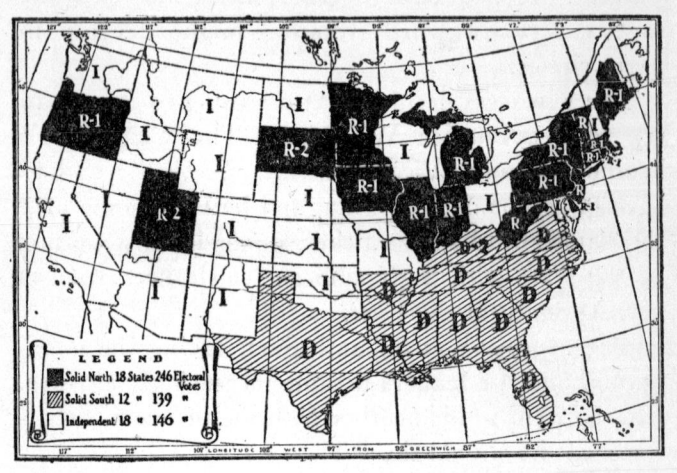

POLITICAL MAP OF THE UNITED STATES 1896-1924

*As indicated by the legend there is a solid North more extensive than the solid South.*
*The figures —1, —2, etc., indicate that once or twice the state has not been of the dominant complexion.*
*Several states are listed as solid Republican, even though they have been Democratic twice, because those two times were due first to the split in the Republican party caused by Roosevelt in 1912, and second to the deep-reaching war issue in 1916.*
*New Hampshire, while usually considered a Republican state, is listed here as Independent because it went Democratic in 1916 though in the midst of a territory which went Republican.*
*Note tabulation of the three groups opposite, as well as table on succeeding pages.*

# THE COMMONER AND AL SMITH

## POLITICAL MAP OF THE UNITED STATES
## 1896–1924

| Solid North | No. of Electoral Votes | Solid South | No. of Electoral Votes |
|---|---|---|---|
| Connecticut | 7 | Alabama | 12 |
| Delaware | 3 | Arkansas | 9 |
| Illinois | 29 | Florida | 6 |
| Indiana | 15 | Georgia | 14 |
| Iowa | 13 | Kentucky | 13 |
| Maine | 6 | Louisiana | 10 |
| Massachusetts | 18 | Mississippi | 10 |
| Michigan | 15 | North Carolina | 12 |
| Minnesota | 12 | South Carolina | 9 |
| New Jersey | 14 | Tennessee | 12 |
| New York | 45 | Texas | 20 |
| Oregon | 5 | Virginia | 12 |
| Pennsylvania | 38 | | |
| Rhode Island | 5 | | 139 |
| South Dakota | 5 | | |
| Utah | 4 | | |
| Vermont | 4 | | |
| West Virginia | 8 | | |
| | 246 | | |

| Independent | No. of Electoral Votes |
|---|---|
| Arizona (2 R—2 D) | 3 |
| California (6 R—1 Pro—1 D) | 13 |
| Colorado (3 R—5 D) | 6 |
| Idaho (4 R—4 D) | 4 |
| Kansas (5 R—3 D) | 10 |
| Maryland (4 R—3 D) | 8 |
| Missouri (4 R—4 D) | 18 |
| Montana (4 R—4 D) | 4 |
| Nebraska (4 R—4 D) | 8 |
| Nevada (3 R—5 D) | 3 |
| New Hampshire (6 R—3 D) | 4 |
| New Mexico (2 D—2 R) | 3 |
| North Dakota (6 R—2 D) | 5 |
| Ohio (6 R—2 D) | 24 |
| Oklahoma (4 D—1 R) | 10 |
| Washington (5 R—2 D—1 Pro) | 7 |
| Wisconsin (6 R—1 D—1 LaF) | 13 |
| Wyoming (5 R—3 D) | 3 |
| | 146 |

TOTAL ELECTORAL VOTES . . . . . . . . . . . . . 531
NEEDED TO ELECT . . . . . . . . . . . . . . . . 266

# BRYAN, THE GREAT COMMONER
## PRESIDENTIAL ELECTIONS, 1884-1924

(NOTE: The basis of this tabulation is the *electoral* vote of the respective states. Strictly speaking there is no popular vote for president. Where such is recorded it is actually the highest vote for any elector on either side. Sometimes the popularity of one elector will give him the highest popular vote even though the state chooses the majority of its electors from the opposing party.)

| STATE | '84 | '88 | '92 | '96 | '00 | '04 | '08 | '12 | '16 | '20 | '24 |
|---|---|---|---|---|---|---|---|---|---|---|---|
| Alabama...... | D | D | D | D | D | D | D | D | D | D | D |
| Arizona...... | .. | .. | .. | .. | .. | .. | .. | D | D | R | R |
| Arkansas...... | D | D | D | D | D | D | D | D | D | D | D |
| California..... | R | R | D | R | R | R | R | Pro. | D | R | R |
| Colorado...... | R | R | Pop. | D | D | R | D | D | D | R | R |
| Connecticut... | D | D | D | R | R | R | R | D | R | R | R |
| Delaware..... | D | D | D | R | R | R | R | D | R | R | R |
| Florida....... | D | D | D | D | D | D | D | D | D | D | D |
| Georgia....... | D | D | D | D | D | D | D | D | D | D | D |
| Idaho......... | .. | .. | Pop. | D | D | R | R | D | D | R | R |
| Illinois........ | R | R | D | R | R | R | R | D | R | R | R |
| Indiana....... | D | R | D | R | R | R | R | D | R | R | R |
| Iowa......... | R | R | R | R | R | R | R | D | R | R | R |
| Kansas....... | R | R | Pop. | D | R | R | R | D | D | R | R |
| Kentucky..... | D | D | D | R | D | D | D | D | D | D | D |
| Louisiana..... | D | D | D | D | D | D | D | D | D | D | D |
| Maine........ | R | R | R | R | R | R | R | D | R | R | R |
| Maryland..... | D | D | D | R | R | D* | D* | D | D | R | R |
| Massachusetts. | R | R | R | R | R | R | R | D | R | R | R |
| Michigan..... | R | R | R | R | R | R | R | Pro. | R | R | R |
| Minnesota.... | R | R | R | R | R | R | R | Pro. | R | R | R |

D—Democratic.
R—Republican.
Pop.—Populist.
Pro.—Progressive.
*—Republicans polled the highest popular vote in Maryland in 1904 and 1908, that is to say the elector who had the highest vote was Republican, but a majority of the Democratic electors were elected and hence the state is given in the Democratic column.

In presidential years emphasis is sometimes laid on the possibility of splitting the electoral vote. In such cases, however, the minority has never benefited largely. California, for example, gave one electoral vote to the Republicans in 1892, one to the Democrats in 1896, and two to the Democrats in 1912.

[ 370 ]

# THE COMMONER AND AL SMITH
## PRESIDENTIAL ELECTIONS, 1884-1924

| STATE | '84 | '88 | '92 | '96 | '00 | '04 | '08 | '12 | '16 | '20 | '24 |
|---|---|---|---|---|---|---|---|---|---|---|---|
| Mississippi.... | D | D | D | D | D | D | D | D | D | D | D |
| Missouri..... | D | D | D | D | D | R | R | D | D | R | R |
| Montana...... | .. | .. | R | D | D | R | R | D | D | R | R |
| Nebraska..... | R | R | R | D | R | R | D | D | D | R | R |
| Nevada....... | R | R | Pop. | D | D | R | D | D | D | R | R |
| New Hampshire | R | R | R | R | R | R | R | D | D | R | R |
| New Jersey.... | D | D | D | R | R | R | R | D | R | R | R |
| New Mexico... | .. | .. | .. | .. | .. | .. | .. | D | D | R | R |
| New York..... | D | R | D | R | R | R | R | D | R | R | R |
| North Carolina | D | D | D | D | D | D | D | D | D | D | D |
| North Dakota. | .. | .. | Pop.† | R | R | R | R | D | D | R | R |
| Ohio......... | R | R | R | R | R | R | R | D | D | R | R |
| Oklahoma..... | .. | .. | .. | .. | .. | .. | D | D | D | R | D |
| Oregon....... | R | R | R | R | R | R | R | R | R | R | R |
| Pennsylvania.. | R | R | R | R | R | R | R | Pro. | R | R | R |
| Rhode Island.. | R | R | R | R | R | R | R | D | R | R | R |
| South Carolina. | D | D | D | D | D | D | D | D | D | D | D |
| South Dakota. | .. | .. | R | D | R | R | R | Pro. | R | R | R |
| Tennessee..... | D | D | D | D | D | D | D | D | D | R | D |
| Texas........ | D | D | D | D | D | D | D | D | D | D | D |
| Utah......... | .. | .. | .. | D | R | R | R | R | D | R | R |
| Vermont...... | R | R | R | R | R | R | R | R | R | R | R |
| Virginia....... | D | D | D | D | D | D | D | D | D | D | D |
| Washington... | .. | .. | R | D | R | R | R | Pro. | D | R | R |
| West Virginia.. | D | D | D | R | R | R | R | D | R | R | R |
| Wisconsin..... | R | R | D | R | R | R | R | D | R | R | LaF. |
| Wyoming..... | .. | .. | R | D | R | R | D | D | R | R |

D—Democratic.
R—Republican.
Pop.—Populist.
Pro.—Progressive.
†—Electoral vote divided R. 1, D. 1, Pop. 1, with Populists having largest popular vote.

## CHAPTER XIX

### THE HOLY WAR

New Gods are crowned in the city,
Their flowers have broken your rods.
    *Hymn to Proserpine.*—SWINBURNE

STRANGE times, strange days! The Great Commoner sat on his ample veranda at Miami looking over his estate with its well-clipped lawns and its tropical palms. His wealth in the tax assessor's books exceeded one million dollars. From the standpoint of the taxpayer, whose virtues he had been extolling in the past few years, nothing more was needed to fill his days with comfort, unless it might be the privilege of paying taxes on a second million.

But for Bryan to have money was only another of the ironic touches which fate had added to his career. It was not that he despised money as such, but it was a thing about which he cared little. In fact, it had increased and multiplied to that extent largely because his wants were simple, and he never indulged in display of riches.

But the taxpayer was not content, because being a taxpayer was the thing in which he himself was least interested. Democracy, his Democratic party, had gone down to its second colossal defeat since the

War. They had treated him as a has-been at the New York Convention. Well, the results had not indicated that those who managed the affair were so much wiser than the one whose leadership they had brushed aside. Was the political state, after all, the center of the people's liberties? If his voice was no longer heard in the councils of the party, he had the satisfaction at least that most of the policies which he had championed had become the policies of the nation. The income tax, his provisions in the Federal Reserve Bill, the direct election of senators, the Prohibition Act, the Thirty Peace Treaties, his safeguards in the Banking Act—a good deal for one lifetime.

And yet the world did not seem right. The old ways, the old simplicities were gone. The population was moving toward the cities, and the infidelism of the city was sweeping out into all corners of the country.

He had been leading his fight against Evolution, against teaching it in the colleges, against the proclaiming of it in the state universities and schools.

He did not deny the practical uses of science, but when these guessers invaded the field of the origin of man, they struck at the roots of his essential dignity. In place of a man formed in the image of God, they brought the theory that he was descended from the animals. Growing bolder, many of them taught it as a fact rather than a theory.

And this was what they were offering in place of the religion which had been the comfort of the pioneers who had dared to blaze their way through a wilderness and erect a new civilization. The God of his fathers had built the country which he knew and he would acknowledge allegiance to no other.

All around him there were signs that the new influences were winning their way. True that he had thousands at his Bible Class in Miami every Sunday; true that wherever he spoke the churches and the Chautauqua tents were crowded, but he knew that this represented but a fraction of the world opinion. In his own religious denomination, Fosdick was being permitted to occupy a prominent pulpit. At the state university at Lincoln, where he had once had enough support to name as its President Benjamin Andrews of Brown, there at the university the influence of Evolution was in the ascendency. Morrill, his old friend and supporter, had given the money for a laboratory in which there were elaborate exhibits concerning the origin of man.

Did they not see that their Evolution failed to explain the essence of the human spirit? Did they not see that it broke down that support of the individual soul—the support of an Almighty and Personal Father, which made the common man able to defy any tyrant, trust, overlord or oppressor—confident that all would ultimately be equalized before the Great White Throne!

As valiantly as the negroes of San Domingo made voodoo against the Emperor Jones, and as bravely as the Church of the Middle Ages protected the common man from the feudal barons, Bryan had

## La Paloma
(The Dove)

S. YRADIER

*In his later years this was Mr. Bryan's favorite piece of music. He never tired of hearing it either in instrumental or vocal form.*

been calling to his people not to be misled by the *ignis fatuus* of a half-baked, unproved theory which would strip them of the protection of the Everlasting Arm.

America, who had rejected him many times only to follow his views in the long run, was turning to him in his aging years an inattentive shoulder. If one must choose between service and entertainment, he had held early in his life, service was the better choice. And he had served long. His father had been short-lived and his father's father before him. He knew that there were not many days left. He didn't let Mary know that he felt that way, but he often had to remind Charlie; good Charlie, who had been his organizer, his mainstay through everything. Charlie was still planning how Brother Will would do this and that, and put Democracy on its feet again. He had to remind Charlie to leave him out of the picture.

But it was humdrum to close one's days like this. All right for some folks to sit by the fire and watch the embers fade. A soldier wants to keep going, keep going. . . . In the midst of this quiet, this suspension of affairs in The Great Commoner's life, he received on a bright May morning of 1925 this letter:

We have been trying to get in touch with you by wire to ask you to become associated with us in the prosecution of the case of the State against J. T. Scopes, charged with the violation of the Anti-Evolution Law, but our wires did not reach you.

## THE HOLY WAR

We will consider it a great honor to have you with us in this prosecution.

It was a gift from heaven; in The Great Commoner's eyes, perhaps a direct message from heaven. He wired his acceptance, and the fight was on.

The news rang round the world. What had started out as a petty case in a little Tennessee village (originating, it was later found, as a publicity stunt) became a *cause célèbre*. Bryan was going to try Evolution before the world. Every paper in the nation and all the leading publications throughout the entire world sprang to attention. The old chorus of detractors were at it again, joined by some new voices. They called him a publicity seeker, a bigot, an ignoramus, and a has-been. They pointed out that he was a forgotten nobody, but gave him the place of greatest prominence in their sheets which had to do with the news of the world.

George Bernard Shaw in London said: "Let America look to it and let the newspapers and pulpits of Tennessee rally to their duty, lest their State become a mere reservation of morons and moral cowards."

Mencken could be heard screaming from the rabbit warrens of Baltimore. The *Nation* and the New York *World* were reunited in their familiar chorus of denouncing the man from Nebraska.

But the abuse was of second-rate character. The Great Commoner had lived through the days of '96 and 1900, when voices were more lusty and less shrill. It looked as though the fight might not prove worthy of his efforts.

Then the word came that Darrow would appear for the defense. Nothing could have been more right and no one realized this more than Mr. Bryan.

Clarence Darrow! What a worthy antagonist, and what a history was underlying the lives of the two men! Darrow had been the partner of Bryan's old friend and supporter, Governor Altgeld. Darrow had defended the Chicago anarchists in the nineties, and Altgeld had pardoned them, believing their guilt unproved. Bryan as the friend of Altgeld and Darrow had suffered from the incubus of the Chicago case in the '96 campaign.

If their ways had parted, they nevertheless had much in common, not only in sympathies but in experiences. When Altgeld died, Doctor Frank Crane had preached the sermon, Clarence Darrow had given the eulogy, and Bryan had spoken at the grave. Darrow's novel, *Farmington,* had been advertised and reviewed in *The Commoner,* and read by many of the Bryan followers. Darrow had been a delegate to the Democratic National Convention in 1904, there seconding the nomination of William Randolph Hearst, at a time when The Peerless Leader had none too adroitly sidestepped a political alliance with the Hearst forces.

The appearance of Darrow in the trial meant that the fundamental issues would be faced. He was an agnostic. There would be no halfway attempts to indicate that Evolution and evangelical Christianity could go hand in hand. It would be the word of science against the literal word of the Bible. Bryan went forth eagerly to meet the issue, and he knew that he would be met head on.

Millions of persons all over the world, who had laid their religion on a shelf and not given it a thought since childhood, awoke to a discussion of what it was all about. The world stirred from its preoccupation with radio, automobiles, Mary and Doug, tax reduction, and the myriad other items within the five miles of ether surrounding the globe, to wonder about the origin and destiny of man.

On his arrival in Dayton, The Great Commoner addressed the local Progressive Club before the trial opened. He stated the issue definitely and without equivocation.

"If Evolution wins, Christianity goes," he said to the natives of this village of 1,700 souls, and the wires carried his words around the world, "not suddenly, of course, but gradually, for the two cannot stand together.

"Heretofore, Evolution has been like the pestilence that walketh in darkness. Hereafter, it will be like the destruction that wasteth at noon-day."

The metropolitan papers were about to treat this case and Mr. Bryan with a certain proper condescension, playing up The Peerless Leader as a cross between a tottering old man and a dangerous ignoramus. But the ignorance was not all on one side. A leading New York paper, alluding to Mr. Bryan's comparison of Evolution with the pestilence that walketh in darkness, pointed out sapiently that the Nebraskan's words were a paraphrase of Goethe.

As the crowds gathered for the trial, it was clear that there was a sharp division of the forces not merely along the line of believers and unbelievers, but between the pseudosophisticates from the big cities and the local people who were being represented to the rest of the world as backwoodsmen and mossbacks. Dayton, which read the same fashion magazines, purchased the same radio sets, bought the production of the same trade outlets as Cleveland, Ohio, or Denver, Colorado, naturally resented for itself, and on behalf of all the small towns of America, the unwarranted condescension of its visitors. Bryan, a former Secretary of State, holder of degrees from universities all over the world, a man who had been received by princes and potentates, an American citizen who dared to lecture the Czar on free speech, represented to them not only a defender of the faith, but also the attorney who had served to establish the essential dignity and validity of the civilization whereby they lived.

Some of the newspaper men gathered around the tables in Robinson's Drug Store were indeed openeyed enough to see that these natives were Americans much like every one else, and better fed and educated on the average than the inhabitants of the larger cities. Some of them wrote this to their papers. It was a gathering of well-known names in the newspaper and magazine world. It included William G. Shepherd, Frank R. Kent, H. L.

Mencken, Joseph W. Krutch, Rollin Lynde Hartt and others, most of them appearing unofficially for the defense. In fact, there was very little effort on the part of most of the correspondents for a dispassionate reporting of the trial. Krutch approached the trial with this opinion of The Peerless Leader, which he had written for the *Nation*: "Driven from politics and journalism because of obvious intellectual incompetence, become bally-hoo for Boom Town real estate in his search for lucrative employment. . . ."

Each day as the trial drew near brought its high points of excitement. Patrick Henry Callahan, who had been Director of War Work for the Knights of Columbus, offered his efforts on behalf of the prosecution. While he did not come as an official emissary of the Roman Catholic Church, the offer served as an indication of where Rome stood on the issue. This was not a little embarrassing to some of the Klan-minded persons, who wished this affair to be solely a hard-shell Protestant accomplishment. But Bryan, who was never intolerant about religious dividing lines, welcomed additional support to his cause. Counterbalancing this, Charles Francis Potter, then pastor of the West End Unitarian Church in New York, arrived in town and was announced as a speaker for the First Methodist Church North. A part of the congregation of this body threatened to split the church if Mr. Potter spoke, with the result that Mr. Potter refused to create a situation which would be locally painful and withdrew his acceptance of the invitation.

More like a county fair than a trial of either faith or science was the scene of the opening of this singular event. The main street leading to the Court Square was lined on either side with improvised soda and sandwich stands. Interspersed with these were stalls of religious books, and an occasional counter of watermelons. The green lawn surrounding the Court House was jammed with sightseers in summer attire, crowding as near as possible toward the windows and arguing with the doorkeeper for admittance. The Court House itself looked as though it had been designed by a Congressman. It was a brick building with a stone base, having arched windows on the first floor and square-cornered windows on the upper floors. At one corner it had a square tower surmounted by an octagonal belfry, and capped with a pointed roof. To one part of the tower was affixed a stone balcony. The total effect was a mixture of Moorish and Wesleyan Methodist.

Inside of the Court House every seat was taken, and, in fact, after the jury panel, the attorneys for both sides, and the press had been accommodated, there was room for very few besides. The atmosphere was a good deal that of a camp meeting or of a summer-time political rally. Judge Raulston presiding in a Palm Beach suit permitted counsel and the audience to remove coats. Mr. Bryan sat up forward toward the right of the judge, wearing an open-neck white shirt, and waving a palm-leaf fan. There he sat through most of the event like a large, impassive Buddha, dominating the scene, yet arising only at rare intervals during the trial to make his voice heard. As the argument advanced, the eyes of the press and of the audience turned continually to The Commoner to see how he was taking the progress of events.

The opening details were soon cleared away. Those present learned that there was the following statute on the law books of Tennessee:

> Be it enacted, by the General Assembly of the State of Tennessee, that it shall be unlawful for any teacher in any of the universities, normals, and all other public schools in the State, which are supported in whole or in part by the public school funds of the State to teach the theory that denies the story of the divine creation of man as taught in the Bible, and to teach instead that man has descended from a lower order of animals.

But what was this theory which challenged the Bible? The caption for the act made this more clear, though, as Mr. Darrow pointed out, it was a singular practice to make the caption of an act more inclusive than the act itself. Here is how the caption appeared on the books:

> Public Act, Chapter 37, 1925, an act prohibiting the teaching of the Evolution theory in all the universities, normals, and all the public schools of Tennessee, which are supported in whole or in part by the public school funds of the State, and to prescribe penalties for the violation thereof.

The State alleged that John Thomas Scopes, teacher in a public school of Dayton, Tennessee, had violated this act. The first day, Friday, was taken up with the reading of the indictment and selection of the jurors. Mr. Bryan had nothing to say.

Court adjourned until Monday, and on Monday Mr. Bryan learned the caliber of the opposition that he must face. Darrow led the charge. Here was no dapper city fellow with an assortment of smart phrases and callow thinking which could be easily swept aside. Here was, in fact, a man of singular mental power, a thick-set rugged frame, a head thrust forward in earnestness, a face kindly toward the individual, but merciless in its pursuit of logic, a seamed, dauntless countenance, barren of, and destructive of, illusion.

The Great Commoner knew that Darrow, in tearing the comforts of faith away from others, sought no blanket of illusion for himself. His argument would be as cold and relentless as the agnosticism which he espoused. Yet, the presentation of Darrow was electric not because of its analysis but because of the challenging faith of a different order with which it concluded. When Mr. Darrow rose from his chair on that bright Monday morning to move the dismissal of the indictment, it was immediately clear to the audience that he had out-commoned The Commoner. Bryan had on a white shirt; Darrow's shirt was yellow. The Commoner wore a belt, but the Chicago lawyer's trousers were sustained by bright blue galluses. The attorney argued the lack of definiteness of the indictment and the discrepancy between the caption of the law and the wording underneath, and then described since the beginning of the Republic the history of religious freedom in the United States, pointing to the words of Jefferson, alluding to the terrorism of the Klan. Calling upon the historic liberty of Tennessee, he turned toward the one-time leader of freedom and issued his challenge:

"If to-day you can take a thing like Evolution and make it a crime to teach it in the public schools, to-morrow you can make it a crime to teach it in the private schools, and next year you can make it a crime to teach it to the hustings or in the church. Soon you may set Catholic against Protestant, and Protestant against Protestant, and try to foist your own religion upon the minds of men.

"If you can do one you can do the other. . . .

"It is the setting of man against man and creed against creed, until with flying banners and beating drums we are marching backward to the glorious ages of the Sixteenth Century when bigots lighted fagots to burn the men who dared to bring any intelligence and enlightenment and culture to the human mind."

Mr. Bryan said nothing.

The court refused to dismiss the indictment, though a day passed before this opinion was determined upon. On Wednesday afternoon the court instructed each side to present its case, now that the decision had been reached that the trial should go on under the indictment. The defense soon made it clear that the event was not so much a trial of Mr. Scopes as it was a trial of Mr. Bryan and the particular type of religion for which he stood. The Peerless Leader sat immovable while he listened to the renewed attacks upon his fairness, integrity, and consistency of purpose. If the shafts went home he showed it infrequently, but continued only to wave his palm-leaf fan. He too had his ideas of the issues present in the trial and was ready to state them in due season. Darrow had given his confession of faith the day before, and it fell to Dudley Field Malone, former member of the Department of State when Mr. Bryan was chief, and defender of radical causes, to lead the attack for the defense. Mr. Malone alone of those present at the trial refused to remove his coat, feeling the need perhaps to uphold the sartorial dignity of New York City.

Mr. Malone stated the view of the defense.

"So that there shall be no misunderstanding," he said, "and that no one shall be able to misinterpret or misrepresent our position, we wish to state at the beginning of this case the defense believes that there is a direct conflict between the theory of Evolution and the theories of the creation as set forth in the Book of Genesis."

Mr. Bryan smiled with satisfaction.

"But we shall make it perfectly clear," Mr. Malone continued, "that while this is the view of the defense, we shall show by the testimony of men learned in science and theology that there are millions of people who believe in Evolution and in the story of creation as set forth in the Bible and who find no conflict between the two. The defense maintains that this is a matter of faith and interpretation. . . .

"The defense maintains that there is a clear distinction between God, the church, the Bible, Christianity, and Mr. Bryan."

The audience turned its eyes to The Peerless Leader, who himself smiled at the contrast suggested by Mr. Malone. But he became attentive, and his fan moved restlessly, as the Irish lawyer from New York quoted from an introduction to a book on Thomas Jefferson by a great political leader.

" 'In the preamble to the statute for religious freedom, Jefferson put first that which I want to speak of last. Was the regulation of the opinion of men on religious questions by law contrary to the laws of God and the plans of God? He pointed out that God had it in his power to control man's mind and body, but that he did not see fit to coerce the mind or the body into obedience to even the Divine Will; and that if God Himself was not willing to use coercion to force man to accept certain religious views, man, uninspired and liable to error, ought not to use the means that Jehovah would not apply. Jefferson realized that our religion was a religion of love and not a religion of force.' "

"These words," Mr. Malone pointed out, "were the words of Bryan, and the defense appeals from the Fundamentalist Bryan of to-day to the Modernist Bryan of yesterday."

The State's attorney objected to the personal attack. The court sustained him and asked Mr. Malone not to mention Mr. Bryan's name again. The New York lawyer expressed the view that Mr. Bryan was not sensitive.

For the first time during the trial The Great Commoner broke his silence. "I require no protection from the court," he said. "At the proper time I shall be able to show that my position now differs not at all from my position in those days."

When the time came for the introduction of proof, the State called Mr. Scopes, who admitted that he had taught from Hunter's *Biology*. The State then called Howard Morgan, fourteen years of age, a pupil of Mr. Scopes, who testified as to the instruction. Mr. Darrow examined the boy and triumphantly brought out in the testimony that this instruction had not done the boy any harm. But if Mr. Darrow was satisfied on this point, it might also have been observed that Mr. Bryan was smiling to himself.

On Thursday the defense sought to introduce its scientific witnesses and the court took the matter under advisement.

At this point there was a stir among the counsel for prosecution, and Mr. William Jennings Bryan rose to protest against the admission of scientific testimony.

It was his single speech of the trial and he lost

no opportunity in coming back at what had been said before.

"The principal attorney has often suggested," he said, looking over at Mr. Darrow, "that I am the archconspirator and that I am responsible for the presence of this case, and I have almost been credited with leadership of the ignorance and bigotry which he thinks could alone inspire a law like this."

He raised the question that if the defense were really the champions of liberty that they claimed to be, and if they felt that this law was so hazardous to human liberty, they would have taken pains to watch the course of the state legislatures and appear in opposition to such laws before they got on the statute books.

Mr. Bryan maintained that religious liberty for adults and the teaching of specific theories as accepted facts in the public schools were two different issues. He pointed out that Tennessee prohibited the teaching of the Bible in the public schools in order to keep religious prejudice out of them. He maintained that if this were true it were only equitable that a theory hostile to the Bible should not be forced upon the public by a minority.

And then he turned to the defense and asked what assurance they had to offer that their hypothesis represented the truth.

"Evolution is not a theory," said The Commoner, "but a hypothesis. Huxley said it could not rise to the dignity of a theory until they had found some species that had developed according to the hypothesis, and at that time there had never been found a single species the origin of which could be traced to another species.

"And it is true to-day. Never have they traced one single species to any other. And yet they call us ignoramuses and bigots because we do not throw away our Bible. . . . They not only have no proof, but they cannot find the beginning. . . .

"They take up life as a mystery that nobody can explain, and they want you to let them commence there and ask no questions.

"They do not dare to tell you that it began with God and do not dare to tell you that it ended with God.

"They do not deal with the problems of life. They do not teach the great science of how to live. And yet they would undermine the faith of these little children in that God who stands back of everything and whose promise we have that we shall live with Him forever by and by."

It was 1896, 1904 and 1912 repeating itself, but this time the issues were eternal. The Commoner's being was infused with his message. Every one in the audience was sitting on the edge of his chair. Even those who understood him least and were professionally opposed to him felt the impact of his personality. "His eyes fascinated me," Mencken wrote three years later. "I watched them all day long. They were blazing points of hatred. They glittered like occult and sinister gems. Now and then they wandered to me, and I got my share, for

*Photograph from Wide World Photos*

CLARENCE DARROW AND W. J. BRYAN AT DAYTON

*Mr. Darrow's suspenders and Mr. Bryan's fan were featured in reports of the trial.*

## THE HOLY WAR

my reports of the trial had come back to Dayton, and he had read them. It was like coming under fire."

Mr. Mencken flattered himself. The Great Commoner's zeal was directed against his vision of the Great Adversary, not against the Baltimore journalist who happened to be in the room. And it was directed against Darrow, not the Darrow of many years' friendship but the Darrow who was there to plead for Error under the guise of liberty. The Commoner's eyes were ablaze, too, not with hatred but fervor, and with the knowledge that Darrow had led himself into a *cul-de-sac*.

The day before the Chicago attorney had examined little Howard Morgan and had attempted to bring out the fact that the doctrine of Evolution had not hurt him. The implication was that school children were able to sift truth from untruth, and that right teaching would prevail of itself no matter what doctrine might be offered to the pupils by the instructors.

Had Mr. Darrow always felt that freedom of instruction had no evil consequences? Had he always contended for the sanctity and protection of teachers in offering all philosophies and hypotheses to young minds? Mr. Bryan knew that he had not.

Suddenly in his oration The Great Commoner leveled his finger at Mr. Darrow and said, "It is this doctrine that gives us Nietzsche, the only great authority who tried to carry this to its logical conclusion."

The audience drew in its breath sharply. It sensed what was coming.

"We have the testimony of my distinguished friend from Chicago," said Bryan in his ringing voice, "in his speech in the Loeb-Leopold Case . . . and have him pleading that because Leopold read Nietzsche and adopted Nietzsche's philosophy of the superman, he is not responsible for the taking of human life.

"That is the doctrine, my friends, that they have tried to bring into existence. They commenced in high schools with their foundation in the Evolutionary theory, and we have the word of the distinguished lawyer that Nietzsche is more read than any other philosopher, and more than any other in a hundred years, and then the statement of that distinguished man that the teachings of Nietzsche made Leopold a murderer."

Mr. Darrow sprang to his feet.

"Your Honor, I want to object," he cried, "there is not a word of truth in it. Nietzsche never taught that anyhow. There was not a word of criticism of the professors nor of the colleges in reference to that, nor was there a word of criticism of the theological colleges when that clergyman in Southern Illinois killed his wife in order to marry some one else."

Mr. Bryan: "We do not ask to have taught in the schools any doctrine that teaches a clergyman killed his wife."

Mr. Darrow (to the court): "I want to take an exception."

Mr. Bryan (indicating the report of the Loeb-Leopold trial, which he has in his hand, wherein Mr. Darrow had defended two murderers): "I will read what you said in that speech here."

Mr. Darrow: "If you will read it aloud."

Mr. Bryan: "I will read that part I want; you read the rest."

Mr. Darrow: . . . "I want to object to injecting any other case into this proceeding, no matter what the case is. I want to take exception to it if the court permits it. . . ."

Mr. Bryan: "I want to find out what he said, where he says the professors and universities were more responsible than Leopold was."

Mr. Darrow: "All right, I will show you what I said, that the professors and universities were not responsible at all."

Mr. Bryan: "Here it is, page 84" (reading Mr. Darrow's plea). " 'I will guarantee that you can go down to the University of Chicago to-day, into its big library, and find over 1,000 volumes of Nietzsche and I am sure I speak moderately. If this boy is to blame for this, where did he get it? Is there any blame attached because some one took Nietzsche's philosophy seriously and fashioned his life on it? And there is no question in this case but what it is true. Then who is to blame? The University would be more to blame than he is. The scholars of the world would be more to blame than he is. The publishers of the world—and Nietzsche's books are published by one of the biggest publishers in the world—are more to blame than he. Your Honor, it is hardly fair to hang a nineteen-year-old boy for the philosophy that was taught him at the University.'"

Mr. Darrow: "Will you let me see it?"

Mr. Bryan: "Oh yes, but let me have it back."

There was an exchange between The Commoner and the Chicago attorney on the possible effect of Evolution on young Howard Morgan.

The Peerless Leader proposed to continue to follow up his advantage.

"It is a necessary caution," he said, "to write 'Poison' on the outside of this stuff, so that it will not be administered without even having taken this precaution. It is the parents that are doing that, and here we have the testimony of the greatest criminal lawyer in the United States defending one of the most dastardly crimes in the United States, stating that the universities. . . ."

Mr. Darrow: "I object, your Honor, to an injection of that case into this one."

Judge Raulston (after argument on this point): "Suppose you get through with Colonel Darrow as soon as you can, Mr. Bryan."

Mr. Bryan: "Yes, I will, I think I am through with the Colonel now."

"The Bible is the word of God," cried Mr. Bryan, turning from his attack upon the defense, and proclaiming the affirmation for which the prosecution stood. "The Bible is the only expression of man's hope of salvation. The Bible, the word of the Son of God, the Saviour of the world, born of the Virgin Mary, crucified and risen again—that Bible is not going to be driven out of this court by experts who come hundreds of miles to testify that they can reconcile Evolution with its ancestor in the jungle and man made by God in His image and put here for a purpose as part of the Divine plan."

The issue had been stated, when Mr. Bryan concluded, and nothing further in the trial altered the fundamental positions of either side. Mr. Darrow put The Great Commoner on the witness stand and questioned him on his beliefs in the literal meaning of various Biblical passages. The trial closed before Mr. Bryan could in turn put Mr. Darrow on the witness stand and ask from him evidence of the hypotheses of science. Science or its followers were not to be disturbed. The trial came to an abrupt close on Tuesday, the twenty-first of July, after all the admissible testimony had been introduced, and as the defense did not contest the fact that Mr. Scopes had taught Evolution, the defendant was adjudged guilty. The defense made great flourishes of appealing, but the case was never carried higher. The Baltimore *Sun* provided the five hundred dollar bonds for Mr. Scopes during the period of appeal, and the great drama was over.

Over in fact, but not in its effect.

The Great War Horse had fought his last tremendous battle, but had the cause been as true and clear as he had seen it? Did there not press at last upon his mind some hint of the danger that came from entrusting power to a vast machine, even when that machine was manned by the majority?

The honesty which always came at last into his reflections, even when it disturbed his preferences and desires, crept in again at this last moment.

On an automobile trip with Mrs. Bryan following the trial, he discussed the issues, and Mary Baird Bryan brought up the narrow margin between forbidding the teaching of Evolution as a fact and the encroachment on individual religious belief. She pointed out the hazard that religious zeal might enter in and become intolerance.

"Well," said Mr. Bryan, "I have not made that mistake yet, have I?"

"You are all right, so far," she answered reassuringly, "but will you be able to keep to this narrow path?"

"I think I can," he said, with a happy smile.

"But," Mrs. Bryan persisted, "can you control your followers?"

More gravely, he answered, "I think I can."

## CHAPTER XX

### IS BRYANISM DEAD?

*No man ever wetted clay and then left it, as if there would be bricks by chance and fortune.*
—PLUTARCH

THE Miami house is sold to strangers. In Lincoln, too, old times have passed. On the site of the First Presbyterian Church where Bryan worshiped when he first came to the city stands the new Cornhusker Hotel, with marble lobby, pool of trout in the foyer, and a saxophone orchestra in its dining room.

The simple Westminster edifice where he attended next has been supplanted by a quarter-million dollar building having a huge interior with a wide rostrum on which are seated every Sunday the pastor and an octet of well-fed deacons and elders. The little neighborhood Methodist church at Normal, which he attended after he built Fairview, remains as it was in The Commoner's day, a small frame structure set in a field, equipped inside with cushionless pews and meager pulpit furniture. But this congregation, too, is planning for grander days.

Fairview stands mute, in its architecture a symbol of its times, and in its present use an emblem of the man who built it. It is not dead. The orchards are still bearing. The fields are sown for the harvest. New buildings are being erected on all sides of it. Activity teems around it. The Bryan Memorial Hospital is being built on the historic home site.

Within a week after the Dayton trial, on July 26, 1925, The Great Commoner passed on. He had been to Chattanooga to correct proofs on the manifesto which he was to issue on the evolution case. He had come back in the forenoon to Dayton to rejoin Mrs. Bryan and to make arrangements for their vacation. At the noonday dinner he was in a happy frame of mind. While in Chattanooga, feeling exhausted by the efforts of the trial he had gone to a doctor for examination. All the tests, he was informed, indicated that he was in good normal condition.

"According to that," he said, telling Mrs. Bryan the good news, "I have several more years to live."

After dinner he made several long distance telephone calls with respect to their traveling plans and then laid down for a nap. Mrs. Bryan went out on the side porch and studied touring maps. As the afternoon wore on she was disturbed that Mr. Bryan did not join her.

"Go in and wake Mr. Bryan," she said to their chauffeur at last. "Such a long nap will break his rest to-night."

But The Great Commoner did not waken.

His final ride back to Washington was a triumphal march such as had never been his lot during his lifetime. Yet it was reminiscent of his first campaign.

## IS BRYANISM DEAD?

At every little station, at all hours of the day or night, great throngs came down to greet his funeral train, bringing wreaths. At Jefferson City, Tennessee, a quartet of young men stood by the railroad tracks in the darkness and sang "One Sweetly Solemn Thought" while thousands stood with bared heads.

He was buried, according to his wish, at Arlington. Arlington, the national military cemetery. By what right? Was he not Colonel William Jennings Bryan of the Third Nebraska Volunteers Regiment? Had there been an American Westminster Abbey, he might have chosen that. He regarded war as an outworn measure, but the emblem of the sword and the resting place of the nation's heroes were an appropriate surrounding. In the final test, he returned to that quality which was most himself. The mystic was submerged, the hand of Tolstoy faded from the picture, the gallant fighter remained.

His had been a lifetime of conflict:

He began his fight for the popular election of senators in 1890, and signed the proclamation of this amendment in 1913.

He championed the income tax law in 1892, put it continuously into his party platform, and as Secretary of State put the official seal on it in 1913.

He broke with the strongest elements of his party to campaign for national prohibition.

He fought government by injunction, and obtained a law guaranteeing the right of trial by jury in contempt cases.

He was the author of the law compelling publicity of campaign expenditures.

He demanded regulation of the railroads ten years before Roosevelt took up the cry.

He drew up the Thirty Peace Treaties under which the United States took a new step toward world peace.

These are but a few entries on the record. He was the impresario of the rights of the common man, sometimes originating the bill, often organizing lost causes and bringing them to the forefront, frequently bearing the burden of the campaign before the time was ripe and ultimately seeing others carry off the honor of the victory.

The Commoner has gone and new times have come. The structure of the nation has changed. The rural regions and the small town have a smaller percentage of the population. There is not the same cleavage between country and city, between finance and the public. The thirty years of Bryanism, with many of his projects put into effect by Roosevelt and Wilson, have served to distribute more equably the balances of power. The freebooting practices of '96 are no longer possible to the same degree and in the same way. The people have a feeling of being sophisticated. The automobile, the radio, the motion picture, electricity, mail order houses, and chain stores have served to inform and standardize all sections of the country.

The influence of the political state which was established in an agricultural and trading era has

### HE'S ALWAYS SEEING THINGS

From Chicago "Tribune"

No matter what ground The Great Commoner chose for his battlefield he was always on the front page and a favorite subject for the cartoonist.

become less significant. Men tend to think not in terms of Congressional districts, but in respect to industries, occupations, unions. "The interests" have become diversified in ownership, if not in control. The trusts have been "busted" not at the executive end, but by the wide distribution of shares of stock. The *laissez faire* policy has gained prestige in the nation, because in an age of skepticism the public does not want to be bothered. It feels that the old technique of government is inadequate and new standards have not been drawn.

W. Z. Ripley has stated the complexity of the post-Bryan years in his *Main Street and Wall Street:*

It has been estimated that of the 14,400,000 stockholders in the United States no fewer than 3,400,000 were added within the three years following 1917. This betokens a great incursion into the field of investment by the common people —corporate possession being shared by those of moderate and small means with the wealthy class.

The movement has been called "an economic revolution— the passing of ownership from Wall Street to Main Street." What would be the effect were these newcomers—consumers, employees, or others—to discover some day that ownership and control had parted company, each going its way as ships that pass in the night? Suppose that the ownership of many industrial plants, great and small, continues to reside all through the countryside but that the lodgment of the power of direction has shifted to the great financial centers.

We have had experience, to our sorrow, with the old sectional divisions between the East and West. Is there no smoldering spark in this matter of corporate control, which may some day flare up as a political issue of the first order?

## IS BRYANISM DEAD?

Woodrow Wilson speaking at Chattanooga in 1910 foresaw the direction that the new age was taking and took notice of the hazards which it was creating. "Liberty is always personal," he said, "always a thing inhering in individuals taken singly, never in groups, or corporations, or communities."

Bryan's contribution to his age was primarily his belief in the inherent dignity of the common man. Brought up in the tradition of Jefferson and Jackson, The Peerless Leader opposed the trespassing upon individual freedom either by socialism or by corporate aggrandizement. The modern equivalent of The Commoner's jousts would lie in the saving to the individual of a degree of control in his own destiny and personality amid the complications of a machine era.

There is no paint box of present day colors to create again that figure of purple and silver. His principles are everlasting, and to that extent another may come to be called a Great Commoner. But as a human being, as an individual, he was alone of his kind. The label that his early followers gave him suggests this. What a wealth of adoration, of personality, and of the singular timbre of his times is wrapped up in his title "The Peerless Leader."

In millions of homes throughout the nation he was a hope, a defender, and a personal godfather. The backlog of his strength in the myriad battles which he engaged upon was his devotion to his people and theirs to him.

A stranger entered a small shop in the city of

Lincoln during the summer of 1927, and inquired the way to Fairview. The storekeeper, a round-faced, stubby little man with gray hair, became eagerly alert at the newcomer's query.

"Are you for Mr. Bryan?" he asked the visitor.

The stranger, somewhat taken aback at the unexpected question, hesitated for a moment.

"I'm for him," the shopkeeper stated. "I heard him at his first big Chautauqua. There were twenty thousand there to hear him. Two hundred came on white horses. . . ." The little man's eyes looked off into the procession of the past. After a pause, he continued—"You want to go out to Fairview? Take that car marked 'Normal.'"

As the stranger turned to go out of the doorway, the storekeeper came from behind the counter and tugged at the visitor's sleeve as though there were something yet to be told.

The little man seemed as if hunting for the right words; he still held on to the sleeve; then in a quiet voice as if imparting a vital secret, he said—

"We loved him."

# BIBLIOGRAPHY

ALLEN, LESLIE H. *Bryan and Darrow at Dayton.* 1925, A. Lee and Company.

ANDREWS, E. BENJAMIN. *An Honest Dollar.* Hartford, 1894, Student Publishing Company.

ASQUITH, MARGOT. *My Impressions of America.* New York, 1922, George H. Doran Company.

BAKER, RAY STANNARD. *Woodrow Wilson, Life and Letters.* New York, 1927, Doubleday, Page & Company.

BARCUS, J. S. *The Boomerang, or Bryan's Speech with the Wind Knocked Out.* 1896, Barcus.

BEER, THOMAS. *The Mauve Decade.* New York, 1926, Alfred A. Knopf.

BRYAN, W. J. *A Tale of Two Conventions.* New York, 1912, Funk & Wagnalls.

——— *The First Battle.* 1896, W. B. Conkey.

——— *In His Image.* New York, 1922, Fleming H. Revell.

——— and BRYAN, MARY BAIRD. *Memoirs of William Jennings Bryan.* Philadelphia, 1925, John C. Winston Co.

——— *Under Other Flags.* 1904, Woodruff-Collins.

BRYAN, W. J., and TAFT, WILLIAM HOWARD. *World Peace, a Written Debate.* New York, 1917, George H. Doran Company.

——— "The Old World and Its Ways." 1907, *The Commoner.*

# BIBLIOGRAPHY

BRYCE, JAMES. *The American Commonwealth.* New York, 1909, The Macmillan Company.

CLARK, CHAMP. *My Quarter Century of American Politics.* New York, 1920, Harper & Brothers.

CROKER, RICHARD. *Political Cartoons Gathered by Their Target.* 1902, Mitchell.

DAVIS, HAYNE. *Bryan among the Peacemakers.* 1906, Progressive Publishing Company.

GALE, A. L., and KLINE, G. W. *Bryan, the Man.* 1908, Thompson Publishing Company.

GLASS, CARTER. *An Adventure in Constructive Finance.* New York, 1927, Doubleday, Page & Co.

HENDRICK, BURTON J. *Life and Letters of Walter Hines Page.* New York, 1925, Doubleday, Page & Co.

HERRICK, GENEVIEVE FORBES, and HERRICK, J. O. *Life of William Jennings Bryan.* 1925, Buxton.

HOUSTON, D. F. *Eight Years with Wilson's Cabinet.* New York, 1926, Doubleday, Page & Co.

*House Reports No. 582.* 1912, Committee on Merchant Marine and Fisheries.

LANE, FRANKLIN K. *Letters, Personal and Political,* edited by Anne W. Lane and Louise Herrick Wall. Boston, 1922, Houghton Mifflin Co.

LIPPMANN, WALTER. *American Inquisitors.* New York, The Macmillan Company.

MCELROY, ROBERT. *Grover Cleveland, the Man and Statesman.* New York, 1923, Harper & Brothers.

METCALF, RICHARD L. *Bryan, Sewall and Free Silver Free Coinage—16 to 1—Prosperity.* 1896, Edgewood.

NEWBRANCH, HARVEY W. *William Jennings Bryan, a Concise but Complete Story of His Life and Service.* 1900, University Publishing Company.

*Official Proceedings of Democratic Conventions, 1890-1928.*

# BIBLIOGRAPHY

OSBORN, HENRY FAIRFIELD. *The Earth Speaks to Bryan.* New York, 1923, Charles Scribner's Sons.

RIPLEY, W. Z. *Main Street and Wall Street.* Boston, 1927, Little, Brown & Company.

ROBERTS, GEORGE E. *Coin at School in Finance.* 1895, W. B. Conkey.

SEYMOUR, CHARLES. *The Intimate Papers of Colonel House.* Boston, 1926, Houghton, Mifflin Co.

SHIPLEY, MAYNARD. *The War on Modern Science.* New York, 1927, Alfred A. Knopf.

*Statistical Abstract of the U. S., 1921.*

STODDARD, H. L. *As I Knew Them.* New York, 1927, Harper & Brothers.

SULLIVAN, MARK. *Our Times, The United States, 1900-1925.* Vol. I. The Turn of the Century, 1926. Vol. II. America Finding Herself, 1927. New York, 1926, Charles Scribner's Sons.

THOMPSON, CHARLES WILLIS. *Party Leaders of the Time.* 1906, Dillingham.

*Treaties for the Advancement of Peace.* 1920, Carnegie Endowment for International Peace, Division of International Law.

TUMULTY, JOSEPH P. *Woodrow Wilson As I Knew Him.* Garden City, 1927, Garden City Publishing Company.

TURNER, F. J. *The Frontier in American History.* New York, 1920, Henry Holt & Company.

TUTTLE, C. R. *The New Democracy and Bryan, Its Prophet.* 1896, Kerr.

UNTERMYER, SAMUEL. *Who Is Entitled to the Credit for the Federal Reserve Act? An Answer to Carter Glass.* 1927, Pamphlet published by Mr. Untermyer.

VINCENT, HENRY. *Story of the Commonweal.* 1894, W. B. Conkey.

# BIBLIOGRAPHY

WILLIAMS, WAYNE C. *William Jennings Bryan, a Study in Political Vindication.* New York, 1923, Fleming H. Revell.

*World Almanac, 1890-1928.*

Newspapers and periodicals, especially files of *The Commoner;* Omaha *World-Herald; Nebraska State Journal;* Lincoln, Nebraska, *Star; Harper's Weekly; The Nation;* New York *World;* New York *Journal;* New York *Times; American Monthly Review of Reviews; The Literary Digest.*

## SOURCES

Neither the bibliography just given nor the notations to follow can be considered as complete source material in themselves. The data and newspaper reports vary in bias and emphasis, and have to be reconciled by study, comparison, and further inquiry. The bibliography and notations are given, however, as the indices of basic material wherein the reader interested in a special period or special incidents may find data.

### CHAPTER I

For further details of *Prinz Joachim* shipwreck see *Memoirs of William Jennings Bryan,* newspapers of November 23, 1911, and *The Commoner,* December 15, 1911. For data on the new radio law which resulted see House Report No. 582, April 20, 1912.

### CHAPTER II

More details of Bryan's early life may be found in *The First Battle,* by W. J. Bryan, in the archives of Illinois College, and in the Gale and Kline biography, which carries his career to 1908.

### CHAPTER III

Files of the Nebraska State Journal, the Metcalf biography and the Newbranch biography (the first going to 1896 and the next to 1900), give data on the pre-Congressional years. See *Congressional Record,* 1890-1894, for Bryan's activities at Washington. See also McElroy's *Grover Cleveland.*

SOURCES

For Free Silver discussion see *Our Times,* by Mark Sullivan. For Free Silver literature of the period see *An Honest Dollar,* by E. Benjamin Andrews, *Coin's Financial School,* by W. H. Harvey, *Coin at School in Finance,* by George E. Roberts.

CHAPTER IV

See files of the *Atlanta Constitution,* and other southern newspapers for 1892-1896; also files of Omaha *World-Herald,* same period. In light of these the nomination of Bryan in 1896 is seen to be more logical and expectable than many accounts of the event would indicate. *The First Battle* is the primary source of this period.

CHAPTER V

For the Yale incident see New Haven *Evening Register,* September 24, 1896, the Yale *News* and the Harvard *Crimson* during the same week.

CHAPTER VI

The Newbranch biography and the files of the *Literary Digest* give some of the best source material of the campaign.

CHAPTER VII

See *Congressional Record,* 1897-1899, for trend of official opinion in this period; also *Harper's Weekly* for extreme anti-Bryan attitude; files of *Literary Digest* for current opinion on the issues of the Spanish War and on the 1900 campaign.

CHAPTER VIII

See *Statistical Abstract of the United States* for data on price of farm products, and gold production. Accounts of

# SOURCES

European trip referred to in this chapter and of subsequent trips were carried in *The Commoner*.

### CHAPTER IX

For estimate of Bryan up to and through this period, see *Party Leaders of the Time,* by Charles Willis Thompson.

### CHAPTER X

Detailed accounts of Mr. Bryan's views on various countries are given in his book, *The World and Its Ways*. For the 1904 convention details see the Official Proceedings.

### CHAPTER XI

Data supplied by Nebraska Historical Society, and files of Nebraska *State Journal* and Lincoln *Star*.

### CHAPTER XII

A reading of all the memoirs of members of the Wilson Cabinet (see bibliography), as well as the Colonel House papers and the autobiography of Champ Clark is recommended for the study of this period and the period covered in the three succeeding chapters. See also *Memoirs of William Jennings Bryan*.

### CHAPTER XIII

Official Proceedings of this convention are valuable as indicating in more detail the variety of cross-currents with which Mr. Bryan contended. The various behind-the-scenes incidents have come from different participants, checked with the testimony of other participants in the same scenes.

### CHAPTER XIV

See especially *Memoirs of William Jennings Bryan,* and Houston's *Eight Years with Wilson's Cabinet*.

# SOURCES

### CHAPTER XV

See especially the books given in bibliography by Carter Glass, Samuel Untermyer, Colonel House, Joseph Tumulty. See also: *The Bryan Peace Treaties,* published by Carnegie Foundation for the Advancement of Peace.

### CHAPTER XVI

*Life and Letters of Walter Hines Page* (Burton J. Hendrick) and *William Jennings Bryan, A Study in Political Vindication* (Wayne Williams) give two contrasting points of view on the same events.

### CHAPTER XVII

See *In His Image,* by W. J. Bryan, and Shipiey's *The War on Modern Science.* Also newspaper files of the period (*New York Times Index*).

### CHAPTER XVIII

Files of *The Commoner* indicate in nearly every issue Bryan's friendliness toward the Roman Catholic wing of Democracy.

### CHAPTER XIX

Aside from the stenographic record of the trial the only approximately complete account is Leslie H. Allen's *Bryan and Darrow at Dayton.*

### CHAPTER XX

In addition to the Ripley book referred to in this chapter, and to Sullivan's *Our Times,* previously mentioned, it is suggested that *The Frontier in American Life,* by F. J. Turner, will serve to orient the influence of Bryan and his times.

# INDEX

A. B. C. proposals of Colonel House for Pan-American countries, 325
Acceptance speech of Bryan at Indianapolis, 1900, 140
Addams, Jane, 38
Aguinaldo, General, 128-130
Aldrich, Senator, 288
Alien land laws (California-Japan), 305, 307, 308, 311-313
Altgeld, Governor, 80, 154
*An Honest Dollar*, 74
American womanhood, 155, 350
Ancestry of William Jennings Bryan, 22
Andrews, E. Benjamin, 74, 111, 112, 122, 354, 374
Angell, Norman, 298
Anti-imperialism, Bryan issue in 1900, 140
Arlington Cemetery, Bryan buried at, 399
Article X of League of Nations, Bryan's view of, 347
Asquith, Herbert, 16
Asquith, Margot, 162, 165
Atlanta *Constitution*, foresight on Bryan's nomination, 84

Baker, Newton D., 46, 145
Baker, Ray Stannard, 225
Baldwin, Governor, of Connecticut, 248

Balfour, A. J., 74, 164
Baltimore Convention. *See* Democratic Convention of 1912.
Baltimore *Sun* offers to finance Scopes appeal, 395
Barnard College, 352
Beckham, Governor, of Kentucky, urges one-term plank for presidency, 256
Beecher, Edward, 32
"Behold a republic" speech of Bryan, 140
Belmont, August, 72, 257-262
Bennett Will Case, 158
Bernstorff, Ambassador, of Germany, position on Bryan treaties, 202
Bible, early study, 25
Bimetallism. *See* Silver coinage.
Birth of Bryan, 24
Bland, "Silver Dick," 64, 78, 154
Blockade, British, 340
Borah, W. E., 146
Boston University, 350
Bowdoin College, 355
Brown University, 74, 354
Bryan, Charles W., 122, 257, 258, 367, 376
Bryan, Grace, 158
Bryan, Judge Silas L., 20, 21, 22, 23, 32

[ 413 ]

# INDEX

Bryan, Mary Baird (Mrs. W. J.), 14, 34, 55, 93, 114, 119, 123-126, 168, 169, 172, 202, 226, 227, 260, 278-280, 281, 345, 374, 396, 398
Bryan Memorial Hospital, 398
Bryan Peace Treaties, 298-304
Bryan, Ruth, 41, 55, 158
Bryan, W. J., Jr., 162
Bryce, Ambassador James, 282, 298
Bryn Mawr College, 350, 352
Burke, Governor, of North Dakota, 248
Burleson, A. S., 340, 342
Burns, John, British Labor leader, Bryan's visit to, 166, 170

California-Japanese dispute, 305
Callahan, Patrick Henry, 381
Calvé, Emma, 148
Campaign expenditure, publicity, 400
Campaign of '96, mileage, 106
Carnegie, Andrew, 140
Carranza, 316
Carter, Mrs. Leslie, 17
Carthage, Missouri, Chautauqua event, 149
Catholic. *See* Roman Catholic Church.
Chamberlain, Joseph, 164, 165
Chamberlain, Mrs. Joseph, 169
Charleston, West Virginia, anti-Evolution campaign, 353
Chautauqua, 5, 146, 150, 404
Chicago Union League Club, 104

China, proposed loan to, 306
Chinda, Ambassador, of Japan, 298, 311, 313
Choate, Joseph, 164
Choctaw Indians, statement on Yale, 100
Church life of Bryan, 27, 50
Clark, Champ, qualifications for 1912 nomination, 230; tries to hold straddle position, 231; attends Bryan's 1911 birthday dinner, 232; gets letter from Bryan urging a more definite political stand, 233; House comments on, 237; at Jackson day dinner, 1912, 241; disappointed at Bryan's friendliness with Wilson, 242; receives telegram asking for stand on Parker chairmanship, 247; replies to Bryan wire, 248; campaign at Baltimore Convention, 257-268
Clark, Genevieve, 263
Clark, W. A., 17
Cleveland, Grover, initial difficulties with Bryan, 61; program on silver coinage, 64-66; Bryan's first attack on, 65; takes patronage from Bryan, 66; proposed gold bond issue financed by Morgan-Belmont bankers, 72; Bryan attacks on gold bond issue, 74; notes for compared with '96 total, 118
Cocked hat, Wilson's desire to knock Bryan into, 238
Cockran, Bourke, 261

[ 414 ]

## INDEX

Cockrell, Senator, Bryan supports for presidential nomination in 1904, 185
*Coin at School in Finance,* 76
*Coin's Financial School,* 74
College days of Bryan, 30-38
Columbia University, 350
*Commoner, The,* established, 151
Congress, Bryan's campaign for election to, 51-54; Bryan's tariff speech before, 55
Congressional campaign, Bryan's first, 51; Bryan's second, 62
Coolidge, Calvin, 350, 353, 356
Cornhusker Hotel at Lincoln, 397
*Cosmopolitan,* editor of, entertains Bryan, 96
County option. *See* Prohibition.
Courtship, Bryan's, 33-37
Crane, Charles R., 254
Crane, Dr. Frank, 154
Creel, George, 225
Creelman, James, 108
Croker, Richard, 62, 135, 137, 155, 182, 363
"Cross-of-Gold" speech, 86, 87
Cuba, McKinley's statement regarding, 126
Czar of Russia, 162, 171, 172, 301

Dahlman, Mayor, of Omaha, 216-222
Daniels, Josephus, 80, 238, 240, 246, 280, 320, 321, 340
Darrow, Clarence, 80, 154, 184, 378, 383, 386, 389, 391, 392, 396

Davis, Hayne, 200, 203
Davis, John W., 22, 367
Davison, Henry P., 306
Dawes, Charles G., 49, 146
Dayton trial, 27, 353, 380, 396. *See* Chapter XIX.
Death of William Jennings Bryan, 398
*Delineator,* Coolidge articles in, 350
Democratic Convention of '96, 82, 89; of 1900, 135-138; of 1904, 181, 185; of 1908 (Denver), 204; of 1912, 226, 247-268; of 1916, 344; of 1920, 357; of 1924 (New York), 358
Democratic Party in Nebraska, 50-54; position on the currency, 1896-1908, 295
Demonetization of silver. *See* Silver coinage.
Deserving Democrats, letter unearthed by New York *Sun,* 276
Destinn, Emmy, 148
Dillon, John, dinner to Bryan, 168
Dixon, Thomas, Jr., 110
Donahey, Vic, 146
Dumba, Ambassador, from Austria, conversations with Bryan, 330-333

Editor, Bryan becomes newspaper, 72
Education of Bryan, 24-43
Elkus, Abram, 268
England, Bryan's first visit to, 163

[ 415 ]

# INDEX

Evolution, Bryan's attack on, 372-396

"Fairview," 157, 181, 205, 232, 345, 397, 404
Federal Reserve System, 287-297
*First Battle,* written by Bryan, 123
First Meeting of Wilson cabinet, 280
First Presbyterian Church at Lincoln, 397
Fletcher, Admiral, 321
Florida, Bryan moves to, 346
Foraker, Senator ("Fireworks"), 62
Foss, Governor, of Massachusetts, 248
Frank, Glenn, 148
Free silver. *See* Silver coinage.
Frewen, Moreton, 74, 164
Frick, Henry Clay, 290

Gage, Lyman J., 76
Garrison, Lindley M., 273; comment on alien land laws, 310, 315
Gaynor, Mayor, of New York, ignores overtures of Colonel House, 229
George, Henry, 122
Gerard, James W., 333
Germany, attitude of, toward Peace Treaties, 336; influence against Hague Conferences, 301
Gibbons, Cardinal, 260
Gilroy, Thomas F., 62
Glass, Carter, 80, 288-297, 325

Gold Democrats, 113
Gold standard. *See* Silver coinage.
Goltra, Mr. and Mrs. Edward, 279
G. O. P., Bryan statement of, 51
Government ownership of railroads, Bryan support of, 187, 189, 190, 196, 200, 203, 204
Grand Island Convention of Democrats (Nebraska), 212
Grape juice luncheon, 282-284
Gregory, Thomas W., 273

Hague, peace progress at, 301
Hanna, Mark, 21, 104, 106, 110, 112, 113, 118, 127, 131-134, 354
Harding, Warren G., 345
Harkness, E. S., 98
Harlan, Justice, stand on income tax, 69, 154;
Harmsworth, Sir Alfred (Lord Northcliffe), 163, 167
Hartt, Rollin Lynde, 381
*Harvard Crimson,* article commenting on Yale reception of Bryan, 101
Harvey, Coin. *See* W. H. Harvey.
Harvey, W. H., 74
Hawthorne, Julian, 108
Hayes, Rutherford B., 31, 378
"He kept us out of war" speech by Bryan, 345
Hearst, W. R., first meeting with Bryan, 96, 156, 181-184; support of Champ Clark, 242,
Held, Anna, 17

[ 416 ]

# INDEX

Heney, Francis J., 254
Hepburn, A. Barton, 292
Herndon, William, 32
Hill, David Bennett, 119, 135, 184
Hillis, Newell Dwight, 349
Hitchcock, Gilbert M., 216
Hoar, Senator, view of Philippine issue, 129
Homestead, Pa., steel strike, 58
Hoover, Herbert C., 46, 145
House, Colonel Edward M., early acquaintance with Bryan, 227; suggests Mayor Gaynor of New York as 1912 candidate, 228; starts to work on Bryan to support Wilson cause, 236, 243; sails for England, 250-268; tries to arrange that Bryan go to Russia, 271; discusses appointees for Cabinet, 272; calls Bryan a "spoilsman," 272, 275; bored by inaugurations, 278, 279; becomes interested in Federal Reserve, 288-296; concerns himself with State Department, 322; calls on Bryan *re* mediation in Europe, 323, 325, 326; proposes A. B. C. plan for Pan-American countries, in conferring with Bryan, 324; message to Wilson *re Lusitania*, 328; does not see need of Catholic in Cabinet, 360
Houston, David F., 270, 272, 273, 340
Howell, Clark, foresight on Bryan's nomination, 84

Huerta, 314, 316
Hyde, James Hazen, 17

Illinois College, 30-38; Bryan resigns trusteeship of, 140
Imperialism, as Bryan's issue, 134
Income tax, Bryan's early battle for, 69, 399

Jackson day dinner, 1920, 345
James, Ollie, of Kentucky, 260
Japan, Bryan's visit to, 190-196
Japanese boy educated by Bryan, 16
Japanese-California dispute, 305
Jelke, W. F., 98
Joline letter ("cocked hat") of Wilson about Bryan, 238
Jones, Dr. Hiram K., 28
Jusserand, Ambassador, of France, 282, 298

Kahn, Otto, 290
Kaiser William's attitude toward Bryan treaties, 338
Kelly, John, 31
Kent, Frank R., 380
Kern, Senator, of Indiana, 251, 252, 255
Knox College, oratorical contest at, 38
Knox, Delegate, of Alabama, 266
Kohlsaat, H. H., 76
Kountze, Herman, 98
Krutch, Joseph Wood, 381

# INDEX

Ku Klux Klan, 359, 360, 364, 369

La Follette, 355
Lane, Franklin K., 274, 327, 340, 342
Lansing, Robert, 335
Laughlin, J. Laurence, 76
Lawyer, Bryan as, 39, 49
Lewis, Alfred Henry, 108
Lincoln, Abraham, 22; influence on Bryan, 23, 32
Lincoln, Neb., Bryan arrives in, 43
Lind, John, delegate to Mexico, 315
*Literary Digest,* comment on issues of 1896, 112
Lodge, Henry Cabot, 346
Loeb-Leopold trial, 392, 393
Lovejoy, Elijah P., 32
*Lusitania,* 303; effect of sinking on Cabinet, 328, 335; Bryan comments on, 333, 335
Lusk, Senator, of New York, 349

McAdoo, William Gibbs, 249, 268, 272, 273, 275, 296, 337, 338, 358, 365, 366
McArthur, Rev. Dr. R. S., 110
McClure, S. S., 38
McCombs, W. F., 249, 272, 275
McCorkle, Governor, of West Virginia, 265
McKenna, Justice, 154
McKinley, William, 63, 98, 104, 113, 118, 120, 126, 129, 130-134, 138, 208, 319

McLean, John R., Bryan rejects as vice-presidential candidate, 91
McReynolds, J. C., 274
Madison Square Garden, first address in, 92-94; second appearance at, 202, 203; third appearance at, 358, 359, 364-368
Malone, Dudley Field, 240, 386-388
Manure-spreader story, 4
Marriage of Bryan, 41
Marshall, Governor, of Indiana, 248, 251
Mencken, H. L., 377, 381, 390, 391
Metcalf, R. L., 216
Methodist Church at Normal, 397
Mexican troubles, 305, 314-316, 321, 326, 334
Miami, Bryan's life in, 372, 373, 374, 397
Michaelson, Charles, 163
Michigan, University of, 352
Mikado, Bryan's visit to, 190, 191
Moreton, J. Sterling, 50
Morgan, Howard, 388, 391
Morgan, J. Pierpont, 260, 282
Morgan, J. P. and Company, 72, 306, 367
Morgan, J. P. (the younger), 290, 330
Morgan bonds, Bryan's speech on, in Congress, 72
Murphy, Charley, 242, 253, 257-262
Music in Bryan home, 26

[ 418 ]

# INDEX

Myers, Rev. Cortland, 104

Nebraska, Bryan moves to, 43; early politics of, 212; State Democratic Convention of 1910, 212
Negro question, Bryan's attitude on, 155
New York *Journal* alliance with Bryan, 96
New York State, Bryan orders Democratic Committee to rescind choice of governor, 95
New York *Sun,* comment on Yale reception of Bryan, 101
New York *Times,* comment on Bryan's tariff speech, 59; comment on Bryan's first appearance before Tammany, 62
New York *Tribune,* comment on Bryan's first appearance before Tammany, 62; comment on Bryan's '96 defeat, 115, 116
New York *World,* comment on Bryan's tariff speech, 60; comment on Bryan's handling of alien-land (California-Japan) dispute, 310
News leaks in State Department, 326, 327
Nicaragua, Bryan's policy toward, 319
Nicholas II. *See* Czar of Russia.
Nixon, Lewis, 363
Nomination in '96, 4
Nordica, Lillian, 148
Norris, G. W., 146, 215

North Carolina instructed for Bryan in '96, 82

O'Connor, T. P., 168
O'Connor, Mrs. T. P., 168
O'Gorman, Senator, of New York, 240, 250
Omaha *World-Herald,* Bryan becomes editor of, 72; comments on Bryan's Prohibition stand in 1890, 213, 214
One term for president proposal by Governor Beckham, 256
Oulahan, Richard V., 108
Owen, Senator Robert L., of Oklahoma, 288-297, 325
Oxford, Bryan's plan to attend, 20, 33

Pacifism, conversations concerning, between Bryan and Tolstoy, 173-180
Page, Walter Hines, 16, 272, 274, 324, 327
Parker, Alton B., 184, 185, 188, 208, 246, 247, 250, 251-255, 257, 357
Peace policies, Bryan influenced by Tolstoy, 173-180
Peace treaties, 298-304
Peary, Rear Admiral, 148
Pensions, Bryan's activity in, 15
Pershing, John J., 49
Philippines, American attitude toward, 129-134; Bryan's visit to, 196
Phillips, John S., 38
Pope Leo XIII, 162, 360
Pope Pius X, 360

[ 419 ]

# INDEX

Popular election of senators, 399
Populist party, 92
Potter, Charles Francis, 381
Prohibition, 358, 399; Bryan's personal stand in 1896; 90; Bryan's stand in 1890, 213, 214; why Bryan embraced national, 215-223; Roman Catholic interest in, 220; Lincoln, Neb., meeting to endorse county option, 220; national, Bryan's comment on, 223; Bryan's discussion with Wilson regarding use of liquor by Secretary of State, 272

Radcliffe College, 350
Radical wing of Democracy, Bryan declares leadership of, 186
Radishes, Bryan's fondness for, 14
Railroad regulation, 400
Railroads, Bryan's study of, 40. *See* Government ownership.
Raulston, Judge, 382, 294
Rauschenbusch, Walter, 225
Redfield, W. C., 273
Reed, James A., 46
Reed, Thomas B., 59
Religious life of Bryan, 27, 50
Religious views of Bryan and Smith, 362
Republican Convention at Chicago (1912), 244
Resignation of Bryan as Secretary of State, 337-339
Resolution, Bryan's anti-Tammany, at Baltimore, 260

Ripley, W. Z., 402
Roberts, George E., 76
Rockefeller, Percy, 98
Roman Catholic Church, 381; Bryan's views of, 359-369
Roosevelt, Theodore, 5, 21, 128, 132, 138, 139, 142, 155, 224, 226, 244, 253, 258, 287, 400; statement on U. S. neutrality, 322
Ross, Edward Aylsworth, 225
Russell, Bertrand, 122
Russell, Charles Edward, 225
Rutledge, Ann, 32
Ryan, Thomas Fortune, 257-262

Salem, Ill., days of Bryan, 24-26
Schooling of Bryan, 24-43
Scopes, J. T., 376, 384, 388
Sembrich, Madame, 148
Sewell, nominated for vice-president by Democrats, 92
Seymour, Prof. Charles, of Yale, 303
Shallenberger, Governor, of Nebraska, 216-218
Shaw, G. B., 349, 377
Shepherd, William G., 380
Shipwreck, 1
Shotgun incident, 25
Silk hats owned by Bryan, 40
Sills, Kenneth C., 355
Silver, free, Congress on, 60
Silver coinage, 46, 47, 48, 74, 161; fight in Congress in 1893, 64; effect of gold discovery, 121

# INDEX

Silver leaders battle with Cleveland, 61
Silver manifesto, 78
Simmons College, 3, 50
Smith, Alfred E., 18-46, 145, 358, 362, 365, 366, 367, 368
Smith College, 350, 356
Spanish War, declared, 126; Bryan's military part in, 127, 128; Bryan's statement of purposes, 128, 132-134
Springer, Congressman, 42, 54
Steel strike at Homestead, Pa., Bryan's comment on, 58
Steffens, Lincoln, 225
St. Louis, Democratic Convention of 1904, 181-185
Stone, W. J., of Missouri, 264; Senator, 303
Straight, Willard, 306
Straton, John Roach, 110
Sullivan, Mark, 148

Taft, William Howard, 148, 208, 226, 287, 314, 319
Talbot, A. R., 43
Talmage, T. De Witt, 110
Tammany Hall, 31, 61, 62, 135, 136, 137, 155, 182, 242, 253, 257-262, 359, 363-368
Tariff speech of Bryan in Congress, 55
Telegram, Bryan's, to 1912 candidates, 248
Thatcher, John Boyd, 95
Tilden, Samuel, 31
Togo, Admiral, Bryan's toast to, 195
Tolstoy, Count Leo, 162, 173-180, 298, 305, 338

Trumbull, Judge Lyman, 38, 154
Tumulty, Joseph, 239, 249, 294, 295, 320, 360
Twain, Mark, 148
Tweed, Boss, 31

Underwood, Senator Oscar, 248
Union College of Law, 38
University of Nebraska, 16, 122
Untermyer, Samuel, 268, 288, 289-296

Van Hise, President of Wisconsin, 355
Vanderbilt, W. H., 17
Vanderlip, Frank, 290
Vardaman, Senator of Mississippi, 250
Vassar College, 356
Vera Cruz, 320
Vote for Democracy in 1896 campaign, 118; in 1900, 143, 144; in 1904, 188; in 1908, 205-209

Wadsworth, James W., Jr., 98
Walker, John Brisben, entertains Bryan, 96
Wallace, Edgar, 163
Walsh, Archbishop, 168
War, U. S. enters, 346
Warburg, Paul, 292
Washington, Booker T., Bryan's comment on Roosevelt's luncheon to, 155
Washington *Post,* comment on Bryan tariff speech, 59
Watermelon, carload disposed of by the Bryans, 125

# INDEX

Ways and Means Committee of Congress, Bryan's appointment to, 54
Webb, Mr. and Mrs. Sidney, 162, 167, 181
Welcome to Bryan in New York in 1906, 202
Wellesley College, 350, 352, 356
Westminster Presbyterian Church at Lincoln, 397
Wet issue. *See* Prohibition.
Whipple Academy, 28-31
Whitney, Payne, 98
Wilson, Woodrow, 5, 226; meets Bryan face to face, 235; "cocked hat" letter (Joline letter), 238; comment in 1897 *re* Bryan, 239; comment in 1908 *re* Bryan, 239; Bryan's early support of, 239; conference with Bryan at Jackson day dinner 1912, 241; why his record pleased Bryan, 243, 244; answer to Bryan wire on Parker Chairmanship, 248; managers struggle for his nomination at Baltimore, 257-268; nominated for presidency, 268; of-

Wilson, Woodrow-*contd.*
fers Secretary of State office to Bryan, 272; inauguration, 278-280; stand on Federal Reserve, 287-297; on alien land laws, 307; on Mexico, 314-317, 319; on Vera Cruz, 320, 321, 324; meets with House on State Department matters, 325; reception of *Lusitania* news, 328; censures Bryan for charging Cabinet was pro-Ally, 330; war policy, 333, 335, 336, 337, 338, 340; renominated and reëlected, 344; asks for declaration of war, 345, 346, 400, 403
Wireless law, 3
Wisconsin, University of, 350
Woodson, Urey, 261

*Yale News,* comment on Yale reception of Bryan, 100
Yale University, reception of Bryan, 97
"You shall not press down upon the brow of Labor, etc.," 88

Zimmermann, German minister, 333

# DISRAELI: A Picture of the Victorian Age
### By ANDRÉ MAUROIS,
#### Author of "Ariel: The Life of Shelley"

Who could have written the life of Disraeli more gracefully or in better taste than André Maurois? This surprising Frenchman has a style admirably suited to his method, and a faculty of coining epigrams which set off a character in a single phrase. His sympathy for the tempestuous, storm-ridden soul which he lays bare in this book finds perfect expression in the delicate, yet forceful writing of which he is past master.

"Was there any tale of the Thousand and One Nights, any story of a Cobbler made a Sultan, that could match the picturesqueness of Disraeli's life? There was not. Hence, the enthralling interest of the tale M. Maurois tells so well . . . . . The translation (by Hamish Miles) admirably preserves the brilliance and sparkle of the original French.—*Sir John Marriott, M. P., in The London Observer.*

"Wholly a work of art. It is a fancy picture, staged, lighted, and presented with perfection of wit, style, finesse and humor."
—*John Jay Chapman in The Yale Review.*

"It makes English politics as fascinating as 'Alice in Wonderland'; it is playful without being childish, ironical without being bitter, and as creative as a fine novel."—*Hugh Walpole in the New York Herald-Tribune.*

"The Story of Dizzy's life does not need embellishments to make it romantic. All that M. Maurois adds is deep understanding, wide appreciation, and style. But he also adds wit."—*The Daily Observer (London).*

"Disraeli comes to life in its pages . . . . . . and dozens of others, caught up quickly by the skillful hand of M. Maurois, put into their proper places in the drama which was Disraeli, and made to live and move and have their being before our delighted eyes."
—*Herschell Brickell in the New York Evening Post.*

$3.00

### D. APPLETON AND COMPANY
Publishers                                                                 New York

## INTERESTING BIOGRAPHIES

**SHAKESPEARE: ACTOR-POET**
By *Clara Longworth de Chambrun*. "Most convincing and complete life of Shakespeare yet written."—Richard Le Gallienne in the *New York Times*. Illustrated. $3.00.

**SIXTEEN TO FORTY: A Woman's Story**
By *"Marna."* Writing anonymously, a brilliant woman tells her life story. An intimate revelation of what life and love mean to a woman. $2.50.

**SOME MEMORIES AND REFLECTIONS**
By *Emma Eames*. A great operatic star presents in delightful fashion the memories that gather around her wonderful career. Illustrated. $5.00.

**THE TRAGIC BRIDE: The Story of the Empress Alexandra**
By *V. Poliakoff*. The story of one of the most picturesque of modern figures, the last Empress of Russia. Illustrated. $3.00.

**THE CATASTROPHE: Kerensky's Own Story of the Russian Revolution**
By *Alexander F. Kerensky*. There is a real thrill in this inside picture of the first Russian revolution. $3.00.

**MOTHER DEAR: The Empress Marie of Russia and Her Times**
By *V. Poliakoff*. An absorbing picture of the Russian Empress Dowager who lived to see the downfall of her son's Empire. Illustrated. $3.50.

**GEORGE ELIOT AND HER TIMES**
By *Elizabeth S. Haldane*. A modern study of a great novelist. Illustrated. $3.50.

**JULIA MARLOWE: Her Life and Art**
By *Charles Edward Russell*. A revealing picture of a splendid actress and a study of her contribution to the American stage. Illustrated. $5.00.

**BOB DAVIS RECALLS**
By *Robert H. Davis*. A distinguished editor tells sixty stories of love and laughter and tears, treasures of a rich memory. $2.50.

D. APPLETON AND COMPANY
PUBLISHERS NEW YORK

# BIOGRAPHY and AUTOBIOGRAPHY

### THE LIFE OF ELBERT H. GARY
By IDA M. TARBELL.
> This is not only the life story of a great and powerful man in our industrial life, it is the story of the steel industry and much of the story of the country itself as well. $3.50.

### DAVID WILMOT: FREE SOILER
By CHARLES B. GOING.
> An historical biography of one of the most intense personalties in the great Free-Soil struggle which culminated in the Civil War, the originator of the Wilmot Proviso. $6.00.

### FORTY YEARS OF IT
By BRAND WHITLOCK.
> An autobiography—a record of real service in American life. A fine story and a fascinating account of forty odd years of useful activity. $2.50.

### SAINTE-BEUVE
By LEWIS FREEMAN MOTT.
> The story of one of the most striking personalities of the nineteenth century—Charles Augustin Sainte-Beuve, the greatest literary critic of France. $5.00.

### D. APPLETON AND COMPANY
NEW YORK                                          LONDON

# BIOGRAPHY

**MAPE—THE WORLD OF ILLUSION**
By ANDRÉ MAUROIS.
In brilliant fashion the author of "Ariel" takes three characters and gaily, humorously, sympathetically shows them as they lived and loved. Here is the youth of Goethe, the most diverting of literary romances. Then one reads of an episode in which the novelist Balzac has an important role, and finally there is an inimitable rendering of that extraordinary character Mrs. Siddons, the great tragedienne.

**ARIEL: THE LIFE OF SHELLEY**
By ANDRÉ MAUROIS.
Maurois has so triumphantly touched biography with the magic of the novelist's art that everyone is enjoying this maddest of romances and most delectable narrative of facts. Robert Morss Lovett writes in the New Republic, "It is M. Maurois' art to tell this amazing story in the simplest, most limpid style. Now for the first time the personality and experiences of Shelley stand out distinctly in a white light."

**THE NOBEL PRIZE WINNERS IN LITERATURE**
By ANNIE RUSSELL MARBLE.
There is no other literary prize with quite the significance in the eyes of the world that the Nobel Prize possesses. This book about the men and women who have won this honor proves most interesting.

**G. STANLEY HALL—A BIOGRAPHY OF A MIND**
By LORINE PRUETTE.
One of the most eminent psychologists and educators made known to us by another psychologist who writes with sympathy and charm and breadth of vision. President Hall lived a life of drama, a long struggle against odds. Twice his love life met disaster; twice defeat threatened his most precious ambition. But the extraordinary force of his character and personality and the vivid individuality of his genius carried him through.

**D. APPLETON AND COMPANY**
NEW YORK　　　　　　　　　　　　　　　　LONDON